We Were on a BREAK

Lindsey Kelk is an author, journalist and prolific tweeter. Born and brought up in the UK, she worked as a children's editor before moving to New York and becoming a full-time writer. She now lives in LA.

Lindsey has written eleven novels: *I Heart New York, I Heart Hollywood, I Heart Paris, I Heart Vegas, I Heart London, I Heart Christmas, The Single Girl's To-Do List, About a Girl, What a Girl Wants, A Girl's Best Friend* and *Always the Bridesmaid*. You can find out lots more about her here: http://lindseykelk.com and by following her on Twitter.

@lindseykelk
www.facebook.com/LindseyKelk

D0376745

LINDSEY KELK

HARPER

Harper
An imprint of HarperCollins*Publishers*
1 London Bridge Street
London SE1 9GF

www.harpercollins.co.uk

First published by *Harper* 2016

This edition published by *Harper 360* 2017

1

A catalogue record for this book
is available from the British Library

ISBN: 978-0-00-817560-3

Set in Melior LT Std by Palimpsest Book Production Ltd.
Falkirk, Stirlingshire

Printed and bound in the United States of America by
LSC Communications

Find out more about HarperCollins and the environment at
www.harpercollins.co.uk/green

Dear Della, Terri and Kevin,
What's worse, looking jealous or crazy?
That's what I thought, thanks.
Love, Lindsey & Beyoncé

1

It really doesn't matter how brilliant your life is, the last day of your holiday is always depressing. I'm talking Monday dread plus post-Christmas blues multiplied by a maxed-out credit card with the added bonus of knowing there are at least another twelve holidayless months stretching out in front of you before you'll be able to get away again. Unless you're Beyoncé. I imagine nothing other than dinner with Kanye is quite that depressing if you're Beyoncé, but for the rest of us, the last day of a holiday is right up there with doing your taxes, getting a bikini wax and that time you went to the fridge for your favourite bar of chocolate and found out someone had already eaten it.

Kneeling on the sofa, I rested my chin on my forearms and stared out the window. Bright blue skies bled into dark blue seas with flashes of pink and purple smeared through the middle to let me know that night-time was on its way. The sun was literally setting on my vacay and it just wasn't on. I had a tan, seventeen insect bites, a suitcase full of tat I didn't need – but I still didn't have the one thing I'd been waiting for which could only mean one thing.

Tonight was the night.

'Liv?'

'Adam?'

'Is it me or can you see my knob through these trousers?'

Not exactly the question I was waiting for him to ask.

I craned my neck to see six feet four inches of blond boyfriend framed by the bedroom doorway, thrusting his crotch in my general direction with a vexed expression on his face.

Hmm. He was wearing his Best Trousers. My heart started to beat a little bit faster.

'I don't think so?' I said, squinting at the general area. You could sort of see it, but only if you were looking for it and, really, how many people were strolling around Tulum on a Monday night, staring at my boyfriend's crotch? I hoped it wasn't that many. 'I can't see anything.'

'"I can't see anything" isn't exactly what I want to hear when you're looking down there.' Adam bent his knees slightly and bounced up and down in front of the mirror. 'You sure there isn't, you know, an outline? I forgot how thin these trousers are.'

'You look nice,' I reassured him with a smile while he shoved his hands deep into his pockets and checked his reflection at every angle. 'I like those trousers.'

'I'm going to get changed,' he said, more to himself than me. 'I can't put anything in these pockets. And you can totally see my knob.'

'What do you need to put in your pockets?' I asked, the attractive high pitch of desperation squeaking into my voice. 'I can put your wallet in my bag.'

'My phone?' Adam muttered, giving the mirror one last thrust then pottering back into the bedroom. 'Stuff?'

'Stuff?'

I glanced down as my own phone buzzed on the windowsill.

'You know,' he called from the other room. 'Stuff.'

'Oh, OK,' I replied, nodding as I opened the text message. 'Stuff.'

HAS HE DONE IT YET?????????

Cassie had sent me the same text thirty-six times in the last fourteen days. Anyone would think she was the one whose blood pressure had been hovering around stroke-inducing levels every day for the last two weeks. And that wasn't an exaggeration, I'd been checking, such were the perks of a background in medicine.

No, I tapped out as quickly as my little fingers would allow, *not yet.* I added three sad faces just in case she wasn't sure how I was feeling and then a unicorn, just because. There's always room for a unicorn.

Three little dots thrummed across the bottom of the screen while Adam sang an off-key Rihanna song to himself in the bedroom.

Maybe he's nervous? Cassie suggested. *Give him an in.*

I looked up from my phone just in time to see our very large, very hairy neighbour in nothing but a pair of tiny trunks walk right by my window and raise his hand in a polite hello. There were downsides to staying in a cottage on the beach. They certainly hadn't shown him on the website. Waving back quickly, I stood up and leaned against the arm of the settee, shaking out the creases in my long skirt.

Give him an in?

That was easier said than done. Maybe I could start a

casual conversation on the way to dinner with 'Did you know nine out of ten boyfriends that want to live to see another day propose to their girlfriends on holiday?' Or perhaps 'Hey Adam, the third finger on my left hand is cold; do you have anything sparkly I could borrow to warm it up?'

Working on it, I replied, despondent.

No emojis this time.

Truth be told, we'd had a lovely holiday but it would have been considerably lovelier if I hadn't been constantly waiting for Adam to drop the P bomb. Nothing kills the mood like waiting for a proposal that never comes. And I want to be clear, it's not as though I've been sat around the house for the last three years, draped across a fainting couch and waiting for him to swoop in with the promise of a yearly allowance of a hundred pounds and a new topcoat every winter. The chance would have been a fine thing. When you're the only local vet in a five-village radius, you spend most of your time in surgery with your hand up a Chihuahua or in your bed, fast asleep. After you've washed your hands, of course. Ideally, at the end of a dog-bothering day, all I wanted was to be up to my eyeballs in a *Real Housewives* marathon and two-thirds of a bottle of rosé with Adam by my side. Marriage hadn't really crossed my mind. There were so many other things I still had to accomplish, I wanted to travel, I wanted to start drinking whisky, I wanted to finish watching the last series of *Doctor Who* before the new one started.

However, things had changed. Supposedly, Adam had told his brother he was going to propose in Mexico, then his brother had told his wife, who just so happened to be my best friend. Of course, everyone knew Cass couldn't keep a secret and it only took half a bottle of Pinot Grigio before she was bursting to tell me everything, and now here I was at the end of our trip, still unengaged. I had been told there was a ring, I had been told the ring was coming in Mexico – and now I *wanted* the bloody ring. I was Gollum, only with slightly better hair.

'Ready?' Adam re-emerged from the bedroom, best trousers replaced by regular jeans, paired with a nice, but hardly special, shirt.

I looked at him and wondered. Why would you tell someone you were going to propose to your girlfriend and then not do it?

'Ready,' I replied with a curtsey, dropping my phone in my bag, out of sight and hopefully out of mind.

He frowned for a moment, giving my ensemble the once-over before fastening and then unfastening his top button. 'Is that what you're wearing?'

'What's wrong with it?' I stood up and let my long, floaty white dress drift down to the floor. 'I love this dress.'

It was a great dress. It was loose around my backside, tight around my boobs and, most importantly, I could eat in it without feeling like I was wearing my nana's girdle. It had also cost an obscene amount of money but Cassie had assured me it was The Dress and I'd put it on my credit card without thinking about the damage. That was until the bill came. He had better propose – I needed a joint income to pay for this bugger.

'Makes me feel a bit of a scruff, that's all. Are you sure you're all right to walk in those shoes?'

5

'I could run a marathon in these shoes.' I picked up a foot to inspect my three-inch heels. Maybe a marathon was pushing it. 'We're not walking that far, are we?'

'Google Maps says it's ten minutes,' he replied, patting himself down then sticking his thumbs in his jeans pockets like a Topman-clad cowboy and all the while his eyes were still on my sandals. 'You can do ten minutes?'

I nodded and made a disgusted noise in the back of my throat. Of course ten minutes were doable. Generally I was of the opinion that no good could come of strapping tiny stilts to your feet after a particularly nasty incident involving a spiral staircase in a club called Oceana during Freshers' Week. More than a decade may have passed but if you'd spent your first semester of university on crutches, you'd be wary of anything higher than a kitten heel as well.

'I really do like that dress,' Adam said, crossing the room to rest his arms on my shoulders. I shuffled my feet apart and pulled him in closer until we were nose to nose. 'Is it new?'

'Quite new,' I replied, hoping there were no follow up questions. Adam hated spending a lot of money on clothes, hence only one pair of Nice Trousers.

'It's like a proper lady dress.' He nuzzled his face into my hair, pressing his lips against the nook where my neck met my shoulder. I shivered from head to toe. 'It might be the nicest thing I've ever seen you wear.'

'Just checking that's a compliment,' I whispered as he slid his hands around my waist and a flush bloomed in my cheeks. Adam was no slouch in the bedroom department at the best of times but on holiday it wasn't just the bedroom that got him going. The living room, the bathroom, the beach, the toilets at a restaurant we could never go back to . . . Not that I was complaining. The restaurant manager maybe, but not me.

I ran my hands down his broad back and rested them on his hips. 'Perhaps we should stay in tonight?'

'No, we're going to the restaurant.' Adam checked his watch then dropped me like a bag of burning dog shit and backed away, jostling the front of his jeans to dispel the beginnings of a boner. 'And we need to leave now or we're going to be late.'

'Adam, we're in Mexico. Nothing has happened at the time it was supposed to happen since we got here,' I said, brushing my blonde hair forward to cover the stubble rash on my throat and delicately draping my dress back down over my thighs. 'What's the rush?'

'They were really funny about it when I made the reservation. It's supposed to be dead fancy,' he insisted as he checked his reflection and smoothed down his eyebrows. What a weirdo. 'Plenty of time for doing it when we get back.'

My boyfriend was such a romantic.

'Dead fancy,' I repeated. Dead fancy sounded like the kind of place where you would propose to your girlfriend, or at least the kind of place that would have proper toilets and honestly, either of those things would have been welcomed at this point in the trip.

Following him outside, I nabbed a quick glance in the mirror as we went. Hair looked good, make-up looked good, but nothing I could do about my sunburned nose except filter it into oblivion. I was as ready as I'd ever be.

The next time we walked through that door, we would be engaged.

Or I'd have stabbed Adam through the heart with a spatula. Or a teaspoon. Or whatever was handy, really; I was a resourceful girl.

'Do we really have to go home tomorrow?' Liv skipped along beside me as I tried to slow down.

'Aren't you ready?' I squeezed her hand and smiled, hoping that my palm wasn't as sweaty as I imagined it was. 'I'm gagging for a proper cup of tea.'

'Yeah, this is just awful,' she replied, waving at the white sand and screensaver-worthy sunset. 'I'd trade it all for a cup of Tetley.'

'You know what I mean,' I said, looking at the time on my watch. We were definitely going to be late. 'Come on, let's pick up the pace.'

'We have definitely been walking for more than ten minutes,' she said in a tight voice, a few minutes later. 'How much further is it?'

'Not far?'

A dark look crossed her face as she gripped my hand hard and attempted to match my long stride. A word of advice: if you're over six feet tall and you end up going out with someone under five-five, you will never not be frustrated with how slowly they walk.

'I will miss the sunsets,' I admitted as she walked on beside me in silence. I wrapped my right arm around her red shoulders, keeping one eye on the time. 'The sunsets are good.'

'The sunsets are good?' Liv repeated, one eyebrow raised. 'If it weren't for the cat, I wouldn't be going back at all. We've got everything we need right here. Sun, sea, sand and surprisingly good internet service? I'm in no rush to go home.'

As casual as possible, I ran a hand over my hip, checking for the telltale bump in the tiny pocket. I was certain she'd found it back in the cottage when she was packing up my clothes, but if she had, she was doing a fine job of pretending and there was no way she could fake something like that: she was a terrible liar.

'Loads going on when we get back though . . .' She carried on talking, twisting the ends of her hair in her fingers. 'Are you excited to get started on the bar?'

'Yeah.'

'Nervous?'

'Nah.'

I was so nervous I was bricking it. Just before we left, a friend of a friend of a friend had set me up with a guy who was opening a bar in London and needed someone to design and build the interiors. Since he had next to no budget and I was looking for a project, we'd managed to come to a financially dubious but still exciting accord. But it was still my first major project and there were a million things that could go wrong. Was my estimate right? Was my timeframe realistic? Was I even capable of pulling something like this off without it looking utterly crap? But Liv didn't need to know how worried I was. Men shitting themselves over their big break wasn't exactly a turn on for most women to the best of my knowledge.

'It'll be amazing,' she said, with an assured nod I couldn't return. 'And there's my dad's sixty-fifth coming up, Gus's christening, your birthday, my birthday . . .'

I made a noncommittal noise, trying to hold her hand, remember if I'd had a response to my last email from Jim, the guy who owned the bar, and open Google Maps to check where this bloody restaurant was supposed to be. All I could see was beach, beach, and more beach. We'd already been walking forever and I certainly couldn't see a five-star restaurant with sunset views and a ridiculously-expensive-to-hire string quartet hiding anywhere nearby.

'Things have been mental at the surgery, it feels like everyone on earth just adopted ten dogs and they've all got ear infections or worms or something else disgusting—'

'Liv?' I interrupted.

'Yes?' she looked up at me with big blue eyes, all smudgy with make-up but in a good way.

'No.'

There was nothing like a woman talking about putting her hand up a dog's backside to put you in the mood for a romantic proposal – not.

'Sorry,' she opened her mouth to say something else and then clamped it shut, staring out to sea. She didn't look happy.

'Liv?'

'Yeah?'

'What do you think Daniel Craig is doing right now?' I asked.

She turned round, shielding her eyes from the sun and gave me a look.

'The actor or the cat?'

'The cat.'

'Eating, sleeping or having a shit,' she replied, pulling on my hand as she began to lag. 'That's more or less all he does these days.'

'What do you think Daniel Craig the actor is doing right now?'

'Eating, sleeping or having a shit? That's more or less all he does these days.'

'Weirdo,' I laughed, flapping my elbows slightly as I tried to find a phone signal and hoped there wasn't a massive sweat stain on the back of my shirt. Should have worn an undershirt. Should have put deodorant on my back. Should have done a lot of things.

Liv pressed her lips together into a thin smile. '*You're* a weirdo.'

'Yeah, but that's why you love me.' I choked on the words as the map came up. We were nowhere near the restaurant – it was a ten-minute drive away, not a ten-minute walk.

'I knew there had to be a reason,' she said, trying to subtly pull a strand of hair out of her lip gloss. 'Are you excited about the christening?'

'I can't believe my brother is a dad,' I replied, still staring at my phone. 'He wasn't even allowed to bring the school guinea pig home during the holidays and now he's got a baby.'

Recalculating the route, I looked down at Liv, wincing with every step she took.

'Anyway, it really has been the best holiday ever,' she said slowly. 'I can't imagine anything nicer.'

'Yeah, incredible,' I agreed, a cold sweat running down my back. How could I have messed this up? 'Total once-in-a-lifetime thing.'

'And I can't imagine anyone I'd rather be with, yeti.' She looked up and gave me the smallest, sweetest smile and I thought I was going to be sick. In a good way. Sort of. 'Ever.'

Oh god, I was actually going to be sick. Everything had been planned so carefully, right down to the smallest detail, and I had cocked up the directions. Maybe it was a sign. Maybe I wasn't supposed to propose after all.

'You obviously haven't given it enough thought,' I said, forcing out a laugh to distract from the fact I was dying inside. 'You're saying you'd rather be on holiday with me than Channing Tatum?'

'Why Channing Tatum?'

'I don't know,' I admitted. 'He's good looking, isn't he? All buff and that. And he can dance. Women love men who can dance.'

'You can't dance – and I love *you*,' she said, curling her fingers tightly around mine. 'And I'd definitely pick you over Channing Tatum.'

'Really?'

'You've got better hair,' she nodded thoughtfully. 'And I couldn't do that to his wife. She seems lovely.'

I'd been so worried about what to wear, about getting the music right, the menu right, about fixing my massive *Teen Wolf* eyebrows, I'd completely messed up our timing. We were supposed to get to the restaurant in time to watch the sun go down. At this rate, it would be the middle of the night before we got there.

'Really, though,' Liv started with a crack in her voice and my stomach turned over again. 'I don't want to be with anyone other than you, Adam. There's no one else for me, ever.'

I let go of her hand and wiped my sweaty palms on the back of my jeans.

'Yeah, better the devil you know,' I said, my tongue tripping over my words. 'It's like *Star Wars*. You've got the original trilogy and they're great, but then George Lucas says he's going to make new films and you get all excited but you end up with *The Phantom Menace*.'

Liv knitted her perfectly groomed eyebrows together. I always hoped our children would have her eyebrows. 'You've lost me.'

'I'm saying, our relationship is like the original *Star Wars*,' I explained. 'So I can't dump you in case I end up with *The Phantom Menace*.'

The sun had already started to slip away over the horizon but it was not difficult to make out my girlfriend's expression. She didn't look nearly as pleased with the analogy as I was.

'What I'm saying is . . .' I rubbed my palms together then took her hand back in mine. 'You're *A New Hope*. That's good! And it's better to stick with you because who knows if the next girl is going to be a *Force Awakens* or a *Phantom Menace*.'

'If I were you, I'd probably just stop talking.' She looked around the deserted beach, clearly confused. 'Yeti, where is the restaurant?'

'So, there's a small chance I was looking at the driving directions when I said it was ten minutes away,' I replied, reviewing the map. 'It's further than I thought?'

'How much further?' she asked, a noticeable hobble in her walk.

I bloody well knew those shoes of hers would be trouble.

'The good news is, we've already been walking for twenty minutes,' I replied with a tentative smile. 'And it's only fifty minutes away altogether.'

'Fifty minutes!'

Liv stopped dead in her tracks, looking at me as though

I'd just told her she had to walk the rest of the way barefoot, over hot coals.

'I can't walk another half an hour in these shoes.' As she leaned forward, her blonde hair fell in front of her face, showing off her long neck as she messed around with the miniscule gold buckles. I hated those shoes but I loved that neck. I wanted to kiss it. But this really was not the time. 'My foot is killing me.'

I bloody knew it.

'Well, take your shoes off and we'll walk on the sand,' I suggested, looking at the uneven path that ran down the side of the beach. Even my leathery Hobbit feet wouldn't fancy that much.

'I can't,' she said, wincing as she removed her left shoe. 'My foot is a bit of a mess.'

'Oh my god, there's a hole in your foot!' I made an involuntary gipping sound as she pulled the shoe away to reveal what must have been a particularly nasty blister about fifteen minutes ago. 'Why didn't you say something?'

'You were in such a rush.' She leaned against the low tidal wall and poked gently at the weeping mess formerly known as her foot. 'I didn't want to be late.'

'I told you not to wear those shoes,' I said, mad at her foot, mad at Google and possibly, very slightly mad at myself.

'You also told me the restaurant was ten minutes away,' she snapped back. 'I can't help it.'

I checked my phone one more time before taking another look at Liv's gammy foot. It was utterly disgusting but I couldn't tear my eyes away.

'If we walk around the beach, we'll be there in ten minutes,' I said, enlarging the map to make sure of my short cut. 'Then we can clean that mess up there.'

'There's no way I'm walking down the beach,' she said, folding her arms across her chest. 'It's filthy. Do you want me to get an infection in my foot? Do you want me to get septicaemia?'

No, I almost shouted, I want to bloody propose to you! Instead, I took a calming breath, put my phone away and smiled.

'Have you got a plaster?'

'Of course I haven't got a bloody plaster!' she exploded. 'Why would I have a plaster?'

'Because you're a vet?' I suggested. 'Don't you carry that sort of thing?'

'What, in case we pass an Alsatian with a splinter?'

I turned my back on her and looked out at the setting sun, the last sliver hovering over the sea, and fingered the ring in my pocket. We were supposed to be there by now. We were supposed to be drinking champagne, surrounded by white roses and enjoying all the other amazing things I'd paid an arm and a leg for Pablo the events manager to organize in The Arse End of Nowhere, Mexico. I should have been the one down on one knee with a ring in my hand, instead Liv was crouching on the floor and tending to an open wound.

'Maybe we should go back to the hotel,' I suggested weakly as the sun drowned itself in the ocean. 'It's dark; it's late. We're not going to get there on time.'

'You want to go back?' she asked, hesitating over every word. 'You don't want to go to dinner?'

'Well, I don't want to sit here,' I replied. 'What would you suggest?'

Do it now, hissed the little voice in my head. Do it now, do it while she's not expecting it.

'Fine,' Liv pursed her lips and stood up, limping along to the edge of the path. 'We'll just go back.'

That's right. For some reason, the voice sounded an awful lot like my big brother. *Go back to the hotel, don't propose, wait for Liv to leave you then you can die alone with a massive beard, tissue boxes on your feet instead of shoes and hundreds of bottles full of your own wee to keep you and your eighteen cats company.*

'Fuck it,' I murmured, fishing around in my pocket for the ring and bending down. Slowly. I really needed to see someone about my back.

'There's a taxi!'

Before I could stop her, Liv hopped off the path and into the street, flagging down a white car with a red stripe down the side. It screeched to a halt at her side. I watched her, the headlights of the car lighting up her flowing white dress as it swirled around her slender legs, her hair flying out behind her. She was beautiful. She was clever and caring, she made me laugh, she took care of me even when I didn't know I needed taking care of and she always watched *Star Trek Next Gen* with me, even if we'd seen it a dozen times before. Olivia Addison was perfect.

And I couldn't even get her to a bloody restaurant on time.

'I can't,' I realized, staring at my grandmother's engagement ring. 'I can't do it.'

'Adam?'

It was too late, Liv was already inside the taxi, staring back at me. 'What are you doing?'

It felt as though everything inside me had stopped working, like even my organs were waiting to see what came next before they bothered to carry on keeping me alive. Her eyes widened and she blinked at the sight of me kneeling on the dusty street.

'Fastening my shoelace,' I replied, dropping the ring on the floor and covering it with my shoe. 'Sorry.'

Better start saving up my tissue boxes and adopting those cats, I thought, as I stood up, stashed the ring back in my pocket and forced one foot in front of the other to join her in the back seat of the taxi. You couldn't just walk into an RSPCA and take eighteen. Could you? Surely there was a limit.

The taxi driver pulled out into the speeding traffic, turning the radio up full blast and soundtracking my misery with a song I had loved until that moment. Now I was going to have to hunt down Mumford and all of his sons and murder them all to death.

Liv stared out the window with her shoes in her lap as I closed my eyes, trying to work out just how I'd managed to get everything so wrong. Slipping my finger into the tiny pocket of my jeans, I traced the setting of the sapphire in my grandmother's engagement ring and squeezed the bridge of my nose, trying not to cry.

Well. That went well.

2

'Have you got everything?'

'Yeah,' Adam replied, looking back over his shoulder. 'I think so.'

'Did you check all the drawers?' I asked. 'The little ones in the nightstand?'

'I'll double check,' he said, disappearing back into the bedroom.

The second we got back to the cottage, Adam had retired to the bathroom, claiming an upset stomach and didn't reappear until I'd given up any hope of a romantic proposal and swapped my beautiful white dress for my Garfield pyjamas. The whole evening had been a complete waste of make-up. Neither of us had slept a wink but neither of us was prepared to admit anything was wrong. Adam kept saying he still felt unwell, even though he'd managed to put away all the beer left in the fridge after I'd gone to bed, and I was only just keeping my shit together.

'Are you not taking all this sun cream?' he shouted, waving half-empty bottles of Ambre Solaire in the air. 'There's loads left.'

'I couldn't fit it in my case,' I said as I heaved said case out of the front door and onto the deck, waving at our very early taxi driver. 'Leave it.'

'But there's more than half left in one of them.' He appeared in the living room with the three bottles in his hands. 'Why didn't you use one up instead of starting all three?'

'Why didn't you use any sunscreen the entire fortnight?' I replied. 'They're all different. SPF 50 for the first week, 30 for the second and 15 for my legs.'

'That doesn't make any sense,' he muttered, opening his suitcase and jamming the bottles inside. 'Such a waste of money.'

'It's sunscreen, it doesn't matter, we can buy more. And it's going to explode all over your sodding case if you keep shoving it in like that.'

He looked up, defiance all over his broad features.

'No, it won't.'

I raised an eyebrow and shrugged. 'Fine.'

'You're not right about everything you know.' He yanked the zip closed and pushed past me, chucking the case through the door. 'It's such a waste of money.'

'Arsehole,' I muttered under my breath. 'I'm totally right.'

He stood on the deck, staring at his phone as I locked the cottage door behind us. I'd already checked out when Adam went for his morning swim. Because like I said, he wasn't feeling well.

'All right?' I asked as he began to type madly, all fingers and thumbs with his phone. His hands were so big, they even dwarfed his iPhone 6. 'Is something wrong?'

He shook his head without taking his eyes off the

screen. 'I need to call someone, I won't be a minute. It's not a problem.'

I stared at him as he strode across the beach but kept my mouth closed for fear of accidentally screaming 'Where is my riiiiiing?' right in his face. Instead, I nodded and wheeled my suitcase over to the waiting taxi while he paced up and down the sand, shouting at someone in Spanish. For someone whose only opinion on weddings before finding out about Adam's supposed proposal was that if it wasn't an open-bar reception, I wasn't going, I was beginning to worry I'd lost my mind.

'*No!*' Adam barked in his laboured accent. '*Eso no es lo que acordamos.*'

It was strange to see him so close to losing his temper. Generally speaking, my boyfriend was so laidback and offensively agreeable that I once went round to his house to find Jehovah's Witnesses trying to come up with an excuse to leave.

'Who was that?' I asked, intensely casual as he clambered into the back of the taxi beside me.

'No one,' he replied, clicking in his seatbelt and turning towards the window. 'Nothing.'

Oh good, I thought, smiling beatifically. I was going to have to kill him.

'No one,' I repeated. 'Right.'

He looked back at me for a moment, seemingly on the verge of telling me something.

'Really,' he said with fifty per cent less huff. 'No one. The manager of that restaurant wanting to know why we missed our reservation.'

He was such a terrible liar.

'OK.' I kept my eyes on the horizon as we sped away

from our beautiful cottage, in the beautiful resort by the beautiful beach, and realized I had wasted two weeks waiting for a proposal that wasn't going to happen. 'OK, then.'

'Yeah,' Adam replied, shifting back towards the window. 'Everything's fine, don't worry about it.'

Because that was definitely a sensible thing to say to a woman, wasn't it?

'Here, give me that.'

Adam held out his hands for my suitcase as I jostled it up onto the headrest of the seat in front of me, hair stuck to my sweaty forehead.

'It's all right,' I said with a tired but determined smile. 'I can do it.'

'I know you can,' he replied, lifting the case out of my hands easily and sliding it neatly into the overhead locker before kissing me on the top of the head. 'Just let me help.'

'Thank you,' I said, hurling my handbag onto my seat. He shrugged agreeably, staring at his ticket as I curled up in my uncomfortable seat.

'Oh.'

'Oh?' I looked up to see Adam staring at his ticket. 'What's wrong? Are we not sat together?'

'We are,' he said, jamming his ticket into the back pocket of his jeans. 'But you're in the window seat.'

I looked out of the tiny porthole at the steaming tarmac below and saw three men in orange hi-vis vests chucking suitcases onto a conveyor belt. I watched as one fell off, bouncing along the floor before one of the men came over to kick it all the way back to the conveyor belt to try again.

'Did you want the window?' I looked out at my little square of sky reluctantly. 'We can swap?'

'No, I don't mind,' he wrestled his man bag from across his chest and dropped it in the aisle seat. 'It's just, you had the window on the way out.'

'You can have the window,' I told him, nursing my handbag. 'You sit here and I'll sit in the middle.'

'I said I don't mind.'

It was funny, because he certainly looked like he minded. He looked like he minded a lot of things but since he'd been almost silent ever since we got in the taxi it was impossible to know what was going on in his head. I had read every single gossip magazine the airport had to offer while he paced up and down the terminal, shouting at the supposed restaurant owner in broken Spanish. It had been a long three hours. I wasn't a woman renowned for her patience when it came to human beings and the thought of a twelve-hour flight back to the UK was not helping me be my most sensitive self. If he wasn't going to explain what was going on and the rubbish app I'd quickly downloaded to translate him couldn't explain either, I was just going to have to pretend it wasn't happening.

'Uh, I think I'm sitting next to you guys.' A young woman with an American accent waved her hand awkwardly behind Adam's immense shoulders. '22C?'

'Oh, hi.' I gave her a manic smile and nudged my boyfriend in the thigh. 'Adam, can you move your bag.'

'I'm Maura,' she said, slipping travel-sickness bands onto her wrists and sliding assorted medications and sick bags into her seatback pocket. 'I'll probably sleep the whole flight, so if you need to get by to use the bathroom, just like, climb over me.'

'No problem, I'm Olivia, Liv,' I replied, pointing at myself before gesturing at the six-foot-four human partition standing between us. 'This is Adam.'

'We're not supposed to change seats before take off.' He grabbed his bag from Maura's seat without acknowledging her and hugged it like a sulky toddler. She sat down, cheek to cheek against his backside. 'But whatever. You sit in the window, I'll sit in the middle. Again.'

I looked up at him, all tanned and sullen, and hoped against hope that my ring was wedged right up his arse.

'Why can't we change seats before take off?' I asked, watching as Maura in 22C swallowed a handful of little white pills without so much as a sip of water. Total pro.

He sat down in the middle seat with a heavy thump. 'Because if we blow up during take off, they might not be able to identify the bodies so they need to know where everyone was to distribute the remains.'

Maura in 22C froze.

'I think it's actually something to do with weight distribution,' I replied loudly. 'And I don't think it really matters that much, let's just swap.'

'No, that's helicopters,' Adam corrected, still cuddling his backpack. 'With planes it's in case all the bodies get burned up beyond recognition, then they can bury the right remains in the right—'

'Just swap with me.' I stood up and hoisted him to his feet while Maura in 22C began to cry. 'And for god's sake, shut up.'

'What?' he asked, wide-eyed and completely oblivious to my neighbour shaking silently as she stared at the safety card through red eyes. 'What did I do?'

'Nothing,' I muttered, hiding behind my hair. 'Sit down.'

Adam kicked his bag under the seat in front and pulled

his hood over his head, smiling for the first time in I couldn't remember how long.

'Liv.'

From deep inside a dream about going out for ice cream with Brad, Ange and all the kids, I felt a stiff poke in my shoulder.

'Liv? Liv.'

Why? Why would he wake me up when it took me so long to fall asleep?

'Liv.' Adam tapped my shoulder over and over again. 'Are you awake?'

'No,' I replied without opening my eyes. 'I'm really not.'

'I'm bored.'

I cracked open one eye to find his face so close to mine that everything but his freckles was a blur.

'Talk to me,' he pulled the strings on his red jumper so that the hood cinched in tightly around his face until just his eyes and nose were showing, the strain showing on his stupid, handsome face. 'We've still got ages.'

'I know, that's why I was asleep,' I said, swiping at his hood. 'Can you take that down? You look like Little Red Riding twat.'

'You love it.' Adam tied the strings in an elaborate bow underneath his chin. 'I look amazing. I'm the amazing red-hooded yeti.'

'If you say so,' I replied with a yawn. 'And I'm not just saying that because you've got food in your hand.'

Abi had been the one to christen him 'yeti' when we first met. She always labelled our dates, refusing to acknowledge their real names until the relationships had been established. Adam came to be known as the yeti because none of us really believed it was possible for an eligible, handsome man over the age of thirty to move to our village with his family and therefore she considered his kind to be as rare as the abominable snowman. With his sandy blond hair, longer and shaggier than it was now, yeti worked, and yeti had stuck.

'Open your mouth,' he ordered, opening a packet of M&Ms. 'I bet I can do it in one.'

Somewhere far, far away, I felt my grandmother spinning in her grave. Somewhere closer, I heard Maura in 22C let out a stuck-pig snore.

'You're not throwing sweets at my face on a plane,' I said quietly, holding up a hand in front of my face. 'Stop it.'

'You know I can do it,' Adam repeated, readying a blue M&M. 'Open your mouth.'

With lips pursed tighter than the average cat's arse, I shook my head, still mad about being woken up and slowly remembering all the other reasons I was upset with him. Last night's weirdness, the airport phone calls and, oh yeah, the complete and utter lack of a bloody proposal.

'Fine, whatever,' he muttered, emptying half the bag directly into his mouth, slumping back down in his seat and producing a tiny can of Coke from his backpack. 'Sorry, Mum.'

'Excuse me?' I turned so sharply a curtain of my own sun-bleached blonde hair slapped me in the face. 'What did you call me?'

'Nothing,' he replied with a smirk. 'Mum.'

'Oh, be quiet,' I replied, mostly peeved because he was right. It was happening more and more often, I would open my mouth and my mother's voice would come out instead. I had Motherettes. 'That's so not funny.'

'Oh, it's *so* not funny?' He let down my tray table without asking and placed his can in the little indentation without a napkin underneath. 'I hate when you talk to me like a child, you're not my mother, you know.'

'Thank god,' I quipped without thinking.

The smirk wiped itself off his face.

'And what's that supposed to mean?'

I should have known better, I really should. I knew I wasn't allowed to make comments about his mum, ever, no matter what he felt like saying about mine. It was the number one unwritten, unspoken rule of dating a mummy's boy. Never make a joke about his mother, ever.

'Nothing.' I picked up his drink and snapped my table back in place to cross my legs without hitting my knees. 'Is your tray broken or something?'

'At least my mum's fun,' he muttered, nipping the can out of my hand and glugging. 'At least my parents aren't boring.'

'Don't start.' I closed my eyes and tried to think of happy things like my friends and my cat and advent calendars and Tom Hardy and the Topshop summer sale. Nothing was really that wrong, it was just the enclosed space and the lack of sleep and the night before and . . . oh god, I really was going to kill someone. At least Maura was completely unconscious so there wouldn't be any witnesses.

'I can't be arsed with you right now.'

'*Me*?' Adam replied, incredulous. 'What have *I* done?'

'Other than all those weird phone calls? And the moody silences?' Once I'd started, I couldn't stop myself and an unpleasant feeling began to fizz up in my chest.

'Or, I don't know, completely ruining the last night of our holiday?'

'I didn't feel well,' he protested. The strings of his hoodie were still tied in a neat bow under his chin and it was all I could do not to choke him with them. 'You couldn't walk in those stupid shoes anyway; you would have ended up moaning all night. You should be grateful.'

'I would not have moaned.' My foot was still throbbing underneath the four layers of plasters. Ten minutes away, my arse. 'You were the one who said it was ten minutes. And can you please take that hood off when I'm trying to talk to you?'

Adam yanked the hood down, his hair springing up around his face, all fluffy and dry from the recycled plane air. He looked like a furious Pomeranian and it was very hard to take him seriously.

'So, I made a mistake.' He chugged his drink and crumpled the can like a slightly less impressive Incredible Hulk. He was, in fairness, almost as green. Adam was not a good flier. 'I'm sorry I'm not perfect all the time like you. And it wouldn't matter if you hadn't been wearing those stupid shoes in the first place.'

'I'm not perfect,' I said, brushing my hair behind my ears as my eyes began to burn. It was just the dry air. My eyes were watering because I'd gone to sleep in my contact lenses. I definitely wasn't crying. 'I'm just not stupid.'

I felt Maura seize up at the side of me, not nearly as unconscious as I had originally thought.

A condescending sigh escaped his mouth and he flipped his hood back up over his head, pulling it down over his eyes.

'That's me, so stupid. Not like Professor Liv. I'll shut up before I say anything else that offends you.'

I didn't know what to do. We never argued, ever. Well, there was that one time he'd deleted the *Downton Abbey* finale off my Sky+ but he'd replaced it with the DVD and all was forgiven. What was I supposed to do? Let him calm down, I told myself. Take Elsa's advice and let it go. That would be the clever thing to do.

'Arsehole.'

I closed my eyes the second it was out, ashamed. Elsa would never call her boyfriend an arsehole – Olaf, maybe, but never Elsa.

'I'm an arsehole?'

Adam yanked the hood down and turned in his seat to give me his full attention.

'I'm an arsehole?' he repeated.

I opened my mouth but nothing came out. Oh brilliant, *now* I couldn't think of anything to say.

'You've been acting like a mentalist for two weeks,' he said in an angry whisper that woke anyone still sleeping in a three-row radius. 'Whining, sulking, constantly complaining and *I'm* the arsehole.'

'When was I whining? What have I complained about?' I replied, trying to keep my rage to an appropriate volume level. My grandmother would have come back to life just to die again if she'd seen us arguing in public. 'What are you talking about?'

'"What are we doing today, Adam? Where are we going tonight, Adam? Adam, I need a drink. Adam, it's so hot. Why don't you carry me, Adam? Why didn't we hire a donkey, Adam?"'

'I was only joking about you carrying me,' I replied, flushed. 'And obviously I didn't really want to hire a donkey. You're totally exaggerating.'

Admittedly, I had googled the donkey thing when a

girl rode one past us halfway up a mountain but apparently you had to buy it outright and I knew my credit card limit wouldn't stretch to it. Not after that bloody stupid frock. For the most part, any questioning on my part was because I was anxious about the supposed proposal, but I could hardly tell him that.

'I'm very sorry the Mayans didn't build their ancient civilization closer to the hotel,' Adam seethed. 'What a bunch of selfish fuckers.'

'It *was* hot and I *was* thirsty,' I glanced around the plane and everyone quickly looked away. 'But that doesn't mean I wasn't having a good time. Don't make out like all I did was complain.'

'Oh, I'm sure you enjoyed yourself,' he said, either oblivious to or unconcerned by the scene he was creating. 'You love complaining, you complain constantly.'

'I do not.' At least, no more than any other self-respecting Englishwoman. 'I tell you when I'm upset about something, that's not the same thing.'

'Then you must be constantly upset. Liv, how do you cope?' Adam said, sharpening his spine and wrapping his arms around himself, pulling himself further and further away from me, severing every point of physical contact. 'Nothing's ever good enough for you, is it?'

'What are you talking about?' I was so incredibly angry I could barely see, and worst of all, I was almost certainly about to cry. 'You've totally lost me.'

'Mexico's not good enough, my family's not good enough, *I'm* not good enough,' he carried on ranting in a mad whisper, banging his elbows on the armrests and his head hitting the ceiling as he threw himself around in his seat like an overgrown toddler. 'Nothing's ever good enough.'

I stared at my boyfriend and he fannied around with his seatbelt, yanking on the strap trying to extend it, only succeeding in restraining himself even more tightly. Not a terrible idea, as things were. It was so out of character. Adam never lost his temper. Something was definitely wrong.

'Adam,' I laid my hand on his arm to calm him, trying to ignore the prying eyes up and down the plane and be the bigger person. 'What's wrong?'

He shook his head and pulled away. My hand hovered in midair for a moment and I literally didn't know what to do. What had happened? How had we gone from kissing in the cottage to shouting at each other on a plane?

'What's wrong with me?' he asked with a laugh. 'Amazing. There's nothing wrong with me, what's wrong with you?'

Without waiting for an answer, he pulled his phone out of the seatback pocket and opened up one of his games, completely ignoring the stunned expressions on me, Maura in 22C and everyone in row 23. Nothing I wanted to say could be helpful, nothing I was feeling made sense. All I could do now was sit quietly for the next five and a half hours and hope we were flying through the Mexican equivalent of the Bermuda Triangle.

Dabbing the corners of my eyes with my sleeve, I stared straight ahead, burning with embarrassment, confusion and most of all, the unshakeable feeling that I had done something wrong only I didn't know what. And if he hadn't apologized by the time we landed, I could always push him down the escalators at Heathrow and say it was an accident.

*　　*　　*

We spent the rest of the flight in silence, listening to Maura's choked sobs every time the plane shook, followed by another wordless hour in customs and nearly two more driving home. I was half awake, half asleep, delirious from jet lag and unwelcome tears. I didn't care about the ring at all any more, all I wanted to know was why Adam was so incredibly angry.

A sharp left turn jolted me wide awake as we pulled off the main road and into the village. Enough was enough, I thought, rubbing my eyes and blinking at the clock on his dash. Perhaps the holiday wasn't going to end in a proposal but there was no way it was going to end like this.

'Here already?'

Adam nodded as we pelted down the country roads.

'I wonder what's gone on while we've been away,' I said, my voice so croaky I could barely hear it myself. 'Dad was supposed to be getting the surgery painted. I hope he got the colours I suggested.'

Adam stared straight ahead.

'I bet Gus has grown,' I went on. 'He gets bigger every time I see him. I think he's going to be tall like you and your dad. I bet he'll be bigger than Chris by the time he's seven. Definitely going to be a heartbreaker, like your mum said.'

I stole a sideways glance at my boyfriend. Nothing.

'It's a long way from Tulum, isn't it?' I clucked as we flew past the supermarket my dad swore he would never shop at until he found out he could get a free coffee every time he went in. The little village Co-op had closed within six months, it never stood a chance. 'Makes you think.'

About what, I wasn't sure.

Another left turn took us off the high street and down the little lane that led to the surgery.

'We're going to mine?' I asked, sounding like I'd sandpapered my throat on the way home.

We never stayed at mine because Adam hated staying at mine. Mine being a tiny one-bedroom flat above the veterinary surgery as opposed to Adam's three-bedroom house with a great big garden and no attached neighbours. Adam claimed the flat was haunted by the Ghosts of Pets Past and their late-night howling kept him awake but I had an inkling it was more to do with the fact he didn't like being away from his fancy coffee maker and king-size bed. Out of the three years we'd been together, I could count the number of nights we'd spent together in my flat on one hand. Most of my things were over at Adam's but since my parents were oddly old-fashioned about these things, I had never officially moved in. I slept at mine once, maybe twice, a week, if my evening surgery ran late or Abi demanded a sleepover but really, it was little more than an unnecessarily well-furnished storage locker.

Adam's Land Rover crunched along the gravel outside the surgery and the motion-activated security lights shone accusingly into my eyes. Exhausted and frustrated, all I wanted was to go to bed. Maybe a couple of hours of decent kip would help, things always got blown out of proportion outside of daylight hours and everyone knew things seemed worse when you were tired. I opened the passenger side door and stumbled out onto the drive – Adam's car really wasn't made for a short arse like me. Retrieving my suitcase from the boot, I was staggering down the path with my suitcase, halfway to the front door, keys in hand before I realized Adam was still in the car. Still wearing his seatbelt. Still gripping the steering wheel as though the car might tear away all on its own.

'Are you planning on sleeping out here?' I asked, the sharp edges of my house keys cutting into my fingers. 'It's a bit cold for a camp-out.'

'No,' he replied, eyes straight ahead. 'I'm going home.'

I took a deep, calming breath.

'Adam,' I said as softly as I could. 'Come inside—'

'I need to sort some stuff out,' he cut me off, nodding once at his windshield. Even though he was looking in my general direction, his eyes didn't quite meet mine. 'I need a break, Liv.'

'Well, you've just had a holiday,' I pointed out, trying not to yawn. 'That was a two-week break.'

'I don't mean that kind of break,' he tailed off with a huffing noise and then turned the key in the ignition. 'I need a break from this, a break from us.'

The security light blinked out above me, leaving me in disorienting darkness for too long a moment. The only thing I could make out was Adam's profile, etched in orange light from his glowing dashboard.

'What?'

My handbag slid off my shoulder, landed on my foot and then hit the ground, its contents spilling all over the floor. Inside the surgery I heard a few drowsy barks and whimpers as the security light flashed back into life, dazzling me with its angry white light.

'I'm tired, Liv,' he muttered, gunning the engine. 'I'm going home and I'll talk to you later.'

Without any further explanation, he reversed quickly and peeled out of the driveway, showering me with gravel as he went. Stunned, I reached down to grab my handbag and felt an unexpected tear roll out of my dry eye and off the end of my nose. Inside the bag, my phone was flashing with a text message. It was Cassie, up for a three a.m. feed.

ARE YOU ENGAGED???? DID HE DO IT??????

'No,' I whispered to my phone, tears falling freely down my face as I knelt on the floor. 'I'm just knackered, miserable and desperate for a wee.'

The sharp stones of the driveway dug into my knees, and underneath all the plasters my foot was screaming but I couldn't feel any of it. I couldn't feel anything at all. Swiping the back of my hand across my face, I scooped all my things back into my handbag then dragged my suitcase through the gravel, up to the door of my little flat, alone.

3

'Morning, Nutsack.'

There was nothing like waking up to a phone call from my brother to ruin a perfectly good Tuesday before it had even begun.

'You there or did the kidnappers answer your phone?' he said when I didn't reply. He laughed at his own joke, still waiting for a response. 'If this is the kidnappers, we don't want him back. Do what you've got to do.'

'Very funny, Chris.' I yawned loudly, grinding my fists into my eyes. Why was I asleep on the settee? Why was I still wearing my coat? Why did I have a horrible feeling that I'd ruined my life?

Oh.

Yeah.

I stretched out the crick in my neck and squinted at the devastation in my living room, suitcase dumped open by the door, jumper thrown across the floor, duty free bottle of whiskey left open, knocked over by a flying shoe and emptied out onto my rug.

'What do you want?'

'Nothing you want to tell me, little brother?' he asked. 'Nothing you'd like to share before I see it plastered all over social media?'

'Nope.'

'Really?'

'Really.'

I stretched as far as I could without getting up and dug around in the suitcase for the little square box I'd been carrying around for three months. It wasn't there.

'You didn't do it?'

'I really don't want to talk about it,' I assured him, panic rising. Where was the ring? 'What do you want?'

'Whatever you say, dude,' he replied, letting go far more easily than I had anticipated. 'Dad needs a lift to the supermarket and I can't take him. Can you pick him up?'

'I just got off a plane.' I lay back down, head spinning from my ill-advised three a.m. nightcap and felt something digging into my hip. It was the ring box, nestling in between the sofa cushions. 'Why can't you take him?'

'Because I've got a job, Adam, and I'm on my way into the office. You can't tell I'm in the car at all, can you? I got this new Bluetooth hook up for the Jag and it's so clear I—'

'Can't you take the day off?' I interrupted, picking up the ring box and letting the sharp corners dig into my palm. 'I thought you were your own boss.'

'No such thing as a day off when you run your own company,' he scoffed. 'I've barely had a minute to myself in the last month. Honestly, I'm out for a morning and my number two doesn't know whether to shit or wind his watch. I've employed idiots, Adam, it's a miracle we're even still going, let alone doing so well. I've got to go in today, we're pitching for this—'

'I'll take him,' I said quickly. I didn't have the stomach for another Chris Floyd lecture on how Very Important he was. 'I'll be there in an hour; let me have a shower and I'll go over.'

'OK, I'll let him know,' Chris replied cheerfully. 'So, what went wrong? Did you not have a good time? Cass is dying to hear all about it.'

'Yeah, something like that,' I said, rubbing my temples. 'I'd better go.'

'Well, I hope you're planning to be more talkative tomorrow night. You're both still coming round for dinner, aren't you?'

'Uh, I don't know,' I said, sitting up and faking a cough. I'd forgotten, I always forgot. Liv managed our social calendar. I was in charge of making sure she ate solid food and she was in charge of making sure I entered the outside world. It had been a good system until now. 'I've not been feeling brilliant. I don't want to come if I've got a cold. You know, the baby.'

'Oh yeah,' he replied. 'I suppose not. You pick it up on holiday?'

'On the plane, I think,' I went for another cough, trying to get a bit more of a hack into it and putting Chris on speaker while I checked my emails and messages. 'Been feeling shit all night.'

At least that part wasn't a lie.

'Well, let me know, twatfink,' Chris said. 'Cass was going to cook some ridiculously complicated Chinese thing that takes ten years to make. If you're not going to come, for fuck's sake text me tonight or I'll never hear the end of it.'

'Tell her we'd be just as happy with a takeaway,' I replied, scanning one of half a dozen emails from Pablo the restaurant manager who seemed dead set on screwing me out of all my money for the non-event of a proposal. How could not showing up and eating dinner be costing me more money than actually going to the restaurant? I definitely hadn't told him to organize a firework display. Had I? 'I'll bring a pizza or something, the woman just had a baby.'

'Yeah, but you know how she is,' he said with half a sigh. 'She wants to do something nice and, you know, I thought we'd be celebrating.'

I did know how she was, and I thought we'd be celebrating too. The ring box was not supposed to be in my hand right now, or at least the contents weren't. Actually, I wasn't sure where the box went once the ring was on her finger. Did she keep the box? Did I? Did we throw it in the sea in a glorious celebration of love and the giddy assumption that it would never, ever come off her hand ever again?

'Don't let her mess about cooking.' I stuck my left big toe into the ankle of my left sock, wriggling it down over my heel. 'I'll text you later, but right now I feel like shite. I really don't think we'll be coming over.'

'OK, let me know, I've got to go, almost at work.'

'Yeah, I get it,' I said, tackling the second sock, so much easier now the first one was off. 'I'm honoured you found the time to call to ask me to do you a favour in the first place.'

'You should be,' he said. 'Now go and get Dad before he eats one of the dogs. Love to Liv.'

Kicking my socks across the wooden floor, I let my phone slip between the sofa cushions and held the ring box in the palm of my hand. Such an inconspicuous little thing. For something so small, it felt very heavy.

'Adam, what did you do?' I wondered aloud while Jim Beam tap-danced on my temples. My mouth was dry and my eyes were sore and every part of me ached. 'What did you do?'

It was all a bit of a blur and for that I was thankful. I remembered losing it on the plane, driving home in silence and then an argument at her front door although exactly what had been said was a mystery. And after that . . . nothing. I couldn't hold my ale at the best of times but Jim Beam and jet lag were an evil combination and I knew I wasn't in a rush to call her for the details.

Very carefully, I stood up and placed the ring box carefully inside a tall ceramic vase on the mantelpiece. Somewhere it couldn't escape, somewhere I couldn't see it.

Stretching, I picked up the almost-empty whiskey bottle and set it on the coffee table, gagging at the stench of booze coming from the rug. I was a mess.

'Shower first, Dad second,' I told my greyish-green reflection. 'Grovel to Liv third.'

I had a feeling the last one could take a while.

'You're shitting me?'

'I shit you not.'

'I don't believe you.'

'Because I'd make this up? Can you hand me the thermometer?'

David, my nurse and work-husband, picked up the requested instrument without taking his narrowed brown eyes off me. Bruiser, a French bulldog who couldn't stop

passing foul gas, kept his huge green eyes on the thermometer.

I really hadn't slept after Adam dropped me off and,
instead, I tossed and turned for a couple of hours before
changing out of my pyjamas and into my scrubs. I'd done
the rounds, checked on our overnight patients and called
all their owners before David even got to work. As far
as I could tell, nothing majorly dramatic had happened
while I was away, other than my dad being called out
to tend to an epileptic guinea pig in the middle of the
night a week last Friday.

'Adam didn't propose?' David wrapped his rubber-
gloved hands around the unwilling pup. 'Hold still,
Bruiser, it'll all be over in a minute.'

'That's what he says to all the boys,' I whispered to
Bruiser as I lubed up the probe.

'Honestly, I'm not telling you anything ever again,' he
replied with an affected toss of his head. 'It was one
time and I didn't care for it one bit. I went to public
school, Liv – everyone was doing it.'

Even when I was sleep-deprived, jet-lagged and desperately trying to convince myself nothing was wrong, David
could still make me smile.

'Don't change the subject. What the cocking hell
happened?'

'Not only did Adam not propose,' I said, watching the
numbers jump around on the little digital monitor while
Bruiser the Farting Dog made a horrible high-pitched
noise I had not missed in the slightest. 'He went
completely mental on the last evening, we had this really
weird fight on the plane, then he dropped me off at mine
at three o'clock this morning and announced he needed
a break.'

He lowered his chin and raised an eyebrow. 'A break?'

'Temperature's normal,' I nodded. 'A break. Isn't that weird?'

'Let me get this straight . . .' David gave Bruiser a well-earned scratch behind the ear before turning his full attentions to me. 'You went all the way to Mexico to get engaged and instead you came home dumped?'

I looked up sharply to see a confused look on my friend's face.

'He didn't dump me, he said he needed a break,' I said, nudging my wonky blonde topknot with my wrist. 'That's not what I said.'

'OK, then what happened to the proposal?' He swabbed Bruiser's behind before carefully carrying him back into the blanket-lined cage behind him. 'I thought this was a done deal? I missed out on so many pastry-eating opportunities so you could look skinny in the engagement pictures.'

'And for that I apologize,' I said, peeling off my latex gloves. 'I have no explanation. Maybe he never was going to propose. It's nearly three months since Cass told me about the ring. The ring I'm not even supposed to know about, remember?'

'You mean, maybe he bought the ring then realized he didn't want to marry you but he didn't want to break up with you before the holiday because he'd already paid for it, so he waited for you to get back?'

Both Bruiser and I gasped in unison.

'You are a very mean man,' I told him as the idea squirrelled itself away into my brain. What had been said could never be unsaid. 'This is why you haven't got a girlfriend.'

David, resplendent in Dalmatian print scrubs he had

ordered in from the States, stared at me from across the room. 'I haven't got a girlfriend because I'm too awesome for one woman,' he assured me. 'And because Abi still won't put out.'

'Abi will never put out for you,' I tossed my gloves into the bin but felt nothing as they swished into the basket the first time. Things were really bad. 'And Adam did not break up with me. We had an argument, he needed a good night's sleep. That's all that happened.'

He fixed me with a sympathetic smile.

'As a man and as your friend,' he replied. 'It's my duty to tell you you're being really stupid right now.'

A wave of jet lag and nausea washed over me. I probably should have eaten something other than half a packet of Jammy Dodgers before coming down to work.

'And you're being really unpleasant,' I said. 'You're not getting your present now. Shut up.'

'I'm only trying to help,' he said, shrugging as though I was the one who was being unreasonable. 'I mean, you're not engaged, are you?'

I turned on the cold tap and held my hands under the water, trying to wake myself up. He had said he was tired and that we'd talk later and that he needed a break from us. Did he really mean he wanted to break up?

I turned off the tap slowly, waiting for another, more rational explanation to present itself.

'You really think he's dumped me?' I asked, the prospect hitting me like a sound slap. 'He meant a break-up break?'

'This is going to come as something of a shock given that I constantly anticipate your every need,' David replied, 'but I'm not actually a mind reader. I don't know what he's thinking, Liv, any more than you do. I thought this proposal was a done deal; I was just waiting for you to ask me to be your bridesdude.'

'So did I,' I replied, still reeling from the possibility I might have been dumped without even realizing it. 'But just so you know, I wasn't planning on bridesdudes.'

'You're so cruel,' David said as I flipped blindly through Bruiser's chart to cover my hot face. 'To be honest, Liv, I'd blame Cass for this whole thing. If she hadn't told you about the ring, you wouldn't have been so stressed before you went away.'

'She knows I hate surprises,' I couldn't help defend Cass but in my heart of hearts, I agreed with him. My relaxing holiday had been ruined before it had started. 'It's stupid, I wasn't even thinking about getting engaged until this all kicked off. Oh god, David, did he dump me?'

He looked up at the buzzing fluorescent light in the ceiling that Dad was supposed to get fixed while I was away and shrugged.

'I don't know, Livvy,' he said. 'Men can be shits. Last time I had to break up with a girl, I asked my neighbour to answer my phone and shout at her in Japanese until she stopped calling. Have you tried to call him this morning?'

'No?' I replied, still stunned. 'When he said he'd talk to me later, I assumed I would talk to him later. I didn't know I'd been bloody dumped, did I?'

'So you took one part of his conversation literally but not the other?' He bent over, nose to nose with Bruiser. 'Women.'

Bruiser growled in agreement. Then farted.

'Not women, *Adam*,' I corrected as David reeled backwards into the sink. He really was noxious, the poor pup. 'He's the one who's being a knob. Who would dump their girlfriend like that? You need to be clear about those kinds of things, you need to be specific. There is no room for ambiguity in a dumping!'

I grabbed hold of the stainless steel examination table and replayed the entire incident. Had he said break-up and not break? Had I misheard? It was possible; I was so tired. But why? Why would he do that? All the stress and hurt and uncertainty bubbled back up inside me. Bruiser gave a quiet growl and licked my hand. Even the flatulent dog felt sorry for me.

'Liv.' Fanning the air in front of his face, David leaned against the back door and crossed his black-and-white spotted arms in front of him. 'Pick up the bloody phone. You won't know what's going on until you talk to him.'

Stupid David and his stupid common sense.

'I'll do it after my next appointment,' I said, stretching my naked fingers out wide and pressing into the cold metal of the table. I was not going to lose it at work, I just wasn't. 'It's Zoe Gustar isn't it? I could do with some pug time.'

'Are you sure?' he asked with a furrowed brow. 'I'm sorry, I shouldn't have said anything. I'm sure you're right and this is just a big misunderstanding.'

'It's fine,' I said, my hands shaking. 'Really, I'm fine.'

'I'll talk to Zoe and the pug,' he said, snatching up the clipboard from the table. 'Go and call him now. You're not going to be good for anything until you do.'

'OK,' I said, nodding as I opened the door that led to the back passages of the surgery, taking the used instruments with me. 'I appreciate it.'

'You'll figure this out,' David said, patting me on the topknot as I went. 'And I'm glad to have you back.'

'Yeah,' I agreed with enthusiasm I did not feel as I closed the exam room door behind me. 'Me too.'

There really was nothing like sticking a thermometer up a dog's arse then finding out you'd been stealth-dumped to let you know your holiday was over.

4

'And apparently that will blow up a microwave.'

Dad pulled two boxes of cereal from the shelf and held them both at arm's length, considering the packaging over the top of his glasses.

'I don't understand why you were trying to microwave yoghurt in the first place,' I said, taking the Frosties out of his hand and putting them right back on the shelf. 'How bored were you?'

'Have you ever cooked yoghurt? Maybe it's delicious.' He handed me the Coco Pops without a fight and resignedly replaced them with a box of muesli. 'I thought it might be a bit like Ready Brek.'

I looked at his all organic, sugar-free selections and tossed the box of Coco Pops back in the trolley. 'Make sure they're gone before Mum gets home.'

'Oh, they will be,' he said, leaning heavily on the trolley, his walking stick wedged in his shopping bag and resting up against his shoulder like a flagpole missing its flag. 'Maybe you and Chris can come round tonight and help me finish them. Or we could even order a pizza. It's bin day tomorrow, your mother would never know.'

'Pizza?' I asked in a doubtful tone. 'I thought you weren't allowed dairy or gluten any more?'

'Or meat,' he added. 'Let's get a pepperoni pizza.'

'I don't know if I can do tonight,' I said, walking ahead. 'I've got some stuff on.'

'Oh. OK,' he shuffled forward, a martyred smile on his face. 'Your mum'll be back tomorrow night. Would have been nice to have a boys' night but, of course, I know you two are very busy.'

I picked up a packet of Weetabix. We were all out and I knew Liv would want to get back on her healthy eating kick now we were back from holidays. Right after she'd given me the kicking I was almost certain I deserved.

'Has she had a good time?' I asked, also remembering I had told Liv I wanted to take a break at three o'clock in the morning and I put the Weetabix back, swallowing down the dark feeling in the pit of my stomach. 'It was a yoga retreat, wasn't it?'

'Yoga retreat *and* a sugar detox,' he corrected, turning a corner and staring wistfully at a packet of chocolate Hobnobs. 'And something to do with mindfulness.'

'Intense.' I raised my eyebrows at my dad in his freshly pressed shirt and trousers with a crease so sharp they could have sliced bread. Not that he was allowed to eat bread. Mum's middle-aged interest in all things healthy had completely passed him by, but Coco Pop bans aside, they both seemed to be adjusting to her new path with relative ease. Probably because Mum didn't know he was sneaking down the café for a bacon sandwich every other morning when he went out to get the paper. That was the thing about villages: too small for secrets. I'd seen him, hiding in the back behind his *Telegraph*, brown sauce all over his mush.

'That's the one,' he nodded. 'Are you sure you can't do tonight? I mean, Chris has got his own business and a new baby but he said he could find half an hour or so. Early doors? Four-ish?'

Sighing, I picked up the Hobnobs and put them in the trolley next to the Coco Pops.

'If Chris can make it, I suppose I can.'

'He's a good lad,' Dad said with a nod. 'He's got a pitch, you know.'

'I do know,' I replied, folding the sleeves of my jumper over my knuckles. 'He mentioned it. Twice.'

'He's doing so well.' He smiled brightly at a furious-looking woman in a tabard and kept talking. 'And little Gus, what a pumpkin. Healthy as an ox, he is.'

'Total pumpkin,' I agreed, unsure as to whether or not that was a good thing but Dad had been a doctor before he retired so I assumed positive things.

'You should get some babysitting in,' Dad advised. 'Before it's your turn.'

'Yeah,' I replied, focusing on the nutritional table on the back of a jar of Horlicks.

Ever since that fateful night Friday night at Sadie Jenkins' house party in Year Twelve, me and my mates had spent almost every waking second trying to work out how to have sex as often as possible without knocking anyone up. Sex good, babies bad. Now they were popping up all over the place and I never knew how I was supposed to react. When Cassie first got pregnant, Chris was a wreck, hiding in the back of his garage and singing Oasis songs to himself while he played with his original, mint condition 1992 Game Boy. Now he was posting topless black-and-white pictures of himself on Facebook, holding the baby in the air like he was the FA Cup. As Liv pointed out, it was all very Athena poster and not in a good way. Chris was not a man who should be appearing shirtless in the world.

'All right, out with it,' Dad demanded as we headed for the toilet paper aisle. 'You haven't said a word about your holiday and quite frankly, Adam, I can't remember a time you've had less to say for yourself since you went through puberty. Is something the matter?'

I shook my head and grabbed a twelve-pack of Andrex. 'Nope.'

'Your mum doesn't like those ones.' He fished them back out of the trolley and put them straight back on the shelf. 'Ever since they put the dogs on the paper. She says it makes her uncomfortable.'

'Fair.' I swapped for an overpriced, unbleached organic, recycled brand and waited for Dad's approval, which was given in a slow nod. 'I'm just tired, we got in late.'

'But you had a nice time?' he asked. 'And Liv's well?'

'We had a brilliant time the whole two weeks,' I said. Not technically a lie, it didn't really go to shit until the last night. 'Liv's fine.'

'And she won't mind me borrowing you tonight?' He pushed his glasses up the bridge of his nose, smiling brightly. 'Pizza, Coco Pops and a bit of *Newsnight*?'

'How could any woman begrudge any man pizza, Coco Pops and Kirsty Wark?' I replied. 'Other than Mum, obviously.'

'Sugar is more addictive than cocaine,' he said wisely. 'And meat is murder. And I'm sure there's something about pizza but I can't think of it right now and, to be frank, I don't care to. I've earned the right to a slice of pizza once in a while.'

Couldn't argue with the man.

'When do you think she'll pack this all in?'

'I'm not sure she will.' He tapped his fingers on the top of his walking stick while contemplating the different types of wet wipes. 'She's stuck to this a lot longer than she did the ballroom dancing or the pottery.'

'Any joy on selling the kiln?'

'Not a lot of demand for a second-hand kiln round here,' Dad replied. 'And you never know, she might take an interest again.'

'You're a saint,' I said, thinking of all the oddly shaped bowls and redundant ashtrays filling up my kitchen cupboards. Mum's hobbies must have cost them a small fortune. Almost as much as a half-completed law degree, suggested the little voice in my head that sounded an awful lot like my brother. 'I don't know how you cope sometimes.'

'I knew what I was getting into when I married your mother,' he said with a little shrug. 'The only thing she's ever stuck to for more than six months is me, so I can't really complain. I know it's different nowadays but I won't say I wasn't glad when Chris tied the knot. It changes things. You'll understand when you get married.'

'Yeah,' I shivered involuntarily, not sure if I was more afraid of going over to apologize or the thought that she might not want to see me in the first place. 'Maybe you're right.'

There was, after all, a first time for everything.

I've never been a smoker but there were times when the idea of popping out for a cigarette sounded so great.

Hiding at the back of the surgery and checking Instagram was not relaxing. All those photos of other people's holidays, overdrawn-lip selfies and artfully shot pasta might have been easier to stomach with a lungful of nicotine. Every time I scrolled through, I thought of an old framed photo of my granddad hanging in my parents' living room. He was standing in the surgery in his operating gown, enjoying a pipe with his colleagues immediately after performing his first successful spinal surgery on an Alsatian. I'm not saying it was the healthiest thing for my granddad or the dog, but everyone in the picture looked incredibly relaxed and every single one of them was puffing away. Here I was, squinting at a smudged phone screen, looking at what one-quarter of Little Mix had for breakfast and my anxiety levels were off the charts.

For sixteen minutes I'd been pretending I was about to call Adam and in those sixteen minutes, I'd done a full lap of my social media channels and checked three different websites to make sure it wasn't Mercury retrograde. I wasn't usually someone who was lost for words but it was one thing knowing how to say 'I'm sorry, Mrs Stevens, your hamster didn't make it' without hesitating but quite another to call your boyfriend when all you had to work with was 'So, I was just wondering, did you by any chance dump me at three o'clock this morning?'

'Liv?'

I looked up to see Adam right there in front of me, same red hooded sweatshirt as the night before, a different, more sheepish expression on his face.

'Hello,' he said.

Well, at least he'd saved me a phone call.

'You look knackered.' There was a sad-looking bunch

of pink roses in his right hand and he was hanging onto them for dear life. 'Busy morning?'

'Very,' I replied. 'And, you know, I didn't get a lot of sleep.'

'Oh, yeah,' he looked down at the flowers in his hand and blew out a big, heavy breath. 'These are for you.'

He stretched as far as his long arms would reach, only taking two extra steps towards me when he was absolutely certain they were necessary.

'Thanks,' I said, trying not to notice the remains of the price sticker he hadn't quite managed to remove. There were a bunch of Sainsbury's bags in the back of his car and my stomach rumbled loudly. Would it be impolite to trade the flowers for a loaf of bread? 'They're pretty.'

They weren't.

'Least I could do,' Adam's words were stilted and uncomfortable. 'I'm sorry about last night, I don't know what was going on in my head, I must have gone mental from the flight.'

'You mean about the break thing?' I asked, concentrating on the bouquet of flowers. Even though he was here to apologize and take it back, having David's theory proven right hurt. Really hurt. Hurt like I'd been kicked in the stomach by a donkey. That really had happened once and donkeys do not mess about.

'Um, yes?' He dug his hands in his pockets, looked at his feet for a moment then peeped back up to see whether or not he was forgiven. 'Sorry.'

He was not.

'You're sorry?' I asked. He *had* dumped me. There had been a dumping and I didn't even know. Standing there, in the car park, phone in one hand, crappy supermarket flowers in the other, I was so close to meltdown. Anything

I said or did would be wrong. If I cried I would feel foolish, if I shouted, he would shout back, and if I punched him in the throat, well, in theory I could go to prison but really shouldn't I get some kind of prize? I didn't know which was worse, to be angry, crazy or heartbroken, because, in that moment, I was all of the above.

'Yeah, I'm sorry.' He gave me a small, handsome smile and lifted his head a little bit more. 'Uh, so, I know we were supposed to go round to Chris and Cassie's tonight but Mum's away and Dad asked if me and Chris would go round there, so I think we're going to do that instead. Me and Chris, I mean.'

My grip tightened around the stems of the roses and I thanked the supermarket overlords for removing the thorns.

'What?'

For some bizarre reason, I couldn't quite seem to get over the part where my boyfriend had dumped me and then magically changed his mind overnight. Turned out it was incredibly hard to forgive something in the past when you had only just found out it happened in the first place. I wasn't a saint, I wasn't Beyoncé, more's the bloody pity.

'Me and Chris are going to my dad's for tea,' he repeated, a smile fully realized on his face, his body easy and relaxed all while a tiny version of me ran around circles in circles inside my brain, screaming at the top of her lungs and drowning out my thought process. 'So dinner at their house is off. Didn't Cassie call you?'

That was all he had to say? Sorry I broke up with you, I'm going to my dad's for tea, here are some shit supermarket flowers now let's pretend it never happened, cool, OK, bye?

'I'm sorry,' I said, resting the flowers on the wall and rubbing my shiny, sunburned face with both hands. 'I think I've missed something. What exactly happened last night? What exactly happened in Mexico?'

A wave of tension swept over my boyfriend and he rocked backwards on his heels, tugging on the strings of his hoodie and pushing out his bottom lip.

'I don't know,' he said, kicking the gravel with the toe of his Converse and squeezing his shoulders up around his ears. He did the same thing when I found out he'd eaten all my Jaffa Cakes so at least I was certain he knew how serious this was. 'It was stupid, I wasn't thinking. I was just tired, Liv.'

'Well, it came from somewhere,' I pointed out, still processing. 'You must have meant it at the time.'

I could feel my face getting hot, not just hurt, not just angry but consumed by feelings I'd paid no mind to in years. Adam had never made me feel anything other than safe, loved and, very occasionally, mildly irritated but that was only when he shoved Penguin wrappers down the side of the settee. All I wanted to do was go back to bed, pull the covers over my head and pretend this wasn't happening. Instead I had to resolve it like a grown-up then explain to a sixty-two-year-old man that his cat's neon pink furballs and the fact he kept forcing it to wear neon pink hand-knitted jumpers were related.

'I don't know,' he said. Even though he didn't look nearly as shit as I did, I could tell by the bags under his eyes he hadn't got a lot of sleep. As was right and proper. 'I was pissed off. All that shit on the plane and then you wouldn't stop talking and I needed some space to calm down.'

All that shit on the plane? Like that was my fault?

'I was only upset because you were being weird all Monday night,' I reminded him, sending the heat in my face to fuel the fire in my belly. Rage was better than tears: angry, I could work with. Tired and emotional, I could not. 'And I'm not the one who caused a scene on the plane.'

'I'm sorry,' he said stiffly. 'What else do you want me to say?'

'And now you don't need space?' I asked, still processing as I spoke. It wasn't fair, he'd had a whole morning to think about this and I had been blindsided. If anyone needed space, it was me.

'Oi, Liv, Mr Harries is here—' David stuck his head out of the door, took one look at Adam, one look at me and slammed it shut again. 'Never mind,' he shouted through the letterbox, 'I'll sort it.'

'Look, I said I'm sorry,' Adam said, ignoring David's interruption. 'I don't understand why you're so pissed off.'

'I'm so pissed off because at three o'clock this morning you apparently broke up with me,' I explained, beating the flowers in the palm of my hand until there was a carpet of baby pink petals under my feet. 'And now you want me to pretend it never happened. It was only nine hours ago, Adam. What is going on? You've changed your mind now? Nine hours was a long enough break, was it? I. Just. Don't. Understand.'

'Maybe it wasn't long enough.' I could tell he was annoyed now. Clearly he thought his five-quid apology flowers were going to be enough. 'If you're going to be like this, maybe I could use a bit more time.'

'Fine!' I shouted.

'Fine!' he shouted back.

For a moment, we stood in silence in the car park,

neither one of us moving or speaking and I was unsure whether to carry on arguing or run and hide. Adam clenched and unclenched his hands and I could see the same options spinning around in his eyes, like a human fruit machine.

I would not speak first, I would not speak first, I would not speak first . . .

'So what?' he said eventually. 'What do you want?'

Less than three days ago my answer would have been 'to get engaged'; now I didn't have a clue what to tell him.

'You're the one who wanted something,' I reminded him, bitterly pleased he had been the one to break the awkward silence. At some point, our conversation had turned into a competition I was desperate to win, even though I didn't really know what that meant. 'You can't say you want to break up one minute and pretend everything is all right the next without some sort of explanation.'

He straightened himself up to his full height, towering over me as he nodded, either because he agreed or he was trying to convince himself that he did, I wasn't sure.

'Fine,' he said again. 'I mean, yes. A bit of space might be a good idea, you're right.'

It was such an Adam thing to do, turn the situation around to make it seem like it was my idea in the first place. But there was no point making this worse than it already was by pointing that out. I rolled my eyes, turning back towards the surgery so that he wouldn't see. David's head was just visible through the frosted-glass pane in the door, and I realized he was listening to everything through the letterbox.

'I've got to get back to work,' I said, pointing behind me with my battered bouquet. 'I really can't get into this now.'

Or possibly ever.

'Fine,' he replied. So help me god, if he said 'fine' one more time . . . 'I'll talk to you later.'

'When?' I asked. 'Specifically?'

'I don't know,' he admitted. For the first time since he'd shown up, he actually looked like he was in pain. Without warning, all my fire and brimstone burned away, leaving nothing but a stick figure, holding onto a bunch of broken flowers with a lump in my throat. 'But I will call you.'

'OK.'

My gaze settled on his shoes and I couldn't even look at him. I didn't think I'd ever felt so unsure around him and that included the time I got so drunk, the second time I stayed over at his house that I puked into his pillowcase.

He automatically stepped towards me for a kiss but stopped just before he reached me. My shoulders seized as he pressed his lips against my cheek instead.

'See you later, Liv.'

I watched as he climbed into the car and drove away, shopping bags bouncing around in the back seat.

'You all right?' David asked behind me, opening the door slowly. 'Want me to tell Mr Harries to stop being such a daft twat and send him home?'

'No.' I turned on my heel, handing him my flowers, taking a deep breath. Not yet, not yet, not yet. 'I think doing that myself might actually make me feel a bit better. There's only an hour of surgery left, I'll be OK.'

'Sainsbury's?' he turned the bouquet over in his hands

57

Lindsey Kelk

and gave it a disapproving sniff. 'Even I know better than that. Shall I put them in water?'

'Water or the bin, I don't really care as long as I don't have to look at them.'

'Excellent choice.' David closed the door behind us as I strode back into the surgery. 'Glad to see you're OK. I heard some of it. What a tosspot.'

'Not now,' I said, taking out my topknot, winding it up and wrapping the elastic band around my hair so securely, I looked like one of the *Real Housewives*. All of the *Real Housewives*. 'Give me a minute and then send in Mr Harries, please?'

I swallowed hard and the edges of my vision began to blur. Not yet, I told myself, not until I was alone.

'Whatever you say, doc,' he said, unconvinced. 'I might pop upstairs and put a bottle of wine in the fridge as well. Just in case we fancy an after work bevvy.'

'Make it two,' I called after him. 'Dinner and dessert.'

'That's why you're the boss,' he said, shooting me the double guns. 'You're so wise.'

I watched as he sauntered off down the hallway, holding my flowers to his chest like Miss World. Despite being considerably younger than me, and one hundred per cent more male, he was usually right about most things, but in this instance I wasn't so sure. I certainly didn't feel very wise. I closed the back door to the examination room and made sure the other door that opened into the waiting room was securely latched. Safely locked away, I lay back on the steel examination table and popped my stethoscope around my neck, bouncing the weight of the drum in the palm of my hand until I calmed down. I loved my stethoscope so much, sometimes I put it on with my pyjamas while I

58

was watching telly but today it wasn't enough. I wasn't sure if anything was.

'What is happening?' I whispered, staring up at the flickering fluorescent tube above me.

Two fat tears slid out the corners of my eyes, ran over my temples and into my hair. Had I spent so much time fretting over when he was going to propose, I'd missed the signs of an impending break-up? This wasn't my first rodeo; I'd been the dumper and the dumped in my thirty years on this planet but I hadn't seen this coming. Adam and me weren't supposed to break up, ever. He was mine and I was his, why would I have looked for signs?

Was this why he was so anxious on Monday night? Not because he was going to propose but because he knew he was going to break up with me when we got home. Another warm tear plopped out of my left eye and made a beeline for my inner ear, making me shiver. But then he'd changed his mind. Probably got home to an empty bed and realized it was easier to keep me around than to find someone new. Probably couldn't be bothered to work out which DVDs were mine and return them.

I laid the drum of my stethoscope on top of my chest and listened for my heartbeat. It was still going which was something of an achievement in itself.

'Hello?'

The handle of the waiting-room door turned and the door knocked against the latch. Sitting up, I wobbled for a moment, almost falling off the table before catching myself, wiping my face and giving a loud, satisfying sniff.

'Just a moment,' I called through the door as I splashed my face with cold water. 'I'm almost ready, Mr Harries.'

Just three more appointments, just one more hour to get through.

With a deep breath that stuck in my throat, I pushed myself out of my mind and opened the door. A sandy-haired older gentleman carrying a long-haired black cat in a shopping bag held up his hand politely as he walked in. The cat was wearing a hand-knitted jumper with a picture of what I took to be Olaf from *Frozen* emblazoned on the back.

'Mr Harries, I thought we'd talked about getting rid of Jeremy's woolly jumpers?' I said as gently as possible, turning away to dab my runny nose with my sleeve. 'They're what's causing all the hairballs.'

'But he loves them,' Mr Harries protested. 'What am I supposed to do?'

'I don't know,' I said, sharing a despairing glance with poor Jeremy. 'I really don't know.'

5

'And that's how I blew up the microwave,' Dad finished his story with pride. 'It was only a small fire and I put it right out, no problems. Scorched the curtain a bit but you can't tell unless you look.'

'It was time we replaced that microwave anyway,' Chris said, waving his hand as he laid down his decree. 'I'll get you a new one, a better one. Mine's brilliant, does everything except wipe your arse. Amazing.'

'You could get a gold-plated microwave that shits unicorn droppings, it'll still blow up if you put metal in it,' I pointed out.

'I still can't understand why you were trying to heat up a yoghurt.'

'I wanted to know what would happen,' Dad replied. 'Now I do.'

'You should sue them,' Chris went on. 'It should say on it that you're not supposed to microwave yoghurt pots.'

'You can't sue the manufacturers for human error,' I said. 'I think you just need to be more careful, Dad.'

'And I think you shouldn't take legal advice from a law school dropout.' Chris twisted around in Mum's favourite armchair to give me the full benefit of his smug, older-brother expression. 'I'll get a new microwave sent over before Mum gets back. She'll never know.'

'She doesn't use it any more anyway.' Dad merrily ignored the pair of us, having done a wonderful job of developing selective hearing over the years. 'I'll tell her I got rid of it because of the radiation. She'll be made up.'

'I'll get you a good one,' Chris said, already looking at microwaves on his phone. 'Can't have you and Mum getting into accidents. We probably ought to replace the whole kitchen.'

'We're not senile quite yet,' Dad said, pushing himself up to his feet as the doorbell rang. 'You don't need to put a catch on the toilet to stop me falling in.'

'He was dicking about with a microwave, not trying to burn the house down,' I whispered after he left the room. 'Stop patronizing him, they don't want a new kitchen.'

'Calm down, Ad.' Chris popped the top on a bottle of beer, wrinkling his nose at my provided beverages. He only drank craft ales so I'd brought Bud Light with Lime. It was the little things that got you through the difficult days. 'You shouldn't feel inferior because I'm in a position to help them out.'

'If they wanted a new kitchen, they'd buy a new kitchen,' I replied, turning my phone over to check the time. Between the night on the settee, the Mexican jet lag and whatever the hell had happened with Liv, I was dying on my arse.

'And if I want to help my parents out, I will,' he replied with serial killer calm. 'Maybe if they hadn't spent half their savings on paying for the barrister's qualification you jacked in a year before you finished, they might have bought themselves a new kitchen before now. Or at least had a lawyer son who could afford to buy one for them.'

'Oh, fuck off.' I burrowed backwards, praying for the settee to swallow me whole 'They don't want a new kitchen, Chris.'

'You're very touchy this evening.' He leaned forward over his designer denim-covered knees and fixed me with a smile. 'Anything to do with the distinct lack of a post-Mexico engagement?'

'Nope,' I replied, sipping my beer with great difficulty. It really did taste like piss. 'And I don't want to talk about that here.'

'She say no?'

'Fairly certain I just said I didn't want to talk about it.'

'Shame that,' Chris said with a deep, satisfied sigh. 'Especially since Cassie was on the phone to Liv when I left. What's all this about a break?'

When my brother started going out with Liv's best friend, I was wary. He'd come to Long Harrington for my birthday and Liv had thrown me a party and warned Cassie and Abigail, her two best friends, not to touch him with a ten-foot pole. Abi listened, Cass did not. Chris had always been a bit of a shit with the ladies – well, a shit in general – but that had been even more of a worry than usual. I didn't want to get in trouble with Liv when he inevitably broke her best friend's heart. We hadn't been going out that long and my brother had never been able to keep it in his pants for more than three months at a time and, try as I might, I could not see a scenario in which his relationship went well for me. What I couldn't have predicted was Chris falling head over heels in love with Cass, leaving London and buying a house in the village after three months, proposing after six, then getting married and knocking out a baby less than a year later. Whatever magical spell Cassie had worked on my brother had worked and he was a new man. At least for her, anyway. Where the rest of the world was concerned he was still a total prick.

'What did she say?' I asked, taking another sip of my disgusting drink. Hoisted by my own lime-flavoured petard. I was happy it had worked out but it was massively annoying that he always seemed to know what was going on in my life before I did. Cassie and Liv were constantly texting each other, updating one another on every last little thing that went on. I'd tried to read their texts but since I couldn't speak emoji I couldn't understand most of it anyway.

'I can't believe you brought this piss; I don't know if it's cat's, gnat's or rat's but I'm not drinking it.' He took one more drink then put the half-full bottle on the fireplace. 'She said you and Liv had some sort of barney and now you're taking a break. What's going on? I thought you had it all planned.'

'I did,' I said, fixing my eyes on a photo of the village millpond that Dad had taken when me and Chris were kids and visiting our grandparents. 'And then I didn't and now we're sort of on a break.'

My brother fixed me with an unimpressed gaze.

'That's it?'

'That's it,' I confirmed. 'And I don't want Dad to know, so don't say anything.'

'If I'm honest . . .' Chris stood up and strode across the living room to the reusable Waitrose bag on the table. He wasn't quite as tall as me but he was still pushing six foot. Add to that the same blond hair and blue eyes and there was no mistaking we were brothers. Unfortunately. 'I never saw it working out with you and Liv.'

'What?'

'Eh . . .' He pulled a six-pack of Samuel Smith ales out of the bag. 'I'm not saying she's not pretty but she's not properly hot, is she? And you know you look like you could be brother and sister, don't you? It's all a bit too master race for my liking.'

'Liv is hot!' I couldn't decide if he was trying to make me feel better about my situation or if he was just being Chris. 'Liv's really hot. And we do not look like brother and sister.'

'You do a bit though,' Chris said, pouring one of his special beers into a pint glass and returning to his chair without offering one to me. 'I've seen her look all right, bare materials are there, but she doesn't really try, does she? Always got her hair up, never got any make-up on. And I don't think I've seen her out of jeans more than what, twice?'

'I like her hair up.' I settled on him just being himself. He'd been acting up ever since he arrived, barking about his big deal at work and talking about the baby like he was the second coming of Kanye. 'And she looks good in jeans. You're talking shit.'

'And I've always thought it's weird, her being a vet. Doesn't it bother you, her stuck in a surgery all day?'

'Where would you rather have her?' I asked. 'Chained to the kitchen sink, baking me a pie?'

'Hardly,' he said, sinking back into his seat. 'You know I like an ambitious woman but the thought of her hand up a cow's arse all day makes me gip.'

'Cassie was a vet,' I reminded him. 'That's how she and Liv know each other. From vet school. Where they both trained to be vets.'

He shrugged. 'Yeah, but Cass doesn't put her hands up anything's guts for a living. She's a science teacher now.'

'I think it's brilliant Liv's a vet,' I replied. And it was true. I'd gone out with a fair number of girls before her and none of them had such cool careers. Dating a yoga instructor sounds like it would be fun until she's dragging you out of bed at five a.m. for sunrise sun salutations and refusing to eat, well, anything. 'She helps animals, she helps people, she has a stethoscope. And it's good money.'

'It'd have to be given she's shacking up with a dropout,' he replied. I wondered how upset Dad would be if I glassed him. I probably shouldn't – we'd never get the Bud Lime smell out of the carpet. 'Only kidding. I know you've got a job.'

It was the air quotes around the word 'job' that pushed me over the edge.

'We can't all be a technowiz,' I declared, banging my bottle down hard. 'I wish I'd thought to start an app that delivers condoms and rolling papers to students for three times the price of the corner shop.'

'Yeah, you really do.' There was an edge to his voice that hadn't been there before. 'That app paid for my house. Remind me how you got yours again? Oh, that's right, it's *Granddad's* house and Mum and Dad gave it to you.'

'They tried to give me the wrong pizza.' Dad walked slowly back into the room, weighed down by a pile of Domino's boxes, just as I was about to leap across the room and choke my brother with our great-grandmother's handcrafted quilt. 'He had to call the shop to check. I wonder how many people don't check what they've been given before the driver leaves? Can you imagine ordering a pepperoni and ending up with tuna? I'd be devastated.'

'If Liv's so hot and so brilliant, why are you on a break instead of engaged?' Chris asked while Dad fannied around in the kitchen with plates and the world's biggest wad of kitchen roll. 'You're not making any sense, little brother. She's had enough of you playing carpenter and packed you in for someone with a proper job, hasn't she?'

'It was a mutual agreement,' I replied, swigging my pissy beer. 'No one has packed anyone in, we're taking a break, working out some stuff.'

I didn't even know if that was true, but since I'd spent all afternoon literally passed out, face down in my workshop from jet lag, I hadn't had much time to think about it.

'Now leave it. I don't want Mum and Dad to know until we've sorted it out.'

'Getting married a big commitment,' he said loudly, with an added cluck for emphasis. Chris Floyd, the world's greatest authority on relationships. 'It's a lot to take on.'

'What's that?' Dad asked, gleefully presenting us both with two slices of forbidden pizza.

'Marriage,' Chris said. I shot him a warning look but he went on regardless. 'I was just telling Adam it's not something to be entered into lightly.'

'True enough,' Dad agreed before taking a bite and closing his eyes, enraptured. 'Is there something you want to tell me, son?'

'He's going to propose,' Chris answered before I could. 'Aren't you, Ad?' He smiled at me across the room and mouthed the word 'what?' before stuffing his mouth with pizza.

Dad's eyes opened up wide and I couldn't think of a time I'd seen him happier. Pizza, his boys, and important family gossip Mum hadn't heard first. He was living the paternal dream.

'That's bloody marvellous news, that is,' he said, setting down his plate and hurling himself across the settee to give me a hug. Dad had become quite the hugger in his old age. 'You know your mother and I love Olivia. Do you have an idea when you're going to ask her? Have you asked her dad for permission yet?'

'No.' I chewed and chewed and chewed on the same mouthful of pizza but I couldn't seem to swallow. 'I haven't decided anything yet. Probably best not to say anything to Mum until I've, you know, worked out all the details.'

'Surprised you didn't do it on holiday,' he said, dumping himself back in his chair and nibbling at his leftover crust. 'That would have been nice.'

'Oh yeah.' Chris looked at Dad as though he was a genius. 'Why didn't you think of that, Adam? Why didn't you propose on holiday?'

'Anyone want any more pizza?' I asked, getting up and loading my plate with greasy, sausage-laden Domino's before helping myself to one of Chris's expensive beers. 'Beer, Dad?'

'Oh sod it, I will have one,' Dad said, holding out his hand for the freshly opened bottle. 'We'll be dry again tomorrow. Your mum poured all my booze down the drain.'

'I'm sure she'll let you bend the rules to toast the happy couple,' Chris said as Dad happily glugged his beer. 'As soon as you do it, let me know, Ad. I've got a bottle of vintage Bollinger from the year you were born. Cost me a grand but it's perfect for a celebration, don't you think, Dad?'

The senior Floyd beamed around the room at the fruit of his loins.

'I know it's cheesy but I am glad the two of you have stayed such good friends,' he said. 'It's so sad when siblings grow apart. You're making an old man very happy.'

'I can't imagine the world without him,' I said, raising my bottle and giving my brother the filthiest look I could muster. 'I've tried but I can't.'

Chris nodded, his cheeks flushing from the booze and the pizza and the general adulation while Dad carried on putting away his pizza, gazing at his children in such a perfect state of joy I couldn't help but think Mum had wasted her money on a two-week yoga retreat. Forcing my pizza down my throat with a mouthful of beer, I stared at the wall and waited for someone else to change the subject. Now I was really buggered. There was no way my dad could keep schtum about this and there was absolutely no way Mum would leave me alone until I fessed up about what was going on. Meaning I really should make an effort to work out what that was before she got home.

'You all right, Adam?' Dad asked, red sauce all round his mouth. 'You look a bit peaky.'

'Right as rain,' I assured him, raising my pizza up high as Chris stifled a laugh. 'Never been better. Never been better.'

If only Liv were as easy to placate as my dad, I thought to myself as he carried on munching until his plate was clear. I knew I should have taken her a pizza instead of flowers.

6

Thursday night drinks at the local pub had been a tradition for Abi and me well before our eighteenth birthday but in honour of my relationship implosion, we took the unorthodox move of bringing it forward to Wednesday. It was necessary. After Adam left and I finished up all my appointments, I sent David home early and spent the rest of the afternoon hysterically crying in a corner of the surgery while all the doggy in-patients howled along in sympathy. It was like a really terrible deleted scene from *Lady and the Tramp*. Without going into the details, I summoned my girls to the pub and steeled my liver in preparation.

'Evening all.' Abi shuffled into our regular corner of the Blue Bell, setting a bottle of white wine on the table. Her chin-length brown hair was half up, half down, secured by endless hair grips and her accidental cool girl glasses were so smudged it was a wonder she could even see. 'I've had a shit day, let's get smashed.'

I shuffled along the seat to make room, banging my knees on the underneath of the table as I went. Booths were the devil's invention; it was impossible to get in or out of one without laddering a pair of tights and yet we always sat here. It was hard to break a habit after more than a decade.

'What happened?' I asked, pouring for everyone, my hand still shaking.

'My lab assistant broke a very expensive piece of equipment, buggered three months' worth of test results and I really don't want to talk about it,' she said as Cass picked up the bottle I had just put down and filled it up to the top. Cass and I had already talked. 'Liv, you're back, yay. You look nice.'

'No, I don't,' I replied, my eyes dry and sore from all the horrible, horrible crying. 'I look like shit. I haven't had a proper night's sleep since Sunday and an Alsatian had explosive diarrhoea all over the examination room when I tried to give him a rectal exam and – well, we'll get to the rest.'

'Good tan though,' she said with a shrug. 'Go on, then, what's the big news that couldn't possibly wait until tomorrow?'

It was only as she sank half a bottle of wine in one swallow that I realized she was expecting me to announce my engagement.

'Nothing major,' I said as Cass, who had already heard the story at least a dozen times since I arrived at the pub, held my hand under the table. 'Me and Adam broke up.'

Abi picked up her glass, emptied the second half of her glass and put it back down. 'Well, my dishwasher's been on the blink for a week, so, you know, we're all going through stuff right now.'

Determined not to cry in the Bell, I covered my face

with my hair and snorted a half laugh, half sob as she bundled me up in a hug. Apart from a brief flirtation with Impulse Vanilla Kisses in Year Seven, Abi never wore perfume, so her hugs always smelled the same. Burying my face in her armpit was almost enough to push me over the edge.

'He didn't break up with you,' Cass said, stroking my back. 'You're on a break, that's not the same thing. Don't freak out.'

'I love how you know more about this than I do,' I said, sniffling as I extricated myself from Abi's hug. She stroked loose strands of my topknot back into place. 'Feels a lot like a break-up, Cass. I mean, it's six thirty on a Wednesday night, there are two open bottles of wine on the table and my friends are telling me not to freak out. That doesn't paint a scene of everything being hunky-dory, does it?'

'I didn't tell you not to freak out,' Abi said, refilling her glass as I leaned forward to sip from mine without taking it from the table. 'I'd definitely be freaking out if I were you.'

'Not helping,' Cass said with narrowed eyes. 'Adam told Chris it's just a break. Chris thinks he's got cold feet, that's all, nothing to panic about. Everything will be back to normal by the weekend when he's calmed down.'

'Liv, what happened?' Abi's phone was flashing with a picture of a half-naked man with ridiculous muscles. She frowned and cancelled the call. 'I thought you were coming back engaged. I've spent all day practising my excited face for when you ask me to be your bridesmaid.'

'What makes you think I'd ask you to be my bridesmaid?'

73

I asked, sliding my glass back and forth across the table. 'And more importantly, who was on the phone? Are you shagging Fabio?'

'He's no one. I was warming him up as a wedding date, but if you're not getting married any time soon, I don't need to answer that call.' She tossed her phone into her bag then hid it underneath the table. 'Seriously now, what's going on?'

'Technically Cass is right, we're on a break,' I explained, turning over my own phone to check for messages. Nothing. 'All holiday, Adam kept going on about this amazing restaurant in town, how he'd heard it was so great but we couldn't get a reservation until the last night, and so obviously, I'm thinking he's going to propose then. But there we were, on our way out, and then I don't even know what happened. One minute we're walking down the beach on our way to a fancy night out, and the next thing I know, we're in a taxi on our way home. No swanky restaurant, no proposal, not even any last-night-of-a-holiday shag. It was all very confusing.'

'Chris said Adam said he wants to work out some stuff,' Cassie said, twisting the wine bottle to check the label. I wasn't sure what she was expecting to see: the Bell had two kinds of wine, red and white. We were drinking the white. It was not good. 'He definitely said you hadn't broken up.'

'Chris said that or Adam said that?' Abi looked distinctly unimpressed.

'Adam said it to Chris, who then said it to me,' she clarified, stroking the ends of her sleek, black ponytail. Everything about Cassie Huang was sleek. The word most commonly used to describe her was 'willowy' which I especially enjoyed hearing from my mum who had generally referred to her own teenage daughter as 'sturdy'. And she wondered why I'd gone on the Haribo and Diet Pepsi plan in the first year of university.

'They had an early dinner at his dad's house. I saw Chris for, like, ten seconds before I came out.'

'Sounds like a real keeper,' Abi said. She'd never been one to mince her words, Abi subscribed to the philosophy of calling a spade a spade. Or a wanker if she deemed it more appropriate.

'Chris says it's totally normal,' Cass declared as they continued to argue over me. It was fine, I was perfectly happy to keep quiet and drink my wine. And their wine. And everyone else on the planet's wine. 'Chris says all men go back and forth before they pop the question, even if you don't know it. Steve Harvey basically says the exact same thing in *Think Like a Man*.'

Abi gave her a stern look. Abi didn't care for Cass's reliance on self-help manuals. Abi really only believed in truly relying on herself. 'Could you tell Chris to tell Adam that when he has made his mind up do you think he could find the time to tell Liv himself rather than have her wait for it to trickle through you and his brother first?'

'I'm only telling you what Chris told me,' she said, her phone fluttering across the table, buzzing against the almost-empty bottle. 'Speak of the devil, I'll be back in a minute.'

I half-stood, half-shuffled out of the booth until she could squeeze past, smiling at Mrs Moore, the landlady, as Cass dashed for the door. She smiled back, giving me the once-over as she passed. She'd been serving me since I ordered my first Malibu and Coke at fifteen. If she didn't like what she saw, she only had herself to blame.

'Liv, I'm so sorry.' Abi straightened my collar as I sat

back down, her huge green eyes full of concern and just a hint of murderous rage. 'How are you really?'

'I don't know,' I said, raising a hand to wave at Melanie Brookes, my mum's neighbour, mother of two children and owner of three rabbits and a diabetic cat. There had been a dog as well at one point but he got into a cupboard and ate an Easter egg and there really wasn't anything anyone could have done about that. 'I feel sick when I think about it. I just really want Cass to be right, I really want this to be a wobble. Because if it's not, I don't know what I'll do.'

Abigail Levinson and I had been friends ever since her dad brought her puppy into the surgery when we were both eleven. I was hanging out there, looking for animals to bother, when a little, skinny, dark-haired girl with Coke-bottle glasses and what I thought was a super cool Mickey Mouse T-shirt walked through the door. She sat down beside me as our respective fathers disappeared into the examination room, looked me in the eye and whispered, in her most serious voice, that the dog was not going to make it. I held her hand in silence until both dads reappeared with the dog who, despite my new friend's most assured diagnosis, bounded out towards us, happy, healthy and a hundred per cent alive.

After they left, my dad explained Abi had been watching too much *Blue Peter* and took it upon herself to try to clean her dog's teeth with her electric toothbrush and an entire tube of Colgate. In the interest of the dog surviving the summer, Dad took her on as his second junior intern (we were only allowed to clean out kennels and feed the cats but we felt terribly important) and we'd been joined at the hip ever since. After we graduated, she'd stayed on at uni to do her PhD and now she was such a super shit-hot veterinary research scientist. Even I didn't really understand what she did and I was an actual vet. While I was taking pieces of Lego out of the Youngs' Labrador's stomach, Abi was curing cancer. Dog cancer, but still, it was impressive. She was Superwoman as far as I was concerned.

'Sod what Adam wants.' Abi tucked her short brown hair behind her ears and drew her eyebrows together behind her glasses, still Coke-bottle thick but considerably more stylish than they had been when we were kids. 'What do you want?'

I looked at her blankly.

'You, Olivia, what do you want?' she asked. 'You do know who I'm talking about? Short, split ends, fiddles with animals for a living?'

'I haven't got split ends,' I muttered, pinching together an inch of hair and holding it up to the light. 'I don't want to break up. I want everything back how it was.'

'Why?'

'What?'

'Why do you want things back how they were?' she asked. 'It should be an easy question.'

'I don't know,' I confessed, busying myself by peeling the label from the wine bottle. 'This wasn't my idea. Leave me alone, I'm sad.'

'Your idea or not, someone needs to set some boundaries before this gets messy,' she said in the nicest voice she could manage. 'And that should be you. He doesn't get to dictate this entire situation, Liv, even if you are going to be back together tomorrow. You need to think about you a little bit. First he decided you were going to get engaged; now he's decided he wants a break. You need to know what *you* want.'

'I want to know what you want,' I said, nudging her in the shoulder and taking a sip.

'For you to be happy,' she replied. 'And for Mini Eggs to be available all year round.'

'I don't want to break up with him,' I said, slowly pulling on the label, trying to move it in one piece. Life without Adam didn't seem like an actual possible thing. 'I can't even process the thought of it. If he says he needs space, I should just give him space. This seems like a classic rubber band situation to me, don't you think?'

'You know I won't answer that,' Abi replied, cursing our best friend's name as the wine bottle label ripped in two. 'One, *Men Are from Mars, Women Are from Venus* is a shit present, and two, it's full of shit advice. Cassie should be shot for giving it to you in the first place.'

'Sorry, it was Chris.' Cass bounced back into the booth and grabbed her glass. I shuffled around, glad of her interruption. 'Gus was crying but he was just hungry. I'm going to head back soon, I don't like leaving him alone for too long.'

'Chris or the baby?' I asked Cass.

'Liv, don't be mean,' Abi admonished. 'Surely you don't expect Chris, a grown man, to be able to take care of his own child for more than forty-five minutes at a time?'

'It's not the same as asking him to record *Gogglebox*,' Cass replied tartly. 'Gus gets fussy when I'm not there at night. Sometimes he won't settle.'

'Chris or the baby?' I asked Abi.

'We should meet at mine some time,' she said, throwing cardboard coasters in our general direction.

'Then I won't have to run off so early. Plus, we've got much better wine. You two have to come over more often, Gus barely even knows his Aunt Abi.'

'He doesn't know anyone, Cass, he's five months old.' Abi swirled her wine, coating her glass and taking a sniff. 'And I've Stockholm Syndrome'd myself on this wine. Whenever I drink wine anywhere else, my brain doesn't recognize it as the same substance.'

'That would be because all other wine is good,' Cass explained. 'And this is very bad.'

'Cass only drinks the finest wines, these day,' I explained, ignoring the look on her face and topping off her glass. 'Cass married up.'

No one was going to say it but our weekly meet-ups had been much more like monthly meet-ups over the last year or so. I understood sitting around a dank old pub was hardly the most alluring idea to a pregnant woman but Cass had started making her excuses well before Gus was so much as a twinkle in Chris's eye and I hadn't realized how long it had been since we were all in the same place until I really needed to be there. I glanced over at Abi and wondered how many times I'd cancelled on her to hang out with Adam instead.

'If you didn't want me to marry your boyfriend's brother, you shouldn't have introduced me to him,' she said, knocking back her drink and sticking out her tongue. 'It's your fault.'

'It's true,' Abi agreed. 'You should have introduced him to me first so I could bone him then never speak to him again. I'm much better at alienating the opposite sex than Cass.'

'You just haven't met the right man,' Cass said, making me splutter into my wine glass. Having a baby had made her brave. 'You work too hard and you don't give relationships a chance.'

'You're so right,' Abi framed her face with her hands and blinked her big, anime eyes. 'Teach me everything you know, oh wise married one, help me be like you.'

'I'm going home,' Cass said, ignoring our loud, squawking pleas for her to stay. 'I know, it's early but I'm knackered and I want to put Gus to bed. You should think yourself lucky I'm here at all. If my grandmother had her way, I'd still be housebound. She thinks I bring evil spirits back into the house every time I go outside.'

'That's not a very nice way to describe me and Liv,' Abi said, shaking her head.

'Isn't your nan from Reading?' I asked, slapping Abi's leg.

'She's being ridiculous,' Cass nodded, opening a text and smiling to herself before showing the two of us. It was a photo of Gus and Chris in the bath and the bubbles weren't covering nearly as much as I would like. 'Mum said she wasn't like this at all when I was born but she's gone crazy with all the old Chinese traditions this time. She doesn't even like Chris holding him. Apparently, I wasn't supposed to get out of bed for the first month at all.'

'Can I stay in bed for a month if I have a baby with a Chinese father?' Abi suddenly perked up while I made the expected cooing noises. Gus was a cute baby, if you were into babies. 'Do you have any single cousins? Uncles? Would your mum lend me your dad for an hour or so?'

Ignoring Abi, Cass gave me a hug before shuffling out of the booth.

'Don't get too upset about this, Livvy, it's going to be

fine,' she promised. 'Let Adam have his mad half hour and I bet you anything, you'll be back together with a ring on your finger before the end of the year.'

'Maybe,' I said, scratching at an indeterminate green stain on the hem of my shirt. Hmm. Gross. 'But do me a favour? Please don't go home and tell Chris everything we just talked about? It's not like I don't appreciate you trying to help but I don't want him reporting back to Adam.'

'I won't say a word,' she said, a look of surprise on her face. 'You know I wouldn't.'

'Because you've done such a good job of keeping secrets so far?' Abi pointed out. 'You're the one who told Liv about the ring, you're the one who told her he was going to propose in Mexico, and all you've done tonight is spill what Adam has told Chris about this situation.'

'Sisters before misters.' Cass brushed off the indisputable accusations and rolled her eyes. 'I tell you what he says but I don't tell him what you say. Promise you won't sit here all night and get upset.'

'Brownie guide promise,' I said, holding up three fingers.

'Wrong hand,' Abi whispered.

'Whatever,' I muttered, burying my face in my wine glass. 'Bye, Cass.'

'Bye Cass,' Abi said, stretching out for her own hug. 'Say hello to Chris for me.'

No matter how much they bickered, they loved each other really.

'I honestly don't know what to believe,' I said as the door swung shut on Cass and Abi poured the remnants of her wine into my glass. 'Chris is such an arse to

Adam most of the time. Why would he pour his heart out to him?'

'Because he's his brother,' Abi replied. 'You're an only child, chick, you don't get it. You hate each other one day, you're giving them a kidney the next.'

'You gave your brother a kidney?'

'Clearly not,' she said, patting me on the top of the head. 'I was making a point. I just mean, that's how it is with siblings.'

'Yeah, maybe,' I poked my finger through a tiny hole in the velvet seat covering. This place really was starting to look tired. 'Chris is always such a bully, always making fun of Adam for leaving law school then going on about how well his own company is doing.'

'Probably just insecure,' Abi rationalized. 'Does Adam have a bigger dong?'

'I really haven't thought about it.' I washed away the very thought of Chris's penis with a mouthful of wine. 'Adam's taller, he's definitely better looking and he's a hundred per cent cleverer. I don't know what Cass was thinking, I really don't.'

'She was thinking she'd marry a rich dude and get her parents off her back,' she replied. 'Let's be honest about it, all Cass ever wanted was to get married, have a kid and not worry about anything else, ever again. Now she's got that, so good for her.'

I pushed my finger all the way inside the seat until the tiny hole wasn't so tiny any more.

'Bit harsh,' I said. Abi's expression suggested she stood by her assessment. 'Cass is more old-fashioned than we are. She does love him, I think. And he definitely loves her.'

Abi picked up the second bottle of wine and refilled

her glass. Abi had an iron constitution, nothing could put her down, but I was a complete lightweight. One very full glass in and I was already light-headed. I held my hand over my glass before she could give me a refill.

'I can't,' I said sadly. There was nothing I would have liked more than to fall into a white wine coma as soon as I got home. 'Tomorrow is spay and neuter day, probably shouldn't have a hangover because I'm going to end up doing all the surgeries. Dad's been really off it lately.'

'Is he OK?' Abi asked. 'I can't believe he's going to be sixty-five, it doesn't seem like two minutes since his fiftieth birthday.'

'I think he's OK,' I nodded, without wondering whether or not it was true. I had too much else on my mind to spare any space for my dad's commitment to the surgery, or lack thereof. 'He hasn't been around much but that suits me. I deal with the patients and he deals with the paperwork. I'd rather not see him while I'm upset, though. You know how my parents are.'

'There has to be a happy medium between your family's stiff upper lip and Cassie's self-help library,' she replied. 'You know, like me!'

'I don't know how the human race has survived this long,' I said, clinking my glass against hers. 'Relationships are so difficult. It's a miracle that both mine and Adam's parents are still together. You'd think that would be enough for him to seal the deal – who has two sets of parents who are still together in one relationship these days?'

'Did I tell you my dad's on about going off travelling again? Without Karen?' she asked with a pinched expression.

'Is this divorce number three?'

'Four.' She paused as Bill Stockton walked past, throwing a wink in her direction. 'You're probably forgetting Lisa. A bit like he did.'

I watched Bill cross the bar and take a seat with his friends. He looked back at Abi and then quickly shifted his gaze to somewhere vaguely over our heads when he realized I was watching.

'Um, what's going on with you and Bill?' I asked, looking back at my friend to see her almost as red-faced as he was. 'Is there something you want to tell me?'

'No,' she said quickly. 'There's nothing I want to tell you.'

We lived in a small village, not as small as it used to be but if you wanted to actually leave your house of an evening, there weren't very many options. We had one supermarket, one chip shop-slash-greasy spoon and two pubs, meaning it was more or less impossible to keep any kind of secret here for more than fifteen minutes. Abi and Bill had been a thing when we were in the sixth form for almost a year but then Bill got off with Caroline Higgins round the back of the sports centre and Abi vowed never to talk to him again. As far as I knew, she had stayed true to her word for the last thirteen years but from the looks on both of their faces, they'd done more than talk to each other while I was away.

'When there's something to tell you, I'll tell you,' Abi informed me. I picked up my wine, unable to keep the smile from my face but didn't push it any further. There was no point trying with Abs, she'd tell when she was ready. 'Promise me you'll think about what you want out of this break, not just sit around waiting for Adam to make his mind up.'

'I promise,' I declared, giving the Brownie salute another go. 'I will.'

'That's still the wrong hand,' Abi sighed. 'I'm glad you're not operating on my dog tomorrow.'

Two hours later I hung my keys on the hook at the bottom of the stairs and collapsed onto my settee. A three-legged tortoiseshell cat unfurled himself from the armchair by the window and meowed loudly.

'Hello, Daniel Craig,' I said, reaching down to scratch underneath his chin before he leapt up onto my stomach, his little paws digging into my boobs as he walked up and down my torso, trying to decide where he wanted to settle.

'It's nice to be missed,' I muttered, pulling my phone out of my coat pocket. I should have taken it off before I lay down, I realized, as Daniel made himself comfortable, right on top of my bladder. I should have gone to the loo as well.

It felt so strange to be ending the day without Adam around. If I spent the night in my flat, it was usually because I'd worked so late I was so tired, I passed out the instant I walked through the door. Now I was here because here was the only place I had to be. It felt so wrong. I wanted to collapse on the sofa with my head in his lap while he stroked my hair and we told each other tales of our day. I wanted to turn down his offer of a glass of wine or a chocolate biscuit only for him to bring it anyway and tell me we deserved it because we worked so hard, even if we hadn't worked that hard at all. I wanted to hear him, to touch him, to make him laugh. Not knowing when I would see him again made things even worse, I was trapped, slightly tipsy, in relationship limbo – was there a worse place to be?

'Do you think your dad misses me?' I asked the cat.

Daniel opened one bright, sea-green eye and then slowly closed it again. I held my phone up in front of my sulky face with both hands.

'I'll take that as a no, then.'

Abs was right. I needed to set some ground rules with Adam before I went insane. Telling me we'd talk without putting a specific date in the diary had already driven me over my two glasses of wine on a school night limit, I refused to let this evening end with my face covered in the emergency bar of Galaxy I kept in the back of the fridge.

'I'll send him an email,' I told Daniel Craig, who was happily purring himself to sleep on my belly. 'I won't be a dick about it, I'll just send him an email to let him know what I think and then I'm going to turn off my phone and go to bed.'

Daniel raised his head, meowed loudly and then went back to the serious business of sleeping. I took that to mean he supported my actions.

'*Hey Adam . . .*' I tapped out the message. 'No, too casual. Just "Adam", no "Hey".'

I corrected the message, squinting at the bright screen above my nose and started again. '*Adam. Hope you're OK.*'

Daniel yawned.

'Do we hope he's OK?' I asked.

He did not reply.

'*Hope you're OK. Wanted to clarify some stuff RE: the break. Agree it's a good idea to think about things but would appreciate some sort of timeframe.*'

I stared at the message for a moment. Was I writing to my boyfriend or my bank manager?

'An email is ridiculous,' I decided. 'I'm going to text him. He is still my boyfriend after all. I think.'

Opening my messages, I scrolled down to Adam's name, finally finding it all the way down at the bottom of my inbox. Usually, we texted constantly, stupid links, sweet messages and there was a certain gif of a St Bernard slapping a man in the face that we'd sent back and forth at least a hundred times but now he was underneath Abi, Cass, David, my mum, my dad, my hairdresser and that man who came round to the surgery trying to sell me pirated DVDs. It felt wrong.

'*Hey,*' I began, poised to write something brief, friendly, clear, to the point, unambiguous and constructive.

Then I hiccupped and deleted it.

'How is it possible,' I said, staring at the blank white screen, 'that I cannot think of anything to say to a man I have talked to every day for the last three years?'

There were a million things to talk about in this world. The weather, the price of bananas, Jon Snow theories, but when it came to Adam, I had less than nothing. I didn't want to be too formal but I couldn't be too casual. If I was too jokey he might think I wasn't upset, but if I was super serious it didn't feel right. On Monday he was asking my opinion on whether or not I could see his penis through his trousers and by Wednesday I couldn't say so much as a simple hello.

Leaving my phone on the floor, I sat up slowly and moved Daniel Craig to a cushion at the end of the settee. After one displeased yowl, he rolled over, showing me his belly and tossing his head from side to side. I shrugged myself out of my coat and tickled him until he reared up and nipped my wrist with his sharp little teeth. Cats were so fickle.

'Just like your dad,' I told him, staring at my phone and willing him to respond. But I got nothing.

'Oh, sod him,' I announced loudly to the living room. 'Abi's right. I'm not going to sit here and feel shit while he gives me the silent treatment. As of right now, I will not feel sorry for myself, I am taking control of this situation.'

The cat looked at me, seemingly supportive for a creature that had just bitten me hard enough to draw blood, and waited for me to do something.

'Only I do feel a bit sorry for myself,' I admitted quietly.

Adam was everywhere and I didn't just mean in the framed photos on the wall. I saw him building the cat bed he'd bought for Daniel, puffing up the cushions on the settee before we lay down for a solid night of Netflix. One of my dining chairs was still in the corner of the room from where I'd made him sit and think about what he'd done when he deleted the *Downton* Christmas special off my Sky+ box in August. I dropped my head between my knees, already regretting that last glass of wine, and saw the unwelcome corner of a secret bridal magazine peeking out from underneath the settee. I pulled it out slowly, the Post-it notes I'd stuck on my favourite dresses rustling.

'Maybe I feel really sorry for myself,' I said out loud, turning the pages of the magazine slowly, running my fingers over the beautiful gowns. DC stretched out his back leg until it was touching my knee. He got it.

'And maybe I could open the Galaxy and just have a little bit.'

Daniel yawned again, cocked his one remaining back leg over his head and began his nightly cat bath.

'I'll take that as a yes then,' I said, heading straight for the fridge, determined not to end another night in tears. I'd never cried so much in one day and that included the time me, Abi and Cass watched *Beaches*, *The Notebook* and *Titanic* all in the same day when we were supposed to be studying. 'I'd love it if you could stop licking your bum when I'm talking to you. The human Daniel Craig would never do that.'

Or at least I assumed he wouldn't, but if I'd learned nothing else from the last few days, I at least knew you shouldn't make assumptions about anything in life.

7

'What do you think of this one?'

I held the jacket up in the air, waving it around to get Tom's attention.

'Nice,' he replied, hands shoved deep inside his jacket pockets. 'Blue.'

'Yeah.' I considered the shirt again. It was blue. Too blue? I hung it back on the rail and flicked through the alternatives. 'Hmm.'

It was Saturday and I'd driven down to London for the day, desperate to get out of the village. Three days of radio silence from Liv was deafening, and with every passing second Long Harrington felt as though it was closing in on me. As far as I could see, I was the one who was owed an apology. Yes, I'd been out of order when I dropped her off at home but I'd apologized, I'd brought flowers, I'd done all the things I was supposed to do. Whether her silent treatment was punishment or she was truly angry with me, I did not know but if I knew one thing about women, it was that until she picked up the phone, all I could do was steer well clear.

Thursday and Friday I'd been able to concentrate on work, finalizing designs with the owners, literally forcing myself to sit in my workshop until I couldn't keep my eyes open any longer, but by Saturday I couldn't stand it any longer. I needed a break from my break.

'Got a big occasion coming up?' Tom asked. 'I don't think I've ever seen you in a suit outside of a wedding or a funeral.'

I shuddered involuntarily at the 'W' word.

'No,' I said, frowning at the suit section. He was right. I hardly ever wore a suit. 'Just looking. I'm broke.'

And after several terse exchanges and threats of Mexican lawsuits from Pablo the events organizer, that was true. I was fairly certain his case wouldn't hold up but there was a chance I'd want to go back to the country without having to worry he was waiting at the airport to break my legs.

'Right, well, do you want to look later?' Tom leaned against a display case full of cuff links, jumping back to his feet when he realized it wouldn't take his weight. 'I'm dying of thirst over here.'

'Can I help you?'

A tiny redhead with a name badge appeared at my elbow, a deliberate pout on her pretty face. 'Looking for anything in particular?'

'No,' I picked up another jacket and immediately put it back down, 'not really.'

'Thanks,' Tom added on my behalf. 'He's not sure what he's looking for.'

'I could help if you like?' the girl offered. I tried to check her name badge without looking at her chest but since she was wearing an insanely low-cut T-shirt and had pinned her badge directly at cleavage level that was

near enough impossible. Rebecca. Her name was Rebecca
and she had a fine pair.

'If it's a suit you're after, I'd definitely go with something slim fitting, single-breasted. Maybe a dark charcoal
or a midnight blue rather than a black? We've got some
really nice options for taller guys actually. You would
look so amazing in a Paul Smith or – oh, there's a new
Tom Ford suit just in that would really just hug your
shoulders.'

'There you go, Ad,' Tom said elbowing me in the ribs.
'You need a Tom Ford to hug your shoulders.'

'I don't wear suits all that often,' I told the sales
assistant as she looked me up and down slowly before
picking two shirts up and throwing them over her arm.
'I'm just looking.'

'I would really like to see you in the Tom Ford,' she
insisted, stroking the lapel in a manner that suggested
what she would actually like to see was me *out* of a
Tom Ford suit. 'What do you think?'

'I would also *really* like to see him in the Tom Ford,'
Tom agreed, utterly gleeful. 'But you know, he never
listens to me.'

'Oh.' Rebecca's eyes widened for an instant and her
face relaxed into a wide smile. 'Oh. Well, he should
listen. I love your shoes.'

'Thanks.' Tom looked down at his brown leather lace-
ups and then back at the girl with a goofy smile on his
face. 'They're my favourites.'

'I don't have a lot of call for suits,' I told her, keen to
get out of the shop and into the pub. I wasn't sure what
had possessed me in the first place. I hated shopping.
'I'm a carpenter.'

'Just like Jesus!'

'Yeah,' I said, glancing back at Tom who was struggling to hold himself together. 'Only, you know, not.'

She cocked her head to one side and pulled a comically sad expression. 'It's such a shame,' she reached out a hand and squeezed my forearm. 'Everyone needs a suit, you know. Even if you're not wearing it while you're working, you need one for best. Don't you agree?'

'One hundred per cent,' Tom nodded, flipping the arm of a shirt hanging beside him back and forth. He was starting to get bored, I could tell. The pub really was calling.

'Maybe if you tried a suit on, you'd see how amazingly sexy you look and we could convert you.' Rebecca said. 'What do we think?'

Tom failed to stifle a laugh while I shuffled on the spot, staring at her long, pointed bright-blue fingernails. 'I think you should try one on,' he said. 'I definitely want to see how amazingly sexy you look.'

'There you go, your better half has spoken,' Rebecca said, clapping happily. 'You're so lucky to have such a fashion forward boyfriend. Let's start with the Tom Ford.'

'Actually, we have somewhere to be and we're running late.' Tom stood up straight, the smile vanishing from his face. 'Come on, Ad.'

'Thanks,' I said, throwing Rebecca and her blue nails a wave as I chased my friend out of the store. 'Thank you.'

'At least she said you were the better half,' I said, catching up with Tom as he marched down the high street as fast as his legs would carry him. 'I know for a fact you've been called worse.'

'What made her think we were gay?' Tom complained,

adding an out of character swagger to his stride. 'It's that haircut. You need a haircut.'

'Maybe it's your "favourite shoes",' I suggested. 'You could not have sounded more camp.'

'They *are* my favourite shoes,' he replied, defensive. 'Maddie bought them me for my birthday. They're Church's.'

I looked at him and didn't say a word.

'They're nice shoes,' he muttered. 'Shut up.'

Minutes later, we were in the pub with two pints, two packets of crisps, and the Arsenal game Tom had made vaguely interested noises about playing on a screen above the bar.

'They are nice shoes,' he said again, sticking out one leg to admire his lace-ups. 'I wear them all the time, they're not gay.'

'She didn't think we were gay because of your shoes,' I said, opening my crisps with a satisfying pop. 'But I don't think it helped when you called me amazingly sexy.'

'Brad Pitt, George Clooney and then you,' he replied, stacking his hands one above the other over the table. 'And then probably David Beckham. He's a good-looking bastard.'

'I am better looking than David Beckham,' I confirmed with a thoughtful nod. 'That's fair. George Clooney though? Really?'

'I'm a mug for a silver fox,' Tom said, craning his neck to check the score.

'Just as well.' I pretended to squint at his temples while inhaling salt and vinegar crisps five at a time. 'Going a bit at the temples there, son.'

'I am not.' He looked back at the TV, brushing his hair when he thought I wasn't looking. 'I'm not sure what we were doing in that ridiculous shop in the first place. Have you come into some money or something?'

'Just looking,' I replied, wincing at a particularly nasty tackle. 'Bored with everything in the wardrobe and I haven't bought any new clothes for ages.'

'I know I'm supposed to hate shopping,' Tom scooted his chair closer to the table, as though he were about to impart a great secret, 'but I actually really like it. Maddie won't even go with me any more, we have to go our separate ways as soon as we step foot into Selfridges.'

'And you wonder why she thought you were gay,' I said, brushing crisp crumbs off my jeans and accepting the punch in the arm as due course. 'I'm joking, I'm joking. I don't hate shopping, I don't have the time or, quite frankly, the money.'

'How are things going with work?' he asked. He tore open his packet of crisps as I folded my empty bag into a neat square and wedged it underneath the condiment holder. 'Not that busy?'

'Busy enough,' I replied. 'But there's only so much I can do on my own and I can't afford to pay anyone else full-time. I'm doing the interior design and build for a new bar not that far from here, actually. We can have a look on the way back to the car if you want?'

'Yeah, cool,' Tom said. 'You going to be down here working on it then?'

I nodded.

'In a few weeks. I'm building everything in my work-shop up at home but I'll be coming down to install it, obviously. It's going to be cool – the sign's up already,

Camp Bell on Norville Street? It's a brother and sister ˃ who own it.'

'I think I've seen it.' He winced at a nasty tackle on the TV. 'You should come and stay next time you're down here. I'm really glad it's working out for you, Ad. You'd have been miserable if you'd stuck with the law.'

'Is that a cry for help?' I asked, stretching my long legs out alongside the table. 'Because you can leave at any time.'

He laughed, resting his elbows on the table. 'Maybe,' he said. 'Maddie's company is doing really well. Maybe I'll take a sabbatical and let her be the man of the house for a while.'

'Like she isn't already,' I replied before nicking a handful of his crisps.

Tom looked happy and I was pleased to see it. We'd been friends for a long time, ever since university. It was Tom who I turned to when I realized my heart wasn't in it and it was Tom who helped me work out my next steps. When my brother was busy taking the piss and I was too afraid to tell my parents, he was the one who reminded me it was my life I was wasting. I was pleased to see him finally getting it together with a decent girl – his ex and I had never seen eye to eye. It's not like I was happy when he found out she was cheating on him, but I was downright ecstatic when he packed her in and started going out with Maddie. Good looking, funny, and not afraid of a pint, she was a winner in my book.

'It's good, things are good,' Tom said, a huge smile on his face that made me think of Liv. Every time she crossed my mind it was a punch in the gut. 'Even better since she moved in, to be honest. I wish we'd done it months ago.'

'That's brilliant.' I offered him a vague smile and then returned my attention to the game. 'I can't see how anyone's going to get anything out of this, the way they're playing.'

'How are things with Liv?' he asked, polishing off the rest of his crisps and rolling the empty packet into a long, narrow tube. Weirdo. 'How was the holiday?'

'Holiday was good,' I replied. I sat behind Tom at his dad's funeral. I went to the hospital with him when his mum had her thankfully minor heart attack and he came in the ambulance with me when the dodgy fake Viagra I bought on our boys' trip to Ibiza ended in a six-hour erection and a very painful draining procedure but, for some reason, I was finding this incredibly difficult to talk about.

I clucked my tongue against the roof of my mouth and looked over his shoulder at a couple trying each other's food in a booth by the window. 'And we are. Taking. A. Uh . . .'

I paused, pouting my bottom lip. Tom took a sip of his pint with raised eyebrows.

'Come on, Adam, you can do it, use your words.'

'We're taking a bit of a break,' I said quickly. As soon as the words were out, I realized how ridiculous they would sound to Tom. 'It's nothing serious. A time-out, that's all.'

'Nothing serious?' Tom looked as though I'd just told him I had cancer of the puppy and it was terminal. 'You broke up with her? Or she broke up with you? Adam, why haven't you said anything?'

'We haven't broken up,' I said, trying to play everything much cooler than I really was. 'We're taking a break. I suggested it, she agreed it was a good idea, it's no big deal.' We just hadn't spoken since. That was fine, that was normal. Right?

'I don't want to be an arsehole,' he replied, presumably because he was about to be an arsehole. 'But there's not a woman on earth who thinks it's a "good idea" when their boyfriend suggests they take a relationship sabbatical. I know what Mads would say if I told her I wanted to take a break.'

I responded with the best argument I had. A shrug. It was just as well I'd given up as a lawyer.

'Are you thinking about knocking it on the head?' Tom asked, a look of abject horror pasted on his face. 'You're not seeing anyone else, are you?'

'God, no,' I answered immediately. There was no grey area with cheating as far as Tom was concerned. Chris referred to seeing one woman before breaking up with another as 'taking the car for a test drive', but for my best friend it was an entirely black-and-white situation.

'We're taking some time off from each other, definitely not breaking up. To be totally up front with you, I was planning to propose and it sort of went wrong.'

Tom sucked the air in through his teeth.

'She said no?'

Why was that everyone's first assumption?

'I didn't actually get the chance to ask her.'

'What stopped you?' he asked, a look of disbelief on his face. 'Pirates? Snakes? Pirate snakes?'

'I was about to do it,' I began, momentarily distracted by the idea of snakes in pirate hats. 'And then, well, there were some logistical problems. Then I started thinking about everything. How getting married is a big deal, you know? And how Liv's great but what if I can't take care of things properly.'

'Oh god.' Tom looked around and leaned over to rest his arm on my shoulder. 'Is something not working right? Was it that tablet you took in Ibiza?'

'Not like that, you cock,' I said, shoving him back across his side of the table. 'Everything is fine in that department, thank you. I mean, in general. Like I said, work isn't that steady, I'm hardly bringing home a small fortune and yeah, I know I've got the house and she'll always have a job, people will always need a vet, but right before I did it, I had this vision of everything going to shit.'

He kept his eyes on the table and knitted his brows together. Tom had great eyebrows. I wondered whether or not he tweezed. But there are some questions a man couldn't ask even his best friend.

'How so?'

'What if my work dries up?' I replied. 'Working on the bar is brilliant but this is my first proper job in six years. I don't know when I'll get my next commission. I could go back to law if I'd finished my BPTC but I didn't. And what happens if we have kids? I know Liv wants a family, and now Cassie's got a baby Liv's definitely going to want one, isn't she? What if she wants to pack in work once she's had it and I'm not making enough money? I'm not Chris; I can't afford to support a wife and a child. What happens if I get ill? What happens—'

'What happens if you get hit by a bus?' he countered. 'What happens if zombies attack? What happens if Liv realizes she's really a man and decides to get gender-reassignment surgery? You, sir, are being ridiculous.'

'*You're* being ridiculous,' I countered. Liv would never get gender-reassignment surgery. She had to be the only vet on earth who is terrified of going through any kind of medical procedure herself. The drama we went through when the dentist said she had to have her wisdom teeth out. But she'd looked so cute with her big chipmunk cheeks afterwards. 'It's sensible. It's the opposite of ridiculous.'

'Ad, Liv isn't Cassie and you're not Chris, thank god,' he said. I drank down half my pint in one gulp. 'Have you been talking to him about this? Because this sounds a lot more like your brother than it does you.'

'I don't want to let anyone down,' I said, pushing my pint back and forth in front of me, condensation leaving trails along the shiny wooden table. 'I know my mum and dad were really cool about me changing careers but it still felt like shit. I can't do that again.'

Tom shook his head and sighed.

'And breaking up with your girlfriend who you were about to propose to feels amazing?'

'We're not broken up,' I said quietly. 'We're on a break.'

The awkward silence was broken by a cheer from the bar: Arsenal had scored in the ninetieth minute.

'And none of this occurred to you before you bought an engagement ring?' Tom asked, completely ignoring the game. That's how good a friend he was.

'Didn't buy one,' I said. 'My nan left me hers, I was going to give her that.'

And instead of sparkling on Liv's finger, it was hiding in the bottom of a vase on my mantelpiece.

'No one can see the future.' Tom's chair creaked under his six-foot frame. He would look great in a Tom Ford suit and he could probably afford one as well. Rebecca had been barking up the wrong tree. 'I can't tell you what's going to happen six months from now, but I do know if anything was going to happen to me, I'd want Maddie there when the shit hits the fan. If you don't feel that way about Liv, then maybe you're doing the right thing.'

I stared at the toes of my trainers for a moment then looked over at Tom's fancy, grown-up lace-ups. He was right, they were nice.

'But if you're on the verge of cocking up a perfectly good relationship because you're scared, you need to do something about it.'

'OK,' I said, entirely noncommittal.

'Silly question,' he said, waiting until I had the balls to make eye contact again. 'But have you talked to Liv about any of this?'

'Uh, not as such,' I admitted. 'Or, you know, at all.'

Tom didn't say a word.

'She hasn't been in touch with me!' I said, defensively. 'And I don't really know what to say. That's why I said I wanted a break, not a break-up. I didn't want her to think I was definitely knocking it on the head.'

'She's such a lucky girl,' Tom said, finishing up his pint. 'For fuck's sake, Adam. Finish your pint then go and say you're sorry. Or at least bloody well tell her what you just told me. If you're incredibly lucky, she'll take you back without too much suffering.'

'I don't know, she's got her dad's sixty-fifth birthday party tonight.' I was making excuses when I knew full well that he was right. 'I don't think she'd want to see me right now.'

'Now is exactly when she needs to see you,' he argued. 'Surely you're invited to said party? Surely her parents are expecting to see you there?'

'Of course I'm invited,' I replied. Now who was being dense? 'Her parents love me. Everyone's going – Mum and Dad, Chris and Cassie, I think . . .'

Tom stared at me, eyebrows raised.

'What?'

'Have you told your mum and dad and Chris and Cassie that you're not going to your girlfriend's dad's big birthday party?' he asked.

'Oh. Fuck.'

'Present for her dad, flowers for her mum and I'd recommend kneepads for all the grovelling you're going to be doing,' Tom suggested. 'Keep that ring handy as well, you might have to bring out the big guns.'

I pulled my phone out of my pocket to check the time. It was only two fifteen, the party didn't start until six. It was a good two-hour drive back to Long Harrington but I could definitely still get over to Liv's before it all kicked off.

'I've got to go.' I stood quickly, dramatically knocking my chair over and then awkwardly picking it up.

'Agreed,' he said, standing up to give me a hug. 'Let me know how it goes. Call me if you want.'

'I will,' I promised, patting myself down; phone, my wallet and keys, all present and correct. 'Thanks, I mean it.'

'No worries,' he replied, standing up and following me out of the pub. He pulled his own phone out of his pocket and I saw he had a photo of Maddie as his wallpaper. I had Liv and me as mine, dancing at Chris and Cassie's wedding, looking so happy and so stupidly in love. 'Now piss off.'

'Tom, can I ask you one question.' I stood directly in front of him, eye to eye.

'Of course,' he said. 'Anything.'

Smoothing my hands over my face, I squinted into the sunlight outside the bar.

'I want you to be honest.'

'When am I not?'

'Do you think my eyebrows are too bushy?'

'On second thought,' he said, clipping me round the back of the head as we left the pub, 'leave Liv alone. She's a nice girl, she deserves better.'

8

My parents had never been ones for a big celebration. Major milestones passed the family by, celebrated with nothing more elaborate than a Viennetta and a bottle of Marks and Spencer's own-brand sparkling wine. And only if the Viennetta was on offer. Mum and Dad's idea of a wild time was opening a packet of Fox's Crinkle Crunch and watching some Michael McIntyre or, if they were feeling terribly controversial, fifteen minutes of Graham Norton.

When I demanded a thirteenth birthday party, hot on the heels of Abi's impossibly extravagant bat mitzvah, they did the best that they could. Five girls from my class in our living room, a Take That birthday cake, Dad playing DJ with my tape deck and Mum hovering in the doorway with a bin bag and a Dustbuster. Not so much as a crumb of that cake touched the carpet. It was better than a kick in the tits, but not exactly what I'd been dreaming about, especially compared to Abi's live band, ice cream sundae bar and light-up dance floor. And so, given my birthday party was still the pinnacle of their entertaining career, I was naturally suspicious when my dad announced he was putting on a 'proper do' for his sixty-fifth birthday in the upstairs room in the pub and inviting half the village.

'Olivia!'

Jeanette Riley, owner of the local newsagents and Persian cat enthusiast, greeted me with an over-familiar hug as I attempted to slink into the party. I thought I was early, but from the looks of it the half of the village that had been invited had brought the other half as their plus one. I wasn't entirely surprised; my dad had lived here his entire life. He knew everyone and everyone knew him, a fact that had often come back to haunt me as a teenager. The last thing I wanted was to spend the evening making small talk with every Tom, Dick and Jeanette, knowing they would all ask about Adam and I had no idea what to tell them. It was Saturday and I still hadn't heard from him. It was beginning to look more and more like things were over and I refused to believe there was a woman on earth who wanted to spend her first weekend as a potentially single thirty-something nodding and smiling over cheese and pineapple on a stick with the woman who refused to sell her *Cosmo* until she was twenty-one because it was 'full of nothing but smut' when she could be eyeball deep in Häagen-Dazs, watching *Dirty Dancing* and sobbing into her cat like a proper spinster.

'Olivia Addison, don't you look lovely,' Mrs Riley said, eyeing my outfit as though she didn't quite believe what she was saying.

'Hello, Mrs Riley,' I said, returning her once-over. I don't care what anyone says, there is an age when you're too old for hot pants. 'How are you?'

'I haven't seen you outside of that vet's in a dog's age,' she replied, ignoring my question and planting her fists on her hips. 'Must be a relief to get out of those pyjamas you wear all day.'

'They're scrubs,' I explained, allowing her to lead me directly to the bar without argument. 'You're be surprised, they're very comfortable.'

I'd given up wearing proper clothes to work as soon as I found out you didn't need to iron scrubs, it just made sense.

'Comfort isn't everything though, is it?' she asked. 'My eldest is the same, you know. Never thinking about how she looks, always running around, dressed like a man.'

'Not really any point dressing up for what I do,' I replied. 'I hate being uncomfortable, don't you?'

'Hmm, your dad and your granddad always wore suits to work,' she said, flicking her eyes up and down my polka-dot dress once more. 'Now, would you mind having a quick look at this picture of my Hermione? She's got some runny stuff in the corner of her eye and I can't decide if it's just runny or there's an infection. I took it earlier, since I knew I'd be seeing you.'

'Well, it's hard to tell from a photo,' I started but it was too late, her phone was pressed up against my nose before I could finish my sentence. 'It would be better if you could bring her in.'

'I'm sure it's nothing,' Mrs Riley said, waving her smudged phone screen back and forth, two inches from my face. 'Just have a look. What do you think?'

'I think bring her in on Monday,' I replied as politely as I could. 'And I'll have a look at her for you.'

Slowly putting her tiny phone back into her giant

handbag, Mrs Riley treated me to a long and accusatory scowl.

'Your granddad always had time to look out for his friends.' She squinted at me through her elaborate eye make-up. 'He wouldn't have had a poor old woman with bad hips trek all the way down to his office just for a cat's runny eye.'

Jeanette Riley was forty-seven.

'I can always come to you,' I suggested with a bright smile. 'Give us a call and we'll set up an appointment.'

'It's a racket,' she muttered, walking away. 'That's what it is. You'll want an arm and a leg, all to look at a runny eye. It's criminal, that's what it is.'

'You all right there?' Abi emerged from the ladies while I stood at the bar, nodding and smiling politely to thin air. 'You look like you're about to cut someone.'

'I've been here less than a minute and I've already been accused of running a pet protection racket,' I explained. 'This is why I stopped leaving the house, isn't it?'

'It's funny,' she replied, straightening my necklace. 'No one ever asks me to diagnose their pet's problems.'

'That's because the last time someone did, you told them it looked like their dog had herpes,' I reminded her. 'And then you told them to fuck off.'

'What did they expect?' she asked, ordering two glasses of wine from the barmaid. 'I was at a christening.'

'I know,' I replied. 'It was the vicar.'

'Eh . . .' Abi rested her elbows on the bar and checked out the guests as they swarmed from one end of the room to the other. 'This is an awfully fancy do for the village. Is it really your dad's birthday party or is he actually about to help us all ascend to the next reality? Is the punch safe to drink?'

'He didn't say anything about mass murder but you never know with my dad, he's a taciturn man,' I said, clutching my wine but not drinking. It had been a rough week on that front already and I was such a lightweight. The thought of even taking a sip made my stomach turn. 'You're right though, something's up. They've actually spent money on this. They literally told me nothing about this evening – I thought it was going to be a bottle of Blue Nun and a bag of dry roast peanuts. But you know what my mum and dad are like, they never tell me anything.'

Admittedly, my mum had done a much better job of this birthday party than she had with mine. The room looked lovely. A dozen round tables covered with elegant white tablecloths and elaborate floral centrepieces filled half the room while gold and silver balloons floated above the dance floor, swaying out of time to the Sinatra that was playing over the PA system. It was all very swish and there wasn't a single bin bag or handy vac in sight.

'And I don't want to scare you but it's an open bar,' Abi whispered. 'Something's definitely going on.'

'Oh god,' I said, gulping the wine straight down with a shudder. 'Do you think he's dying?'

She shrugged and nodded. 'Or transitioning.'

'It can't be either,' I said, peering into the crowds to search for my parents, just in case. 'They bought a new car a month ago and there's no way he'd waste money on a Volvo if he thought he was about to die and when I tried to explain Caitlyn Jenner to him, he said he was too old to bother with all that and left the room.'

I hadn't seen Abi since our summit on Wednesday evening and we'd been playing telephone tennis ever since. To be fair to my friend, I really hadn't felt like talking. It had been a long three days of ridiculously long shifts in the surgery followed by unwelcome paperwork sessions and, most evenings, I'd topped off the day with a fun cry in the bath. It was a mystery to me how Adam could even consider walking away from such a prize.

'So, I'm going to ask you before everyone else does . . .' Abi fiddled with the plunging neckline of her beautiful deep green dress. She was not dressed for the sixty-fifth birthday of a family friend, unless she was trying to finish my dad off. 'Is you-know-who coming?'

'Adam?' I asked.

'No, Voldemort,' she replied. 'Of course, Adam.'

'I don't know,' I said, pushing up onto my tiptoes to peer over the crowd. 'I really don't. We still haven't spoken—'

'This is ridiculous, Liv.' Abi's face was a picture of empathy with just a hint of homicide in her eyes. 'He's your boyfriend, you can't just rattle on like this. I'm going to call him.'

'No, you're not,' I said, slapping her phone back into her bag. 'I spent all afternoon trying to come up with excuses for why I haven't heard from him that didn't end with me crying and drinking vodka under a table. This is not the time to make that dream a reality.'

'I would have been under the table with a bottle by Thursday night,' she said, dropping her head onto my shoulder, giving me an unrestricted view of her rack. She had amazing boobs. 'You're my hero.'

'Then I won't tell you about the empty bottle of vodka under my dining table,' I replied. 'You still think it's going to be all right, don't you?'

Not even all the music and laughter and happy chatter

that filled the room could fill the pause before she spoke again.

'I'm trying to think of a way to make not hearing from him all week positive,' she said. 'But I'm struggling. Is this the part where I'm supposed to take you shopping then we both get makeovers and disappear on a life-changing holiday to Tuscany?'

Ooh, Tuscany.

'Well, you're shit out of luck.' She emptied her wine glass into mine, filling it to the brim. 'Because I haven't got any money, I can't take any time off until April, and your hair is really nice as it is. Don't be ridiculous.'

'You're such a failure.' A small smile worked a group of muscles in my face that hadn't been used in almost a week. 'I think you need to check your "best friend" job description, Abigail Levinson.'

'They definitely sound like Cassie things to me,' she replied. 'Are they coming?'

'Couldn't get a babysitter,' I told her, watching three teenagers huddled together on the back of a bench outside, passing a bottle of something underneath their coats. I wondered if they needed a fourth. 'You're stuck with all the BFF duties.'

'I thought *you* were *my* best friend?' Abi waved to David who was edging into the room with a total lack of conviction. He hated what he referred to as 'old people parties', especially when the majority of the attendees were the same old dears who asked him when he was going to find a 'nice girl and settle down' every time they came into the surgery. 'You should take David to Tuscany. He'll be better at it than me anyway.'

'Better at what?' he asked, giving me a fist-bump. It was always best not to start any rumours at a village party; gossip spread like wildfire in Long Harrington and the two women who ran the library would have me barefoot and pregnant with his triplets in under three minutes if they so much as saw a hug.

'Olivia Addison's Magical Break-Up Makeover,' Abi replied with elaborate jazz hands. 'I'm thinking haircut, boob job, burn all her clothes and then we move to Paris to live in a five-star hotel. Shenanigans ensue.'

'I thought you said I had nice hair?' I asked.

'Or, we could move to Las Vegas,' he suggested, one hand swooping in a wide arc in front of my face, painting an invisible picture, the other on Abi's shoulder before she knocked it off. 'And I meet a wonderful, gentle but feisty stripper named Harmony who is only dancing to earn money to pay for medical school, she takes us to her favourite blackjack table, Abi wins it big and we all live happily ever after in the high roller suite.'

'And where will I be during all of this?' I asked, taking one more sip of wine to confirm my hangover and putting it back on the bar. 'How does that help me?'

'Taking care of the lions at the MGM casino,' he said, picking up my glass of wine and chugging half the glass. Great, now we'd all had a go at it. 'Obviously.'

Abi reached out to take hold of my hand. 'I know this isn't easy and I know we're taking the piss.'

'We are?' David said. 'Oh. Shit.'

'But you've got to look at the opportunities here.' She grabbed a handful of peanuts from the bowl on the bar and shovelled them into her mouth. 'Firstly, you haven't actually properly broken up yet. And secondly, OK, things might not work out exactly as you thought. That doesn't mean things can't be great. If you could be anywhere right now, where would you be?'

'Miami, on the beach, cocktail in one hand, Karlie Kloss in the other,' David replied.

'And back in the real world,' Abi said, eyes on me. 'What would you be doing, if you'd never met Adam? If you could be anywhere in the world, doing absolutely anything, what would it be?'

Once upon a time, I would have had a thousand answers tripping off my tongue but now I had nothing. It was too easy to get stuck in your own life, wrapping yourself in layers of the every day. I was too busy paying the electric bill, bingeing on the new series of something I wouldn't remember in six months and making sure I always had milk to bother with dreams. I wasn't just stuck behind my break-up blinkers, I'd built so many walls around myself, I could barely see the sky.

'Japan,' I said, scratching around in my brain for anything that had been parked on the 'maybe' or 'not right now' shelf. 'I've always wanted to go to Japan but I haven't suggested it because I knew Adam was worried about money and it's so expensive.'

'Three tickets to Japan!' David said, easy as that. 'What else?'

'I'm not paying for all three of us,' I corrected.

'One ticket to Japan!' David said. 'What else?'

'I always thought I'd end up somewhere other than here,' I said, casting an eye over the room that was filled with faces I'd seen almost every day since I was a little girl. 'I mean, Abs, we only made it fifteen minutes down the road for uni.'

'I know,' Abi said with a consoling sigh. 'I thought we'd move to London afterwards. How come we're still bloody here?'

I gazed out the window and indulged in a vision of myself skipping through a cityscape in heels I couldn't possibly walk in and wearing a far too colourful outfit. This was why Carrie Bradshaw was a journalist and not a vet, I realized. Significantly more opportunity for glamour and significantly less chance of going home covered in something's vomit. I really had made some poor life decisions.

'You don't have a mortgage, you're not tied to anything.' Abi gave me a tiny smile, even though I knew she didn't love this chain of thought. 'Nothing stopping you, babe.'

A tiny spark of something that could be lit up inside me, and it was almost too frightening to look at directly. I couldn't even choose between two different flavours of ice cream, the idea of the entire world opening itself up to me was terrifying.

'The world is your lobster,' David waved a hand off into the distance. 'As long as you promise to always send me and Harmony a Christmas card, wherever you end up.'

'Liv, did your mum invite Adam's parents to the party?' Abi asked, taking the double glass of wine out of David's hand and putting it back into mine.

'Of course,' I replied. 'But they didn't RSVP. I think his mum's away.'

'His mum is not away,' she said, nodding across the room. 'His mum is here.'

I followed her gaze across the room to see two older men, each hugging an older woman. My parents and Adam's parents.

'Oh god, they're talking to each other,' I whispered, desperately looking for an escape route. I wasn't ready for this. I didn't know what to say to them. 'Is he here as well?'

'I can't see him,' Abi said, craning her neck above the crowd, her boobs threatening to burst free as she went up on her tiptoes. 'Do you want me to do a lap of the room?'

'I'll go,' David offered. He leaned forward and took a slurp out of our group wine glass. 'If I find him, I'll signal.'

'What's the signal?' I asked, a flush creeping up my chest and neck as both sets of parents continued to chat.

'Oi Liv, Adam is here,' he suggested, waving his arms around in the air. 'Does that work?'

'Perfectly,' Abi said with a grim nod. 'Now, let's get you sorted out.'

Without another word, she bundled me backwards into the ladies, pushing our sixth form French teacher out the door in the process.

'*Pardon*,' she called as the door swung shut. '*Je suis désolée.*'

'Why are we in the toilets?' I asked.

'We are in the toilets,' she replied, turning me around and shoving me into a toilet stall, 'because if Adam's parents are here, Adam is probably here too and you are dressed for your dad's birthday party.'

'It is my dad's birthday party,' I replied as she yanked her obscenely low-cut dress over her head and tossed it over the toilet door, her hands on her hips in her bra and pants. They matched. I was impressed.

'Abi,' I said calmly. 'You appear to have removed your dress.'

'Take that off,' she ordered, pointing at my delightful, very ladylike, navy-blue polka-dot ensemble. 'Right now.'

'But if I take it off, I too will have removed my dress,' I replied. 'I'm not sure what you're going for here, Ab.'

She rolled her brown eyes and crossed her arms over

her magnificent bosom. 'You haven't seen Adam since the car-park incident, correct?'

I nodded.

'And regardless of his recent behaviour, you do still want to be with him, don't you?'

I nodded.

'Then take that bloody frock off, you look like you're dressed to meet the queen,' she commanded. 'And then stuff your bra with bog roll. We're going to need to pad you out a bit if you're going to pull this off.'

My heart was pounding at the thought of seeing Adam and also at the thought of stripping half-naked in the lavs of the Bell. This was not standard Saturday night behaviour for me.

Any more.

We'd all done things we weren't proud of as teenagers.

'Do you really think wearing your dress is going to magically make our relationship all better?' I said, yanking handfuls of Kimberly-Clark toilet paper out of the dispenser.

'No,' she admitted as she zipped me up. 'But it will make you look amazing. And Liv, if you really love him and you really want to sort this out, looking amazing the first time you see him can't hurt.'

The edges of my mouth began to flicker as I smiled at her. Abi had little faith in relationships and I knew she must be itching to call Adam everything from a pig to a dog. She'd always been protective of me, ever since we'd met.

'I'm guessing he hasn't said anything to his parents,' Abi, ever the analyst, theorized while she dressed me. 'They seemed awfully chummy with your mum and dad. If my boyfriend had packed me in and then his parents turned up to a family party, my mum would run them through with a chainsaw.'

'Yes, but my parents are a lot more repressed than yours,' I reminded her as she pulled my sophisticated dotty number over her head and attempted to restrain her chest so I could zip her up. 'My mum is probably apologizing for raising such a disappointing daughter and offering to reimburse all the Christmas presents they bought me.'

'What are you going to say to him?' she asked, rolling her shoulders uncomfortably. This was a sacrifice that would not soon be forgotten. Mainly because she was unlikely to let me forget it. 'If he's out there?'

I looked down at my chest and my elevated rack looked right back up.

'I'm not sure I need to say anything,' I said, meeting Abi's eyes.

I burst out of the toilet stall, prodding at my tissue boobs. They weren't as impressive as Abi's by any stretch of the imagination but I wasn't used to seeing so much of them outside of my own bathroom. Adam wouldn't know where to look which I supposed was the point.

'He's here,' David shouted, bursting through the toilet door, making me, Abi and the hand-drier jump. 'He's here, Adam's here.'

'It's definitely him?' I asked, my heart pounding so hard I could actually see my bog roll padding move.

David nodded. 'Yeah. I think so. I mean, yeah. Pretty sure it was him.'

'It's not that hard a question,' Abi said. 'You've met the man before.'

'Well, I was trying to get to the vol au vents before your mother ate them all,' he told her. 'Then I saw a very tall blond man bothering Liv's dad so I left the buffet empty handed and came straight in here to report back. You're welcome.'

'Such a martyr,' she said.

'Can I go now?' David cast his eye around the pink tiled bathroom. 'I really don't like to spend too much time in the ladies unless there's a BJ in the offing.'

'Then you'd better go,' Abi said.

'You'll succumb to my charms eventually, Levinson,' he replied, waggling his eyebrows before slinking out the ladies' loos. He was wrong, she wouldn't. Other than being six years younger than we were (and Abi never dated younger men), he had once drunkenly informed Abi that she was his great white whale and asked if she would like to see his Moby Dick. He had more chance of getting Adam into bed.

'You'd never know I spent all week weighing mouse spleens, would you?' Abi asked, fluffing out my hair. 'Right. Let's do this.'

'Do what exactly? I whispered, still staring at my boobs. There was so much boob.

'That part is up to you,' Abi said, patting me on the backside. 'Remember, you can do anything you want to do.'

'Go home?' I asked weakly.

'Anything but that,' she replied, pushing me out of the bogs. 'Go get 'em tiger.'

'Olivia . . .' My mum, neat and tidy in her navy blue Jacques Vert special, opened her arms to give me a very tiny almost hug. 'What are you wearing?'

'Nice to see you too,' I said, hoisting up my plunging neckline as far as it would go. Across the room, over by the buffet table, I saw Adam's dad leaning on his walking stick while his mum, unmissable in a fuchsia sari, repeatedly reached out for a canapé before frowning, shaking her head and moving along to the next platter. Wherever Adam was hiding, he was not with his parents. It felt ever so slightly as though there were a spider in the room but I wasn't sure where it was lurking.

'I was just speaking to Adam's parents,' Mum said, inclining her tasteful bob towards the Floyds. 'His mother just came back from India. Did you know she'd been to India?'

'Oh, India, that's right,' I replied, not sure I did know. Adam's mum was always off somewhere. Wellness retreat in Costa Rica, watercolour lessons in the Lake District, wine-making course in the South of France – all while his dad sat at home, watching the snooker. And they were just about the happiest couple I'd ever met. 'She looks well on it.'

'Where is Adam?'

Someone was bound to ask sooner or later, I supposed I should have been thankful it was my mum.

'On his way,' I lied. I'd spent hours coming up with answers to that question, he was at work, he'd joined the army, he'd become a Scientologist and no longer believed in celebrating birthdays other than those of Tom Cruise and John Travolta. And that was the best I could come up with?

'I'm sure he'll be here soon,' Mum said. Bugger me, it worked. 'Is that a new dress, dear?'

'Where's Dad?' I asked. Over at the bar, Abi and David raised shot glasses in my direction but I still couldn't see Adam.

'Oh, he's about somewhere,' she replied. 'He's been bouncing around all day.'

I nodded. No sign of any tall, blond men at all. David must have been seeing things.

'Anyone would think it was his birthday,' I said.

Mum placed a hand on my forearm and smiled. We looked so much alike, it sometimes scared me. Same round blue eyes, same small, upturned nose and, thanks to the good people at Nice 'n Easy, the exact same shade of soft, ashy blonde hair. It wasn't difficult to look at my mum and see exactly where my life could go if I let it carry on running its untended course and that wasn't an entirely comforting thought.

'Olivia,' she said, gently squeezing my arm. 'You do know, your father and I love you very much, don't you?'

I felt all the colour leave my face and the floor rushed up towards me.

'Oh god,' I whispered, steadying myself with a hand on her shoulder. 'He's dying, isn't he?'

'And of course, you know we adore Adam.' Mum's face brightened at the mention of my sort-of boyfriend's name, ignoring my question and doing a good job of distracting me. They adored Adam? This was news. Even though they hadn't exactly openly dismissed him, Mum never failed to remind me how well Darren McLachlan, my date to the Year Seven Valentine's dance, was doing. Darren was a dentist in Australia, owned his own surgery as well as a four-bedroomed house, and flew his parents out to visit twice a year. Of course, Darren was also incredibly gay, something that seemed to have escaped their Facebook notice.

'His business is going well, his dad tells me. He's working on a big project?'

'He's designing a bar,' I said, searching the room and still coming up empty. Why did David think he'd seen him? No one in the room topped five foot six, including himself. 'Down in London.'

'That's . . .' she rolled her gold locket around in her fingers while she searched for just the right word. 'Nice.'

All that effort for 'Nice.'

'It's huge,' I corrected. 'It's amazing actually.'

Regardless of what was happening between us, I still felt defensive of him. Winning a job like this wasn't nice, it was wonderful. He'd been up against so much competition and he'd worked so hard on his proposal. Adam had been working away on tiny projects and assisting other people for years. This was the first chance he'd had to really design something big, something impressive, and I was jump-on-the-table, shout-it-to-the-world-and-not-even-care-if-my-knickers-were-showing, proud of him.

'If you say so,' Mum said, such a mixed expression on her face. 'I'm happy if you're happy. Oh, Olivia. It's all happening at once, isn't it?'

And the rush of pride rolled away, leaving me alone in my uncertain relationship status, standing in the middle of my dad's birthday party, wearing a borrowed dress with a fistful of loo roll shoved down my bra, defending a man who couldn't even bother to dump me properly.

'Hello, everyone.'

I looked up to see my dad on the stage wearing a smile and his best suit, leaning over a too short microphone stand. The last time I'd seen my dad anywhere near a microphone, he was three brandies over his Christmas limit, Abi was trying to teach him how to play *SingStar* and he was half-singing, half-sobbing along with a Benny and the Jets, while my mum took herself off to the kitchen with an unopened bottle of Baileys. Adam had been an absolute champion, sitting through three rounds of high-pitched 'Bennys' before joining in. I had rewarded him with a very quiet quickie in my childhood bedroom. My cheeks got hot at the memory and I gave myself a shake, turning my attention back to the stage.

'I wanted to thank you all for coming along tonight, it's lovely to see so many people in one place and it not be a funeral.'

Everyone in the room laughed uncomfortably while Mum gripped my hand tightly and began to shake. Bless everyone for not realizing he wasn't joking.

'I wasn't terribly excited about being sixty-five,' he went on, still leaning awkwardly over the mic stand. 'That's nearly nine and a half in dog years and I was very worried I might have to put myself down.'

Abi and David howled. Mum and I whimpered. The rest of the room fell silent.

'Ah, bit of vet humour there,' Dad added. 'Anyway, I wasn't looking forward to my birthday, wasn't looking forward to becoming a pensioner. It's not a sexy word, is it? Pensioner.'

'Did he just say sexy?' I asked.

'He's been watching Channel Four when I go to the WI,' she replied. 'It's the only possible explanation.'

'But just now I was talking to some friends, I'm sure you all know Mary and Clive Floyd—' Dad paused to flap a hand at Adam's parents who gave regal waves to the assembled guests. 'And they reminded me of a very good point. Life isn't over just yet. In fact, it really is just beginning, and Lesley and I have got a lot of adventures ahead of us.'

Adventures? Dad's idea of being adventurous was to drive out to the big Tesco on a Saturday.

'There are so many wonderful things ahead of us.' He peered into the crowd, pushing his glasses up his nose, eyes finally settling on Mum and me. His face lit up and he straightened slightly. 'I definitely owe Lesley a few holidays. And who knows what else, hopefully a few grandchildren eventually.'

A murmur ran around the room and I wondered how many text messages I'd get before the end of the night to congratulate me on the baby.

'But before she runs off and makes me a granddad, I'd like to ask my little Livvy up to the stage. Come on, Dr Addison, don't be shy.'

No one was ever going to refer to me as an attention-seeker but I'd definitely never been described as shy. I could hold my own at karaoke and that one time me and Cassie saw Helen Mirren in the street, I was the one who asked her for a selfie, but there was something decidedly terrifying about being hauled on stage unexpectedly by your dad, in front of a room full of people you'd known since birth. I'd rather be eloquently told to fuck off by any number of celebrities than stand on stage in front of my next-door neighbour, my former French teacher and the boy I'd forced my virginity upon at Abi's eighteenth birthday party after one too many Bacardi Breezers. Or at least I was fairly certain I had, the memory was still hazy.

'Go on,' Mum said, pushing me gently towards the stage. 'Let's get this over with.'

'Get what over with?' I asked, forcing myself to put one foot in front of the other. 'What's going on?'

The crowd parted like a poorly dressed red sea as I made my way up to the stage.

'Can you believe this is my little girl?' Dad asked the crowd to a mixture of clapping, sniggering and one very inappropriate comment about my tits that came from Abi's general direction. 'As you all know, Olivia has been working with me at the surgery for almost, what is it now? Six years?'

I nodded, sticking to the edge of the stage. People always said the best way to handle a crowd when you were nervous was to imagine them in their underwear. Those people had never spent a great deal of time with my neighbours.

'Six years.' My dad took a couple of short sidesteps, grabbed my hand and dragged me to the microphone. There was nowhere to hide. 'I can hardly believe it. I took over the surgery from my dad when I was forty-two and he was sixty-six. Before him, his uncle worked as a vet on the local farms. I've always been so proud that Olivia followed me into the family business and I'm sure you'll all agree, she's a wonderful vet.'

In the corner of the room, I saw Mrs Riley raise an eyebrow. She wouldn't agree that I was a wonderful vet and neither would her scabby-eyed cat.

'I've always thought of retirement as a bit of a cop out. Never saw the appeal but as my friends—'

He paused to tip a wink to the Floyds. Adam's mum giggled behind her hands while his dad gave her a stern nudge. 'As my friends the Floyds reminded me, there's a lot of life to live and, as much as I love my job, I've decided it's time for me to step aside. It's time for me to step aside and let a younger, cleverer – and if I do say so myself – better-looking Addison take over.'

Oh. Oh dear god.

Polite applause rippled through the room, punctuated

by David hammering on the bar and hollering his approval. Only Abi wore the same expression I felt on my own face. Complete and utter horror.

'Very shortly, the only Dr Addison in Long Harrington will be Dr Olivia Addison!' He wrapped me up in a huge hug, crushing me and my tissue boobs against his scratchy suit and peppering the top of my head with kisses, just like he did when I was five years old. 'For as long as you are an Addison, anyway,' he whispered in my ear. 'My lovely Livvy.'

'What?'

I stumbled backwards as he released me, stunned by the flashes of camera phones and the rousing chorus of 'Happy Birthday' that started somewhere near Adam's mum and rolled around the room until everyone was singing.

'I'm very proud of you,' Dad said into the mic, feedback screeching out of the speakers. 'I can't tell you how happy I am to be able to pass on my father's work into my daughter's hands and I very much hope to see the next generation of Addisons working alongside her one day.'

The birthday chorus came to an end and the assembled guests began to clap and cheer. Dad was going to retire and I was going to have to run the entire surgery. I knew how to be a vet but I didn't know how to run a business. I didn't even know where the electric meter was. I couldn't run the surgery, I didn't want to run the surgery. Shit. Shitshitshit. Shit.

'To Dr Addison!' Dad cried into the microphone. 'Our village vet.'

And as the entire village chorused their approval, I saw Adam charge through the door, sweaty and red-faced and wearing a far-too-snug T-shirt with a cartoon parrot making an obscene gesture on the front.

'Olivia,' Dad whispered, waving a hand in the general direction of my cleavage. 'There's something, um, just there in the front of your frock.'

I looked out into the crowd to see Abi manically grabbing her chest while David held his head in his hands before I eventually looked down to see one of my tissue boobs escaping from the front of my borrowed dress.

Because, of course it was.

None of this would *ever* have happened to James Herriot.

9

The drive from north London to Long Harrington should have taken two and a half hours, three at worst with the Saturday traffic going against me. But that would have been too easy. That would have left me time to go home, jump in the shower, put on something decent and arrive at Liv's flat so we could have a proper talk, iron everything out and possibly even sneak in a make-up shag before the party.

An hour after I'd left Tom, buzzing off my tits on the Red Bull I'd found in the glove box, I was pulled over on the hard shoulder of the A1, kneeling in six inches of mud. A flat tyre was not in my schedule, or pulling my shoulder out of its socket trying to unscrew a dozen rusted wheel nuts.

'Fuck you then, you fucking piece of shit!' I threw the wrench into the field behind me, narrowly missing a particularly judgmental-looking cow. 'Bollocks.'

The cow turned, pretty quickly for a cow, and carried on chewing even though she looked thoroughly scandalized.

'Sorry,' I told her, rubbing my shoulder and smearing it with five filthy oil stains. 'I didn't mean you. You're not bollocks, obviously.'

She mooed in acknowledgement before dropping a giant steaming pile of shit on top of my wrench. Apology not accepted.

I hated calling the AA – it always felt like admitting defeat. The man who answered didn't help, asking me a million obvious questions before finally relenting and sending someone out to save the day. I had thirty-five minutes – he'd said – to sit on the side of the road and think about what I'd done. At least it was a nice day for hanging out on the side of a motorway, choking to death on exhaust fumes and watching Middle England buzz by. Where were all the people going? What had they been doing with their day? I stared into the cars that went by slowly enough for me to make out faces.

Almost everyone sat in the passenger seat, starring at their phones while the drivers kept one eye on the GPS, too busy listening to the match commentary or Taylor Swift to talk to each other. I watched as an elderly couple passed close to my parked Land Rover in their Volkswagen. The husband sat close to the steering wheel, his wife by his side, chattering away as they drove along at the kind of sensible speed that would drive Liv insane. Whether she liked to admit it or not, both the Nottinghamshire constabulary and myself were very familiar with her heavy left foot. I needed my Land Rover to cart around wood for work. Why on earth did she need a souped-up Fiat Punto that rattled the windows in their frames whenever she came round to mine? I couldn't think of a single vet emergency that needed subwoofers taking up her entire boot.

When we first started going out, we would drive out
to the seaside when she got off work just to get fish and
chips for our tea. I still had a video of her on my phone
singing along to Adele at the top of her voice, as we
cruised down the dark country roads late at night. Even
though I'd washed my hands, I remembered the unmis-
takable stink of vinegar and coppers from the arcade
games we'd played, and the smell of her conditioner
which always seemed to fill the car as soon as she sat
down in the driver's seat, as I held my phone up close
to my face to capture the moment. I always threatened
her that I'd show it to our kids one day and she always
countered by threatening to render me unable to have
kids if I didn't delete it.

'WANKER.'

I looked up to see one teenage boy hanging out the
window of a Vauxhall Corsa, waving a curled palm and
a bent wrist in my general direction, baseball cap on
backwards while his friend in the back seat recorded the
incident for posterity. Or, more likely, for the millions
of people subscribed to their YouTube channel.

'You're shit! Ahhhhh!'

'God, I wish I was seventeen again,' I smiled and waved
after them, instantly cheered. 'Happy days.'

'You can hardly go in dressed like that,' announced Brian,
the man from the AA, as we pulled up outside the
Millstone at exactly six o'clock.

'I haven't got time to go home,' I said. I was impossibly calm given the circumstances. An hour, I'd waited.
An hour on the side of the road, followed by another
hour of watching Brian try to do the exact same thing
I'd spent an hour trying to do, followed by the split

second it took for him to break one of the nuts and fuck my car up entirely. After that, it was an easy ninety-minute whizz up the A1 in a tow truck. I was Liv's knight in mucky armour, arriving at the castle on my giant yellow steed. Basically, all her dreams come true.

'I've got a T-shirt in the back,' Brian said, cocking his head towards the shelf of a seat behind us. 'You can have it. It's designer.'

'Oh, I couldn't,' I replied, wiping my sweaty palms on my thighs and peering into the upstairs windows of the pub. The low sun shone directly onto the glass, reflecting the tall trees back instead of giving me any sort of clue as to what was going on inside. 'I'll be OK.'

'Going to a party, innit?'

I stared at the tiny, bald man and tried to work out whether he was asking me a question or not.

'I am going to a party,' I said hesitantly.

'You've gotta get changed.' He grabbed hold of my arm as leverage, further filthying said rag, as he curled around his seat and produced a crumpled Sainsbury's bag. 'You can't wear that.'

'I can't now . . .' I looked down at the new black handprint on my white sleeve and frowned.

'Top of the line, this is,' Brian said proudly. 'Too big for me, though. My cousin got it for us on holiday in Milan. Right into fashion, he is. I was going to give it to this bender what lives round the corner but you're a big lad, it'll fit you a treat.'

'Right.' I took the bag under my arm and gave him a tight smile in return. 'I appreciate it.'

'No worries, son.' He slapped me on the back, branding me one last time. 'Now, get in there and give her one from me.'

'I'll do my best,' I promised, hoping against hope Brian never ever popped into my head when I was giving anyone anything, as long as I lived.

I hadn't felt like getting into the details with him but ninety minutes is a long time to sit in a car with someone and not talk. We exhausted his conversational offerings (football, fly fishing, the demise of *FHM* and why he had considered voting for UKIP in the last election but ultimately decided not to bother at all) within the first half an hour, and there's nothing like sitting in the passenger seat to force false intimacy with a complete stranger.

'Garage'll have the car back with you on Monday, I should think,' he said, leaning out of the cab as I clambered to the ground, screwed Sainsbury's bag in one hand, phone in the other. 'I can't imagine they'll be open tomorrow.'

I held up a hand in as manly a farewell as I could manage before heading inside. Downstairs was fairly dead, a few young families dotted here and there, but the day drinkers had all left and the night was still young for everyone else. The room upstairs hummed with the crowd-pleasing sounds of the sixties and the staccato steps of everyone's best shoes.

'Been in the wars, lad?'

The barman, whose name I couldn't quite remember, gave me a nod as he polished up a tankard. I headed straight for the toilets, plastic bag in hand. Nothing like getting changed in a shitter to really set a Saturday night off to a great start.

There weren't any mirrors in the gents at the Millstone, save for a misty piece of shined up steel by the hand-drier but I was well aware of how bad I looked. Liv's parents were – I suppose the most polite description I could think of was . . . traditional. They would not appreciate me turning up to her dad's big birthday party covered in oil. There was every chance they might not appreciate me showing up at all and I definitely didn't want to make matters any worse. I unbuttoned myself quickly and threw the ruined shirt in the bin, scrubbing my hands with pearlized pink soap and drying them roughly on the back of my jeans. Red raw but cleaner than before, I pulled my Italian designer T-shirt out of the plastic bag and held it up under the fluorescent yellow light.

'Oh, come on.'

It was short-sleeved, v-necked, and bright pink. And it that wasn't enough, on the front of the shirt was a crude drawing of a cartoon parrot I didn't recognize, bending over and showing the world his parroty arse with one wing pressed against his beak. Despite not being the one with a veterinary degree, and never having considered a bird's arsehole before, I was fairly certain the drawing of the bird was not anatomically correct. What it was, however, was obscene. Without hesitation I pulled my other shirt out of the bin. Oil-stained shirt or pervy parrot T? It was a classic case of you're damned if you do and you're dressed like an extra from *RuPaul's Drag Race* if you don't.

It took me far too long to pull the trigger on the parrot shirt but after ten minutes of trying to wash oil out of cotton with hand wash, I gave up and went with the Italian job. Maybe Liv would think it was funny. Maybe I'd trip on the way upstairs and break my neck. Or as it turned out, when I finally got upstairs, I'd find Liv on stage beside her dad, with half a roll of toilet paper hanging out the front of her dress. And what a dress. I couldn't remember seeing it before; there was significantly more cleavage than Liv was usually comfortable with, and while I was absolutely fine with it, I didn't love the fact that everyone on the floor could see right up her skirt.

'Dr Addison!' Her dad raised his glass and everyone in the room did the same. 'Our village vet.'

He was toasting himself? Well, that was a bit sad.

He stepped away from the microphone and joined in the rhythmic clapping that echoed around the room, his usually placid face flushed as he pointed at the front of his daughter's dress. Liv turned her back to the room, flashing her knickers as she spun, and when she turned back around, the toilet paper was only just visible. Her giant left boob was a bit of a giveaway as to where she'd hidden it though.

'Hello . . .' Liv leaned right into the microphone. It squealed in protest and she jumped back. 'Oh, bugger.'

There she was, love of my life, stuffing her bra and showing her knickers to the entire village. After the week we'd had, I couldn't help but feel equal parts protective and amused but I knew she would not find this funny in the slightest.

'This is not my dress,' Liv stuttered into the microphone, with the same look on her face she'd had when I told her Tesco was out of Mini Eggs and they didn't know if they'd be getting any more in. 'This isn't my dress. It's my friend's dress. It's not mine.'

I saw Abi, her oldest and most hard-to-please friend, raise a hand and wave to the room while David, Liv's nurse, clapped appreciatively.

'Why is she talking about her frock?' an old lady covered

in dog hair whispered to another old lady covered in dog hair. 'I don't care about her frock.'

'If she wore more frocks like that, our Paul might be more inclined to take the dogs down for their check-ups,' her friend replied. 'I hate those scruffy things girls are wearing today.'

'I don't think it's a coincidence that she's not married,' the first one agreed. 'Make a bit of effort dear, you can't walk around all day looking like you've just got out of bed and expect a man to want anything to do with you.'

'Excuse me,' I said as I pushed my way in between their furry shoulders.

'And don't get me started on what they've got men wearing in this day and age,' one of them whispered. 'Look at that.'

'Hey, this is designer,' I replied, giving them both the glaring of a lifetime. 'It's from Milan.'

'Should have left it there,' the first cackled. 'You look a right plonker.'

'Yeah, well.'

Best comeback ever.

'I'm not especially keen on public speaking,' Liv was still talking on the stage, shuffling on the spot and clutching the microphone with both hands, 'and this is all a bit of a surprise, I don't know what to say.'

'Thank you?' called out one particularly unhelpful heckler.

'Thank you, of course,' she said quickly, pasting on what I knew was a fake smile and turning to her dad. 'Thank you, Dad, you're a brilliant vet and a brilliant dad and I don't know what we're all going to do without you.'

The room erupted in a polite smattering of not-drunk-yet applause. I'd missed something, clearly.

'Adam, over here!' I heard my mum hissing my name across the room and moved through the crowd, keeping one eye on Liv as I went. 'That's a nice shirt love, very colourful. What's that he's doing with his hand?'

'I don't know.' I gave her a hug while my dad shook his head over her shoulder. He did not agree with my fashion choices but then he was in a suit and Mum was in a sari so it was safe to say he was always going to be the more conservative of the two. 'What's going on?'

'Dr Addison announced he's retiring,' she said in her soft, scratchy voice. 'And Liv's taking over the practice. That's exciting, isn't it?'

I didn't know if exciting was the word I'd choose. Liv hated surprises. An unexpected piece of sparkly jewellery attached to a marriage proposal was one thing, but something like this? She would hate it. I had to rescue her.

'It's all a bit much, isn't it?' Liv went on. 'How can Dad be retiring?'

Oh wait, she wasn't finished. Liv was a prize waffler when she was nervous. She began to walk up and down the stage, microphone in hand, toilet roll making a break for it once again.

'And he's giving me the surgery?' She shook her head, sharing every thought that fell from her brain and out of her mouth with the entire village. 'That's a lot to take in; it's a lot to think about. I'd literally just decided I'm going to Japan.'

'What's she on about?' Dad asked as the natives became restless. 'Japan?'

'Oh, I've always wanted to go,' Mum said, adjusting her sari. 'Maybe we could all go together. Family honeymoon!'

Family honeymoon? Christ on a bike. I wondered how long it had taken Dad to tell her everything he had sworn that he wouldn't.

'I'll be back in a minute,' I told her, hurtling through the crowd and leaping onto the side of the stage in a single bound. Well, two single bounds. Two and a half, round the corner, and up the steps.

'Liv,' I hissed. 'It's OK, I'm here.'

'What are you doing?' she asked. Her hair was all piled up on the top of her head with those little loose bits hanging around her face. She looked perfect. Apart from the bog roll hanging out of her dress, obviously.

A murmur ran around the room and I asked myself the same question.

'Nice shirt, Justin Bieber.'

I didn't have to look to know the very helpful comment came from Abigail.

I pulled at the hem of my shirt. Every time I raised my arm, it peeled up over my stomach.

'In case you were wondering, this isn't actually my dress.' Liv walked away, ignoring me. 'And yes, I'm going to Japan. I'm not sure when.'

I stared up at her as she made her speech, no idea where it was going. It was just like the end of *Dirty Dancing* only a thousand times more shit. Someone really needed to put Baby in a corner.

'But still, never mind what I might have planned, Dad's retiring!' The microphone screeched with feedback. 'I mean, who doesn't like massive, life-altering surprises chucked at them during family functions? And—'

The speakers on either side of the stage screeched into life and 'Congratulations' by Cliff Richard boomed through my bones as a swarm of red balloons and glittery streamers fell from the ceiling much to the delight of, well, no one.

Liv looked at her dad with an expression I couldn't remember seeing on her face before, then dropped the microphone and rushed down the stairs, pushing me out of her way as she went.

'Liv out!' David ran up the staircase and put the screeching mic back on its stand, saving everyone's ears. 'Give it up for Dr Addison!'

'What were you doing?' Liv asked, wild-eyed. 'You totally distracted me.'

'I did or my T-shirt did?' I replied, looking down to meet the parrot in the eye. 'Because there's such a good reason I'm wearing this, trust me—'

'I think I want to leave.' She cut me off, looked me in the eye and then nodded. 'Sorry, Adam. Not now.'

'Then when?' I was starting to feel very slightly annoyed. I'd gone through hell and high water to get to the party on time, I'd tried to show my support and now she was mad at me? 'You've got to talk to me sooner or later.'

'No she hasn't,' Abi interjected, swooping an arm around Liv and whisking her away. 'She'll tell you when she's ready.'

I was very glad Liv had good friends who loved her, but at that moment, I would have happily seen Abigail Levinson elsewhere. And that was putting it politely.

'Cool T-shirt, bro,' David said, giving me a thumbs up and quickly waving his mobile phone in my face. 'You don't mind if I Snapchat it, do you? Thanks.'

And before I could say otherwise, all three of them were gone.

10

I didn't bother turning on the living-room lights. Instead, I walked directly to the kitchen, opened the fridge and pulled out the half-empty bottle of white wine, pouring myself a full glass in the yellow half-light. Daniel Craig looked up from his prawned position on the settee and meowed loudly, displeased at being woken from his rock-and-roll Saturday-night nap.

'Sorry, DC,' I said, closing the door and drinking my wine in reassuring darkness. 'Don't mind me.'

The cat gave a cursory squeak and settled back down on the settee, eyes darting around the room. It had been a confusing week for him and I was almost certain he did not approve of my presence. I was never home this often and he didn't quite seem to know what to do with himself. Most of the time, I hung out with him during the day when he wandered into the surgery to taunt the in-patient cats in their cages, but this week he'd been treated to almost full five nights of me huddled under a blanket at two a.m., unable to sleep and binge-watching reality shows while intermittently sobbing and stuffing my face. Less Netflix and chill, more Amazon Prime and Kill Yourself.

I wandered over to the settee and sat down beside the cat as my eyes adjusted to the dark. Resting my head backwards, I stared up at the ceiling, focusing on a great big crack running from the outside wall all the way over to the light fixture in the middle of the room. How long had that been there? I'd really let this place go. I couldn't remember the last time I'd decorated. Wait, had I ever decorated? I'd painted three different rooms in Adam's house over the last twelve months and I couldn't even remember the last time I bought toilet paper for my own home. Thankfully, my bra was currently full of it.

But then, I realized, when I was spending my days of decorating Adam's house, I had thought it was *our* house. I was decorating our home, for our family. Now I was lying on the settee with Andrex spilling out of my dress and staring at a crack in my knackered ceiling. How wrong could you be?

On the coffee table, my phone started ringing.

I stared at Adam's name and a picture of a panda holding a machine gun that accompanied it. Without moving, I sipped my wine and waited for the call to end. As quickly as the screen went dark, it lit up again. He wasn't going to give up.

After one last large gulp, I put down my wine and picked up the phone.

'Hello?'

'Liv?'

'Adam?'

I mean, who else did he think it was?

'Are you at home?' he asked.

'Yes,' I said, kicking off my shoes and walking up and down the living room. 'I'm home.'

'None of your lights are on,' he replied. 'Not to sound like a stalker or anything.'

He was outside. I padded through to the bathroom and peered out of the window.

'Can I come up?' he asked.

I stared out into the yard. It was dark but not quite dark enough for the security lights to turn themselves on. Regardless, Adam and his neon T-shirt were easy enough to spot. He gave a small, contained wave.

A car went past, its headlights highlighting his profile more clearly.

'Liv?' he called. 'Are you there?'

'Yes,' I nodded, even though he couldn't see me.

'Can I come up? Or can you come down? I need to see you.'

I pressed my fingertips against the window and shook my head. If I went downstairs and he said he was sorry, I would forgive him and he would kiss me and we would pretend the whole thing never happened. It was what he expected me to do; it was what everyone expected me to do. But it had happened, and if I let this go now it would eat away at me forever. Abi was right. I'd been coasting, waiting for Adam to propose, trotting on with the surgery without thinking about the future, and look where it had got me. Things had to change and they had to change now.

'No,' I said clearly, surprised by the strength in my own voice. 'You've had all week to come and talk to me, and instead you sail into my dad's birthday party, wearing god knows what, and expect me to fall into your arms? One minute it's radio silence and the next it's everything's OK? Didn't you want to break up with me four days ago?'

'I tried to explain,' he replied, the hint of a whinge in his words. 'That was a mistake.'

'Mistake or not, it still happened,' I said, turning away from the window and perching on the edge of the bath. 'I don't know what was going through your head when you said you wanted a break in the first place but it doesn't matter any more. I can't pretend I'm not thinking about it.'

The bathroom window was still open and Abi's dress was nowhere near enough protection against the cold. Goose bumps shivered all the way down my arms and legs and I heard Adam's pace quicken below.

'I know I cocked up,' he was talking fast, tripping over his words as he spoke, 'I know I did. It was stupid, I got in my head about nothing and I'm sorry. I know what I want now, I don't need a break, Liv, I don't want a break.'

'That's great,' I said. 'But maybe I do.'

I held the phone steady between my shoulder and my ear and, resting two fingers on my wrist, measured out my pulse while Adam breathed heavily down the line. It was faster than it needed to be but it was steady. That was something.

'I feel like I've forgotten what I want,' I said, trying to explain to him and myself at the same time. 'In fact, I'm not even sure if I ever knew.'

'I can help you with that,' he assured me. 'You want a Terry's Chocolate Orange, an early night and two sugars in your tea. Occasionally you want to eat an entire tuna and pineapple pizza even though everyone knows it's disgusting.'

'It's not disgusting, it's delicious,' I said with a laugh

that turned into a sob. Now I wanted a pizza as well as someone to make all my major life decisions for me. This was what I missed – the fact that he knew my disgusting secret eating habits and thought it was OK. Well, maybe not OK, but forgivable. What if we broke up and the next man refused to let me have tuna and pineapple pizza in the house? Unthinkable. 'I just need some time. I want to figure everything out in my own head and I can't do that with you around.'

'I don't understand,' Adam said. I could tell he was frustrated and part of me hated him for it. He'd bloody started this, after all. 'Is this about your dad? Have you suddenly decided you don't want to be a vet or something?'

'That would be mental,' I replied immediately. 'What kind of person wakes up and decides to completely change careers?'

'Point taken,' he said curtly. 'So, what do you want? What can I do?'

'I wasn't having a go at you,' I replied, even though I clearly was, just a little bit. 'Yes, Dad telling me he's retiring has thrown me but it's not just that. I need time and you can give me that.'

I could hear all the different replies ticking over in his head. Adam was a practical, logical man who hated to lose an argument. Even though he had decided not to become a lawyer, there was no doubt in my mind he would have been a great one. I knew how hard this must have been for him, asking him to walk away from an argument he couldn't understand or have any hope of winning.

'So, that's it?' he asked. His voice sounded so much further away than he really was. 'We're done until you say otherwise?'

'I'm not breaking up with you,' I replied with closed eyes, biting my lip so hard, I was certain I'd soon taste blood. 'I'm trying to explain to you I need to work some stuff out on my own. Not necessarily us stuff. Life stuff, everything stuff.'

I wished he would go away and let me sleep on everything going on in my head. This was too much to deal with in real time; even I didn't really understand what I was saying so how could he be expected to follow?

'Liv, if you want to punish me for the other day,' his words came quickly and his footsteps stopped right below the window, 'let me tell you, this week and this bloody T-shirt have done the job for you.'

'It's not that,' I said, uncertain but determined. I would not be swayed; I would not be a walkover. 'I'm not punishing you, this is about me.'

'That old chestnut,' he almost laughed. 'It's not me, it's you?'

I smiled weakly into the phone. Why was this so hard? It was the right thing to do, I was sure of it.

'Sorry to be such a cliché,' I replied. 'If I don't work this out now, I never will and everything just keeps happening and one minute it was Christmas and then it was summer and now—'

'Liv,' Adam interrupted, 'have you met someone else?'

'No,' I replied quickly.

Why would he think that? Why would he think that? Unless he had met someone else? 'Have you met someone else?'

'No, of course not,' Adam said, just as fast off the mark. 'OK, you want some time. How long is this going to take?'

'As long as it takes,' I said. My pulse was still steady.

This was the right thing to do, my body knew it, even if my brain was struggling to catch up. 'But I promise by the end of it, I'll know where I was going with this whole thing.'

'A likely story,' he replied with softer words. 'So what now? Am I allowed to call you? Are you still my girl-friend?'

'I am definitely still your girlfriend.' I gave myself a questioning look in the door of the bathroom cabinet. 'And you can call. I'm not going to fall off the face of the earth or unfriend you on Facebook. It's just my whole life is you and the surgery at the moment and I realized it's a really long time since I took stock of everything. What I want to do with my life, where I want to go.'

'I'm not sure I love the sound of this,' he said after a moment's consideration. 'But I'm in, whatever you need, we'll work it out.'

'And just so we're clear,' I said, digging my fingernails into my palms. 'I'm thinking we're not seeing other people while we're on this break thing. Is that all right?'

'Definitely not seeing other people,' he agreed. 'That's not even a question, you moose.'

'Good.' I stood up, the cold ceramic of the bath sticking to the backs of my legs, and peered out the window just as the security lights decided it was dark enough for burglars and Adam took a step back into the light. 'It's OK, you know, everything's fine.'

'That's not entirely true, is it?' he said, meeting my blue eyes with his. 'I love you, Liv.'

'I love you too, yeti,' I said, touching my fingers to the window before shutting it. 'I'll talk to you later.'

Adam raised his hand in a wave, phone still close to his face as he took a few slow steps backwards out of the yard and disappeared out of the circle of the security light. I could still see that hideous T-shirt though. Nodding to myself, I went back into the living room and curled up on the sofa as Daniel Craig crawled up my body and pressed himself against my stomach. I pulled my grandmother's blanket over the two of us and closed my tired eyes, hoping against hope that I'd still believe I'd done the right thing in the morning.

Liv would often tell me how the village had grown since she was a little girl, how they never used to have a proper supermarket, how the post office did half days on Wednesday and everything shut on a Monday but no matter how many times she tried to impress upon me the importance of our very own proper coffee shop inside our very own proper Tesco, it was hard for me to adjust from London life.

I took the long route home, in no rush to get back to an empty house and a cold bed, wafting my hand past privet hedges, tapping low stone walls as I walked by and crossing the street to avoid a gaggle of teenage girls, loitering with clear intent, round the corner from the little shop. It had a proper name, the little shop, but that was what everyone called it and referring to it as anything other the little shop only incurred looks of confusion and assured everyone within hearing distance that you were not a local.

It had been a true arse of a day. If I still lived in London, I'd have called Tom or one of my other law-school mates, summoned them to the pub and drunk myself into a stupor or at least until *Match of the Day* came on, whichever came first. Now, that wasn't an option. I'd spent my first year in the village working like a dog, trying to convince Mum and Dad I'd done the right thing by leaving law school. Then, when I started seeing Liv, I didn't really bother trying to make new friends. We were joined at the hip from the beginning and I wouldn't have had it any other way.

'More fool you,' I muttered, pretending to ignore the catcalls from the girls on the corner when really, I was filing them away in my 'still got it' mental folder. I glanced back over my shoulder only to see them making obscene gestures and high fiving each other. I picked up my pace: the last thing I needed was a reputation as the village perv.

This break could be a good thing, I told myself, as I uncoiled the cable of my earphones from around my phone and scrolled through my iTunes, looking to drown out the tame Saturday-night sounds of Long Harrington. Liv clearly said we were not breaking up and she wasn't seeing other people. This happened, didn't it? Couples needed a time-out from time to time. All she was really saying was that we wouldn't see much of each other for the next couple of weeks. That was all. No big deal.

Besides, I had enough on my plate right now. We both needed to get our other stuff taken care of without worrying about the other. If her dad really was retiring and she was taking over the vet's she'd be even busier than ever and I had the bar to worry about. I'd been so excited when I won the job I hadn't really stopped to think about how much work it would be, going into a major build like this on my own. If I had proposed to Liv and she'd accepted, I'd be losing my mind. The last thing I needed was to be choosing centrepieces when I ought to be focusing on my first proper project and, knowing my girlfriend, I would absolutely end up taking care of all the details. As much as I loved that woman, she was not good at working out the little things – that was my department.

The only real problem was, I didn't want to be on a break. I wanted things back how they were before we went to Mexico: Liv in my bed when I woke up, Liv secretly swearing at the Keurig coffee maker because she'd buggered it up again, Liv rubbing my shoulders after a long day in the workshop, Liv curled up in my arms at night.

'It's a good thing,' I argued with myself out loud. 'People do this all the time.'

Just to make sure, I opened a browser window and typed out *girlfriend wants a break* and held my breath. 46,700,000 results. At least I wasn't alone. Skipping past the troll-dwelling Reddit boards, I scrolled down until I found actual advice from an actual woman in what seemed like a reputable Australian magazine.

If your girlfriend tells you she wants to take a break from your relationship, your most obvious reaction might be to assume the worst. But don't! Women communicate differently to men and even if her request seems like a bolt out of the blue, she may have already given you some subtle signs that flew under the radar. Before you panic, look back over the past few weeks and above all else, remember the three Cs of successful relationships; care, communication and compromise.

Seemed sensible, I thought, reading on. There could have been signs. I'd been so wrapped up in the proposal I could have missed something.

1. Have you been less available to your girlfriend lately?

And I don't necessarily mean physically! Perhaps you've been busy with work or preoccupied with a family matter and she has been bumped down on your priority list. Men sometimes fail to vocalize their concerns with their partner, either because they want to resolve the issue alone or don't want their significant other to see them struggle. If this is the case, your girlfriend might be asking for a little more of your attention. Contemporary society has conditioned women to be afraid of asking for what they want for fear of being seen as too demanding. She could be letting you know she needs more of your time without wanting to seem too needy.

I looked up to cross the road in front of the junior school. I had been less available! Emotionally and physically! But only for the last week. Before that, Liv was my morning, noon and night. If anyone had a right to feel sidelined, it was me. If I had a pound for every time I'd had to microwave my own dinner because she was on an emergency call, I would have at least thirty pounds. Which might not sound like a lot but really, it was. Not that I minded, I knew how much she loved her job, but I was pretty sure that one didn't explain our situation.

2. Did she say she wants a break or needs a break? The choice of language here could be a clue. Saying she wants something suggests your girlfriend is open to a compromise and simply requires your understanding. If she told you she needs the break, it may be that she genuinely feels smothered or overwhelmed and is trying to shock you into changing your behaviour. In this instance, reassure her that you love her and show her you're there for her, then see what happens.

Did she say want or need? It was so hard to remember. Maybe the next point would be more helpful.

3. A woman who knows herself and her needs is a true prize and you should be proud to be with a woman with such a degree of self-awareness and self-worth. For the most part, if a woman wishes to end a relationship, she will do so. If she is truly asking for a time-out, the best thing to do is establish ground rules right away – how long is the break? Are you allowed to date other people? – then give her the space she's asked for. Don't keep calling – let her miss you! Constant, overwhelming communication when she's asked for a break won't help anyone.

So, according to this article, I needed to respect her request for a break, be there for her, communicate but leave her alone and give her more attention as well as more space at the same time. Piece of piss. Swiping back to the search page, I opened the first Reddit article in hope of finding something more reassuring.

'She's dumping your arse, she's shagging somebody else, don't be such a moron,' I read out loud under my breath as I turned the corner to my house. 'No wonder she's had enough of you, how stupid can one man be?'

'Sorry?'

Mrs Johnson, my next-door neighbour, blinked at me as her Boston terrier piddled up against a street light.

'Evening, Carol,' I said with a nod at the dog. 'Lovely out, isn't it?'

'What's that on your shirt?' she asked, staring at the finger-flipping parrot I'd somehow managed to forget about.

'Shouldn't worry about it, Carol,' I assured her, heading up my driveway. 'Have a nice night.'

She was hardly one to judge, I thought, looking back at her disapproving face. I knew for a fact the doggy dumps I regularly saw dotted up and down the street were from that terrier and if you couldn't be bothered to pick up after your own pet, you really had no place commenting on the latest men's fashions fresh from the catwalks of Milan.

11

'She's almost ready.'

I wasn't quite sure how my night of not drinking had turned into birthing a cow with a white wine hangover but there I was at seven thirty on a Sunday morning, wearing rubber gloves up to my armpits, kneeling in a shed full of soiled straw while my dad whistled the theme tune to *Hollyoaks*. Mum was right; he'd definitely been watching Channel Four.

'Can you see the water sac yet?' he asked, ruddy cheeked and a hundred per cent hangover free.

Holding in a not-so-dry heave, I shook my head. I'd woken up in the middle of the night and attempted to put myself back to sleep with a brand-new cocktail of my own creation, half a glass of chardonnay and half a glass of sparkling rosé, washed down with the dregs of a bottle of cabernet and three strawberry Pop-Tarts. Every time I closed my eyes, I remembered my conversation with Adam and every time I opened them, I second guessed myself. Was a break the best idea? Had I made a huge mistake?

'You look exactly how I feel,' I whispered to the cow. 'Only, I've got a load of booze in my stomach instead of a miniature cow. Basically the same though.'

'I'm not sure we needed to come out, Peter.' My dad dusted off his knees and stood up beside another ruddy-cheeked pensioner while I gipped quietly at the side of the cow. 'She seems as though she's doing fine to me.'

'She was making a god-awful racket before you got here,' Peter replied. I still had trouble taking Farmer Jones seriously. Jonathan Roberts, Abi's cousin, claimed he had shot him in the arse with an air rifle when he was little but he'd never been able to prove it and I was still too scared to ask.

'I'd appreciate it if you could hang around until the calf's out. Karen is one of my favourites.'

I looked up quickly. Karen? Karen the cow?

'Absolutely,' Dad said, thumbs in his belt loops, smile still on his face. 'We're happy to stay as long as we're needed. Aren't we, Livvy?'

I nodded my head slowly, lips sealed together. I would not vomit.

'Sorry to have called you so early.' Farmer Jones gave me the same look he had given me when he caught me climbing over his back wall with a tiny backpack full of Kiwi 20/20. 'Jack's on his holidays or I wouldn't have bothered the pair of you.'

Jack Townsend was the closest thing Dad had to a nemesis. And by nemesis, I mean he was also a vet. They used to belong to the same golf club and Dad insists that, once upon a time, Jack Townsend called him a 'shithouse' at the Rotary Club Christmas dinner. It seemed unlikely to me but who's to say what those crazy kids used to get up to at the Rotary Club? Technically, Jack wasn't even

a business rival of Dad's. Townsend & Townsend special-
ized in livestock and large animals, they didn't look after
pets like we did which was why I was not used to
spending my Sunday mornings, hungover, with my arm
covered in cow-friendly KY Jelly, preparing to shove it
into a cow's birth canal.

'Always good for us to keep our hand in,' Dad said,
casting a glance down at me and my lubed-up limb. 'So
to speak.'

'I'll go and make some tea,' Farmer Jones said, hands
deep inside his waxed jacket pockets. It was bloody
freezing for September. 'Looks as though we could be
here for a while. Milk and sugar?'

I gave him a thumbs up from the business end of the
cow while Dad settled himself on an old milking stool
by her head. I'd set up a dustbin by the side of us,
ostensibly to be used for birthing related business but
in reality, it was my puke station.

'Now then,' he picked up the bottle of vet lube and
squinted to read the tiny writing, 'what was all that about
last night?'

I tried to swallow without throwing up.

'I didn't mean to give you a shock,' he said. 'Mum
and I discussed it and we both thought you'd be excited.
You're more than ready to take things over, Liv, I don't
need to tell you that.'

I pouted and tried a shrug. Didn't feel great.

'And you're old enough to take on the extra responsibility.' He sounded as though he was reassuring himself
as much as me. 'I'm not going to be around forever, Livvy,
and I don't want to work myself into the grave.'

I took a deep breath through my nose and tried to open
my mouth. Nope, not ready. I really didn't want to have

this conversation with him until I'd sobered up and considered my response. As it was, all I had right now was me shouting 'I don't want to and you can't make me' before storming off to my room and I had a feeling that wouldn't work any better at thirty than it had at thirteen.

'It means a lot to me that you're doing this,' he said. 'Your mother was always worried about me pushing you into the business but you were a natural. And thank goodness you've got a good head on your shoulders, your granddad never thought much to lady vets but you would have proven him wrong, love.'

Thankfully, I didn't need to speak to let him know how I felt about that.

'I know, I know,' Dad said, chuckling at my expression. 'But things were different back then. He'd have had you sitting out front, taking names and numbers. And what a waste that would have been. You're twice the vet I ever was.'

And a million times more hungover, I added silently. My dad really was a brilliant advert for sobriety. A brilliant, annoying advert that I would have gladly sacrificed to the first god who offered to get me out of this shed and back into my own bed with a bacon sandwich, a cup of coffee and the first two seasons of *The O.C.*

'Of course, I'll be around if you need me,' he assured me, getting up from his perch in order to get wrist deep inside Karen again. I couldn't work out whether he hadn't realized that I had yet to breathe a single word or if he was simply thankful for the opportunity to get his speech out without argument. I tried to look humble and appreciative and engaged, all while investing every atom of my being into not chucking up. Squatting beside a cow's dilated cervix was not helping. 'And we should start interviewing for another vet as soon as possible, lighten your appointment load so you've got more time to get to grips with the business.'

It hadn't occurred to me that we would have to bring someone else in. Interviewing was not a skill that came naturally to me: the last person I brought in was the nurse we had before David and that had been terribly tense after I came in early one morning to find him locked in one of the dog crates, wearing a leather gimp suit and covered in, well, the exact same stuff I was covered in. We had to let him go. As did his wife.

'A family business is a wonderful thing,' said the half-man half-cow beast that had been my father. 'The thought of you carrying on the surgery, it makes an old man very happy, Livvy. And who knows, maybe one day your children will take it over?'

I'm never having children, I replied silently. Just cats. And cat vets are even less likely to be accepted by the patriarchy than women. Probably. Karen the cow let out a heavy, loud moo, distracting my dad just long enough for me to retch over my shoulder. Oh, dear god.

'Oh, she's not happy.' Dad pulled his arm free and clapped his hands. 'Action stations, Livvy. Have you got the chains?'

I held up the chains and the calf puller as the cow howled.

'Right, it's all go from here,' he said, getting down on his hands and knees and inspecting the area. 'Watch how I grip his legs. You'll be doing the next one on your own, after all.'

All at once she began to squirm and a round, opaque bag full of yellow fluid fell out of the cow and straight onto my feet. Without missing a beat, I turned away and puked into the dustbin.

'Ah,' Dad frowned as I stood up, trying to work out how to wipe my face when my arms were covered in heavy duty lubricant. 'Are you not well?'

He couldn't hide his disappointment but I knew if I told him I was hungover he'd be even more upset.

'I had a kebab on my way home last night,' I said, sacrificing my jumper by sliding my hand inside my sleeve and wiping off my face. 'Must have had a dodgy one.'

'That'll be it,' Dad agreed readily. When I proudly announced my first period at the dinner table, he had excused himself and I heard him crying in the downstairs toilet. He might think I was old enough to run a business but he wouldn't deal well with the thought of me getting leathered and upchucking an entire bottle of wine while we were working. 'Well, don't worry about that. Birthing a calf isn't strictly in your everyday job description anyway. Perhaps you can send the other vet out on farm calls.'

I nodded and watched as two little legs appeared from a place that did not look as though little legs belonged. Dad took hold of them gently and pulled in time with Karen's contractions.

'Easy, girl,' he said. 'Nice and easy.'

'No epidural, no gas and air.' I peeled off one of my gloves, seeing the calf was almost all the way out, and patted Karen on the head. 'You bloody champion.'

I couldn't wait to tell Cassie about this. Karen was being way cooler about childbirth than she had been. Chris had Snapchatted the whole thing and Cass had not taken to nature's greatest miracle with the grace she was generally known for.

'And there she is.' The little calf rolled out onto the floor between my dad's knees, all slime and legs and big eyes. 'Oh, I do beg your pardon. He.'

'Good work,' I told Karen, snapping off the other glove and sinking to the ground, close to my puke station. It was done. Everything was OK and surely I was less than an hour away from my own bed. Hallelujah, praise be to Karen. 'I hope Farmer Jones has got you a push present.'

Karen turned her head and mooed while my dad gave the calf a good rub down, chatting to him as he went.

'Cassie got a fancy handbag from Chris but you've probably not got much use for that,' I said, patting her on the head. 'Still, can't hurt to ask.'

Having spent half of my morning watching a cow give birth, spending half the evening making sure my godson didn't die shouldn't have been such a daunting prospect but I'd never been a natural with kids. Animals were so much more resilient. Whose idea was this soft spot nonsense? Why didn't we just keep them in for another week until they were fully cooked? I couldn't work it out.

'You're sure this break is a good idea?' Cass asked. 'I know you're stressed about the surgery stuff but are you not worried you're throwing the baby out with the bathwater?'

'How is that a saying?' I asked, poking a sleeping Gus gently in his pudgy belly. 'Who has ever thrown a baby out with the bathwater? How drunk would you have to be to do that?'

'I know Adam is a really good bloke but he is still a

bloke,' she went on, applying her bright red lipstick perfectly without a mirror. 'What if he meets someone else?'

'We're not seeing other people,' I reminded her, already having explained the terms of our break at least three times since I arrived. 'He gets it, he knows I need time to work out my stuff.'

Cass frowned, utterly unconvinced. 'Well, I don't. When it was Adam who wanted a break, you freaked out, but now you want one you expect him to be totally cool with it and not so much as look at another woman?'

I pushed out my bottom lip and considered my already chipped fingernails. So much for this afternoon's efforts at self-care.

'Yes?'

She sighed, raised her eyebrows and turned her attention back to making sure her handbag was fully stocked with, well, as far as I could see, absolutely everything on earth.

'We haven't broken up; we're taking a time-out to make sure we know what we want. Not just from each other, you know, from life in general.'

'You watch way too much telly,' Cass said, shaking her head at me. 'You should just have a baby, that'll sort your priorities right out.'

'Speaking of which, what do I do if he throws up?' I asked as Gus opened one brown eye and stared at me, all puckered up like a miniature Popeye.

'If it's just spit up, wipe him off and he'll be fine.'

'What if it's proper 360 degrees *Exorcist* vomit?'

'Call a priest.'

'What if he poops himself?'

'He will poop himself, Liv, he's a baby. You know how to change his nappy.'

I stared down at the tiny thing in the Moses basket and for the first time that day was thankful my stomach was empty. Knowing how to change a nappy and actually having to change a nappy were not the same.

'Does baby poop affect nail polish?' I asked, considering my newly home-painted talons. I had planned to spend the afternoon really getting to know myself, working out what I wanted from life and creating a plan to make my dreams a reality. Instead I ate two packets of Wotsits, painted my nails and watched fourteen different YouTube make-up tutorials. Deep and meaningful was so difficult when you were hungover.

'You will both be fine,' Cass said, combing her fingers through the roots of her stick-straight black hair to give it just the right amount of tszuj. 'You're really worrying too much.'

'What if he starts crying and won't stop?'

'You leave him in his basket, lock yourself in the bathroom, turn on the shower and the taps and cry just as loudly until he stops.' She flicked at a smudge of mascara on her cheek. 'Next?'

She was joking. She was probably joking.

'This one's more for you.' I settled down at the huge table Adam had given them as a wedding present and wrapped my hands around my blue-and-white striped mug. I had come up with exactly one good idea all afternoon. It had hit me halfway through a fantastic video on how to properly highlight my earlobes. 'What do you think about joining me at the surgery?'

Cassie stopped dropping things into her Chanel bag and laughed out loud.

'Funny,' she said. 'You're funny.'

'I'm serious,' I replied. 'If my dad really is retiring,

and I really have to take over, I'll have to bring someone else in, and why shouldn't it be you? Think about it, Cass, it would be so much fun.'

Across the table, all long dark hair and perfect make-up, dressed in sleek black trousers and chiffon shirt, Cassie stared at me. Bundled up in a giant turtleneck jumper, baggy leggings with a greasy mess of a topknot and not so much as a smudge of mascara, I smiled back.

'You want me to come and work at the surgery?' She dropped a shiny silver lipstick into her bag then changed her mind, took it out and handed it to me. 'Doing what?'

'Professional Marilyn Monroe impersonating,' I replied, pulling the lid off the lippy and giving it a sniff. 'The pay isn't that good and you'd have to wear a wig but I think you'd enjoy it. What do you think I want you to do? I want you to be a bloody vet.'

She pulled a face and settled on a stool by the breakfast bar. Because Cass had a kitchen table *and* a breakfast bar. And a dining room and a family room and a living room and all kinds of other rooms she didn't need. But then, if I was married to Chris, I'd want lots of rooms to hide in as well, it seemed fair.

'Liv, I haven't worked in a surgery forever,' she said, absently resting her hand inside Mingus's basket. 'And I've got Gus now, I can't go back to work yet.'

'Not right away,' I agreed readily. 'Whenever you're ready. Two, maybe three days a week if you feel up to it to start with. We can work the hours around Gus's nursery schedule and you and I would get to work together. It would be like *Animal Hospital*, only without Rolf.'

'I always said he was creepy,' she insisted, pointing at me across the table. 'I always said it.'

'You did,' I admitted, swatching the lipstick on the back of my hand. 'You did always say that.'

Cass looked down at her baby, thankfully fast asleep, and frowned.

'You don't have to commit to anything right now,' I told her. 'Talk to Chris about it. I'm sure he'd rather you were doing a couple of days at the surgery in the village than five days a week in your school. That place terrifies me – when did teenagers get massive? Every single one of them looks like the scary kid from *Grange Hill*. I can't imagine you're in a rush to go back?'

'They are all giants. It's hormones in milk apparently,' she replied. 'And no, I'm not in a rush to go back. Chris isn't keen.'

'Then this is perfect!' I said, a little too loudly, a little too excited. Gus stirred in his basket, objecting to my enthusiasm by blowing a raspberry before going back to sleep. 'It's going to be amazing, Cass.'

If I had to choose someone to work with, it would always be Cass. Abi was an amazing friend. She was clever and funny, she never judged me and I knew, if push came to shove, she would know the best way to get rid of a body, but Cassie was a sweetheart, everyone loved her and even though she had retrained as a science teacher, I knew she could still be a fantastic vet. She'd had a run of bad luck in her first job at an RSPCA centre in Reading but I was certain I could convert her. Surely the lure of working with your best friend would be stronger than the trauma of having to bust through polystyrene ceiling tiles to escape a rabid Alsatian?

'If I was going to go back into practice, I would only do it with you,' she said, shifting in her seat and tapping a black high heel against the leg of the stool. 'But I'm actually thinking I'm not going back to school after my mat leave is up.'

'I don't blame you, schools these days, not safe places,' I nodded quickly, my hair bobbing back and forth on the top of my head. 'Come and work with David and me. He makes a really good cup of tea and he will do all the gross bum stuff you don't want to do. With the animals, obviously.'

'It's not that . . .' Cass glanced up at the clock on the kitchen wall. Chris was running late, as usual. I could hear him singing off-key in the bedroom, just like his brother. 'I'm really enjoying being a mum. And we're thinking about trying again quite soon – I don't want too much of an age gap between the kids.'

'We have a brilliant maternity policy,' I said quickly. Or at least, I assumed we did. There had never been a pregnant woman working at the surgery as far as I knew, but if I was going to be in charge, maternity leave would be at least twelve months at full pay and all the Haribo you could eat. 'We'd work around you. We could definitely offer you something better than any school.'

'I'm not going back to any school, Liv,' she replied. 'I don't think I'm going back to work at all. I'm going to stay at home with the baby.'

I sucked in my bottom lip and rolled my mug between my hands.

'Oh.'

'I know what you're thinking,' Cassie said, an awkward look on her face. 'I never thought I'd want to be a stay-at-home mum but the thought of missing out on any of this—'

She paused to point at the baby. He stared at me with

his mouth wide open, as surprised by this turn of events as I was.

'It physically hurts to be away from him. Isn't that crazy? Chris makes good money and it's an amazing opportunity not many women get. I'm not going to drag myself back out to work on principle. What's the point in that?'

'I think that's what principles are,' I replied quietly. 'You do it because it's something you believe in, even when there's an easier option. You do it on principle, that's what that means.'

'Then maybe it's your principle, not mine.' She jumped off the stool and went over to the vintage mirror by the door to needlessly check her make-up. 'I want to be there for my family, Liv. I don't think there's anything wrong with that.'

She was right; working *was* a matter of principle for me. When I was growing up, every time we went out people would come over to thank my dad for helping their pets, then they would nudge my mum and congratulate her for marrying such a good man, telling her how proud she must be to have secured such a wonderful husband as if she didn't have anything of her own to celebrate. She was just his wife, just my mother, nothing else, and I hated myself as much as anyone else for treating her the same way.

'There's nothing wrong with being a stay-at-home mum,' Cassie said, her voice harder than I was used to. 'Although I know you and Abi are going to have a lot to say about it.'

'No, Cass, not at all,' I forced myself to disagree with her. She was right, if that was what she wanted, I should be supporting her. It was her choice. That's what we were fighting for wasn't it? A choice? 'I'm surprised, that's all. And you know, disappointed, because I wanted to work together. If staying at home with La Ming is what you want then that's awesome and I'm glad it's an option for you. If you're happy, I'm happy.'

She turned on her heel and glared at me so hard I almost fell off my stool.

'What do you mean, you're glad it's an option?'

Oh god, I'd woken the beast. Cassie hardly ever lost her temper, but when she did the only option was to duck for cover until she calmed herself. I wondered if me using her baby as a human shield would calm her down or make her even madder.

'Nothing!' I replied quickly, trying to smother the fire before it really took hold. 'I'm happy for you and Gus-Gus, I am.'

'You'd understand if you had kids,' she said, grabbing a rose-gold compact from her bag and jabbing herself in the face with the powder puff. 'Or if you had a partner who actually earned a living.'

Too late. She was officially pissed off.

'Evening, ladies.' Chris's aftershave entered the kitchen ten seconds before he did and I buried my nose inside my mug like it was a giant Cornishware gas mask. He buried his head in Cass's hair and she softened instantly. I didn't get it, I really didn't, but in this instance I'd take the assistance without complaint.

'Evening,' I said, still holding my breath. 'Nice tie.'

It wasn't a nice tie.

'Thanks.' He waved it in Gus's face and the baby stuck his tongue out at his father's poor fashion sense. 'You look . . . well, you're only babysitting, I suppose.'

I looked down at my black leggings and soft grey jumper and tucked my hair behind my ears.

'So what's going on with you and Adam?' Chris asked, earning a swift elbow in the ribs from his wife. 'What? I can ask her, can't I? She can always tell me to sod off.'

'Sod off,' I replied, tugging my sleeves down over my chipped nails. 'Go and have your dinner.'

'No, really, what's going on?' Chris reached into the Moses basket and lifted Mingus, holding him against his chest and smiling at his googly faces. For all his faults, no one could argue with how much he loved that baby. It was like watching a YouTube video of the gorilla that had its own kitten. 'You had enough of that slacker or what?'

'Where are you going for dinner?' I asked, politely declining to answer his question. 'Somewhere nice?'

'This amazing new farm-to-table place in Nottingham, called Fetch,' Chris replied, bouncing the baby up and down on his potbelly. I used to make fun of Adam for all the time he spent running but I made a mental note to be more supportive in future. If we were still together, of course. If not, I would be stealing his trainers and digging potholes in his favourite routes to make sure he got as fat as possible. 'Have you heard of it? I can make a call if you want to go, I know the owner.'

'So do I.' I kept trying to make eye contact with Cass but she was too busy looking at everything in the room except me. 'I pulled dental floss out of his dog's arse twice last summer.'

He handed the baby off to Cass and gave me a double thumbs up.

'Sounds fun,' he replied, brushing out his dark blond hair and smoothing down his eyebrows in the mirror. He kissed Cass on the cheek and opened the kitchen door. 'I'll get the car out.'

'He's been fed.' Cassie laid a grumpy Gus back down in his basket and shook off our disagreement. She was so good at brushing things under the carpet it was a wonder she hadn't tripped over and broken her neck. 'So he'll go to sleep soon. We'll be home before midnight, text me if you need anything.'

'I really do think it's nice that you want to stay at home with your kids,' I said, standing as she hung her bag on her shoulder, her expression perfectly placid. 'I'm sorry; I really thought it would be fun for us to work together. I hadn't taken any of this into consideration, obviously.'

'Obviously,' she replied, folding her arms across herself. I wasn't forgiven just yet. 'That's half the trouble with you and Adam. You're both thinking about yourselves and not each other. If you really wanted to be together, none of this would be happening. You'd just be together. You're going to ruin your life because of FOMO, Liv.'

She followed Chris out the kitchen door, leaving me and Gus alone to stare at each other, brown eyes to blue.

'I hate your mum,' I whispered.

He blew another raspberry in response before slapping himself in the face.

'Only joking,' I said. 'Your dad can be a right cock though.'

I could have sworn I saw him nod.

12

'Evening, Nutsack.'

'Don't worry about knocking,' I said as my brother walked straight through the front door on Monday evening. 'I could have been doing anything.'

'Like what?' he asked, immediately walking over to the fridge and helping himself to a can of Coke. As he closed the fridge, I saw baby Gus hanging from his front in an elaborate sling-type contraption.

'I don't know,' I mumbled, pushing away my beans on toast. 'Anything.'

'God, she's really done a number on you, hasn't she?' He sat down across the kitchen table and clicked open the can. 'Sitting in your pants eating beans on toast at six o'clock in the evening. You're a sorry sight, Adam Floyd.'

'Not just my pants,' I replied, looking down at my worn grey T-shirt. 'And I like beans on toast.'

'So you're not sulking?' he asked, flipping through my designs for the bar.

Without a response, I picked up my plate and dropped it in the sink before washing the butter off my hands.

'And I thought Liv was a state last night.'

'You saw Liv?' I spun round and saw the grin on his face. Too late to pretend I didn't care now. 'When did you see her?'

'Last night.' He lifted Gus out of his carrier and rested him on his knee. My nephew stared at me with huge brown eyes, tufts of black hair shooting straight up in an accidental static mohawk on top of his head. 'She was babysitting.'

He held the baby up and I took him, bouncing him up and down in my arms until he smiled. If only the rest of the world was so easy to impress.

'And?'

'She looked a state,' he said again. 'Like she hadn't slept a wink.'

'Oh.'

I turned my back to my brother and danced Gus back and forth, trying not to look as pleased as I felt.

'Or she could have been hungover,' he suggested.

Gus stuck out his tongue as the smile wiped right off my face.

'If that's all you came over to tell me then I'm busy,' I told him, wedging the baby under my arm. 'I've got a meeting with the people I'm building a bar for tomorrow.'

'How's that going?' he asked, showing no desire to leave. 'You nearly done?'

'I've only just started,' I replied, shaking my head at my nephew. His dad never listened but I was grateful to be off the topic of my relationship woes. 'They've approved the design, now I've got to buy all the materials and then actually build the bloody thing.'

Chris squinted at the plans on the table and nodded slowly as though they made any sort of sense. 'Do they pay for that up front or does that all come out of your pocket?'

'They pay part of it up front,' I said while Gus chewed on my finger. Good job I'd just washed my hands. 'But most of it is out of pocket. I took out a business loan.'

Chris sucked the air in through his teeth and made a clucking sound.

'Should have asked me for a loan,' he tutted. 'Lending rates are mental at the moment, you'll be paying that back forever.'

'Yeah, borrowing money from my brother, that sounds like a good idea,' I replied. My brother who never failed to remind me how much money my parents had spent on law school, my brother who never failed to remind me how lucky I was to be living in our grandparents' house. Not that moving in here had ever been at the top of my to-do list but when my dad suggested it after I dropped out before finishing my exams, I didn't really feel as though I had that many alternatives.

Besides, everything had worked out, more or less. I hadn't been desperate to leave London but if I hadn't moved to Long Harrington, I might never have taken up carpentry and I might never have met Liv and now they were the two most important things in my life. Provided I still had Liv in my life at the end of all this.

'Let's hope you don't cock it up,' Chris wiggled the metal tab back and forth on the top of his can until it snapped off in his fingers. 'Last thing you need right now is the bank on your arse.'

'Thanks for the vote of confidence,' I said, raising my own can to his in a toast. 'I can do this.'

It was funny, but I sounded so much more certain than I felt.

'So, I'm sure it won't mean anything to you but Cass says Liv offered her a job,' he said, scratching the back of his neck. 'At the surgery.'

Whenever my brother wanted to talk about something important, he had to pretend he really, really didn't care about your opinion, just in case you didn't share the decision he'd already made.

'Did she now?'

It was strange not to know anything about it. If we hadn't been 'on a break', Liv would definitely have discussed something this huge with me before she spoke to Cass and I hated that she hadn't. It felt like another shove backwards out of her life.

'Because you know her dad's retiring.'

I nodded. I did know that.

'And she needs to bring another vet into the surgery. So she asked Cass to do it.'

'But Cass is a teacher now,' I replied, trying to remember the story as to why Cass had packed in working as a vet. I knew she'd told me but for the life of me, I couldn't remember. 'Doesn't she have to go back to school soon?'

'We've been talking about her maybe not going back,' Chris said, tracing the metal tab from his can up and down the grids of my bar designs. 'She might not go back to work at all.'

He stared down at the squared paper, his tongue sticking out the corner of his mouth as he concentrated on sounding not at all concerned.

'And that's OK with you, is it?' I asked, settling back in my chair with Gus in my lap.

'We don't need the money,' he replied quickly. 'She doesn't need to work.'

'That doesn't mean she shouldn't work,' I said. I stared at Gus who stared back with a funny smile on his face. 'Although I can imagine how much she must want to stay at home with this one.'

'Yeah,' Chris agreed, flipping the metal tag through his fingers. I waited patiently, tapping Gus on the nose and waiting for him to finish his thought. 'Never really thought she'd pack in work though.'

For all his bluster, one thing I could never take away from my brother was his work ethic. He'd always had a job, a paper round when we were kids, McDonald's when he was a teenager, bartending through uni, and the very day after he graduated he started his first day of work. While I was off getting a kidney infection in Chile, he was working an IT job, somewhere in Kettering, taking night classes and online courses in coding and constantly looking for the next big thing. But it had never really occurred to me that he'd expect the same level of ambition from his missus.

'I get why she doesn't want to go back to that school . . .' He tapped his fingers on his can of Coke, much to Gus's delight. 'It's a right hole, but I didn't think she'd want to give it up altogether. Now she's talking about trying for another baby but I don't know if I'm ready.'

'Have you told her that?' I asked.

He looked up, totally gone out.

'Of course not,' he replied, as though I'd suggested he kick her in the crotch. 'I don't want her to think I don't want to have another baby.'

'But you don't?'

'Not right now,' he said. 'But you know, sooner or later.'

'So you do want to have another baby but not right away,' I said, trying to get to the bottom of the enigma that was Chris Floyd. 'And you're fine with her not working but you'd rather she did.'

'I didn't say that,' he said. 'We don't need the money, Adam.'

I closed my eyes and took a calming breath.

'I know that,' I said slowly. 'But that doesn't mean you can't prefer her to work. I'd probably feel weird if Liv packed in working and all the responsibility was on me.'

'That's because you wouldn't know responsibility if it kicked you up the arse,' he said with a grunt.

'OK,' I said, passing the baby across the table. Gus kicked his little legs in protest as I handed him off. 'I was only trying to help, I won't bother next time.'

Chris jostled my nephew back into the carrier, squeezing his chubby legs back through the cushioned holes.

'Sorry,' he said, stiff. 'I feel like it's a lot of pressure on me, that's all. Single income, two kids, wife not working. It feels like a lot.'

'I'm sure it is. Just like me taking out this loan to do the bar,' I replied, trying to empathize. 'I get it.'

'Not really the same,' he muttered, chugging from the can over Gus's head. 'But yeah.'

'Talk to your wife,' I ordered, quickly running out of patience. 'It's hardly like she's running around pissing your money up a wall, is it? She just wants to be a stay-at-home mum. Cass is beyond reasonable.'

'I suppose.' Crumpling his empty can of Coke, Chris stood up and bounced up and down on the spot, making sure Gus's carrier was secure. 'I'm going round to Mum and Dad's if you want to come? She's got her photos back from India.'

'I'll pass,' I replied quickly. 'Like I said, I've got a meeting with the owners of the bar tomorrow and I want to make sure everything is in line before I get started.'

'Oh yeah,' he agreed, grabbing his key fob from the table. No actual car keys of course, he had keyless entry. 'You can't be messing clients around once you've agreed your terms.'

'Maybe you can help me build an app once I'm up and running,' I suggested, walking the two of them out to the door. 'Like, a catalogue of my work or something.'

'Yeah, that's not really what I do,' he said with an annoying smirk. 'But I could probably put you in touch with someone who does that kind of thing. My interface is a lot more complex.'

'Of course it is,' I said, patting Gus on the head and pushing them backwards out the door. 'Night, Chris.'

'Night, Nutsack,' he called through the door. 'Oh. Evening, Mrs Johnson.'

After turning on the deadbolt in case he decided to come back, I went back into the kitchen to stare at my designs and go over the budget again.

'Just once,' I told myself, sitting down at the table to stare at the pale blue paper in front of me. I brought up the calculator app on my phone to go through the numbers and instead found my fingers hovering over Liv's name. What would she think about Cassie quitting work? If she wanted to pack everything in and start a second career as a baby factory, I was sure we'd at least have a conversation before she announced her decision.

'I could call her,' I said to my reflection in the window. 'She said I could call.'

But that one random article you read on the internet told you not to, the reflection reminded me. Give her some space.

I stared down at her name and the little picture of Daniel Craig that popped up beside it before swiping back to the calculator. Maybe I'd call her tomorrow, after my meeting. Good news about the bar plus Cass and Chris gossip was a surefire combination for a successful phone call after all. She couldn't possibly be mad at me calling with all of that.

I would definitely call her tomorrow.

'Knock, knock.'

'If you're a burglar, can you take the rubbish with you on your way out?' I shouted from my mess in the middle of the living room.

Daniel Craig, who had been fast asleep for hours, shot to his three feet as soon he realized the front door was open. Without so much as a second look at his loving human mother, he raced down the stairs, startling my visitor and wailing off into the night.

'Cat got out,' Cass said as she trotted up the stairs. Cass was not a cat person. 'Is that bad?'

'Not until he wants to be let in at two in the morning,' I said, waving to her underneath a pile of magazines. 'The cat flap is broken, it only works one way.'

'And you call yourself a vet,' she asked, placing a large canvas tote bag on my dining room table.

'Did we take different courses in uni?' I pushed away my poster board and Pritt Stick and stood up to give her an ever so slightly awkward hug. 'I don't remember the cat flap fixing class.'

'Fair point.' She squeezed harder and I squeaked as my breath left my body. 'About yesterday.'

'I swear, the TV was all in Spanish when I got there,' I said, breaking free of her oppressive embrace. 'And I thought you had more milk, really.'

'No, I mean all the stuff I said about the job business.' She heaved the tote bag from the table and kicked a path clear to the sofa. 'I was out of order. Possibly a little bit defensive.'

'And a little bit right,' I said, following in her wake. 'Why should you go back to work if you don't want to and don't have to? I was out of order.'

'Maybe, but I shouldn't have had a go at you and a certainly shouldn't have brought Adam into it. I was tired and stressed and I didn't want to go out for dinner but I absolutely shouldn't have taken it out on you.'

I gave a noncommittal sniff and turned my attention to filling the kettle. I was terrible at arguing and I was even worse at accepting an apology but I was relieved to have cleared the air and at least part of my world felt right again.

'Where's Gus?' I asked, searching for clean mugs.

'Chris took him over to his mum's.' Cass shook out all three cushions on the sofa, one after the other. 'I told him I had to drop off your phone charger and I'd meet him over there later.'

'I didn't leave my phone charger,' I said, looking over to the little white cable still plugged into the wall where it lived.

'But if Chris asks, you did,' she replied with a bright smile. 'How are you feeling today?'

'Still hungover from Saturday,' I admitted, dropping two teabags into the teapot. 'And generally a bit shit. I was thinking about what you said, that maybe chucking Adam was a kneejerk reaction. Do you really think it's a mistake?'

'I really don't know,' she replied. 'Does it feel like a mistake?'

Turning away, I continued with the business of tea. Cass sat in silence while it brewed and I poured milk into both our mugs. Silence was one of her gifts, something Abi and David were utterly incapable of. She had never felt the need to fill a moment with needless chatter when you didn't know quite what to say, truly a rare and wonderful quality. Cass wasn't afraid to let a moment breathe, unlike Abi who had to hammer it to death with logic and debate.

'I'm still really upset about the nonexistent proposal,' I started slowly when I returned to the settee, tea in hand. 'And the not-a-break-up-break-up.'

'That's reasonable,' she said before taking a cursory sip of tea instead of adding her own opinion the way most people would, myself included.

I blew on mine and felt my shoulders tighten as thoughts of Adam and my dad began to tick over in my head. I couldn't even think about them without getting mad.

'And I'm annoyed that he thought he could just say sorry and expect me to be over something so huge. It's a big deal, isn't it? To say you want to break up when you were supposed to be proposing?'

'Yes,' she agreed tentatively. 'But you have to remember, he doesn't know you knew about the proposal.'

'He doesn't know I know,' I repeated. 'And he doesn't know you know?'

'No,' she shook her head. 'Although, he did tell Chris which means the postman's cousin's wife's dentist probably knows. I find it really difficult to believe he wouldn't assume Chris would tell me.'

'Well, regardless, even if it was just the three a.m. dumping we were talking about, I'd still be well within my rights to be peeved,' I said, accidentally kicking an issue of Condé Nast *Traveller* across the room. 'And then there's all the surgery nonsense to deal with on top of that.'

'You're mad because your dad wants you to take on the surgery?' she asked, trying to check her phone without me seeing her check her phone. Thankfully, Chris seemed to be surviving without her for once. 'Explain to me why that's bad.'

'It's not bad per se.' I blew out a long, thoughtful raspberry. 'Obviously, I love being a vet, I love working with the animals and most of the people. I just wasn't expecting it, especially not in the middle of his birthday party in front of a million people, without having discussed it with me first.'

'How many people?'

'A million,' I insisted. 'At least sixty-five.'

Cass gave me a look.

'At least seventy.'

She raised an eyebrow.

'About forty-five.'

'Talk to your dad,' she ordered. 'He is a painfully sensible man, Liv. He's hardly going to dump the business on you and skip off into the sunset if he knows you need help. The surgery is just as much his baby as you are.'

'I know that,' I replied, curling my leg underneath me. I was still wearing my scrubs and everything smelled a little bit too much like antiseptic for my liking. 'It's not the doing it, it's the way it was done. Shouldn't there have been a discussion or something? What if I wanted to run off and join the circus? Or knock out fifteen babies? I could be pregnant for all he knows and this would be terrible timing.'

'You're not though, are you?' Cass looked alarmed. 'Because that would probably change things.'

'No.' I poked myself in the belly. 'Although I could pass for it right now. Why am I a stress eater? Why can't I be one of those women who starves herself when she's sad?'

'You have to find the positive in this,' she said, showing off her patented brand of Cassie Huang optimism and bypassing my potbelly pity party. 'You've got to admit you've been frustrated with your dad recently, haven't you? This is a chance to make the business your own.'

'If he lets me.' I thought back to our conversation during Karen the Cow's delivery. 'He seems to have some very clear ideas about how he thinks things should be run.'

'Let him have them,' she said simply. 'It won't matter once you're running the show, will it?'

'Maybe you're right.' I looked at my mess of a living room and brushed my hair back from my face. 'Maybe I've been overreacting about all of this.'

'I didn't say that.' Cass squeezed my knee gently and gave me a small smile. 'The Adam stuff is tough. I don't know what I would do in that situation. I think asking him for a break is really brave, it would be a lot easier just to take his apology and get on with things.'

'And go slowly mad, waiting for him to break up with me again?' I added. 'It's the right thing to do, I think. The only problem is, I have no idea how I'll know when the break is over. I feel like I'm testing both of us but neither of us know the right answer. I'm scared to be the one to make the first move in case he's decided he doesn't want to be with me after all. I know I wasn't chasing him down the aisle or anything but it just hadn't occurred to me that we would ever not be together. And now I don't quite know what to do with the possibility.'

'In three days?' Cass looked doubtful. 'I told you, he told Chris it was cold feet. Add jet lag and lack of sleep and male ego and you have a recipe for disaster.'

'And does Adam know that you and I know what he told Chris?'

Cass looked up at the ceiling as she tried to work out my question.

'No,' she replied. 'I don't think so.'

Sipping my tea, I stared at the magazines and poster board on the floor.

'What's all this?' Cass asked, pointing at the mess with a perfectly polished black Chelsea boot. 'It all looks a bit *Blue Peter.*'

'I was trying to make a vision board for what I want my life to look like,' I replied, shaking my head sadly. 'But I got distracted by a story about how much Gwyneth Paltrow spends on facials every month. Do you know I've never had a facial?'

Cass held up a forefinger to make an unspoken point, put down her tea, then dumped the contents of her tote bag onto the settee between us. Every self-help book I'd ever heard of, as well as several I hadn't, lay in front of me. *Keeping the Love You Find*, *Act Like a Lady, Think Like a Man*, *The Five Love Languages* and something called *Why Men Love Bitches*, a theory I had heard much about but had never been able to make work, myself.

'These are for you.' She waved her hands over her bounty.

'I had assumed they weren't for you,' I said, picking up *Why Men Love Bitches*. 'Unless there's something you want to tell me about your relationship.'

'They're not all about relationships,' she replied, filtering through the pile until she found what she was looking for. 'This one is great. *Becoming Your Truest You*.'

'Do you feel like you are too nice?' I read aloud from the back of the book in my hands. 'This no-nonsense guide reveals why a strong woman is much more desirable than a yes woman who routinely sacrifices herself.'

Cass nodded sagely along with each and every word.

'I don't think this one's for me,' I said, tossing it back in the bag. 'Let me have a look at *Think Like a Man*. I like the chap on the front, he looks like a laugh.'

'These helped me a lot,' she said, defensively, piling the books in her lap and shielding their nonexistent ears from my criticism. 'You can take the mick but you don't know, they could help. You're the one making a vision board, after all.'

'*Trying* to make a vision board,' I corrected. 'Trying to work out what to do with my relationship, trying to work out what to do with my job, trying not to throw myself out the window.'

'At least you are,' Cass encouraged. 'Trying.'

'As in making an effort or as in testing your patience?' I asked, scratching my head. 'Because I'm not sure.'

'If you wake up with all the answers tomorrow morning, could you give me a call?' she said, draining her tea. 'Because I'm married with a baby, I haven't got a job, and I still haven't got a clue what's going on.'

179

'Then there's very little hope for the rest of us,' I said, smiling at my current favourite friend. Not that it was a competition. Except for when it was. Downstairs, Daniel Craig hurled himself at the broken cat flap and meowed impatiently to be let back in.

'That's my cue to leave,' Cass said, folding up the canvas tote and slipping it neatly inside her handbag. 'Promise me you'll at least have a look at them.'

'I promise,' I said with a Brownie salute.

'That's the wrong hand,' she replied, tiptoeing over my craft station. 'And remind me to send you the number of my cleaner.'

'And a cheque to pay that cleaner?' I called as she disappeared down the stairs.

It was funny how everyone seemed to have selective hearing these days.

13

'Uh, wow, I love what you didn't do with your hair.' David kicked open the door to the staffroom with a coffee in each hand and a Waitrose bag swinging around his wrist. 'I feel so special when you make an effort for me.'

'Thanks, I knew you'd like it,' I replied, bouncing my hand on top of my straggly bun before grabbing one of the coffees from my seat behind the reception desk. I'd been awake until three a.m. reading *Why Men Love Bitches* and slept right through my alarm. If it weren't for the furry three-legged alarm that jumped on my face and demanded to be fed at seven thirty every morning I was at home, I'd have been late.

'We're really quiet this afternoon so, if we don't have any emergencies, I think I'm going to leave a bit early if that's all right with you?'

'No problem,' he said, flipping through the diary on the computer to check. 'Where are you off to?'

'I'm doing . . . paperwork,' I replied.

David's eyes lit up like Blackpool and I knew I should have come up with a more convincing lie.

'The only paperwork you're capable of is a BuzzFeed multiple-choice quiz. What's going on?'

'Nothing,' I insisted. 'Paperwork. If I'm going to take over the business, I'd better learn, hadn't I?'

I was not going to do paperwork. My late-night self-help session might not have taught me much about relationships but it did convince me of one thing. Sitting around cutting out pictures of cherry blossom and geishas, then sticking them to a bit of cardboard, wasn't going to help me get anywhere with Adam. And the only thing I had achieved by cutting him out of my life was cutting him out of my life. All the books agreed on one thing and one thing only. Communication. We needed to talk. We used to talk for hours when we first started going out. The books were right: we needed to talk. We needed to resolve this before he forgot all about how amazing it was to be part of us.

So obviously, as soon as I'd fed Daniel Craig, I texted my hairdresser to see if she could do me a quick shampoo and blow dry before I invited myself over to his house for an unscheduled pow-wow. The element of surprise was important: the less time he had to prep, the better. You had to think about these things when you were dating a semi-trained lawyer. Reaching up to pat my greasy hair, I longed for simpler times, the days before I felt the need to pay someone twenty-five pounds to wash my hair before any vaguely important life event, but there was nothing I could do about it now.

David stared at me for another minute, not saying a word.

'I'm doing paperwork,' I repeated. Until I knew what was going to happen with Adam, I really didn't want to discuss it with anyone. 'Didn't you want something?'

'Mr Beavis is here.' David's mouth turned down at the edges. 'Nasty old bastard.'

'Well, technically we're more interested in the nasty old bastard's cat,' I explained, setting my coffee on the shelf and wiping off my hands on the front of my scrubs. 'And, you know, his money.'

'Gotta get dem dollar, dollar bills,' he nodded, rubbing his thumb and forefinger together. 'Do you need me in here? Or can I go and key his car?'

'Key away but I can't imagine he'll be in here long and I'm not bailing you out.'

'I never get caught,' he replied, sneaking backwards out of the door. 'I'm a car-keying ninja.'

I considered whether or not he was joking for a moment, but really, I didn't want to know. I couldn't put anything past David.

'Morning, Mr Beavis,' I said as David opened the door for a short, squat old man and made not-so-subtle vomiting gestures over his head. 'How can I help you and Valerie today?'

'Oh.'

He stopped short of the examination table, clutching his cat carrier to his chest and looking me up and down in a manner that did not seem entirely appropriate to the situation. I glanced down at my top to check nothing was hanging out. Nope, all present and correct and nothing about my person that could possibly be deserving of the look on his face.

'Mr Beavis?' I asked when he failed to move. 'Are you all right?'

'I'm supposed to see Dr Addison,' he said, face as sombre as the grave. 'My appointment is with Dr Addison.'

'That's me,' I replied, a sunny smile fixed to my face.

'Do you want to get Valerie out on the table so I can have a look at her?'

'No,' he replied. 'I want to see Dr Addison.'

This was not the first time this had happened. There were a certain number of people in the village, older people to be entirely honest, who could not get their head around the idea of me as a vet. Half of them because they still thought of me as the little girl in bunches, running around the surgery with a bag of pick and mix, and half because they believed that having a vagina rendered me incapable of putting a thermometer up their pet's backside and telling its temperature. Even now, after all these years, it was still a problem, as if the Spice Girls, Margaret Thatcher and *The Vicar of Dibley* had never happened. And while I rarely name-dropped Margaret Thatcher as a poster girl for feminism, I couldn't help but think if she'd wanted to put a thermometer up a dog's backside, Nigel Beavis would not have tried to stop her.

'I am a vet, Mr Beavis,' I said, trying not to sigh. 'Fully qualified and everything. I don't know if you've heard but my dad has actually retired.'

'Good lord.' He coiled his arm around the front of the cat carrier to shield Valerie's eyes and took a step back. 'Are you closing down?'

'No,' I said, cupping my chin in my hands and resting my elbows on the table. 'But I'd better find a man to cover for me when I've got my monthlies, hadn't I?'

He wasn't crying but he was definitely close.

There was something about living in a village that brought out the best and the worst in people. I loved the sense of community, having people I knew around every corner, but there were also times when I would have happily driven the entire population off the edge of a cliff, lemming style. When you did all the same things and went to all the same places as your parents and your grandparents before them, it was hard to shift your perspective.

And it was even harder if you just couldn't be bothered.

'Please can you put Valerie on the table,' I asked, pulling a fresh pair of rubber gloves out of the box on the side. 'Let me take a look at her.'

'We'll come back when Dr Addison is here,' Mr Beavis said, chin held high. 'No disrespect meant, but Valerie likes who she likes and I don't want strangers fiddling with her.'

'Mr Beavis, I've known you my whole life,' I reminded him, snapping my gloves against my wrist. 'And my dad is retired. I'm afraid Valerie is going to have to get used to some unfamiliar fiddling sooner or later.'

Valerie yowled inside the cat carrier and it was impossible to say whether she was cheering for me or against.

'But he hasn't completely finished yet, has he?'

Ah, selective hearing at its very best.

'No,' I admitted slowly. 'He's still doing a couple of hours a week while we work out the handover.'

'Then we'll come back when we can see Dr Addison,' he said again, either totally unaware or totally unconcerned with how offensive he was. 'No disrespect, mind.'

I watched in disbelief as he trundled out of the examination room, Valerie clawing at the back of her cat carrier, meowing wildly as they went. Clearly not as picky about who 'fiddled' with her as Mr Beavis would like to think. I yanked off the gloves and chucked them at the wall, missing the bin entirely. Stupid man. Stupid village. Stupid me for staying here. And this was what I was supposed to sign up to, for the rest of my life?

'Bugger,' I breathed, splaying my fingers out on the cold metal table and trying to take deep, calming breaths. 'Bugger bugger *bugger.*'

'Are you OK?' David popped his head around the door. 'Did you do him with the slow release poison?'

'I keep forgetting we've got that,' I replied, flicking the tubing of my stethoscope. 'Beavis wouldn't let me and my vagina look at his supposedly sick cat.'

'You use your vagina to diagnose the animals?' he asked. 'Wow, I never knew that.'

'We don't tell you everything,' I said, rewinding my bun tightly. 'Did you key his car?'

'He walked,' he said, looking as disappointed as I felt. 'But if it's any consolation, you're free for the next hour. Want to sit on the back wall and watch me have a fag?'

'Yes,' I said with a heavy sigh. 'Yes I do.'

'Come on then.'

He held out his arm and I took it. Maybe I should stop encouraging him to get out and meet people and just marry David. We could sit in our front garden and grow old together, shouting at people and bemoaning what passed for fashion in this day and age. David already did both of those things, so I'd be learning from a master. Of course there was the problem of him being a twenty-four-year-old he-slag with a not-so-secret boner for my best friend but surely anyone could be dragged down to my level if I was persistent enough?

'He's a doddering old fool,' David said as I followed him out into the back yard. It was a beautiful day, all fresh crisp air with just enough late-summer sun to take the edge off.

'Don't pay any attention,' he pulled a packet of Marlborough Lights out of his clown-dog pocket and sparked up. 'He's a foul, irrelevant old grunt. Your dad'll kick his arse.'

The rush of cigarette smoke didn't really go with the idyllic English country garden I'd been trying for when I bought that apple tree in a barrel, but beggars can't be choosers and if I was planning to spend my twilight years as a grumpy old hag, I needed to start putting the time and effort in now.

'He's not a Year Seven bully, I shouldn't need to get my dad to tell him off for me,' I said, tilting my face up into the sunshine. 'I want him to come in and say, please could you look at my cat, O wonderful veterinarian who studied for donkey's and gets up at six a.m. every day to make sure Mittens' diabetes is under control, hardly ever gets a full day off and constantly smells a little bit like cat piss.'

'Mittens?' he asked, post-inhale. 'Shit, did I miss a patient?'

'Mittens is a nonexistent example. Shit like this is why I don't want to be stuck here forever. Shit like this wouldn't happen in a big city,' I explained. 'It would be nice to be appreciated for once, that's all.'

'I appreciate you.'

'Not by you.'

'Your dad appreciates you.'

'My dad takes me for granted, it's a different thing.'

David took another drag and blew it out slowly. 'What do you want? A medal?'

'A million pounds, my own private island, and to always be a size ten, no matter what I eat,' I replied. 'And forty-eight hours with Roger Federer.'

'He's married,' David said. 'And you wouldn't want him

if he shagged around on his missus because that's half the reason you like him.'

'It is,' I admitted. 'That and the fact that he owns his own cow. Maybe I could be his personal vet?'

'You know what I do when I feel as miserable as you look?' he asked, grinding his cigarette out on the stone wall and knocking it into the car park. I shot him a look of disbelief, which he brushed away. 'I'll get it in a minute. You know what I do when I'm as pissed off as you look right now?'

I thought for a moment.

'Listen to Justin Bieber?'

'He's relevant now and you know it,' he replied before clearing his throat to recover himself. 'No, when I'm feeling shit, I go on Tinder and I swipe right a few times and then I watch the matches come rolling in.'

'With all due respect,' I said, pulling out my hair tie and letting my manky hair fall around my shoulders, 'I don't think a one night stand is the answer to anyone's problems right now. Except for possibly Mr Beavis. Or Valerie the cat.'

'Not for a shag.' He held out his hands, offended. 'It's an ego stroke, that's all. You go in, you swipe left, you swipe right, after a couple of minutes someone swipes right on you and, ta-da, all of a sudden, all is right with the world.'

I took my phone out of my white coat pocket and stared at the black screen.

'So, I'm feeling crappy, I'm second guessing ten years of career choices and I'm suddenly uncertain about the man I thought I was going to marry but you think I'll feel better if I allow a load of strangers to objectify me on a dating app?'

'More or less,' he replied. 'Only it's mutual objectification. So it's OK!'

I had to admit, this was a lot quicker than Cass's suggestion of reading every self-help book on earth. Instant online gratification versus four hundred pages on why I should start being a complete cow and demanding Adam pay for my dinner every time we left the house.

'I've never even been on an online date,' I admitted as David took out his own, matching phone and started jabbing away at it, squinting at the screen against the late summer sun. 'I think I signed up for one of them years ago but I don't even remember my username. God, I have to fix things with Adam, don't I? I can't do this, David. I can't start dating again now, I don't even know how to set up a Tinder account.'

'You don't need to,' he said, waving his phone under my nose. 'I've done it for you.'

And there it was. My face in a pulsating red circle. It was looking for my matches, no, wait, it had found my matches. Bruce, 39, Mark, 45, Jonathan, 45, Joey, 44, Roger, 52.

'How?' I demanded, watching as David flicked through faces faster than I could fathom. 'How did you do that?'

'When you get around to changing your Netflix and your Just Eat passwords, I'd change your Facebook password as well,' he said. 'Joey4Pacey4eva? You should be ashamed. You have two degrees.'

'Shut up,' I watched as the men kept flashing by. Josh, 45, Amin, 38, Will, 37. 'Wait, why are they all so old?'

'Uh, how old are you again?' he asked, taking the phone back and fiddling again as I gave him a thunderous look. 'Just give me your max oldest, max youngest.'

'Forty and thirty,' I said, confidently. 'Never married, no kids, good hair, nice teeth.'

'No fat chicks?' David suggested. 'You might want to dial it down a bit, Liv. We're looking for an ego boost, not your soulmate. Although, even I wouldn't kick this one out of bed for eating biscuits.'

He handed me the phone and I actually gasped out loud. There on the screen was an actual god. Tall, bearded, thick brown hair with glowing green eyes that stared straight out of the screen and right into my pants. Henry, 36, obscenely good looking and apparently, single. Or at the very least, available, according to the internet.

'Did he like me?' I asked. 'Did he swipe on me?'

'Calm down, Glenn Close,' he replied as my hand hovered over the screen. 'We don't know if he's even seen you. You have to swipe on him to find out.'

'Left or right?' I demanded. 'Left or right?!'

'For Christ's sake.' David snatched his phone back and flicked his fingers quickly across the screen, to the right. 'The whole point of this game is to get some attention, not to find your Prince Charming. You already have a boyfriend, remember?'

'I do remember,' I replied, peering over at the screen. 'But you're right, my ego would feel a lot better if the very attractive man gave me a swipe.'

'Is that what the kids are calling it these days?' he asked. 'You can't get all into one person, Liv. Tinder Fishing is a numbers game, we swipe on a dozen or so you wanna bone, and the odd dog for shits and gigs, and then we sit back and let the matches roll in. See? It's like online shopping. You don't have to buy everything in your basket, you're just having a look.'

The screen went grey and the phone proudly declared myself and Bob, a lanky, dark-haired streak of piss David must have swiped on, were a match.

'I don't have to message them or anything though?' I asked, taking back his phone and feeling smug and appalled in equal measure. Bob liked me! Although as I didn't actually like Bob, it was something of a hollow victory but I could see the appeal. I could also see a bottle of wine, Abi, and Cass making this game even more fun than it was right now.

'You don't have to do anything,' he confirmed. 'Even if they message you, you can delete them out of your likes and then they can't contact you. Which you should probably do in case they turn out to be wankers.'

'What do you mean?' I asked, looking down at Bob's kind face.

'Some people take a lack of response too personally,' David replied. 'I've heard they can get a bit shirty and, you know, send you a photo of their penis.'

'You've heard?'

He shrugged and looked away.

'I don't want to see unsolicited penises,' I wailed. 'Isn't there an app for that? Isn't there a blocker?'

'Invent it and you'll be a millionaire.' He hopped off the wall and gave me a small salute. 'As much as I'd love to sit here and play fantasy boyfriend all afternoon, I've got a ton of work to do. Unlike some people.'

I waved David back inside, in no rush to leave my sunny spot in the garden.

I pressed the button on the side of the phone to check the time but instead of finding the time and a photo of Daniel Craig curled up on the bottom of my bed, I saw a Tinder notification.

'You and Henry like each other. Why not say hi?'

I stared at it until the screen went black. David was right, it was nothing but a fun ego stroke. It didn't mean anything. That was the joy of the internet; none of it was real. Only, somewhere out there, within a twenty-five mile radius, was a tall, bearded man called Henry who had seen my photo and didn't hate the look of it. But I had no idea if it had been a casual, ego-boosting swipe in the back yard of his office or a serious, looking for love in all the wrong places, soul searching swipe, made in an independent coffee shop while he sipped his third espresso of the day and wrote poetry in his Moleskine notebook with his grandfather's fountain pen. Or, you know, whatever.

It didn't mean anything. Not really.

Adam and I met in the supermarket. He was there with his dad and I had gone for toilet paper and tampons but ended up taking home two bottles of wine and a bag of apples. I knew who he was, of course, ever since he'd moved into his grandparents' house I'd been watching him like a hawk from afar, this tall, handsome man who Abi had nicknamed the yeti, whom we'd always assumed was married. But it turned out he wasn't married, he was single. And sweet and charming and so very funny. It was hardly a story to tell the grandkids, that Granddad wooed your granny in the pasta aisle of the local Tesco, but realistically, how many people had great romantic moments in their life? And of those that did, how many ended up with that person? My grandparents met at school, my mum and dad met at a village dance. So even though getting chatted up over a box of penne was hardly how I'd imagined meeting the man of my dreams, in this day and age, it really could have been a lot worse.

14

I sat back on my workbench and stared at my phone, willing it to ring. She had said I could call but I hadn't and neither had she. Not because I didn't want to, but because I didn't know what the bloody hell to say. 'Hello love, just wondering if you've decided whether or not you still want to go out with me? No, OK, never mind, as you were.' It was only Tuesday, only three days since I'd seen her but it felt like forever. This was the longest we'd been apart since Chris's stag do and that time I'd been so drunk I didn't even remember calling her up at four in the morning and singing the entirety of Coldplay's 'Fix You' into her answerphone. I'd had to call back several times to complete the whole song – if it weren't so embarrassing, it would be impressive.

I'd been busier than usual, everything in my life seemed to have expanded to fill up the gaps left by my on-hold relationship but every time I looked at my phone, I wanted to punch something and then cry. They say patience is a virtue but hanging around, waiting for your girlfriend to decide whether or not she still wanted to be your girlfriend was a test I was not ready for.

'You could be engaged right now,' I reminded myself, stacking different wood samples on top of my bench in a sad solo game of Jenga. Jim Campbell, the owner of Camp Bell and to all intents and purposes my boss, was supposed to be coming over to choose the wood for the bar. 'And then you wouldn't have these problems but no, you had to pussy out, didn't you? You've only got yourself to blame for this, you knobber.'

'You know they say talking to yourself is the first sign of madness.'

I turned to see a tall, dark-haired woman walking up the driveway towards the workshop. The sun shone brightly behind her, blinding me and blocking out her features, but I didn't need to see her face to know we hadn't met before. This was someone you would remember.

'I was actually talking to the voices in my head,' I replied, wiping my hands off on my jeans and squinting to get a better look. Holy shit. 'So, no need to worry.'

'Yeah?' The sun shifted as she stepped inside the workshop, pushing a pair of huge sunglasses onto the top of her head and fixing me with a blinding smile. 'What are they saying then?'

She was gorgeous. Not fit or cute or pretty – this girl was properly, genuinely beautiful. I might have expected to see her on the pages of a magazine under my bed, but I wasn't ready to deal with her standing in front of me, in my workshop. Long, long, long dark hair that hung right down her back, big dark eyes and those pouty Angelina Jolie lips that made men think terrible things. Even in trainers, she was almost as tall as I was and even her loose, checked shirt, that looked as though she'd picked it up off my bedroom floor, couldn't hide the shape of her body. This girl was a ten. This girl, I would have remembered,

'Uhhhhh.' I stood too quickly, knocking down my tower of wooden blocks and watching as they scattered all over the floor. Smooth. 'It's usually something about snacks. Pringles, Kettle Chips, Hula Hoops mostly.'

'Mine too,' she confessed, tilting her chin forwards and looking down at the ground before slowly lifting her huge brown eyes to look at me. 'When they're not telling me to poison the cast of *Coronation Street* anyway.'

'Oh yeah?' I replied, adding a forced laugh that seemed to make her smile. 'You can't kill Ken Barlow – my dad would be really pissed off. Could you start with the cast of *Emmerdale* and see how you get on from there?'

'I suppose.' The girl stuck out her hand and I took it in mine, trying for the perfect handshake. Not too hard, not too soft, not too long. There was nothing I could do about how incredibly sweaty my palms were, but that was entirely her fault. Nothing I could do about that. 'You're Adam, right? I'm Jane.'

Jane. Did I know a Jane? She was certainly looking at me as though I knew a Jane. Oh shit, I was still shaking her hand.

'Adam Floyd? I'm Jane Campbell. From Camp Bell, the bar?' She raised an eyebrow and looked around the workshop. 'I'm sure I'm supposed to be here today.'

'Oh yeah, of course, Jane from the bar.' I snapped out of my hot-girl trance, ignored the chorus of heavenly voices in my head and nodded over and over. 'Jane. I totally lost track of time. But I was expecting Jim.'

'Yeah, my brother couldn't get away,' she replied,

shrugging off her leather jacket and straddling my bench. 'Sorry, he should have called you or something, let you know I was coming instead.'

'No worries,' I said, clearing my throat. 'It's totally cool. I've got the samples here, we'll get it sorted.'

'Those samples?' she pointed to the wooden blocks littered all over the workshop floor.

'Those would be the ones.'

Even without my incredibly professional inventory of wood chips thrown around the workshop floor, the place was a mess. Not to me, of course, it was perfectly respectable to me. But as soon as Jane walked into the room, I saw it through a woman's eyes – and through a woman's eyes, it was a shithole. My filing system mostly consisted of putting things 'somewhere safe' which meant I had paperwork everywhere, held down by tools clearly not put away in their respective holders and there were empty Coke cans on every surface. It was a creative chaos that I found inspiring. Or at least that was what I told anyone who complained about the mess. But it was not suitable for visitors who had hired me to build a big, beautiful, expensive piece of custom furniture for their bar.

'I like that one,' she said, tapping a large chunk of polished cherry with the tip of her navy blue Converse that matched my own. 'Done.'

'That was easy.' I bent down to pick it up, accidentally checking out her long, slender legs as I bent over. I loved a good pair of legs. It was my mother's fault for making me watch so much *Come Dancing* while I was growing up. 'Shall I price up a couple of other options as well?'

'Why?' Jane held out her hand for the wood and turned it over in her fingers, inspecting every inch.

'In case Jim doesn't like it?' I suggested. 'In case it's out of your budget?'

'I'm sure you wouldn't have shown it to me if it was out of my budget,' she replied simply. 'And if Jim doesn't like it, Jim should have driven up here himself and chosen something else.'

The woman was a goddess. I wasn't usually so useless in the face of an attractive woman but she'd left me with all the social graces of a pork chop.

'I don't want to be rude but I could really use the loo,' Jane said, pulling her sunglasses out of her hair and sticking them into the pocket of her jacket. 'Might I avail myself of your facilities?'

'I've haven't got any facilities out here but there are three toilets inside,' I replied, not at all wondering what she might look like naked. 'Obviously, I'm not bragging or anything.'

'Three toilets,' she whistled and stood up, one long leg on either side of the bench. 'Lead the way, Lord Floyd.'

'If you're very lucky, I'll even put the kettle on,' I said, squeezing the block of cherry wood in my hand and pushing all inappropriate thoughts out of my head. For roughly four seconds.

'Luckiest girl in the world,' she said, following closely behind. 'What a gent.'

Yep, I told myself, one foot in front of the other, not a single thought of what was hiding underneath that baggy checked shirt passing through my mind. *What* a gent.

'It's a mess in here, sorry,' I opened the back door to the kitchen and willed the dirty mugs and plates stacked on the draining board to grow legs and hide themselves away into a cupboard. If I left them alone one more day, there was every chance they'd develop their own civilization, let alone legs. 'I'm not a good housewife.'

'And the missus doesn't do dishes?' Jane's lip curved as she picked up my book from the breakfast table and scanned the back cover. Of all the days to be reading *The Secret*.

'That's not mine and there's no missus,' I replied without thinking. 'I mean, I'm not married.'

It wasn't a lie. I wasn't lying.

'I'd say this place needs a woman's touch but my flat is much worse,' she said, looking around without a reaction. 'Which way?'

'Oh, second door on your left,' I said, pointing down the corridor. I hardly ever used the downstairs lav so I was fairly certain she was safe. 'There should be loo roll in there but shout if there isn't.'

'Yes sir.' She gave me a brief salute and disappeared down the hallway. 'Do feel free to put that kettle on, I'm parched.'

'It's just a cup of tea,' I muttered, filling the kettle straight from the tap. The Brita jug had been empty for days. 'I'm making a cup of tea for my client who has driven a long way to choose some wood for her bar that she's paying for. It's the least I could do. It's polite.'

And I was nothing if not polite. I looked up to see my reflection in the kitchen window and pawed at my hair while the kettle overflowed. The state of me. I needed a haircut. A haircut and, according to a quick whiff of my armpits, at least three showers. This was one of the problems with working alone from home, I'd managed to put on outside clothes this morning but I had not bothered to wash myself. What was the point when you were going to end up rank rotten after a day in the workshop anyway? For the want of a better alternative, I grabbed the can of Febreze from under the sink and gave myself a quick spritz under each pit.

'Nice reading material you've got in there,' Jane called, wandering back into the kitchen, rubbing her hands on the back of her jeans. 'Are you moonlighting as a vet?'

'What?' I spun around, knocking one of my cleanish mugs onto my not-so-cleanish floor.

'There's like, seven copies of the *Veterinary Times* in your lav.' She took a seat at the kitchen table, her eyes travelling all the way around the room before resting on me. 'Interesting hobby.'

'My girlfriend is a vet,' I said flatly.

There. I had told the incredibly attractive woman I had a girlfriend. Clearly I deserved some sort of karmic reward.

'Oh, cool,' she replied, the light in her eyes softening ever so slightly. 'That must be hard though, living with a vet. All those late-night call outs.'

'We don't live together,' I said. 'And we're kind of on a break right now.'

There was a chance I'd lost a couple of karma points there.

'That sounds complicated,' Jane replied, resting her elbows on my table and offering up a sympathetic smile. I could have been fooling myself but I was sure I saw a something flicker behind her eyes.

I leaned against the sink, tapping my fingertips against the cold ceramic and imagined her sitting at the same table tomorrow morning, wearing nothing but one of my giant jumpers and a thong. It was a terrible affliction, being a man.

'It's one of those things.' I turned away as my fast-boil

kettle bubbled into life and considered plunging my hand into it. 'Don't worry about it.'

'Oh, I'm not.'

Without seeing her face, it was a response that could be interpreted a million different ways.

'How long have you been building bars?' she asked as I poured boiling water on top of two teabags and faffed around in the cupboard for a milk jug. The milk had technically expired but a covert sniff suggested it was fine and a milk jug meant no one could see the best before date in the first place.

'Best part of six years,' I replied. Milk jug and sugar bowl on the table. Bills, free newspaper and Liv's bloody useless holiday reading swept onto an empty seat. 'I did a year's course in the basics and then I apprenticed for three years. I set up on my own two years ago this November.'

I held out a mug of tea, wrapping my palm around the red-hot body of the mug and giving her the handle. Chivalry was not dead, it was alive and kicking and disfiguring men with manners up and down the East Midlands.

'Did you always know you wanted to do it?' She added milk to her tea while I gritted my teeth and prayed I still had at least some skin on my palm. 'Were you top of your class in woodworking? Knocking out the odd tree house in your spare time?'

'We didn't actually have woodworking at my school.' I settled down at the opposite end of the table, keeping a safe and respectable distance. 'But I loved building things growing up. I used to come up here in summer and work with my granddad in the workshop. He dabbled – he built this table, actually.'

She cocked her head and smiled, running her long fingers along the smooth, aged wood.

'Haven't you got a coaster?' she asked, picking up her cup of tea and taking a sip. 'I feel like a total shit. This is a family heirloom.'

'No, my granddad was all about building things to be used, things that looked better when they've been lived with.' Underneath the table, I dug my fingernail into the letter 'A' I'd carved there with Chris's compass twenty-five years before. 'This table is more tea stain than wood stain these days.'

'This is your grandparents' house then?' Jane asked. 'That's so cool.'

'Yeah,' I replied, a genuine smile on my face. 'They left it to my parents and they sort of gave it to me. It had the workshop already so it was a perfect set up really.'

'You're so lucky your family supported you.' She piled her long, dark hair over one shoulder. 'Our mum and dad were not happy when we told them we wanted to open a bar.'

'Ah, it wasn't quite that easy,' I assured her. No need to elaborate. I was enjoying her seeing me as Adam, the master craftsman, rather than Adam, the law-school dropout. 'What made you want to do the bar thing in the first place?'

She wrinkled her shoulders and her nose at the same time, tapping short, shiny fingernails on her mug. 'Me and Jim both did marketing at uni,' she replied, 'and I always worked behind the bar in the union. Most people don't believe me, but it was honestly my favourite bit, and when I graduated I got into this grad scheme at a big marketing company and hated every second of it.

Jim went and worked at a summer camp in America for a couple of years and he was the one who came up with the idea of doing the camp-themed bar. Once we'd come up with the concept, it was really hard to think about anything else.'

'Totally understand,' I said. It was almost too much. How could one woman be so cool and so gorgeous at the same time? 'I went through something a bit similar. The hardest bit was making the decision.'

'Ha, if only! The hardest bit for us was finding the money,' she laughed. One of her front teeth was very slightly chipped and even though her skin was a lot more tanned than Liv's there was one tiny fifty-pence-shaped freckle on her left cheekbone. I wanted to lick it. 'But we've both always been savers and Jim managed to rustle up a couple of investors from the marketing place he used to work at.'

As she shifted in her seat, I saw the merest suggestion of black lace underneath her checked shirt and immediately felt the merest suggestion of a boner underneath my filthy jeans.

'You couldn't find investors at your old job?' I asked, my voice pitching up at the end. 'No Mr Moneybags running around the office?'

'I'm surprised I kept my job as long as I did.' Jane pressed her hands over her face, hiding an embarrassed smile. 'I was shit. And I was bartending a couple of nights a week to pay off my student loans faster. It's fair to say I was more committed to one job than the other.'

I was trying not to stare but it wasn't easy. Boners came and went but something else was going on. I understood everything she was saying, it was exactly how I had felt about the law. This wasn't the same as casually wondering what kind of underwear a woman was wearing when you were sat opposite her on the bus, this was deep. I wasn't thinking exclusively with my penis and I didn't know how to feel.

'Yeah, I should have quit and done the bar full-time really,' she said. 'But everyone had an opinion, you know? As though it was beneath me to want to work in a bar when I had a degree. It's so stupid, you love what you love.'

I picked up a teaspoon and turned it in my hands to distract myself. *Teaspoon, teaspoon, teaspoon, teaspoon, teaspoon.* If I said it enough times, the word lost all meaning.

'Has anyone ever told you, you're very wise?' I asked, recovering myself.

'They have not,' she confirmed. 'When I left my job, my mum and dad told me I was a waster and my boyfriend broke up with me. So, yeah. Not that great.'

'You are very wise,' I assured her.

Teaspoon, teaspoon, teaspoon.

For a moment, we smiled at each other across my kitchen and the air felt heavy and thick, and when I looked at her I could see sunshine and rainbows and the two of us gambolling around in freshly mown meadows. Wait, that could have been the Febreze.

'I'm glad I found you.' Jane pulled the cuffs of her shirt down over her hands to accidentally expose a half-inch of her bra and there weren't enough teaspoons on earth to help me in that moment. This was totally unfair. I was nice to animals, I helped old ladies carry their shopping, and I'd never so much as nicked a packet of Monster Munch. Why was the universe testing me?

'For the bar, I mean,' she added. 'I'm glad we found

you to work on the bar. I'm glad you submitted a proposal. The designs look great.'

'I'm glad too,' I replied, picking up a teaspoon and tapping it against the side of my mug. 'I've had some truly shit jobs of late. It's nice to have something where I can flex a bit of creative muscle.'

'Oh yeah?' There was that curved lip again. 'I imagine the building process involves more than creative muscle.'

'Oh yeah,' I echoed, pumping up a bicep. 'Here's your ticket to the gun show.'

'Very impressive,' she said, laughing again. It felt nice to make someone laugh. With this beautiful woman who thought I was funny in front of me, I couldn't remember the last time I'd made Liv so much as smile. My mind was a blank. 'And I'd stay for the encore but I really ought to be going.'

'OK.' I stood up as soon as she did, adjusting the front of my trousers while she pulled on her leather jacket and messed around with her hair. I wondered what it smelled like. I wondered what she smelled like. I closed my eyes and imagined what the nape of her neck smelled like first thing in the morning before she'd had a shower.

Teaspoon, teaspoon, teaspoon, teaspoon, teaspoon, teaspoon.

'I'll walk you out,' I offered, dumping our mugs in the sink and quickly running my hands under cold water. 'You want to get on the road before rush hour.'

'I do,' she nodded. 'I'll be home by four thirty-ish if the traffic gods are willing.'

'I'll pray for you.' I opened the door and held it open, my eyes wandering down to her backside as she walked by. Unnecessary.

'You're such a giver,' she replied, fishing in her pocket for the keys to the Mini Cooper parked in front of my house. 'I'm coming up this way again tomorrow if you're around? I'd love to stop in and see where we're at.'

'I'm not likely to be that much further by tomorrow,' I said, anticipating my progress in my head. 'I'll go to the timber yard in the morning, put the order in for the wood. If they've got it in, I suppose I could make a start straight away but there won't be much for you to see.'

'Oh.' She stared for a moment before pulling the huge sunglasses that were perched on her head down over her eyes. Her car beeped at me twice as she unlocked the driver's side. 'OK.'

'I mean, you're welcome to stop in for a cup of tea,' I blurted out as she walked away. 'You should come anyway.'

Jane paused by the car, pushed the sunglasses back up onto the top of her head and gave me her biggest, most dazzling smile. I returned a small, uncomfortable version while my brain and my boner argued as to which one of them was making my decisions.

'Then I'll see you later.' She walked back towards me and pressed her full lips against my cheek, holding them there just long enough for her breath to tickle my ear. 'For that cup of tea.'

Shit. Her hair smelled amazing.

'I'll get the kettle on.' I took two small steps backwards and held up my hand in something that looked more like I was threatening her with the Vulcan death grip than waving goodbye.

I watched as she pulled away and drove off down the drive, memorizing her number plate and filing it away, along with her black lace bra, her chipped front tooth and the thought of her long legs wrapped around my waist. My hand drifted down to my crotch to cover any activity on little Adam's part as I stared at the space where her car had been. There was no doubt about it, my brain was no longer in control of the SS *Adam Floyd*.

15

I sat outside Adam's house in my car, faffing with my hair in the rear-view mirror. It was too big, too curly. I'd told them to blow dry it straight but they couldn't help themselves, they just had to do the big, silly curls on the bottom. I looked like veterinary Barbie: all I was missing was my stethoscope. Actually, I really wished I had it. My heart was pounding and I would've loved to get a proper listen to my pulse.

'It's going to be fine,' I assured myself in the rear-view mirror. 'We're just going to have a nice casual chat.'

A nice casual chat where I told him everything: how Cassie had spilled the beans about the engagement, how I'd been so stressed out waiting for him to propose, how I was freaking out about taking over the surgery, how I felt completely out of control of my own life and was afraid I was going to wake up to find out I was eighty, alone and incontinent with no idea how to use the latest smartphone. And how I'd missed him every day since we'd got back from holiday and needed his support more than anything else right now. A good shag, too, but mostly him having my back with everything else going to shit. Then maybe we could start fresh and I could resolve at least half the nonsense going on in my tiny mind.

I opened the door and stepped outside, my legs more wobbly than I would have liked. There was a car in Adam's driveway, a dark green Mini Cooper that I didn't recognize. Before I could spy through the windows, Adam and a tall brunette walked out of the house and I dashed back to the car, pressing myself up against next-door's hedge. If this was a client, I didn't want to bother him. We had serious things to discuss and then serious make-up sex to get down to, and both of those things were going to need a clear mind and some concentration.

Hmm. He looked awfully happy for a man taking a client meeting. I squinted, trying to get my three-day-old daily contact lenses to focus. Funny, he hadn't mentioned anything about scoring a job for a Victoria's Secret model. I looked back to Adam and scowled at the goofy grin on his face.

'It's just a meeting,' I reassured myself. 'He has meetings all the time.'

They carried on chatting in front of the green Mini while I picked at the carefully coiffed ends of my hair. No matter how many tutorials I watched, I'd never been able to pull off that sexy, messy hair look. If I tried to do curls with my straighteners, it looked like Sweeney Todd had been at me with a crimper. When I tried it with tongs, I just looked like a knob. Her hair was perfect. Her arse was perfect. Her legs were perfect. I couldn't see her boobs or her face properly but even if they were slightly below average, she was still the best-looking woman I'd ever seen with my own eyes. I had squeezed myself into my skinniest skinny jeans because I knew Adam liked them, but her jeans were so tight they were practically a second skin. They must have been riding right up her chuff, and then, as she raised her arms to wave goodbye, I saw a thong peeking up over the waistband.

The complete and utter slag.

I breathed out slowly as she walked towards her car door, beep-beeping the lock.

'Yeah, it's time for you to leave,' I muttered. Getting a better look at her from the front did not make me feel any better. Combing my hair behind my ears, I shook my handbag as quietly as possible, searching for a lip gloss. I was holding the wand up to my face as she stopped, turned back to Adam, curled her arms around his neck and kissed him.

'Fuck *off*,' I whispered as my hair wrapped itself around my sticky lip gloss. 'Fuck right royally off.'

After what felt like forever, Adam's mystery woman pulled away and got in the car while he stood there, swiping at his eyebrows and waving goodbye. And then she was gone. For a moment he stayed where he was. Stuck to the spot and holding the front of his trousers as though he was about to have an accident. Or perhaps he already had.

It wasn't like they said it was in films. My knees didn't buckle and my legs didn't turn to jelly, they just stopped working. One minute I was standing upright, the next I was folding in on myself and sitting on the cold, dirty ground. His neighbour's well-trimmed hedge poked me sharply in the back of my curly head as I dug my phone out of my bag.

What was that? *Who* was that? It was only two days

since he'd stood on my doorstep and begged me to call off the break. *Two days.*

'Hello, what's up?'

Abi answered on the first ring.

'I just saw Adam kissing another woman outside his house and now I'm hiding behind a hedge and I don't know what to do.'

'No, really,' she replied. 'What's up?'

'I'm at Adam's house,' I said, replaying the scene over and over in my head. 'And I just watched him walk some eight-foot-tall Angelina Jolie lookalike underwear model out to her car with his hands all over her – and before she left, she kissed him.'

'OK, before I start, what are you looking for here?' Abi asked. 'Do you want me to be outraged, threaten to tear off his knob and sew it to his forehead like a unicock, or would you rather I question the accuracy of what you saw?'

'I saw it!' I rocked back and forth, catching my hair in the scratchy twigs. 'With my actual eyes! Also, ten points for unicock.'

'Liv, whoever it was, she wasn't eight feet tall for a start and I very much doubt there was an underwear model randomly knocking around his house at three in the afternoon,' she replied. 'Taking that into account, do you want to calm down and tell me exactly what you saw?'

'I hate you sometimes,' I told her, wiggling my toes and rapping my knuckles against my useless knees.

'Don't be mad at me because I'm logical,' Abi said. 'If you wanted histrionics, you would have called Cass.'

'You're so helpful.' I snapped tiny twigs off the hedge and broke them up into a dozen little pieces. 'But she really was gorgeous and she really did kiss him. Maybe not tongue down his throat – but, god, Abs, you should have seen his face after she left.'

And that was what hurt. It wasn't really the hot girl or the kiss or the handsy nature of their goodbye, it was the look on Adam's face, as though he'd won the lottery on his birthday and James Bond was coming round to deliver the money in the car from *Knight Rider*. He looked at her in a way he had never looked at me.

'Liv, I'm going to suggest something really controversial now,' she said. 'Go and talk to him.'

'Yeah, OK,' I scoffed. 'I'll just go and talk to him, we'll have a grown-up conversation that will make everything better.'

'Why do I get the feeling you're taking the piss?' she asked with a ready tut. 'Go and bloody well talk to him.'

'"Excuse me Adam, I know I said I needed a couple of weeks to sort my head out but you said it first so you can't be mad at me and just out of interest, who was that absolute stunner you were necking at the end of the drive a minute ago? I'd love to ask her where she gets her hair done?"'

'Did she have nice hair?' Abi asked. 'What was she wearing?'

'Yes of course she did!' I yelled. 'She was perfect. Even *I* fancied her. And jeans. Really, really tight jeans.'

She sighed into her phone, the gentle sound blowing up in my ear.

'Liv, go and talk to him,' she said again. 'You're still there, aren't you?'

'Yes,' I said, glancing down either end of the street. 'But I don't know if I can. I'm freaking out.'

'Stop freaking out; go and talk to him and then call

me back. I'm in the lab but I've got my phone and I'll call you back as soon as I can if I don't answer.'

Carrie Bradshaw never had this problem, I thought to myself. Her friends always answered on the first ring. Which was a bit odd when you thought about it; they all had pretty intense jobs, so why were they always picking up the phone? Yep, another tick in the plus column for ditching Long Harrington and starting over as a sex columnist in New York.

'OK,' I said, bouncing my palm up and down on the pavement. I could do this. It was going to be fine. It was Adam, for god's sake, there was clearly an explanation. 'I'm going now. I'll call you back in a bit. What are you working on now?'

'The effects of melamine on humoral immunity with or without cyanuric acid,' she replied. 'Go get 'em, tiger.'

All I had to do was stand up, walk to Adam's door, and have a conversation with him. We'd been having conversations almost every day for three years, why was this one so much harder than any of the others? Two weeks ago I would have marched up to his door, made non-specific threats on her life and already made myself a cup of tea.

Checking myself for stray dog shit, I straightened my shoulders and set off up Adam's driveway. There were tyre tracks on the muddy grass from her Mini. I'd always fancied a Mini. Cow. I fancied a Mini and she fancied my boyfriend, we had so much in common – apart from she had dark hair and mine was blonde, she was nearly six foot and I was only five foot four and I didn't generally wear black lace thongs on your average Tuesday. But then, maybe she didn't either; maybe she only wore them when she knew she was going to get lucky.

I stood in front of the door, one hand ready to knock, my keys in the other. Did I knock or did I let myself in? Did I ask him about her or did I pretend I hadn't seen it? I blinked, my lenses drying out again. I had spares upstairs. I could get my spares after we'd had our talk. I wondered what her eyesight was like. She probably had perfect vision and had flushed all my contacts down the loo, cackling maniacally while smothering my Advanced Night Repair all over her body.

What was worse? Being jealous or crazy? There was no way I could sit down and talk to him until I'd calmed down. As I had already established earlier in this mess, I was not Beyoncé. I could not lose my shit at him then apologize and write an amazing album about it. I turned around, ran back to my car and sat there, shaking. Breathing out slowly, I rested my forehead on the steering wheel and closed my eyes but all I could see was the kiss. Adam kissing another woman. He wasn't supposed to be kissing anyone but me. We had specifically said, 'no seeing other people', and kissing was even worse than seeing.

Go for a drive, a little voice said, pushing the image of the two of them out of my head and replacing it with a vision of open country roads and clearish blue skies. Driving calmed me down, it always had. Nodding to myself, I turned the key in the ignition and flipped on the stereo. A Ford Fiesta honked its horn behind me as I pulled out and I swerved around a parked Mondeo, barely missing its wing mirror, but I really couldn't have cared less. Adele blared out of my speakers as I turned onto the main road, flying past the post office, assuring me that she alone in the universe understood what I was going through.

And then I remembered she was a millionaire who had a kid and a man who loved her and everything she was singing was complete and utter bollocks. I tore at my iPod cable and tossed the whole thing out my open window, watching as it disappeared into a bank of tall grass.

'Fucking Adele,' I muttered, speeding down the road and out into the middle of nowhere.

16

'On your next breath in, sweep your arms up over your head and then, as you breathe out, sweep your arms down as you fold over and plant your hands on the floor in front of you.'

I felt a sharp pull somewhere between my shoulder blades but I didn't dare stand back up to stretch it out.

'Breathing in, send your left leg back in a lunge and then, on your next outward breath, send your right leg back to meet it in plank.'

'Mum?'

'Adam?'

'I think I'm broken.'

'Breathing in, pull your hips up and back and drive your heels down into the floor in downward-facing dog,' she replied. I looked up between my elbows to see her pacing around the living room, barefoot, concentrating hard on her script. 'Don't worry if your heels don't touch the floor, concentrate on the exchange of energy between you and the ground. Feel it channelling up through your hands and feet as you push them away from each other, creating length down your spine and space in your hips.'

'No really.' I collapsed onto the floor, hugging my arms around each other, stretching out whatever I had tweaked. 'I'm broken.'

'Oh dear.' She dropped her piece of paper on the settee and knelt down beside my rubber mat. 'What hurts?'

'I'm fine,' I said, rolling upright. 'You were very good though, I was really into it before I fell over.'

'Adam, five breaths into your first sun salutation and you're lying crippled on the floor.' She pressed her thumbs into my back and dug them in. 'Does that help?'

'It hurts – if that helps?' I replied, pulling away. Before she started training as a yoga teacher, she had qualified as a massage therapist, but as her number one test subject, I had to admit, she wasn't that good at it. She'd done much better when she learned how to speak Russian. And strip a car engine. And play the flute. She didn't get so far with becoming a tattoo artist but that could have been my fault. I had to draw the human-guinea-pig line somewhere. There weren't many things left on this earth that my mum hadn't given her best shot and I'd always admired her for it. Liv asked her why she wanted to try so many different hobbies once and she looked so shocked, as though everyone juggled motorcycle lessons with cheese-making class and figure skating.

'All this time I've put into getting my teaching quali-fication and honestly, I'm starting to think yoga isn't for me.' She hopped up to her feet, turned off the supposedly calming CD and flung the curtains open, flooding the room with mid-morning sunlight. 'I'm not certain I'm getting anything out of it.'

'Anything else in mind?' I asked, following her into

the kitchen and helping myself to a biscuit out the barrel.

'I read about this CrossFit thing that's opening in Newark,' she said. 'I quite like the look of that. It seems more active than yoga, more involved. The yoga community round here isn't that inspiring, to tell you the truth – it's not like it was in India.'

I crunched on the biscuit and immediately regretted it. I didn't know what was in it, but I knew what wasn't and that was flavour of any kind. I'd have given my right nut for a Twix.

'I bet,' I replied, opening the bin and letting the dry crumbs of the world's most disappointing biscuit fall out of my mouth. 'But CrossFit is intense, Mum. Loads of weightlifting and hard-core cardio. Do you really think it's a good idea?'

'Maybe not for your dad,' she gave me the lifted eyebrow that suggested I should not challenge her further, 'but I'm fit as a fiddle. Fitter than you, I bet.'

'I reckon you are,' I laughed. She stirred a spoonful of pale green powder into a glass of water and handed it to me. I downed it as quickly as I could, trying not to smell or taste whatever mank she'd added. 'I've been slacking since I got back from Mexico. We should start running again.'

'Are you still running with Liv?' she asked, sipping her own green slime happily. 'I'm sure she'll be keen to get wedding dress ready. That's what all the magazines say, anyway.'

'Hmm,' I replied. 'Something like that.'

Down at the bottom of the garden, Dad gave me a wave from one of his flowerbeds. Rocking his overall, his hat and gloves, he brandished his trowel with pride. While

Mum went back and forth on her hobbies Dad was forever faithful to his one true love: the garden. Growing up, we'd moved around a lot. My dad had been a medical officer in the RAF but when he was injured in a car crash he took early retirement and moved up here, to be closer to my mum's parents. Over the last twelve years he had developed quite the green thumb, and while I wasn't much of a garden man myself, I had to admit, he'd done an amazing job. There wasn't a plant he couldn't bring to life and he had even taken on the task of landscaping Chris's garden when he bought the old rectory at the other end of the village. I wondered idly if Chris was angry about leaving London now that Cass wanted to stop working. He'd moved up here so she wouldn't have to change jobs – the schools in London weren't safe, he had said – and now here he was, stuck with a two-hour commute from his office and a great big country house in a village he'd never been that keen on, even when we came to visit as kids.

'You can't tell your mother something like this and then expect her to wait patiently without any questions,' Mum said while Dad went back to work. 'What's the plan? Are you going to ask her? Chris says you've already got a ring.'

'I was going to give her Nannan's ring,' I choked, running another glass of water. 'If that's all right.'

'It's more than all right,' she replied, a small sad smile lighting up her face, even though her eyes still filled up at any mention of her mother. It had already been seven years but we'd been close, the three of us. 'Nannan would have loved Liv.'

'Yeah, I don't know.' I sipped my clean water slowly. 'Not about her loving Liv, I'm sure she would have. More about, well, the whole thing.'

Mum finished her green potion with a gasp and ran the glass under the tap until it was clean. She hated the dishwasher, said it wasted energy. Hence why Dad waited for her to go out to whatever class she was in before he ran it and pretended he'd done the washing up.

'What whole thing?' she asked. 'Proposing? I wouldn't worry too much about it, all you've got to do is ask the question, love.'

'Not the proposing, the whole thing,' I mumbled into my chest. 'The whole getting married thing.'

My mum was a small woman but that didn't make her any less terrifying and the Krav Maga class and shooting lessons I knew she had under her belt were absolutely nothing compared with the look on her face.

'And what's that supposed to mean?' she demanded, hands on her hips. 'Are you having cold feet, Adam Floyd?'

'Might be,' I said. I was close to the door. She was smaller and faster but I was much bigger than she was and, worst-case scenario, I could always push her over. 'Don't know.'

'I wonder what went wrong with the two of you, sometimes,' she said, picking up a tea towel and whipping it across the backs of my legs. 'Your brother did exactly the same thing, you realize?'

I did not realize.

'Chris had cold feet? Before proposing to Cassie?'

'Oh yes, he came round here, all het up, crying and talking about how he thought he'd made a mistake buying the ring,' she nodded. 'How he didn't know if he could do it and what if he wasn't good enough for her. It was all very dramatic.'

This was entirely brand-new information. I couldn't imagine Chris thinking he wasn't good enough for anyone. He once said he'd pass on Kate Upton because she didn't seem like she'd have a lot to offer in the conversation department.

'I don't think there's a single man who doesn't go through this,' she said, picking bits of carpet off her leggings. 'At least, not one who was serious about making the commitment in the first place. In a way, I think it's a good thing. It means you're really thinking about what you're taking on.'

'What else did Chris say?' I asked. I just couldn't picture it. My big brother, insecure and crying to his mum? What I wouldn't give to go back in time and watch through the window.

'It doesn't matter what Chris said, it matters what you're going to do.' She had an end-of-conversation look in her eye and I knew not to push it. 'Have you said anything to Olivia?'

Hmm. Given the look on her delicate, pointed face, I didn't want to get myself into any more trouble than I really had to, but even now, after all my years of practice, I found it so hard to keep things from my mum. I was going to have to tell her the truth.

'We're having a break from each other at the moment – she wanted a break,' I said. There. I'd pulled off the plaster and underneath it was only the small scab of a lie. Liv had asked for a break. After I had. But still, semantics . . . 'So I haven't talked to her this week.'

'You broke up?' Mum looked destroyed. She grabbed the kitchen top with one hand and pressed the other against her chest as though she was worried it might cave in. I watched closely from my position near the door, edging closer to my getaway and grabbing an apple out of the fruit bowl just in case I needed a missile.

'Oh, Adam, no. That's awful. You're kidding me? What happened?'

'We haven't broken up.' I don't think, I added in my head. 'It was after her dad's party – she said she needed some time to work out what she's doing.'

'Well, I can't blame the poor girl for that.' She recovered herself slightly, still keeping a firm grip on the kitchen top, just in case. 'I can't say she looked terribly happy about having all that responsibility dropped on her.'

Assured that I was at least somewhat safe, I took a bite out of my Granny Smith-slash-projectile.

'But she loves being a vet,' I said, confused. 'Why would that freak her out?'

'Oh, I don't know, Adam. Maybe because her dad just changed her entire life without asking her? It was clear from the look on her face she didn't have a clue what was going on,' she suggested. 'And whether she wants to be a vet forever or not, imagine how hard it must be to have someone make a decision like that for you, without asking.'

Well, when she put it like that . . .

'I imagine it's not unlike deciding to spend the rest of your life with another person,' she went on. 'It's a good thing and you're happy about it, but it's scary, isn't it? It's a forever thing, and we human beings aren't very good at processing forever things, are we?'

I chomped on my apple and shook my head slowly. 'No?'

'No,' she confirmed. 'And something big like this happens, people tend to go one of two ways. Either they try to keep hold of everything they can in their life or they try to change it all. It's about control, Adam.

She's probably trying to find some control in it all. Just like you.'

My mum always had a way of making things make sense. This wasn't all about me. I'd always been a big fan of running away, that was how I controlled things. By turning my back, moving as fast as I could and never staying in one place too long. I'd gone backpacking for a year after my A levels and then snuck in another two years after I finished my law degree before Dad convinced me to take the BPTC to become a barrister. Both times I was avoiding the fact that I'd chosen a career I didn't really want because people had told me I'd be good at it. It was only when I started working on carpentry projects in my spare time that I realized I didn't have to keep running, that I could actually work towards something I cared about instead.

What if Liv had only gone to vet school because her dad expected her to? What if she didn't really want to be a vet at all? She'd never said anything, but then, I'd never asked. I bowed my head, feeling so stupid. I should have realized all this myself. I shouldn't need my mum to explain how my girlfriend was feeling.

'All you can do is be there for her. Don't try to fix anything or tell her what to do, just listen to her,' Mum said, reaching up on her bare tiptoes to pull a red and black tartan tin out of the top cupboard. She opened it up and revealed three packets of contraband shortbread biscuits. 'Take one of these and don't tell your father,' she instructed. 'Nothing sorts your head out like a cup of tea and a biscuit.'

I did as I was told and took one of the packets before she could squirrel them away again behind tubs of flour and gravy browning.

'Have a think, let her take the time she needs.' Mum came over to give me a hug, the top of her grey curly head only just coming halfway up my chest, then held out her hand for my apple core. 'But don't give up on her, Adam. She's a good girl and she loves you. I've never seen you as happy with anyone else, you're made for each other.'

'You're right,' I said, looking down at the biscuits and felt a wave of shame wash over my cheeks. 'She does make me happy.'

'Then work it out.' She dropped the apple core in the bin and waved at Dad down the garden. 'Will you stay for lunch?'

'Can't. I've got to go, I'm meeting a client later and I need to sort some stuff out.' A gorgeous, six-foot-tall brunette client, I added to myself, feeling guilty about the thoughts I'd had about Jane when Liv was struggling through so much on her own. I pecked Mum on the cheek and waved the biscuits in the air. 'Tell Dad I'll see him later.'

'Always on the go,' she said, following me out the door in bare feet and stopping before she reached the concrete. 'Will we see you before the christening?'

The christening. Gus's christening. The christening where Liv and I were supposed to be godparents.

'Shit, it's this Sunday, isn't it?' I hit myself in the forehead with the shortbread and made a face. They were so much harder than I'd expected.

'It is, and language,' Mum reprimanded as Dad started a slow and steady walk down the garden without his stick. 'Now for Christ's sake get gone before he comes in and sees those bloody biscuits.'

'Language!' I shouted back, jogging out towards the car. 'I'll talk to you before Sunday, promise.'

'And talk to Liv,' she replied. 'Please.'

'I will,' I promised. But first things first, I thought, opening up the Land Rover and chucking the shortbread in the back seat. I had to go, I was meeting a client.

'Afternoon, slacker.'

Jane knocked on the door of the workshop, only to find me leaning back in my battered old armchair, legs up on the workbench, engaged in a particularly aggressive game of *Injustice* on my phone, looking as cool as I could manage. It could have been worse; she could have turned up ten minutes earlier and found me wearing a pair of pink Marigolds and scrubbing the shit out of the bathroom. I had no idea how it got so dirty, I was hardly even in there and every time I was, it felt like I was there to clean something. How could a room designed to clean people get so filthy, so quickly?

'Hi.' I turned off the game without even bothering to check my score. This was intense. 'How are you?'

'Good,' she nodded, loitering around the doorway. 'Some tit tried to cut me up when I was turning off the A1 but apart from that, I'm fine.'

'Should I hunt him down and kill him?' I asked.

'Only if it's not too much trouble,' she replied with her widest smile. 'I'll get my Uzi out the boot and we'll be off, yeah?'

'Sorted,' I nodded, hands in my pockets, shoulders scrunched up around my ears. I wasn't sure of the etiquette.

Ultimately, I was working for her and usually I met my clients with a polite handshake, possibly a half hug if we knew each other and we were being dead modern but this was new ground. We were definitely flirting

– but was it sexless work flirting or one-too-many-drinks-and-oops-that's-my-penis flirting? Jane wasn't dressed like a woman who was trying to get lucky, although I imagined she didn't have to try terribly hard. She was wearing the same skintight jeans and leather as she'd worn on Tuesday, teamed with a plain blue T-shirt and black ankle boots. Nothing overtly 'come and get it' about that.

'So where's my bar?' she asked, searching the workshop. 'Is it not done yet?'

'Not quite.' I straightened the collar of my shirt. Red and black checked, clean, ironed, but not too try hard. 'There's just the cutting and the sanding and the planing and the building. And you know, that's usually easier to do once the timber has arrived.'

'I see.'

Maybe her hair looked a bit shinier than it had on Tuesday and perhaps her eyes looked a bit darker, as though she was wearing make-up. But that could have been the light, I wasn't sure. 'How about a tour of the workshop, then?'

'It's a short tour,' I said, surveying my kingdom. 'Workbench, tools, vice, mini fridge, *Danger Mouse* DVDs, lathe.'

'It's nice,' she nodded appreciatively. 'I like it. What's that?'

'Plane,' I replied, picking up my smallest bench lathe and turning it around in my hands. 'It's for smoothing out surfaces.'

'And what's that?' she pointed to the tool bench by the wall.

'Another plane,' I said, giving it a trusty tap. 'This has a higher pitch than the other, we call it York Pitch.'

'Why?' Jane asked, picking up a chisel and knocking the handle back and forth against the palm of her hand. 'Is it from York or did a man called York invent it?'

'I don't actually know,' I admitted. 'But I'll be using it on your bar. The higher angle is better for cherry wood.'

'Why?' she walked over, her heels tapping against the concrete floor and crouching down until she was eyelevel with the plane.

'It just is,' I said. 'I studied this for a year in college and three years as an apprentice and I don't think I ever asked as many questions as you just have.'

'I'm curious,' she replied, looking up at me from her crouched position, wide-eyed and full-lipped and, oh Jesus Christ, *teaspoon teaspoon teaspoon teaspoon*. 'I like to learn about new things. What if I ever wanted to build my own bar?'

'Is that likely?' I asked, wandering around to the back of the armchair and leaning against it casually. I hadn't had this much trouble with inopportune semis since the sixth form. 'Was commissioning me to design something for you part of an elaborate plan to run me out of business?'

'Damn it,' she bounced back up to her feet, all smiles and easy laughter. 'You got me.'

The radio was on a low crackle somewhere in a dark corner of the workshop and I searched my one-track mind for something else to say. This wasn't me, I was good at people, I always had a comeback. It was one of the reasons everyone was so convinced I'd make a great barrister, I could talk the hind legs off a donkey and then convince him he didn't really need the front legs if he thought about it. Jane just stood there, in the middle of my dusty, dirty workshop, as though there was nowhere else in the world she'd rather be.

'How come you're all the way up here?' I asked as my brain disengaged from my trousers for long enough to form a sentence. 'You said you were going to be up this way, didn't you?'

'Oh, right, I did,' she said. Her mouth hung half open for just a split second, as though her body was ready to speak before her mind had decided what it wanted to say. 'I was visiting a friend.'

'A friend?'

Was she lying? Had she made up a reason to see me again?

'A friend,' she nodded, placing the zip pull of her leather jacket into my table vice and turning the handle until it was caught tight. 'Sorry, not terribly exciting.'

'I'm not sure I believe you,' I said, recovering myself as my semi subsided.

Jane looked up sharply, her olive cheeks flushing pink. 'Is that right?'

She yanked her sleeve upwards but it was caught too tightly in the vice. Certain my crotch was in no way compromised, I crossed the room towards her to free her jacket.

'Yeah, I think you're lying,' I said, spinning the handle towards me, just twelve inches or so between us. My breathing was shallow. Her breathing was shallow. She smelled of something deep and spicy warm. She definitely hadn't been wearing perfume on Tuesday, this was definitely a new thing. 'You're not just trying to take over my business are you? You're an international assassin. You might as well confess now, I've got your number, *Jane*.'

'If that is my real name,' she said, a bubble of tense laughter bursting out of her as she gave my chest a half-hearted slap. The second she touched me I knew I wanted to kiss her and I was almost certain she wanted it too. I'd been out of the game for a while, it was true, but this was not my first hot-girl rodeo. Her hand didn't move and I knew she could feel how fast my heart was pounding. It really was working overtime to get all that blood away from my head and my feet and concentrate it in one particular area it currently considered much more important. Neither of us flinched. I could feel her breath on my throat and hear the rustle of her jacket and that tiny freckle on her left cheek dared me to walk away.

'Cup of tea?'

Walk away I did.

My voice was too loud and too high and I felt my ankle roll underneath my foot as I took a big step back, falling directly into my armchair, arms and legs akimbo.

'I was thinking something stronger,' Jane said, shaking out her hair and wrapping her arms around herself. 'Have you got any wine?'

From my incredibly elegant position in the chair, I noticed that she was gripping the workbench even more tightly than the vice. Jesus H. Christ on a pushbike, what had I got myself into?

'Let's go to the pub,' I suggested, righting myself and making a new plan. Get Jane away from my house, away from any surface that could be considered suitable for boning and out in public where there were lots and lots of other people. 'They've got wine. Amazing wine. First round's on me.'

'Sounds good,' she said, eyeing me with a heavy gaze

for one moment before turning on her heel and walking out into the garden.

Normal service had resumed.

I followed her out of the workshop, closed the double stable doors, and clicked the padlock shut, leaving whatever had just happened far behind.

The Bell was not a good pub; there was no way around that. It was old, tired and generally populated with men so old there was a local urban legend that one regular had died sitting at the bar and no one had moved him for two days. That said, it was still a better option than the Kingfisher, a pub primarily famous for diarrhoea-inducing warm lager and the constant threat of schoolyard violence. In the interest of not being forcibly dekegged before waking up to find I'd shit the bed, I directed Jane to our local. Swirls of dust danced in the air as I opened the heavy door, letting in unwelcome clean air and afternoon sunlight, and followed her towards a small, round table in the corner.

'Nice spot,' she said, settling herself on an unstable stool before switching to the bench built into the wall. 'Retro.'

'I thought it would be good inspiration for you,' I replied, patting myself down for my wallet. 'Just in case you're not totally wedded to the summer camp concept and wanted to go for something a bit more late-seventies, Middle England, bag of shite.'

'It's tempting,' she acknowledged. 'I'm not sure Jim would go for it though. Maybe you and me should buy this place out and make sure no one ever changes a single thing.'

'No one ever will,' I assured her. 'Glass of wine? White or red?'

'Is it going to be drinkable?' she asked, squinting behind the bar. 'Or would I be better with something else?'

'It's not going to be great,' I admitted, exchanging nods with someone Liv had gone to school with but whose name I couldn't remember for the life of me. He immediately clocked Jane, looking her up and down and raising both eyebrows. 'I'd go with a beer if you're not sure.'

'I know this is a bit shit for a career barmaid,' Jane said, scooping her hair over one shoulder, away from the sticky table. 'But I really hate beer. I'm more of a cocktail girl. I know, it's terrible.'

'I'm shocked and appalled,' I replied. 'If I can't get them to make a mojito, glass of white?'

She nodded and pulled her black leather handbag onto her lap, shaking up the contents as I walked to the bar and rooting around inside. 'Sounds good,' she said. 'Thanks, Adam.'

Every time she said my name. *Teaspoons.*

'Afternoon.'

I must have been in the Bell at least two hundred times in the last six years and this man had been behind the bar every single time. Short, stocky and with the most impressive red bush of a beard I had ever seen, he gave me a nod and reached for a pint pot.

'Afternoon,' I replied, snapping back to the job at hand. 'Pint of the Fuller's and a white wine, please.'

'Large or a small?' he asked, pulling the pint. 'For the wine?'

'Umm,' I glanced over my shoulder to see Jane applying lip balm from a small round pot and smacking her full lips together. 'Large.'

'New friend? Haven't seen her around here before.'

'Client,' I replied, quickly before he could think anything else. 'She's a client.'

'If you say so.'

He smiled to himself as I handed him a ten-pound note and watched the head on my drink settle. The idea of me bringing another woman to the Bell on a date was so ridiculous even Liv would have laughed. If I did have someone else on the go, this was the last place I'd bring her. The Bell was the last place I would take my worst enemy if there were a better option in walking distance.

'Thanks, mate.' I pocketed the handful of shrapnel he held out to me without counting it and picked up the drinks. Jane accepted her wine with caution and took a sip.

'Cheers,' I said, holding up my pint.

'Oh, god, yeah.' She clinked her glass against mine quickly. 'Sorry, cheers. My curiosity got the better of me.'

'Hate when that happens,' I said with a gulp. 'How is it?'

'I'm probably not going to put it on our wine list,' she replied, slipping her arms out of her leather jacket. Her T-shirt slouched off one shoulder, showing off a slender collarbone and a spaghetti-thin black bra strap. How was that possibly holding up her boobs? Even now, the engineering of bras astounded me.

'How are you getting on with everything? With the bar?' I asked. It felt weird to be in the Bell without Liv. I doused the ache in the pit of my stomach with cold beer and offered Jane an interested smile. 'There must be so much to do.'

'So much,' she agreed. 'We've got all the paperwork in order and we're talking to the different suppliers now, but that should all be settled soon. Then we've got to find staff, get all the menus printed, decorate. The design is pretty much the only other thing we've got sorted.'

'I've heard you've got a really good man on that,' I said with a nod. 'Best in the business.'

She smiled and rolled her eyes. 'I've heard he's all right. Hasn't got very good taste in wine though, he's lost a few points for that.'

'Doesn't seem to be slowing you down,' I pointed out, tipping back my pint. 'I can't keep up.'

'The faster I drink it, the better it tastes,' she replied. 'I've drunk nicer paint stripper.'

We both stretched our legs out under the table at the same time and snatched them back as our shins clashed.

'I'm going to run to the ladies.' She placed her half-empty wine glass on a warped cardboard beer mat and stood up quickly. 'I'll be back.'

She walked around the horseshoe and every man in the place looked up. There were only half a dozen old boys, as well as Liv's friend, but not a single one of them could keep their eyes off her until she disappeared into the ladies and they all turned to look at me. The ache in my stomach that missed Liv told me to look away and ignore them, but the peacock that had always enjoyed the company of a good-looking woman fought harder and I found myself pulling my shoulders back and stretching out my arms. Everyone looked away and a smile found its way onto my face before the niggling fear that, somehow, this might get back to Liv came back to slap me in the face.

Not that I was doing anything wrong.

Not that I was the one who wanted this break in the first place.

'It's one quick polite drink and then home,' I said quietly, checking my watch. We'd be done inside an hour. 'She's a client, I don't want to be rude, that's all.'

I picked up my pint and sighed. Sometimes I worried that me and Chris weren't that different after all.

17

'I'm really not in the mood for the pub,' David moaned. 'Can't we do something more fun like poke ourselves in the eyes with knitting needles or watch *Keeping Up with the Kardashians*?'

'I thought you liked the Kardashians?' I asked, puzzled. It was his secret straight-man shame. At first I thought he was watching it for the possibility of boobs but it soon became obvious he was genuinely invested. He knew the names of Kylie's dogs; he was legit.

'I like Kourtney and Kendall,' he corrected as he wrung out the sleeve of his sodden sweatshirt. 'The rest of them can get in the sea.'

'Even Kim?'

He fixed me with a horrified stare. '*Especially* Kim.'

It had been a shit day. First the coffee machine had broken, then I'd spilled cat diarrhoea medicine all down my trousers, then I had to explain to a seven-year-old that I had put his rabbit to sleep because it wouldn't stop fitting and his parents didn't want to pay for tests. After all that, I'd spent twenty minutes locked in the toilets, hiding from my dad who wanted to talk takeover strategy, while I ate half a Crunchie and had a little cry. Something that seemed to be happening more and more often; the Crunchie, that is. I'd known Wednesday was going to be a test from the start – dark skies, black clouds, bouncing-off-the-floor rain – from the moment I woke up to the moment we closed up for the evening. And the moment we arrived at the Bell the weather gods decided it would be hilarious to dial things back to a miserable drizzle as we stalked across the car park with our jumpers held up over our heads. Could we find an umbrella in the surgery when we needed it? No, of course we couldn't.

'It's Wednesday, we have to go to the pub,' I insisted in the same way I'd been insisting all day. So much was going on and too much of it was change, so the very least everyone could do was meet me at the shitting pub for a glass of manky wine. If I was being entirely honest, I'd much rather chill out at home with a glass of wine and America's surgically enhanced first family, but a best friend's work was never done. 'Besides, Abi said she might bring Bill and she doesn't want him to think it's a date.'

'Isn't it a date?' David asked.

'Not if we're there,' I replied. 'Which I think is the point.'

He stopped dead in his tracks.

'Sod it, I'm going home. I have to find out if Kim has moved out of Kris's house yet.'

'But you hate Kim,' I reminded him, clutching his arm and dragging him towards the pub. 'Don't leave me with them, please. It's half six now; I promise we'll be home by half seven. Eight at the latest.'

'I do. I do hate Kim,' he admitted with a sigh. 'Fine. One drink?'

'One drink and we can go back to mine and watch all the shit telly you like,' I bargained. 'I need to go back and check on Ronald anyway.'

'He's fine,' David assured me. 'He's eaten something manky, that's all.'

'I hope so,' I mused, thinking back on the big, silly dog currently napping in the sleepover section of the surgery. 'He's one of my favourites – I was there when he was born, you know.'

'I don't know how any animal that throws up on you as much as he did today could be anyone's favourite anything.' David held his hand out to test the drizzle before dropping his jumper from over his head to around his shoulders. 'Did you definitely have a shower? You still smell of it a bit.'

'I do not,' I replied, indignant, before sniffing tentatively at my hair. Arsehole.

Ronald was a golden Labrador who'd come in after lunch and had been throwing up on anyone and anything that came within a six-foot radius all afternoon. We'd given him some fluids, run some tests, and after I had changed my scrubs twice he settled down in his bed and slept happily for the rest of the afternoon. If his owners hadn't texted me to say they were going to the pictures, I would have sent him home, but they were already on their way to the cinema when we closed. Priorities totally in order, obviously.

'Hmm,' I agreed, biting my lips in lieu of lipstick. David immediately handed me his ChapStick. I took it and pulled off the lid to give it a sniff. 'You haven't got anything contagious, have you?'

'Not any more,' he promised as I slicked it on. 'You've got HPV already, haven't you?'

'Get me a drink,' I ordered, slapping the tube back in his hand as we pushed through the double doors. 'I'm going to the toilet to boil my lips.'

Part of me couldn't help but wonder if my terrible, awful, not-at-all-good day was karmic punishment for running away from Adam's house twenty-four hours earlier. After driving all the way to Melton Mowbray and back, I drove around the village three times before heading home to share two fish and a large chips with Abi and Daniel Craig, while trying to convince myself that Adam was a victim of unwanted sexual harassment and the bulge in his crotch was a mechanical, traumatic reaction he had no control over. That could happen, Abi said, she had read it on the internet so it had to be true.

'The internet never lies,' I muttered, hurling myself at the door to the ladies, only to hear the sickening sound of it striking someone on the other side.

'Ow!'

'Oh shit, sorry!'

I covered my mouth with my hands as the door swung back to reveal a girl on her hands and knees, rubbing her forehead with one hand and trying to scoop the contents of her handbag up off the floor with the other.

'Don't worry,' she said, a curtain of long, dark hair covering her face. 'You only hit me in the face.'

'Let me help,' I said, falling to my knees and grabbing a packet of Polos and holding them out like a minty olive branch. 'I'm really sorry.'

'It's OK, I've got a thick head.' She looked up and gave me a dazzling smile. 'I'm sure you didn't do it on purpose.'

Sitting back on my heels, I let the Polos fall to the floor. If I were her, I wouldn't be so certain. It was *her*. The girl I'd seen at Adam's house the day before. I heard my phone singing in my pocket as I sat on the floor, staring up into her beautiful big brown eyes.

'Are *you* all right?' she asked, standing up and leaving me nose to kneecap with her long legs.

'I am all right,' I said in a cold, flat voice. 'Thanks.'

'Right.' She didn't look terribly convinced but she didn't look terribly interested either. 'OK.'

We stared at each other for a moment then silently agreed our awkward interaction was over. The girl pulled the door open and stepped over me, leaving me on the floor, staring at her perfect arse through the frosted glass. She was beautiful. She was beautiful, and she smelled nice, and she had one of those low, husky voices that only worked on incredibly beautiful women. If I sounded like that, everyone would assume I smoked a million a day. But I didn't sound like that and, more to the point, I didn't look like that. I couldn't quite get over how perfect she was close up and in person.

Blinking, I took my phone out of my pocket and saw a text from David.

ADAM IS HERE!!!

Of course Adam was here. Adam was here with *her*. Adam and The World's Most Beautiful Woman were here together, in our local. Before I could respond, another text came through.

It's definitely him this time, FYI.

Dazed, I tapped out a reply from where I belonged, on the freezing cold linoleum floor of a public toilet.

Is he with a really, really gorgeous brunette? I asked.

Three grey dots thrummed across the screen and I waited for David to sugar-coat his response.

She's all right, he replied.

'I have to get out of here,' I told my phone, not quite able to use my fingers to text. 'I cannot walk out there and see them.'

Not because I was upset or embarrassed but because I did not want to deal with it until it was on my terms. I mean, yes, I was embarrassed and flush-my-head-down-the-bog heartbroken, but more importantly, I looked like shit, I felt like shit, a dog had been sick on me three times that afternoon and I'd had to euthanize a very cute rabbit. Enough was enough for one day.

Can I get out the door without him seeing me? I typed, pulling myself together as best I could.

DON'T KNOW, David replied. *THEY'RE PLAYING YE! IN THE BELL!! WTF??? GOT TO LOVE A BIT OF KANYE.*

As much as I loved him, he was useless.

Until Abi got here, I was on my own and I really needed to get out of the toilets before she arrived. What if she saw Adam and Chrissy Teigen's body double before I could warn her and poisoned them with some amazing chemical compound she'd been working on to cure alopecia in rabbits? Maybe if she just poisoned the girl . . .? No, that wasn't fair. I didn't know anything about her; for all I knew she was entirely blameless in this. Totally blameless and incredibly hot and snogging my boyfriend one day and sitting in the pub with him the next and, oh dear god, I was going to have to have her killed.

There was no way I was walking out past the pair of them in one of David's hoodies with no make-up on my face and possibly smelling of Labrador vomit. There had to be another way. Perhaps David could create a distraction or Abi could set the bar on fire. I looked up at the window and felt a breeze on my face. There was always another way.

'This is totally doable,' I announced, making sure my phone and credit card and car keys were safe in the pouch of my jumper, and began my escape. One foot on the pipes, one foot on the sink, both hands through the window and voila! I was out. I was halfway out. Hanging over the pub bins. Hanging out of a window, face first over two massive, filthy dumpsters with nowhere to go but down. Yes, Liv, this was definitely more dignified than walking out of the bar with your head held high, well done you.

'Should I even ask?'

I looked up to see Abi and Cass standing in the middle of the car park. Cassie looked confused, her mouth was moving but no words were coming out, and Abi was simply waiting for a response.

'It looks so easy on telly.' I kicked my legs behind me, swimming in thin air. It felt as though someone had shifted the sink just to mess with me, and the window frame dug into my hip as I tried to find my balance. 'I'm not having a good day. One minute I'm putting Peter Rabbit down and now this.'

'What are you doing exactly?' Cass ran forward in between the bins and placed my hands on her shoulders to take some of my weight off my hip. Ah, sweet, sweet leaning relief.

'Can I tell you the story after you get me down?' I asked, fidgeting around in the window frame and inching forward. I knew I should have stuck with the Pilates classes Adam's mum bought me for Christmas

– my core was not up to this. 'It's a lot further than I thought it was going to be.'

'The safest way to get down would be for you to fall straight into the bin,' Abi reasoned, standing back to review the situation. 'It's the shortest distance and the softest surface.'

'It's also a bloody bin!' I shouted. 'Come and help me. If you take my hands and Cass holds my waist, I think I can get out without too much—'

Before anyone could do anything, I heard the toilet door creak open behind me and I panicked. Pushing all of my weight forwards, I toppled out of the window, crashing down onto Cassie.

'And another way would be for you to fall straight out the window and break Cass's neck,' Abi said, rushing to pull us out from between the bins. 'Are you hurt?'

'I don't think so,' Cass replied from somewhere underneath my arse. 'But I'm not best pleased, either.'

'I'm sorry.' Abi heaved me up to my feet before peeling Cass up off the ground. 'I'm really, really sorry. I heard someone coming.'

'You did.' A face and a hand popped up at the toilet window and waved. It was David. 'What are you doing?'

'I had to get out of there!' I explained, turning from one friend to the next, trying to justify my extreme exit while picking bits of dead lettuce off my jumper. 'Adam's in there, I had to.'

'Oh, Liv . . .' He rested his chin in his hand. 'It shouldn't happen to a vet.'

'I'm lost,' Abi said, while Cass inspected herself for injuries. 'Why did you have to climb out a window because Adam's in the pub? What's happened that we don't know about?'

'He's in there with a girl,' David answered, chin resting on the window frame. 'A really, really, really, really, *really* fit girl.'

After treating him to my best death glare, I looked back at Abi and Cass with a pout.

'What he said.'

'I'm sure it's nothing,' Cass piped up quickly. 'If he was cheating on you, I don't think he'd be squiring her around the village, would he?'

'She's right,' Abi agreed, much to Cass's delight. 'This is Adam, Liv. One minute he's begging you not to break up with him and the next he's snogging girls in the driveway and then bringing super-hot dates to your local? I don't think so. Logically, it doesn't make any sense.'

'Logically, Brad leaving Jen for Angelina Jolie didn't make any sense but it happened,' I replied as David nodded sagely in the window. 'And you'll be pleased to know it's the same girl. The girl in the pub is the girl from the driveway.'

In spite of all my best efforts to remain calm, I felt my bottom lip tremble and my eyes began to sting and burn. It is a scientific fact that it is impossible to stop yourself from crying when you were wearing contact lenses, I was almost certain of it.

'I think I'm going to go home. Sorry, Abi, I can't go back in there,' I said, squeezing my hands together inside the pouch of my jumper, trying not to think about Adam and the Hot Girl in our pub. What if they were at our table? What if Red Roger the barman had seen them? How would I ever look him in the eye again? I was still trying to live down the night I'd decided I was going to start drinking cognac and ended the night falling off a barstool when I was twenty-two.

'You could go in and confront him,' Cass suggested. 'Because I'm certain it's nothing.'

'I wouldn't do that if I were you,' David said fast. 'There's only one thing less attractive than a jealous woman and that's a crazy woman. Unless she's a really smoking hot crazy woman, then it's attractive for a bit.'

'Liv *is* smoking hot,' Cass offered, stroking my shoulder and picking off a cigarette butt. David, Abi and I all gave her the same look. 'What?'

'I just want to go home,' I said, deflating with every breath. 'I will talk to him, but not in public and not in front of her.'

'Then I'm coming with you,' Abi said, whipping her phone out of her pocket and tapping out a text. 'Bill will wait. Or he won't. Whatever.'

'You don't have to,' I assured her, watching as she blew off another potential relationship right in front of me. 'All I want to do is go back to mine to watch crap telly and eat everything in the house. I'm fine, you go and see Bill.'

'And she needs to wash my jumper,' David added. 'There's a brown streak down the back and I don't want to know what it is.'

'I'm coming too,' Cassie said, bending down to pick up a bunch of keys that she held out to me. 'My mum is looking after Gus so I've got the whole evening off. I'll probably pass out by half-past nine, but I swear, every moment I'm awake will be dedicated to you.'

I looked at the keys as I took them from her. Two car keys, two door keys and a gym membership card. Definitely not mine. 'Whose are these?'

'Yours,' she said, straightening her slightly askew ponytail. 'They fell out of your pocket when you landed on me.'

'No.' I shook my head, the keys hot and heavy in my hand. 'They're not mine.' I looked up at my friends, my hand trembling. 'I think they're hers.'

We looked at each other, me horrified, Abi smiling, Cass curious, David downright ecstatic.

'How did you get them?' Abi asked, holding them up and looking for clues. 'Did you pickpocket her?'

'No, we bumped into each other in the toilets,' I explained. 'She was coming out when I was going in, she dropped her bag, I helped her pick up her stuff. I must have put them in my pocket by mistake.'

'Oh, this is too good. Wait there, I'm coming.' David disappeared from the window and I heard the door to the ladies slam shut behind him.

'What do we do with them?' I asked, staring at the keys as though they might come to life at any second. 'We can't burn them. I know we can't burn them.'

'We could drop them back through the toilet window,' Cassie suggested as David tore, red-faced, around the corner. 'She's going to notice they're missing eventually and if that's where she dropped her bag, that's where I'd look first.'

'Or we could do this,' David suggested, snatching them from Abi's fingers and pressing the unlock button on the key fob. In the corner of the car park a familiar little green Mini beeped into life. 'I like the car but I expected better,' he declared. 'It's a bit "look at me, I'm so quirky" isn't it?'

'I like a Mini,' Cass replied as we all began to walk towards the girl's car, before reaching out for my arm and opting for a more outraged expression. 'But obviously, this is a rubbish Mini. Because it belongs to a cow.'

'We don't know she's a cow,' I said, repeating all the arguments I'd had with myself over the last twenty-four hours out loud. 'She might not know Adam has a girlfriend. She might be perfectly nice.'

David shook his head, crouching down to stare through the windows. 'No, I've seen her, she's too fit to be nice.'

'What's that supposed to mean?' Abi demanded. 'Good-looking girls can't be nice?'

'Oh, don't start that with me.' He stared back up at her, a picture of exasperation in rainbow-striped scrubs. He looked like a slightly annoyed, out of work clown. 'You know exactly what I mean. Go in and have a look. If she was on *The Bachelor*, she'd be the first one to say "I'm here to win, not make friends" and then she'd be the first to give him a blow job when she thought no one was looking.'

'That's nice,' Abi replied, kicking one of the car's tyres. 'I'm taking back your "I Am a Feminist" T-shirt.'

'There's something on the back seat.' Cass pressed her hands against the back passenger window and looked inside. 'I can't read what it says though.'

David clicked the key fob again and we all jumped back as the car beeped and flashed its lights. With his mouth open in delight, he gave a magician's assistant flourish and opened the car door.

'He didn't.' I covered my eyes with my hands. 'Tell me he didn't.'

'He didn't,' Cass said, her words bubbling over with glee. 'But he did.'

'She obviously works out.' Abi made it sound like an accusation rather than a statement as she flipped the front seats and clambered into the back. 'A lot, from the smell of this gym bag. It's rancid.'

'You can't break into someone's car!' I stepped backwards out of the car park and into the neighbouring field, tripping over the concrete boundary. 'Put that back.'

'We're not breaking in,' Cass replied as she fished around in the glove box before triumphantly holding up a passport. Her face was flushed with excitement, her ponytail all askew. 'We've got keys. Jane Campbell! Her name's Jane Campbell!'

Jane. Hmm. How dare someone that fit have such an innocuous-sounding name?

David slipped the keys into the car and the stereo boomed into life. 'Eurgh, Mumford,' he said, switching it off as quickly as he could. 'Who likes them any more?'

'Adam,' I replied. 'Loves them.'

'I'm really starting to think you're better off out of this,' he replied as he checked himself in her rear-view mirror. 'You never told me he had such terrible taste in music.'

'We're all going to hell,' I said, sitting down in the wet grass and watching my friends root through the car like truffle pigs. 'Actually, prison first and then hell.'

'You'd be good in prison.' He lowered the driver's window and waved. 'You'd be the dodgy prison surgeon, fixing up all the bitches that got cut up in fights but didn't want to go and see the proper doctor in case they got in trouble.'

'She's been to a lot of places,' Cass said, leafing through the passport with bright eyes. 'This is expired, though. I wonder why she keeps it in the car?'

'Adam keeps his old passport in his bedside table,' I said slowly. 'To remind him of when he went travelling.'

'Oh, yeah,' she nodded, still turning the pages. 'Cambodia, Vietnam, Myanmar. Didn't Adam go there, Liv?'

'Yes, he's been to all those places,' I said weakly. Fantastic. In three days, he'd managed to find his perfect woman. Gorgeous, tall, owned a bar, liked the same music and loved to travel. In the same amount of time I had eaten a packet of chocolate Hobnobs for dinner and only showered twice.

'We should go,' Abi said, looking over at me as I sank into the mud like a miserable blonde hippo. 'Let's go home.'

I stared back at the pub, wondering what they were doing in there. Did he have his hand on her knee? Was she resting her head on his shoulder? That was my shoulder, my hand,

'Guys,' Abi used her sternest boss voice and we all looked up at once. 'We should go.'

'It could still be nothing,' Cass said, ever the optimist. 'It really could be a meeting.'

'I'm going to call him.' I patted myself down for my phone and brought up his number. 'I'm going to call him and ask what he's doing. He'll say he's in a meeting and it'll be fine. Won't it?'

'Yes,' David said, clamping a hand over Abi's mouth while Cass nodded quickly. 'Call him.'

With an audience in front of me, it was impossible to run away, drive two hundred miles and break another iPod. Holding my breath, I pressed the call button and waited. And waited. And waited. Even Cass's keen smile began to flag as I put Adam's answerphone message on speaker. David looked up at the sky as it began to rain again.

'Call him again,' Abi ordered. 'If he's in a meeting he might not answer on the first ring but if he doesn't answer on the second ring, he's officially on my list.'

Wiping drizzle off the screen with my sleeve, I dialled one more time, still on speakerphone.

'Hello?'

He answered almost immediately.

'Is everything OK?' he asked when I didn't reply.

'Yes.' It was so strange not knowing what to say to him. 'I was just wondering what you were doing?'

'Uh, nothing.' Cue far too long of a pause. 'Why?'

'No reason,' I choked. 'Are you at home?'

'Why?' he asked, either nervous or hopeful, I couldn't decide. 'Where are you?'

'Why, why, why?' Abi muttered inside the car. 'Arsehole.'

'I was going to go and see Cass,' I lied, 'but she's not home. I thought they might be with you.'

'No,' he said, clearing his throat. 'No. Actually, I am in the middle of something right now. Can I call you back later?'

'Yeah, OK,' I said, unable to turn away from my friends and keep some dignity intact. 'Talk to you later.'

He hung up before I could. Without a word, I shrugged at my friends, all still hiding inside the Mini, and tucked my phone back into my pocket. Sitting on the floor with a wet-through bum and a broken heart, I didn't know quite what to say.

'He'll be in the middle of my fist in a minute,' Abi said, clambering out of the car and dropping onto the wet ground beside me. 'Don't you dare get upset.'

'This is exactly how I felt when I heard Jay Z cheated on Beyoncé,' I heard Cass whisper to David. 'I can't believe it.'

'What do we do with the keys?' he asked, pulling them out of the ignition and following her out of the car. 'Are we chucking them back in the lavs?'

'We're chucking them somewhere,' Cass replied with wild eyes, grabbing the keys out of his hand, running into the field and hurling them as far as she could into the brambles by the side of the road. She turned back to look at us with her arms held aloft in triumph.

'She didn't.' Abi stared at our friend who was whooping at the top of her voice. 'She did not just do that.'

'She did,' David replied, running at Cass and lifting her up onto his shoulders. 'She's a hero.'

From my spot on the floor, I looked up at Abi with saucer eyes.

'Did that really just happen?'

'This is what happens to people when they have a baby,' she said, nodding. We watched as David ran around in circles with Cass still up on his shoulders, singing the theme from *Rocky*. 'Give them an evening off and they go completely insane.'

'In the best way,' I added, beginning to smile. 'I don't think I've ever been so proud of her.'

'Me either,' Abi said, helping me up to my feet. 'Come on, there's a new episode of *Real Housewives* on tonight. Want to take a bet on who's had the most surgery since last season?'

'Always,' I replied as my phone vibrated in my pouch. I pulled it out, hoping to see Adam's name. Instead, I found a Tinder notification. I had a new message. It was from the handsome hipster I'd matched with the day before. 'Go and get Bonnie and Clyde, I'll catch up.'

Walking slowly across the field as my friends ran ahead, I opened the message, a warm, prickly feeling spreading across my chest.

Hi, it read. *How's your week going?*

It was simple, polite and weirdly familiar from a

complete stranger. But then what else was he supposed to say, *Hello woman I don't know but liked the look of based on one photo from the internet.* At least he hadn't opened the conversation with a picture of his knob. I'd suffered through more than enough second-hand dick pics Abi had been treated to through Tinder. This was definitely better.

'*Not too bad,*' I whispered as I typed the words. It was a blatant lie but he was a picture on a phone, I wasn't ever going to meet him. Like David said, it was nothing but an ego boost and an ego boost was sorely needed. '*How about you?*'

Before he could reply, I put my phone away and raced across the muddy field to catch up with my friends. Running away from the pub before we got caught for something we really shouldn't have been doing. The more things changed, the more they stayed the same.

18

'I can't find them in the ladies and the bloke behind the bar says they haven't been handed in.' Jane dug behind the cushions of our corner again and I winced at the thought of what she might find. 'I must have dropped them when that girl hit me with the door in the toilets but I can't work out where they've gone to. They can't have just vanished?'

'And you don't have a spare set?' I asked, looking around the floor and tapping a probing foot underneath the seat.

'Not with me,' she said, growling in frustration. 'I've got my key code but my spares are at Jim's flat. It's going to cost me a fortune if I have to call a locksmith. I bet it would be cheaper to get the train home and come back up for the car.'

'Then leave it,' I suggested. She turned her eyes on to me without moving her head. 'I'll tell the landlady what happened and I'm sure they won't mind you leaving the car here for a bit.'

'Oh man, that would be amazing.' Jane pulled her

hand out of the cushions and rubbed them hard on her thighs. 'Are you sure you don't mind? I'll be gone first thing in the morning, I promise.'

In the morning? She couldn't get the train back this evening? I looked up at the clock and saw that it was after nine o'clock. We'd been sitting there since three and I hadn't even realized. It was hours since Liv had called and I'd promised myself I would call her back when I got home. Where had the evening gone?

'You'd be my lifesaver if I could crash on your settee,' she said, all hopeful eyes and shiny hair.

I felt myself gripping my knees and staring at my empty pint pot. Why did this feel like the beginning of a wonderful and terrible porno? I was only doing the decent thing. I couldn't expect her to piss away hundreds of pounds on a taxi or a late-night train when I had a perfectly good spare room, could I? Well, one spare room and one very special room, to be truthful. If it were my sister, I'd want to know she had a safe bed for the evening. Besides, even though I didn't feel drunk, I was certain we were both over the limit anyway. She really shouldn't have been driving. It was entirely innocent. Gentlemanly, in fact.

'*Mi casa es su casa*,' I said, checking my pockets for my own keys. This really didn't feel like a great moment to have to ask Liv for my spares. 'And you can even stay in the spare room.'

'I don't want to be any trouble,' she said, beaming. I raised a hand to Liv's schoolfriend, still alone at the bar, but he did not return my friendly gesture. In fact, the look on his face was altogether more disapproving. Wanker. 'This is so good of you, I really appreciate it.'

Really, when you thought about it, I was the hero in this situation.

'Thanks, Adam.' Jane leaned across the bench and curled her arms around my shoulders in a brief hug, confirming my suspicions. I *was* a hero. The man at the bar and the red-bearded bartender exchanged a look and I pulled Jane away quickly. What did they know? 'You're my hero.'

Superman, Batman, Adam Floyd. The people had spoken.

'I'm so excited to see beyond the kitchen.' Jane hovered at my shoulder as I unlocked the front door fifteen minutes later. 'Did you design all your furniture?'

'Not quite,' I replied, wiping my muddy shoes on the mat and watching as she did the same. She sat down on the bottom stair and unzipped her boots, leaving them next to the door. Her little white socks clashed with the rest of her sleek outfit but there was something insanely cute about it. 'Bits and pieces, but a lot of my stuff I inherited with the house.'

'Woah.' She followed me into the living room and stopped short in the doorway. 'Were your grandparents the coolest grandparents ever, or what?'

'My granddad built a lot of it.' I flicked the light switch to reveal my mid-century modern living room in all its grandeur. 'The settee is new but he made the TV cabinet, the side tables, that coffee table. The other cabinet they bought, just after they got married.'

'I love it.' She padded across the hardwood floors in her little white socks and ran her hand along the wood. 'I want one just like it for the bar. Could you make one?'

'I've never tried,' I admitted, stretching one arm above my head and gripping the doorframe before slapping my arms back down by my sides. I wasn't trying to impress her. 'But yeah, in theory. I'm not sure it would go with your décor though.'

'Well, I haven't run this past Jim yet, but I've had an idea brewing for a while and I think I've just cracked it.' She looked back at me with a huge smile. 'We've actually got the upstairs of the bar as well and I was thinking we could open a cool little speakeasy up there and do it all out in sixties stuff. So it's a summer camp downstairs and then upstairs looks like a really cool 1960s living room, only it's a bar. And, basically, I'd need to steal all your furniture.'

'I think that's a brilliant idea,' I agreed, my brain racing ahead with ideas. 'You could do some really nice bespoke pieces and then pick the rest up second-hand.'

'I was thinking we'd do a completely different drinks menu upstairs.' Jane's eyes were bright with excitement and it was hard not to get swept along. 'Proper sixties cocktails like Manhattans and Old-Fashioneds. I've even found a place where we could get original period barware. I think it would be really fun.'

'And really popular,' I agreed, crossing the living room to open the cabinet. 'This was my granddad's whisky decanter. How cool is this?'

'So cool,' she started to put her hand inside and then stopped. 'Is it OK if I touch it?'

I looked away as she burst out laughing, snatching her hand back as I closed the cabinet. Her laughter sputtered out into an awkward sigh as we stood there, inches apart, all alone in my living room at night. There it was again. Not just my semi, but the inescapable something that sparked between us, the something that made me want to rip those socks off with my teeth.

'I should sort out the spare bed,' I said in a hoarse

voice, much closer to a whisper than I'd intended. 'I need an early night, busy day tomorrow.'

'Yeah, yeah,' she replied readily, pressing her hands underneath her armpits. 'I'll need to get up early to get the train anyway.'

'I'll make the bed, won't take a minute.'

Leaving Jane, the decanter, and my confusing feelings behind, I jogged upstairs, opened the spare bedroom door and looked inside. It was so much worse than I remembered. As soon as I'd got home from Mum and Dad's I had cleaned the living room, scrubbed the kitchen and attacked the downstairs toilet, just in case, but I hadn't done a thing to the upstairs. Classic avoidance tactic. Liv told me she never used to shave her legs before a first date but I couldn't say that would have put me off. The state of this place, however, would turn anyone away. Once upon a time it was a delightful spare room, all fluffy pillows and unnecessary cushions, but now it was nothing short of a total boner killer. Dirty clothes in piles by the door, a half-empty bottle of whiskey, several completely empty beer bottles and two pizza boxes. This was not a picture of my finest hour.

'Shit, Adam. Have you been Air BnBing to *Stig of the Dump*?'

I turned around to see Jane at the top of the stairs.

'No. I've been sleeping in here recently,' I said slowly, not sure exactly what I was going to tell her. Or exactly why I had opened my mouth in the first place. 'Sorry.'

'You don't have to apologize for where you sleep in your own house,' she replied as I scooped my mess into the wash bin before she could get a better look. 'Is this something to do with your girlfriend? Does she live here too?'

'No, no she doesn't.' I hadn't mentioned having a girlfriend since that first time but she had remembered. I didn't know if I was happy about it or not. 'We don't live together. I need to get clean sheets.'

'I'll strip these, you get the fresh ones.' Jane placed her hands on my hips and gently pushed me out the way, grabbing a pillow and shaking it out of its case. 'And then we can talk. If you want to.'

Obediently, I went to the airing cupboard and pulled out a stack of sheets, giving them a cursory sniff just in case. In the bedroom, Jane was sitting on the bare mattress, her leather jacket and handbag on the chest of drawers, her bare feet buried into the plush cream carpet.

'So, you said the two of you were on a break,' she said, holding out her hands for a clean pillowcase. 'What does that mean exactly?'

It was a strange thing. I wanted to tell her because I felt so comfortable with her but because I felt so comfortable, I didn't want to say a word. I wanted to keep Liv in the Liv box and Jane in the Jane box where never the twain should meet but there was something about the look on her face and all the pints I'd sunk at the Bell that made it impossible to keep my mouth shut.

'We are on a break,' I started, shaking out the fitted sheet. 'But I don't know what that means in the slightest. It's my fault, I started it, but now she's really mad at me and I don't know what's going on.'

'You started it?' Jane asked, standing up so I could snap the sheet over the top of the mattress. 'You broke up with her?'

'I didn't want to break up with her, I wanted a break,' I replied. Why was that so hard for people to understand?

'To get my head together. But I didn't really. I don't know what I wanted. And last time I saw her she said she wanted to take a break too and now I don't know what to do.'

'Right. I think this should be easy, Adam. Do you want to break up with her?' She sat down on the mattress and placed two freshly plumped pillows at the top of the bed. 'Or do you want to fix it?'

Cross-legged on the floor, nursing the duvet cover in my lap, I stared at my fingernails. They needed cutting.

'I don't know,' I confessed. 'I don't know what she wants.'

'That's not what I asked,' Jane said in a low, soft voice. She sat on the edge of the bed and looked down at me. All I had to do was kiss her, push her backwards against those pillows, and it would be happening. Did she want me to? Could I? Should I? I used to be so good at reading these situations.

It would be so easy.

'What do you want, Adam?'

I couldn't. I shouldn't.

'To get some sleep,' I stood up and dropped the duvet cover on the spare bed. 'Night. See you in the morning.'

'Goodnight, then,' she said, pulling her feet up onto the bed underneath her, her long dark hair falling around her face. Was I imagining it or did she look disappointed? 'Sleep tight.'

Closing the back bedroom door on my guest, I stood still in the cool dark of the landing, listening to the mattress creak as she moved around. What would she sleep in? Should I go back and offer her something? No. No good could come of going back in there. Well, some good, but that would last for about seven seconds, the state I was in, and what would follow was a world of hurt. Instead, I took four steps over towards my bedroom door and rested my hand on the brass handle.

I hadn't slept in my own bed since we got back from Mexico. The first night I'd collapsed on the settee; the second, I'd tried, but as soon as I got into bed, all I could smell was Liv's perfume. Ever since I'd avoided it after the sun went down. The bed was neatly made inside and an almost-full moon shone through the window, reflecting on the spare pair of glasses Liv kept on my bedside table. Her glasses, her moisturizer, her little collection of hair ties. There was even a dried up contact lens that hadn't made it into the bin the last time she stayed over. I couldn't bring myself to throw it away.

I unfastened my belt and shuffled out of my jeans with a heavy yawn, inching across the room to close the curtains. One of the neighbours was walking their dog and waved when he saw me in the window. I waved back, looked down at my boxer shorts and whipped the curtains shut. Unfastening the top three buttons of my shirt, I pulled it up over my head and tossed it into the corner on top of my jeans, yanked off my socks and clambered over the end of the bed. It still smelled of Liv. Her pillow smelled like coconut while the sheets sang with sweet lemons and something herbal, the scent of that big blue tube of body lotion she loved. I pulled the sheets down and crawled inside, cocooning my body and burying my hands under the pillows until I found what I was looking for. It was such a knackered old thing, a baby blue T-shirt with the picture of a wombat on the front. For a moment I clutched it to my chest and inhaled, but instead of being comforting, the whole thing felt incredibly creepy.

I held up the shirt in the dim twilight of the room. I loved the way it looked on Liv, sloppy and cute but cut short enough so I could see her knickers. She had a brilliant backside, probably even better than Jane's, probably the best one ever, but she never believed me when I told her. I felt around for the neck hole in the shirt and stuck my head inside. It was really small. It was really, really small. Forcing my hands through the sleeves, I lay in bed, Liv's wombat shirt stretched tight across my chest, sleeves cutting off the circulation in my arms and tried to sleep.

'Oh, fuck it.'

With a commando roll, I leapt out of bed and crawled over to the pile of clothes in the corner to dig my phone out from the pocket of my jeans. Enough was enough, this break was bollocks and whatever was wrong with her didn't matter, we'd sort it out. We'd sort everything out. With her T-shirt riding up around my belly button and my knees creaking against the wooden floors, I dialled her number and waited for it to connect. It rang three times and then I heard a click, as though it had connected, but there was no sound on the other end.

'Liv?' I said, my voice hesitant, my belly freezing cold. We should have carpeted my room as well, stupid good-looking oak floorboards. 'It's me.'

I heard breathing and shuffling and a deep breath.

'Liv? I'm sorry I couldn't talk earlier, but I'm here now. Are you there?'

More shuffling, and then, 'Don't call again,' she said before ending the call.

I held the phone an arm's length from my face and stared at the picture peeping out behind all my applications. Me and Liv at Chris and Cassie's wedding, arms around each other, nose to nose, laughing so hard I remembered wiping away tears, and even though I couldn't remember what we were laughing about, it didn't matter. Lying on my bedroom floor at the foot of my bed in Liv's shirt and my second-best pair of boxers, I rolled over onto my side and cried.

And the first prize for the greatest twazzock of them all goes to . . . Adam Floyd.

I climbed into bed, closed my eyes and lay back against the pillows.

'Did that really just happen?' I asked.

'Which part?' Abi asked. 'Adam and the girl, you falling out of a window, us breaking into a car or Cass losing her mind and chucking the keys into a briar patch? At least it was nice to see the old Cassie for once.' Abi was full of admiration. 'Do you think she hit her head when you fell on top of her?'

'That or her common sense fell out at the same time as the baby,' I suggested. Abi got up to rifle through the top drawer of my dressing table, produce a packet of face wipes and set about removing her eyeliner. 'She's been so weird lately.'

'She hasn't been weird, she's been completely insane,' she replied, black streaks running up and down her cheeks. 'She is not my favourite example of motherhood. We never see her and then, the first time in forever that she's had more than two hours to spend with us, she goes the full 2007 Britney on the situation.'

I pouted, kicking my legs behind me and stared at the floor.

'What?' Abi said. 'What do you want to tell me but think you shouldn't?'

Such were the perils of knowing someone for twenty years.

'So, don't go mental but I suggested she come and work with me at the surgery,' I started, rolling upright and protecting myself with a pillow. 'We need to get someone in a couple of days a week now Dad's retiring.'

'That's actually a brilliant idea,' she replied, mid-wipe. 'Why didn't I think of that?'

'Because you're not allowed to think of all the brilliant ideas,' I said. 'Anyway, she turned me down. Because she's going to be a stay-at-home mum.'

Abi didn't say anything but instead of removing her make-up, she was suddenly removing several layers of skin.

'I think you're scrubbing too hard,' I said, gesturing at her face. 'You've gone a bit red.'

'Good for her,' Abi said, her voice tight. She tucked her short brown bob behind her ears and threw the used face wipe in the bin. 'That's nice.'

Peeping out from behind my pillow, I raised an eyebrow.

'Really?'

'I couldn't do it,' she replied. 'But whatever, she's got to do what makes her happy. We were always going to drift apart eventually anyway.'

'We won't drift apart,' I argued. 'She literally lives closer to us now than she ever has. Apart from when we were all in the same flat, obviously.'

Abi had the same look on her face she had when she assured me her dog was going to die. 'It's already happening, Liv,' she said. 'How often do we see her? And when we do, what do we talk about? I know she's got a baby and a husband and those things are really important and I don't dispute it, but I can't remember the last time we had a conversation that wasn't about you or the baby. I couldn't even tell you the last time I heard from her without me starting the conversation.'

'That'll change when Ming the Merciless is older,' I said, hoping it was true. 'She's caught up now but she's still Cass.'

'She'll be pregnant again by Christmas,' Abi declared. 'And I don't want you to think I'm saying this to be a massive bitch, but if you and Adam don't work it out, you'll see what I mean. How often do you two go out with the two of them? Or go over for dinner? If you break up and she's still married to his brother, how often do you think you're going to see her? As often as I do now, which is to say, never.'

Things had been different ever since Cassie got together with Chris but the thought I'd lose her altogether if I broke up with Adam hadn't even occurred to me. She was my Cass before she was Chris's – surely he wouldn't get my best friend in a break-up.

'People pick sides, Liv.' Abi walked around the bed and into the tiny bathroom. The deafening extractor fan whirred into life as she turned on the light. 'They say they won't but they always do. You don't like telling her stuff now in case it gets back to Chris – imagine what it'll be like if you and Adam aren't together any more. She'll know everything about his life and he'll know everything about yours. How are you supposed to get over him if he's always around, one friend removed?'

'But we haven't broken up,' I said, hugging the pillow to me. 'Technically.'

'And I'm sure you won't,' she said with a half-hearted attempt at optimism as she closed the bathroom door. 'Everything will be OK in the end.'

Abi was the most cynical woman in the world when it came to relationships; mine, hers, Jennifer Aniston's – it didn't matter, she never believed things were going to end well. Between her parents' multiple divorces and suffering more shitty boyfriends than Taylor Swift, I didn't exactly blame her for throwing out the fairy tale but it would have been nice if she could have lied a little bit more convincingly.

'What is this?' she asked, picking up my borrowed copy of *Keeping the Love You Find* from the bedside table.

'Cass lent it me,' I replied, cringing. 'It's actually not the worst one.'

'I should burn it and help you both.' She climbed across the bed and hopped under the covers. The shortest possible route, of course. 'Still nothing?'

'Nope.' I shook my head and clobbered her around the head with a pillow. 'And honestly, I don't want to think about it right now.'

In my head, there were two ways this could go. The first involved Adam showing up at my door with an engagement ring, confessing to cold feet and a panic fling that never went further than a kiss, begging for my forgiveness which I gave unconditionally and then silently resented for the rest of my days. The second was a long drawn out parade of misery, where he casually swanned around the village with assorted beautiful women while I messaged boys on the internet with no intention of ever meeting up with them and our friends continued to play he said, she said, until our relationship withered away slowly and I died alone.

For some reason, my pride was still erring towards the second option.

'I wouldn't talk to him if he did call,' I said loudly. The louder you were, the more certain you sounded. It was the same technique my granddad had always used to make himself understood when he travelled abroad. 'Fuck him, Abi. He lied to my face. Well, my ear. You know what I mean. We said we wouldn't see other people, so yeah. Fuck him.'

Abi looked worried, but she looked convinced as I got up to clean my teeth, vibrating with righteous anger.

One of the ceiling spotlights was out, lending the bathroom a more flattering light than usual but I was grateful, the overactive extractor fan, less so. I turned to the side and looked in the mirror, electric toothbrush in one hand, fist full of pyjama top in the other. I wasn't in terrible shape – I wasn't in Victoria's Secret swimsuit catalogue condition either – but there wasn't anything going on underneath my polka-dot flannel that would send a man running for the hills. I hadn't been blessed with a massive rack like Abi, but I did have a semi-decent behind that could pass for the kind of arse that did a hundred squats every morning when it was squashed into a pair of black opaque tights.

And then there was my face. Big eyes, small nose, perfectly adequate mouth and nothing skin-wise that couldn't be made decent with a bit of make-up and the right filter. And that was just the wrapping. I was a catch! Probably. I had a job, I liked a laugh. Admittedly I didn't give two shits about football or beer and I couldn't watch a porno without doubling over in hysterics but I was easy-going and kind and really good at the pub quiz. Who wouldn't want a go on that?

There was, of course, one very obvious answer to that question, I thought, giving myself a filthy look and spitting my toothpaste into the sink. Adam Floyd. What did tall, dark and car key-less have that I didn't? Other than six extra inches of leg, Kylie Jenner lips and my boyfriend? *She* didn't know his MOT was due at the end of the month, *she* wouldn't get the special fabric softener because the regular kind brought him out in a rash, and *she* certainly wouldn't know that singing the theme tune to *ThunderCats* but changing the words to 'Thunderpants' was, as far as Adam was concerned, the funniest thing in the world. That stuff mattered, those were the things that made a relationship.

But what happened when those things became predictable and dull, and instead of your lovely girlfriend with her nice blonde hair and reliable old denim jacket, you started to crave a sexy brunette in black leather? I bet she had at least one tattoo and knew all the words to Nirvana songs and only drank black coffee and had never, ever, spent a Tuesday evening googling 'what happened to the cast of *Saved by the Bell*?' I looked into my own eyes and tried to pinpoint the exact moment things had changed. Was there ever such a thing for anyone? One of Cass's books said falling in love was like falling asleep, that it happened slowly at first and then all at once. Was falling out of love the same? Had he really fallen out of love with me and I hadn't noticed?

'No good can come of these questions,' I told myself, wishing I was getting into bed with Adam instead of Abi and wondering if I would ever get into bed with Adam ever again. With half a bottle of wine sloshing around inside my stomach, I slipped my toothbrush back on its charger and turned out the deafening fan and the buzzing bathroom light.

'Are you reading my messages again?' I asked, walking in on Abi holding my phone in her hand. 'Because if you are, you should know I use "wanker" as a term of endearment. Like the kids.'

'Just checking the time.' She popped my phone back on the nightstand, face down, and pulled down the duvet, inviting me into my own bed. 'How is it midnight already?'

'It's a mystery,' I replied. My head found the pillow right away and my eyes closed, heavy and dry. 'Goodnight, slagchops.'

'Love you too,' she whispered, turning her back towards me and burrowing down under the covers while I lay awake, staring at the ceiling.

Abi was already snoring when the quiet click of Daniel Craig's claws pattered around the room. They halted for a quiet moment before a soft grunt sounded by my feet, turned a couple of times, then climbed up my legs and settled on my chest as I stared up at the ceiling. DC was a small cat and couldn't have weighed more than six pounds soaking wet, so I knew the heavy, cold weight that pressed down on my heart was nothing to do with him. I rubbed him behind the ears, picked up my phone and pulled the sheets over my head. Without disturbing Abi or the cat, I opened my photos and went straight to our folder. Two hundred and forty-seven photos of Adam, of the two of us, of DC. Hundreds of photos of our little family that seemed to be all I had left. I flicked through for a minute, torturing myself with happy smiles and awkward kissing selfies before turning it off and sliding it under the bed. With the after-glare of the screen blinding me against the low light in my bedroom, I willed sleep to come and take me away as warm tears spilled out to soak my pillow.

This was the worst part, I reminded myself, everyone went through this bit sooner or later – but even knowing that really didn't seem to help.

19

When I woke up Thursday morning, Jane had already gone. She left a note on the kitchen table to say thanks and that she'd pick the car up later. My first reaction was to be relieved, mostly because I'd woken up, still wearing Liv's wombat shirt and didn't have the energy to take it off when I went downstairs to make a cup of tea. But as the kettle boiled almost instantly and I chucked a teabag in a cleanish mug, I realized I was also disappointed.

'It's not fair,' I said out loud to the kitchen.

All right, yes, I should have talked to Liv when she called me in the pub. Why was everything suddenly so confusing? And why was I talking to myself? I missed Daniel Craig, he always understood. I wondered how he was getting on, stuck on his own at home with Liv. I bet he missed me too, that cat needed a man around the house.

Three months ago, everything had been certain. I was going to propose to Liv, she and Daniel were going to move in and we were going to live happily ever after. I'd even decorated his bedroom in secret but now I was a thirty-four-year-old man with a fish-themed back bedroom with an in-built kitty water fountain. It seemed like a good idea at the time, now it just made me look like I had a very extreme fetish. The giant litter tray did not help.

Now I didn't have a clue what was going on. Yes, I'd had a momentary freak out but that didn't mean Liv had to run off and have an existential crisis of her own and make everything worse. If anything happened with Jane and me, quite frankly, it would be her own fault. I brewed my tea, shook out the last dregs of my cornflakes and sat down at the kitchen table, chomping with great purpose. Women had to make everything so complicated. I remembered the first time I used Liv's bathroom and spent fifteen minutes reading the back of every product in her shower and then smelling them all. I had had one bottle of shower gel and one bottle of shampoo – she must have had twenty things in there. Even having a shower had to be turned into a production. Admittedly, I had added a face scrub and two different moisturizers to my bathroom but that was her influence as well.

'Women can't leave things alone,' I announced to the empty room, imagining Daniel Craig agreeing with me while patiently awaiting the leftover milk from my cereal bowl.

And Jane . . . I could not work her out. She seemed interested, she was definitely giving me signs, I was sure of it. Not that it mattered; I wanted to work things out with Liv. But Jane was so hot. I'd gone out with some really fit girls. Ana, the Colombian girl I'd travelled with in South America, had been improbably beautiful and Jen, my uni girlfriend, was a stunning redhead and then there was Liv, hardly someone you'd kick out of bed for eating biscuits. Still, there was something about Jane that I couldn't put my finger on. She put me on edge, but in a good way. She was the present under the tree on Christmas Eve. You could see it, you were almost certain what was inside but you were still so excited about opening it the next morning, just in case it was nothing like how you imagined. And it wasn't just that she was fit, there was a connection. Before Liv that was something I told myself to explain away the fact that I wanted to get someone into bed and never get out again but with Jane, there really was something there. We had so much in common, travelling, changing careers, annoying older brothers. And we were both tall. That had to count for something.

The phone rang while I was washing out what had been my last clean cereal bowl and I saw Tom's name appear on the screen.

'All right,' I answered after wiping off my fingertips on the back of my shorts. 'How are you?'

'Good, mate, good,' he replied. 'I'm in the car, on my way up to a conference in Norwich. Thought I'd check in.'

'There are so many days when I regret dropping out of law school,' I mused, opening the back door and getting a face full of the clean, crisp September morning. Setting the phone to speaker, I peeled off Liv's T-shirt, looked at it for a moment and then threw it in the washing machine, replacing it with my red hoodie that hung over the back of a kitchen chair. 'Today is not one of them.'

'It's a glamorous business,' he said with a laugh. 'What's going on in your neck of the woods?'

'Not much.' I crunched the first fallen leaves underfoot on my way up the garden to the workshop.

Tom had a beautiful house in London but his back garden amounted to a twelve by twelve square of concrete behind the kitchen, shared by a disposable barbecue, two chairs, a table and an assortment of cats, rats and god knows what else. One thing I loved about living out in the country was the space, the chance to breathe. My grandparents hadn't done much with the house or the garden in their last few years but the sheer scope of it had given me so much to play with. I had a greenhouse, a patio, a little wild flower garden at the very back (because try as I might, I couldn't keep anything alive on purpose) and a huge lush green lawn that just begged you to get outside whenever the sun was shining. While part of me still missed city life, the garden alone was a decent trade.

'The wood for the bar's arriving in ten minutes so I'm starting on the build this morning.'

'And what does that entail exactly?'

'They want it to have an older look, so I'll sand it down a bit, stain it, age it, you know. You've got to rough it up a bit but you want to keep the top smooth for drinks and everything.'

'You realize the only tools I've got in my house are a hand drill and one of those sets of screwdrivers you get in a Christmas cracker, don't you?'

'You're a failure as a man,' I told him. 'There's no hope for you.'

'I already know that, Ad, I don't need you to tell me. I came home the other night and Mads was changing the plug on the toaster. I didn't have a fucking clue what she was doing, I'd have bought a new toaster.'

'Are you coming to the christening on Sunday?' I asked. 'Chris said Maddie had been helping out.'

'Maddie has not been "helping out",' Tom corrected. 'Maddie has been working round the clock to find available Cirque du Soleil performers to perform a flash-mob-style performance to *Circus* by Britney Spears.'

'I have been led to believe there is a circus theme,' I replied gravely. 'My brother is a monster.'

'I'd like to disagree but my girlfriend was practically in tears all night last night because the elephant he wanted has got a cold and she was too afraid to tell him. She's a professional events organizer, Adam, the woman deals with psychotic brides day in and day out – and she's scared of your brother.'

'I refer you to my last sentence,' I replied. 'He's a monster.'

'The last christening I went to didn't even have drinks, it was just a cup of tea and a Fondant Fancy,' Tom replied. 'Who has an elephant? Do you know he wanted lions? He actually wanted her to find lions. For his child's christening.'

I wanted to be surprised but I wasn't. I could still remember the look on his face when I told him I couldn't get Bradley Cooper to show up to his Las Vegas stag do and I was fairly certain he still hadn't forgiven me, Bradley, or the state of Nevada.

'So, things are sorted out with Liv?' Tom's voice was far too cheerful for this early in the morning. 'Or are you still in the doghouse?'

'Doghouse, hundred per cent,' I said, settling down at my bench. 'In fact, I'm not even allowed in the doghouse. I can see it, but I'm somewhere down the bottom of the garden, piss wet through in the mud.'

'Did you apologize?'

'Yes.'

'Did you say it like you meant it?'

'I did mean it.'

'At any point, did she say "I'm not going to tell you what's wrong"?' he asked. 'Because that's a sure sign you're in deep shit.'

'She told me she wanted a break,' I replied. 'And that was after I'd had the "it's not you, it's me" speech.' I left out the phone call the night before, on the grounds of it being altogether too depressing.

Tom made a noise I usually associated with car mechanics and on-call electricians.

'I don't like the sound of that. Sorry, mate.'

'Yeah, well.' I raked my hand through my hair, catching on the tangles I had not brushed out. I was out of Liv's conditioner and I couldn't bring myself to buy more. Not just because it was embarrassing, but because the smell of her hair wafting around my face all day was too much.

'It'll work itself out, won't it?'

'It will if you want it to,' he replied. 'You could always try talking to her again. It can't hurt, can it?'

'I suppose not.'

Tom made the noise again.

I had absolutely zero intention of trying to speak to Liv again after that phone call. She'd come round when she'd calmed down. After all, she was the one who had asked for time and space, I was only giving her what she wanted.

'I hate making rash, sweeping statements but women don't always say exactly what they mean,' he said, a crackly voice down a crackly line. 'Or at least, they're not as black and white in what they say. Is there any chance she's hoping you're on your way round with a massive diamond ring to declare your intentions?'

'Normally, I'd say no,' I replied. She certainly didn't sound like she was waiting for a ring on the phone. 'But I'm at a complete loss right now. She's not acting like herself at all.'

'Then you've got to take her at her word,' Tom said. 'And hope for the best.'

Whatever that meant.

'I'd better get off,' I replied, keen to end this conversation and get started on the far more straightforward sanding portion of my day. That was a part that made sense. 'Busy day – got to clear some space for a wood delivery.'

'Yeah, OK,' he said with a slight sigh, clearly not done with the conversation. 'I'll see you Sunday, mate.'

'See you Sunday,' I agreed, ending the call quickly and stretching my arms high above my head until I heard my shoulders click.

It was the little things that felt wrong. Running out of the conditioner she always bought, not taking her mug out of the cupboard even when all the others were dirty. All week I'd managed to convince myself things were all right but it was getting harder by the second. Liv not being around was like trying to watch your favourite TV show after the main actor leaves: even though it's the same, you know something isn't right and the whole thing isn't nearly as good. That said, if someone had asked me a week ago what my life would look like without Liv in it, I would have described a *Mad Max*-esque, post-apocalyptic wasteland with less Charlize Theron and more electric guitar. But now that had all changed. Life without Liv was strange but not unbearable, just sad. And, even though I still felt guilty even considering it, there was a sliver of a chance that life without Liv could also be known as life with Jane.

Life with Jane. I closed my eyes and pondered the possibilities. Going out with someone in London when I was up here would be a pain in the arse but I could always help out in the bar some evenings, hang out in her speakeasy, drinking Old-Fashioneds like a blond Don Draper, only without the sociopathic tendencies. And maybe we could go travelling once I'd got a couple more gigs under my belt and things were up and running with Camp Bell. She'd told me she'd always wanted to do more of Central America and it was on my to-do list as well. Liv had never been up for backpacking, but Jane's itchy feet sounded even worse than mine.

'It could all turn out for the best still,' I told the giant plank of wood I was shifting. 'Maybe I'm not ready to settle down, after all.'

Like most planks of wood, it had very little to say but my imagination was ready to fill in the blanks. The future I'd envisioned with Liv was pretty simple. We'd get engaged, she'd move in, we'd get married and give Daniel Craig one or two human siblings. The whole thing was so clear in my mind, I almost felt like I was watching a movie when I thought about it: the little boy running around the garden, pregnant Liv chasing after him while I worked on a rocking horse in the workshop. It was a memory of an event that had yet to happen, but like my mum always said, everything happens for a reason. Usually, I wrote that off as bollocks, obviously, but what if the reason I hadn't been able to propose was because I was *supposed* to meet Jane? It was hard to argue with the possibility. Mostly because I didn't want to.

I hadn't done anything wrong, I assured myself. I hated feeling so miserable and guilty all the time for reasons I couldn't even put a finger on. Liv said she needed space to think, then Liv told me not to call. Was I supposed to sit around twiddling my thumbs waiting for her to make a decision? It hardly seemed fair, after all, this could go on for months and when she did finally make a decision, I could still end up on my own. As much as I didn't want to admit it, that scared me. I had permanently flipped off the bachelor switch the moment I decided to propose to Liv and it didn't feel like the kind of thing that could be easily reversed.

All of this really only left me with two choices. I could sit around the house, talking to a plank of wood, sleeping in her T-shirt and crying on the floor or I could get on with things and see what happened. Pursuing Jane would be entirely out of order but I wasn't going to avoid her either. That seemed fair.

'You're not doing anything wrong,' I said again. And this time, I almost sounded as though I believed it.

'I don't know about you but I'm knackered,' David said, dropping down on the little Ikea sofa with a cup of tea as I walked into the breakroom. I nodded and wiped my eyes with my sleeve.

'Liv, please don't cry.'

'I know, there's nothing else we could have done,' I said, massaging my temples as though I could rub my headache away.

'That and it's really unattractive,' he replied, pointing to my cheekbones. 'You get all puffy around here and it does you no favours.'

'Noted.' I patted my cheeks gingerly. 'He was fine when I checked on him last night. God, they were devastated.'

'They're always devastated,' David reminded me as I settled down on the Klippan beside him. 'I'd be more upset if they weren't, wouldn't you? Their dog just died.'

It turned out Ronald, my beloved Labrador, had not eaten something manky. When I opened the surgery on Thursday morning, he seemed fine if not especially chipper. Within an hour, he was vomiting again, turning in circles in his cage and it became very clear Ronald the dog had suffered a stroke. I'd called his owners who confirmed that yes, now I mentioned it, he had been walking a bit funny the day before but they put that down to his puking his guts up so they hadn't thought to bring it up.

'If I'd known more yesterday I might have been able to do something,' I said, my arms flapping down by my sides, as though they weren't properly attached to my shoulders. 'I should have seen it, though, I should have known . . .'

'And done what?' David asked, putting his tea down on the table to give me his full attention. 'Other than put him out of his misery a day earlier? He was fine when we came in this morning, he wasn't in pain. I know it's a shit business but it's done now.'

'He should have been at home with his family and not spending his last night in a cage at the vet's,' I said, still not quite able to let myself off the hook. 'Poor Ronald.'

'You mean Lucky Ronald who had a nice long life with people who loved him and didn't suffer at the end.' He took hold of my hand and squeezed. 'What's up with you? This is hardly the first time we've been through this.'

'I know,' I replied with a sniff. 'Just feels like I missed something, that's all.'

'You didn't,' he said with certainty. 'So pack it in. You need some rest, we both do.'

'Then I've got good news,' I said, patting his scrub-covered thigh. 'It's time to go home.'

We opened early on Thursdays and usually finished up at four, but between the untimely loss of Ronald and several last minute appointments, it was already after eight. I'd promised myself I would take the afternoon off and actually spend it sorting my life out, but instead of sitting in front of my Pinterest vision board and looking for my copy of *The Secret*, I'd been busy with the very worst parts of my job; clearing the anal glands of a particularly rancid tabby and sending Ronald off to meet his maker.

'You OK?' David asked, pulling a packet of Polos out of his pocket and offering me one. 'And I don't mean about the dog. Last night was a bit weird.'

'A bit?' I said, declining the mint. 'Adam was in the Bell with another woman.'

It didn't seem possible when I said it out loud. Not even a little bit.

'We still don't entirely know what was going on there,' he reminded me. 'Has Cass been able to get anything out of Chris?'

I raised an eyebrow.

'I literally do not believe a word that man says,' I told him. 'He's full of more shit than all the toilets in the village combined.'

'You still want to know though.'

'Well yeah, obviously,' I said. 'But I haven't checked my phone in, I don't know, seven seconds? So I've no idea.'

'Anything I can do?' he asked.

I nodded. 'Actually considering having my vagina sewn up. You're good at stitches, aren't you?'

'I've got a rule against seeing my boss's vagina, recreationally or otherwise,' David replied with great certainty. 'All joking aside, really, are you all right? You've not seemed yourself since you got back off holiday.'

'Can't think why.' I dropped my head forward onto my knees and let my hair cover my face. 'I just don't want to think about it.'

'And if I was asking how you felt about deworming a cat, that would be a great answer,' David pulled me back upright by my ponytail. 'It's a lot to deal with at once. You're not Abi the Great and Emotionless and this isn't a casual ghosting we're talking about.'

'Better we break up now than later,' I said, tears stinging the edges of my eyes. 'Now I can concentrate on the surgery.'

'The surgery you don't even know that you want?'

'That's the one,' I confirmed. 'Although to be honest, I'm not sure how not sure I am now.'

'You've lost me,' David said. 'Are we talking about this place or Adam?'

I dug my fingernails into the palms of my hands as it started. First my ears began to tickle, then my eyes. It was something I was getting perilously used to.

'I feel so stupid,' I whispered as my work husband bundled me up into a comforting hug. 'I feel like I don't even know him. My Adam wouldn't do this. He's the same but different, like a same character being played by a different actor.'

'Like Doctor Who?'

'More evil than that.'

'Sam Mitchell?'

'Less evil.'

'The Master?'

'Do you do anything other than watch TV?' I asked.

'No,' he replied. 'Next question?'

'It's all shit,' I said, pressing my thumbnail into the pad of my forefinger to distract me from potential tears. 'I can't believe Ronald died, I can't believe we're breaking up, and I can't believe it's my fault.'

'You can stop that right now.' David pulled away to look me directly in the red, blurry, swollen eye. 'I won't stand for self-pity and you know it.'

'But it feels so good,' I said, smearing my supposedly waterproof mascara onto his nice scrubs. Revlon, you filthy bloody liars. 'I really don't understand what happened. What did I do wrong?'

'Liv, you asked for time and he couldn't give it to you,' he replied. 'That's not on you.'

'But if I hadn't asked for the break,' I insisted. 'If I'd just let it go when he came to apologize in the first place . . .'

'Then we'd be going through all of this in six months' time,' he replied knowingly. 'If he was going to do it, he was going to do it and there's nothing anyone could have done to change a thing.'

'Honest man's opinion,' I started, not sure I really wanted the honest answer I was about to ask for. 'What do you think he's doing?'

'Honest opinion?' he asked. With a gulp, I nodded. 'If something is going on with him and that girl – who isn't *that* hot, by the way – then it's a rebound. I'd have to say he's feeling hard done by and he's flirting with her to make himself feel better. He probably only took her to the Bell because he thought you'd be there to see them.'

It was an honest, considered, XY chromosome response. Even though the girls and me hadn't had a regular Wednesday in the pub for months, he might have remembered. He might have been doing it to make me jealous. The thought of it should have made me mad, but instead it was strangely reassuring.

'I feel like I might have really messed things up,' I admitted. 'I shouldn't have pushed him away because I was freaking out about the surgery, I should have let him help me.'

David stared at his fingernails while he thought about what to say next.

'Maybe,' he replied. 'But you didn't, so what next?'

Blunt, fair and to the point. Exactly what I'd asked for – and exactly what I didn't want to hear.

'I actually do something with my life?' I suggested. 'Instead of sitting around and waiting for life to happen to me? One minute I was that weird girl who cleaned out dog cages on weekends and the next I was that weird grown woman who cleaned out dog cages for a living. I'm thirty already, I don't want to wake up forty and still be sitting here having the same conversation.'

'This *is* something,' David said, waving his arms around in the air. I assumed he meant the surgery in general and not just the breakroom with its curly-cornered Tom Hardy posters and rubbish bin full of Jaffa Cake boxes. 'Just because you haven't won an Oscar or broken the internet with your arse doesn't mean you haven't done anything with your life. If it does, then what does that make me? Sidekick to no one? I don't think so. I'm fucking awesome, Liv. I wouldn't hang around with someone wasting their life.'

'The only way my arse could break the internet would

be if I sat on it,' I replied. 'And yes, you are awesome, but you know what I mean, I want to *do* something.'

He skewered me with a stare. 'You're an amazing vet, you make the best Sunday roast I've ever eaten and, quite frankly, you're probably my best friend.'

I looked up to see bright pink spots in the middle of his cheeks before he clucked his tongue and stood up to collect our dirty mugs from the table.

'Probably?' I asked with a small smile.

'If you were my best friend, you'd put a word in for me with Abi,' he said, dumping them in the sink. 'I know you've got her and Cassie, but ever since I've known you, my life has been better for it. You're so hard on yourself all the time. Just for once, can you take one minute to sit back and see what everyone else sees?'

'You know I'm going to make you say it,' I said, retying my ponytail. 'What, exactly?'

'I see a clever, caring, funny woman with a great arse and nice tits who chose to dedicate her life to making a difference in other people's,' David replied, one fist dug into his hip. 'It pisses me off when you constantly do yourself down. Abi doesn't do it, Cass doesn't do it, I don't do it. You're a good person, Liv, but you're angry with yourself for not being exceptional. Only you're totally missing the point – you are exceptional.'

'Right now I feel exceptionally stupid,' I said, closer to happy tears than sad ones for the first time in forever. 'Thank you. I'm still not entirely convinced but it was nice to hear.'

'And if you were convinced, you'd be a massive wanker and I'd have to take it all back,' he said with a casual shrug. 'Apart from the arse bit, I can't deny that.'

'I'd rather you didn't talk about my arse,' I instructed, shifting awkwardly on the settee.

'Noted.'

'Really though, thank you,' I said. 'You're going to make someone a lovely wife one day. Just not Abi.'

'It's all I've ever wanted,' he replied. 'Now do one before the phone rings and someone wants you to come round and inspect their gerbil or something.'

I didn't need telling twice.

With a quick salute, I grabbed my bag and staggered out the door front, hugging myself against the chill in the air. I checked my phone as I crept around the building: nothing from Adam, nothing from Abi or Cass but there was another message from Henry. A flood of welcome relief washed over me as I opened it and saw a smiley face emoticon. Just a message, no dick pic. Between his decision not to photograph his penis and David's pep talk, it went a small way to restoring my faith in men.

'Livvy!'

The last thing anyone wants to hear when they're walking out of work is the sound of their boss calling their name. Especially when they've been avoiding their boss all week and that boss is their dad.

'Glad I caught you.' He marched up the path, clutching an envelope in one hand and a bottle of champagne in the other. 'I've got some paperwork you need to sign.'

'Can we not do this now?' I asked, wiping my face with the back of my hand. 'It's late, Dad, I'm knackered.'

'No, we need to do it now,' Dad insisted, waving the envelope in the air. 'No point in procrastinating, Livvy, got to get on with the future, live in the now.'

Well, at least I had a better idea where my copy of *The Secret* was hiding.

'My now needs a cup of tea,' I replied, rubbing my eyes with the back of my wrist. 'My now can't read paperwork when I've been at work since half past six this morning.'

'You don't need to read it,' he assured me. 'You need to sign it.'

I closed my eyes and opened them again, just to make sure he was really there and I hadn't accidentally inhaled something I shouldn't and passed out in the examination room. But no, I was wide awake and my dad was standing in front of me, tweed jacket, neat trousers, ruddy cheeks, looking every inch the image of a country vet. I, on the other hand, looked every inch an actual vet: dirty scrubs, messy hair, no make-up and raw, red eyes.

'Come on then.' I gave up and nodded back towards the flat. 'I'll put the kettle on.'

'I brought champagne,' Dad replied, following me down the path and up the stairs inside.

'And you'll be leaving it here when you go,' I said, throwing my keys on the counter and flipping on the already full kettle. 'Don't you worry about that.'

'It's a good job I didn't bring your mother with me.' He cast a disapproving eye over my living room and tapped his envelope in the palm of his hand. 'You want to get this place tidied up, Olivia.'

'What I want is to sleep,' I assured him. 'This week has been manic.'

'I'm sure it's not been that bad,' he said, clearing a spot on the settee and settling down. 'Everything always feels worse when you come back off holiday.'

I glared at the back of his head for a moment.

'No sugar in my tea, by the way, I'm trying to cut it out. Did you know they've said it's more addictive than drugs? Isn't that mad? Adam's mum was telling us all about it at the party. You should throw it out, it's a silent killer, Olivia.'

Gripping the handles of two mugs, I concentrated on making the tea and not bashing him in the head. Murdering your dad was frowned upon, wasn't it? Generally speaking?

'I had the solicitor put together a deed of ownership,' Dad explained while I gathered together enough biscuits to be considered an acceptable spread.

'Mmm-hmm.'

'So, you'll sign all three copies then I'll take them back to the solicitor, he'll sort everything out at his end and then you'll be the sole owner and proprietor of Dr Addison and Associates Veterinary Clinic. Isn't that exciting?'

He turned just in time to see me shovel an entire Hobnob into my mouth.

'I know you'll need another vet,' he went on, 'so I've asked a few of my friends if they know anyone and it turns out Dr Khan's son is looking for a new practice, so he's going to give me a call. Lovely man, Dr Khan, always wears a tie.'

'Shouldn't he be calling me?' I asked, pouring boiling water straight into our mugs and bypassing the teapot entirely. Mostly out of spite. 'He is going to be working for me, after all.'

'Yes, but I thought it'd save you a job,' Dad replied. 'Didn't you just tell me how very busy you are?'

Narrowing my eyes, I dunked the teabags three times before dumping them into the sink.

'Besides, I'd rather have someone I trust in there, Livvy. Your mum is chomping at the bit to get off on a cruise and I need to know the place is in safe hands.'

'And what are these?' I asked, waving my hands in front of my face. 'Flippers?'

'You'd be the first to admit you're not exactly the most business-minded girl in the world,' he said with a smile, picking up an old copy of *Marie Claire*, frowning at the cover lines and putting it back on the table, face down. 'You're going to have a lot more to worry about than you do now, you know, and you'd be surprised at how long the business side of things takes. You'll really need someone to take part of the practice work off your hands so you can look after everything else.'

'I've been thinking about that actually,' I said, skimming little white floaters from the top of his tea. 'You know admin isn't exactly my passion, so I'm thinking about hiring an office manager.'

Dad took his tea and considered it for a moment.

'Did you make this in the teapot?' he asked.

'Yes,' I lied. 'Of course I did.'

'Hmm.' He sniffed his tea and set it on the table. 'I'm not sure about that. This is what's best for the business. An Addison in charge, just like there always has been.'

'And what about what's best for me?' I asked. 'Seriously, Dad, if I have to do all the books by myself, there won't be anything left for an Addison to be in charge of. It makes so much more sense to get an office manager in than it does to hire another full-time vet when that's the part I'm good at.'

'Olivia, don't shout, you're upsetting the cat.' Dad gestured over to DC, who was sleeping undisturbed in the corner of the room. 'And I think your milk is off.'

My dad really had a gift for making me feel like a child. I hadn't been shouting but I was getting bloody close. I was also two seconds away from stamping my foot, running to my room and reminding him I'd never asked to be born.

'Livvy,' Dad took off his glasses, polishing them on the white handkerchief he pulled out of his back pocket, 'come on now, is something else the matter?'

'Many, many things are the matter,' I replied, taking a swig of sour tea. 'But the only thing that matters right now is you steamrollering my ideas. Dad, I'm thirty years old, if you want me to run the surgery, you need to let me run the surgery.'

'Have you had a falling out with Adam?' he asked, a too sympathetic look on his face. 'It's not like you to get so upset about nothing.'

Shaking with anger, I put down my tea before it spilled. How dare he assume I was upset about anything other than the surgery? Poor little girl Liv, she couldn't possibly be questioning his decision once it had been made.

'It's not nothing,' I argued. 'Can you hear yourself? You want me to take over the surgery, you want me to give up treating the animals, the part I love, to do admin, which I hate, and you want to choose who I employ to take over the part of the job you're taking away from me. It's not exactly a treat, Dad.'

He pushed his glasses back up his nose and shook his head at me with a smile. Condescension, thy name is Dad.

'You know you're overreacting?' he said, reluctantly sipping his tea. 'I'm only trying to help. Running the surgery isn't a game, Olivia, you can't take on the parts you want and fob off the parts you don't. That's not how real life works.'

'Actually, that's exactly how it works,' I replied. 'It

doesn't make any sense to take me away from the animals and put me on paperwork when I can employ someone else to do it better than I can.'

'I'm not bringing in a stranger to run my business.' Dad waved his hands in the air and I realized this was possibly the most emotional I'd ever seen him without a sherry in his system. There was a reason why he didn't drink. 'That's not how it's done.'

'It's not how you did it,' I countered. 'But this is going to be *my* business. Not yours. If you don't want me to do this the way I want, maybe you shouldn't be leaving in the first place.'

He gave me a look I recognized from endless arguments across the dinner table. No, you can't go round to Abi's after school when you've got homework to do. No, you can't go to university in London when you can go to Nottingham and live at home. No, you can't make any decisions even though you're a grown bloody woman who has come up with a perfectly sound business plan of her own.

'Right.' Dad stood up and tapped the envelope on the coffee table. 'I'm going to go. You can drop these round when you've signed them. You can bring them round after the christening on Sunday.'

'Dad, sit down,' I insisted, raking my hands through my hair. 'I want to talk about this.'

'I think you've made your point,' he said, fumbling in his jacket pocket for his car keys. 'I'll let you know when I've spoken to Dr Khan's son.'

'Jesus,' I muttered to the cat. Was I hallucinating? Why wouldn't anyone listen to me? David was always threatening to spike my tea with ketamine, he must have finally come good on his promise.

'I'll talk to you later,' Dad said, picking his way through my messy flat. 'And clean this bloody flat, it's a disgrace.'

I waited for him to shut the front door behind him before stamping my feet on the floor, stuffing two more biscuits into my mouth and flinging myself on my back on the settee. Daniel Craig made a quiet roaring sound before stretching out his single back leg and hopping over to leap onto my belly.

'That is not comfortable, you know,' I told him as he padded up and down, his tiny feet pressing into my flesh. 'You've been told before.'

But, like everything else on earth with a penis, Daniel Craig had little interest in listening to anything I had to say. *Almost* everything else on earth, I thought, grabbing my phone and pulling up Henry's message. Henry was interested in what I had to say. Henry wasn't down my local with another woman or forcing me to hire Dr Khan's son who might or might not, in fact, be a very good vet, but that wasn't the point. Henry wanted to trade emoticons and pleasantries and, according to his latest message, get a drink together on Friday night.

Closing my eyes and pulling a blanket over Daniel Craig and myself, I let myself imagine, for just a moment, how it might feel to say yes.

20

As if I wasn't already entirely unconvinced by what I
was doing, the train into town on a Friday night was the
closest thing I could imagine to the seventh circle of hell
without driving all the way down to Basildon. It wasn't
even seven and the sky was only just dark, but as the
sun went down, the hemlines went up and the overpow-
ering scent of Joop! choked everyone on the train over
the age of twenty-five. So, just David and me.

'You look like you're going to throw up,' he said as
I nursed my handbag in my lap. 'Is that the look you're
going for?'

'I was hoping more for hello, how are you, please
don't kill me,' I replied, tapping my toes on the sticky
floor as a group of females of indeterminate ages scrawled
on each other's faces with chunky brown crayons, glued
to their phone screens as they blended, blended, blended.
'Is that coming across too?'

'Liv, don't be so 2007,' he scoffed. 'No one gets murdered
on internet dates any more. You're far more likely to be
bumped off by your Uber driver on the way home.'

'So reassuring,' I said, one eye still on the girls across the carriage. 'Are they drawing on abs?'

'The fact that crop tops came back in the same decade that someone invented an app for pizza delivery just goes to prove that there's no god,' he nodded. 'It's a terrible thing to happen to the British Isles, we're not made for them. We're a naturally soft people.'

'Mmm.' I pinched at my own softness underneath my coat. No one else was wearing a coat. Literally no one else on the train had anything over their brightly coloured and oddly slashed ensembles. 'Is he going to think I'm a weirdo for wearing a coat?'

'I don't know,' he replied. 'But look at those girls. No coats and definitely DTF. You look . . . nice.'

'Oh no,' I shook my head quickly from side to side. 'No, no, no. Nice? I look nice? I'm cancelling, I'm going home.'

'You can't.' He pulled my phone out of my hands before I could text Henry and slapped my wrist. 'It's too late to cancel now. You're going to meet him, you're going to have one drink, and that's all. I will be right there in the bar so you're not on your own, no one has any expectations, and when I said nice, I meant astounding. You're a stud, you're fit as, you're Sandy at the end of *Grease*. You're 2016's Khloé Kardashian.'

'Did we establish where you stand on Khloé?' I asked.

'Not keen,' he replied, watching as the girls across the train swapped their chunky brown crayon for a bright white shimmer stick. 'But you can't argue with that arse. Primarily because if you did, her mum would have you killed.'

Ever since I'd agreed to my date with Henry I'd been regretting it. I'd taken out my phone to cancel at least a dozen times but Abi and David had somehow persuaded me not to. Cass had told me to cancel and, given that I'd regretted telling her the instant the words were out of my mouth, I'd told her that I had. The last thing I needed was her telling Chris and Chris telling Adam and Adam having so much as an opinion. Even if I wasn't sure he would even care. He might be relieved – if I was out on a date, he could crack on with Legs McGee without feeling the slightest bit bad. I didn't know when it had happened exactly, but somewhere between seeing that girl in my pub and getting on the train into Nottingham I'd stopped waiting to hear from him. The disappointment I felt every time I checked my emails and texts had become commonplace and I seemed suspiciously as though I would get used to it rather than get rid of it.

'Look at them.' I watched as the amateur make-up artists drew whiskers on each other's faces. 'Doing their make-up on the train. Forget Kris Jenner, my mother would slap their legs out from under them.'

'They're strobing,' David whispered.

'I know what they're doing,' I whispered back. 'I read magazines, I'm thirty, not dead.'

'The fact you tried to defend yourself by saying you read magazines doesn't really support that statement,' he sniffed. 'Did you watch that link I sent you?'

'Unless it was someone making an omelette in a sandwich bag, I did not,' I confirmed. 'I assumed it was porn.'

'It was, I'm just asking,' he said, brushing his black hair back over his ears and inclining his head slightly at a man sat two seats up. 'I thought it might take the edge off your nerves.'

'Thanks.' I pressed my lips together to redistribute the colour and reached into my tiny bag for a lip balm before remembering I couldn't apply it over my matte lips. Putting on lip balm was one of life's few pleasures – what had possessed me to deny myself such a thing on such a stressful evening? 'I really don't know if I can do this.'

David tapped the back of my hand as the train pulled into Carlton station and yet more stripy, soft girls got on, accompanied by boys in slim fit trousers and buttoned up shirts.

'If you really don't want to go, don't go,' he shrugged. 'NBD.'

But it was a big deal. There was no question about it, I was definitely rushing into this but I couldn't spend another Friday night alone staring at Ming the Merciless while Adam paraded that girl up and down the village. And despite my best efforts, the only alternatives I'd been able to rustle up were Scrabble with my mum, misusing controlled substances with David or killing myself. This was a better option. If he could go on a date, I could go on a date. Even if I felt like throwing up, sobbing and laughing hysterically at the same time.

Poor Henry.

'He seems like a nice guy,' I said, bobbing my head to the Justin Bieber song rattling out of the new group's mobile phone. 'He's thirty-four, went to uni in London. Originally from Newcastle. Tall. Beard. All his own teeth.'

David looked impressed.

'All I knew about my last online date was how much she liked to take selfies in her bathroom mirror,' he replied. 'You're so demanding.'

'Different priorities, I imagine,' I said, patting his knee. 'Now, honestly, do I look OK?'

'More than OK,' he replied and held his phone up in

front of my face. 'Now, laugh like you just saw Donald Trump's penis.'

'Ew.' I wrinkled my nose and the flash on his phone lit up my face. 'That's disgusting.'

'So is that photo,' he said, laughing. 'No filter on earth could save that. Let's try again. Who has a funny penis?'

'Everyone?' I suggested as he snapped.

'That works.' He showed me the screen for just a second, my face a pre-filter blur of white skin and red lipstick. 'You're not laughing but you look fit.'

'Why do you need a photo of me looking fit?' I asked, not really wanting to know the answer. 'You're not whoring me out to your friends are you? It's too soon and, you know, they're all awful.'

'It's going on Facebook,' he replied, too busy filtering the picture to death to actually look at me. 'And Twitter and Instagram. You want everyone to see what a good time you're having. And by everyone, I mean Adam.'

He held up the finished photo and even I had to admit it was actually bloody good.

'Don't tell me what you did to it, just post it,' I said as we pulled into Nottingham station. 'Are you sure you're not gay?'

'Positive,' he replied. 'I couldn't cope with the stubble rash. Come on, we're up.'

Pulling my skirt down over my knees, I stood up and followed him off the train, out into the bright lights of the moderately sized city.

'Right. We're doing this. You go in first and I'll be at the bar in five minutes.'

Two doors down from Tilt, David placed his hands on my shoulders, geeing me up with his best pre-game talk.

'If things aren't going well, give me the signal and I'll come and rescue you. What's the signal?'

'"David, things aren't going well, please come and rescue me",' I said. It was so long since I'd gone on a date, I'd forgotten how incredibly awful it felt. Anxious and nervous and worried he wouldn't fancy me even though I still very much wanted to go home. How had the human race survived this long when it was this difficult? 'How's my lipstick?'

'On your face,' he said, with a double thumbs up. 'How do you feel?'

'Like the man I love has thrown me over for someone way more attractive and if he doesn't want me any more, why should anyone else?'

'Not ideal.' David held out his hand for a fist-bump. 'But you're here now, might as well have a drink.'

The bar was up a narrow staircase and lively jazz accompanied me on my way up. Bluesy guitar and a smoky woman's voice sang a song I didn't know, somewhere I couldn't see, and the low rumble of date night conversation kept tempo with the music and the heartbeat in my ears. It was busy already. I paused in the doorway, trying to work out if any of the men sitting at tiny tables on their own, eyes fixed on the phones, could be Henry. Four of them had light brown hair, three of them had a beard and they all looked tall, sitting down. He could have been any of them. It was the hardest and potentially most embarrassing game of *Guess Who?* ever.

My eyes scanned the bar like a gussied up Terminator as I tried to spot my date until they rested on a man with light brown hair, something of a beard and piercing, bright green eyes sitting alone at a table by the window.

He looked over in my direction and I felt as though I'd been pinned to the wall. Without moving any other part of his body, he raised a hand and reeled me in.

'Hello.'

His voice was calm and deep and even. I liked it.

'Hello,' I replied, pulling out my chair noisily and pulling my skirt down over my thighs. Should have worn jeans, I told myself as I rested my handbag on my knees then hung it on the back of the chair before finally settling it on the floor beside me. I pushed my hair behind my ears, smoothed out the ends and offered my date my best tight, bright smile. Fidgets R Us.

'Drink?' he suggested.

'Probably a good idea,' I replied.

'I'll be right back,' he said.

Henry was handsome, there was no doubt about that. Truly handsome. He had the classic kind of face that my grandmother would have approved of and looked as though he should be wearing a World War Two officer's uniform. As it was, he was wearing dark blue jeans and a light blue shirt but I had to assume he'd look just as good in a bin bag. He definitely had the shoulders for it. The beard he had in all of his Tinder photos was considerably lighter in real life, trimmed back to something that was almost designer stubble, and I couldn't have said for sure that I would have recognized him if he hadn't waved first. He had the rare quality of being considerably better looking in real life than he was in pictures and now, confronted with his high cheekbones, green eyes and complete self-assuredness, I didn't know quite what to do with myself.

'They make amazing cocktails here,' Henry said, returning from the bar and placing a tall glass, shaped like an oversized bamboo shoot, on the table in front of me. 'The rum drinks are incredible.'

'Great, thank you.' I took a sip through one of the two straws sticking out of the glass and sat back. 'Wow. That is good.'

He nodded, stirred the same concoction then discarded his straw, drinking straight from his glass. 'Yeah, I usually drink whisky but these are so good.'

'Is that right?' I asked, grasping for something to say. 'Come here often?'

Henry's wide mouth broadened into a smile. 'Good one.'

It was the strangest feeling. This man was a complete stranger, we had exchanged all of five short messages, not enough words to take up two minutes, and now here we were. Sitting in a bar, pretending this was perfectly normal, neither of us about to acknowledge we were standing at a starting line with no idea where the finish might be.

'I hope you weren't waiting long.' I glanced down at my grandmother's watch on my left wrist and immediately wished I hadn't worn it. She would have approved of Henry's face but she would not have approved of this situation at all. Except for maybe the rum, my nan loved her rum. 'My train was a bit late.'

'And you were talking to that chap down there for a good five minutes,' he said, tapping on the window to where David stood, messing about with his phone across the street. I shrivelled into nothing in my seat, more embarrassed than I actually thought possible. 'Wait, is he texting you?'

My phone pipped its response before I could reply.

'Is this your "*get out*" text or your "*he's not a murderer*" text?' Henry asked.

'It's a bit early for either,' I replied, the rum and the situation flaming in my cheeks. 'I'm not sure.'

'Let's have a look, then,' he nodded and I obediently produced my phone. 'What's it say?'

'*Boneable*?' I said, my hot cheeks turning nuclear.

There was that smile again.

Henry leaned over the back of his chair and waved to David. My best friend, my knight in shining armour, ride or die BFF, looked up, squinted into the window and then ran away. Turned on his heel, ran down the street, and disappeared into the night.

'This bit's always awkward,' Henry said, turning back to the table as I tapped out the word '*wanker*' before stashing my phone back in my bag. 'Do you like the look of me, do I like the look of you, where to start, what to say. You can always tell the people who have done a lot of online dating in the first two minutes.'

'Always?' I took a gulp of my drink and felt the cold sparkling liquor cool me down from the inside out. 'Do you do this a lot?'

He leaned forward slightly, his shirt yawning open at the neck to reveal a sprinkling of chest hair. 'I wouldn't say a lot, but I've definitely been here before,' he replied. 'Is that bad?'

'I feel so special,' I muttered with the straw still in my mouth.

'You should,' Henry replied. 'I could have ended up anywhere in the world tonight, with absolutely anyone, but here we are. I think that's special, don't you?'

I eyed him carefully for a second. The cheesy bastard. I'd put on eyeliner for this?

Adam was the kind of person who was always moving. Unless he was working on something in his workshop, there was always a foot tapping or a hand clenching but Henry seemed so still, even his breathing was calm and steady and I didn't like it. This whole thing was a mistake.

'Does that work often?' I asked, the reality of the situation settling my nerves. Suddenly I knew I could do it. First-date nerves be damned: here he was, armed with his practised lines and steady smile and I was altogether too clever to fall for it. Or at least too cynical. I had been spending a lot of time with Abi, after all. 'It's a great line.'

This would be easy, maybe even fun. I would finish my drink, say goodnight to this joker then hunt David down like a dog and kick him all the way home.

'No,' he said, with a burst of surprised laughter, some of his stillness slipping away. 'Not once. No, that's a lie, it did once but she was not the sharpest knife in the drawer. Lovely girl, and I don't want to be an arsehole but, no, that wasn't going anywhere.'

'So, you've done this before.' I pulled my skirt back down over my thighs with a mental note to tell Abi that I had been right, it was too short, as soon as we both got home. 'Serial dater. I should have known.'

'How's that?' he asked, green eyes still fixed on me, seemingly enjoying himself.

'Well, you were so keen,' I explained as I pushed my drink back and forth in front of me. 'And there was no messing about, was there? Just, hello, I'm Henry, want to get a drink on Friday?'

He considered it for a moment. 'What else should I have said?'

'I don't know,' I admitted. 'But everyone else was a bit more chatty, asked more questions. You don't even know what I do for a living, I don't even know your last name.'

'What do you do for a living?' he asked.

I fought back a smile.

'I'm a vet.'

'And my last name is Maddox.' He held both hands up in the air. 'Done. Can I ask you a question?'

I nodded.

'All those men who asked you all those questions,' he said, kicking back in his chair. 'Where are they tonight?'

Ooh. Sneaky.

'Point taken.' I stirred my drink with the straw. Was it me, or was it getting stronger nearer the bottom?

'Here's how it went . . .' Henry pushed his sleeves up to his elbows. Good forearms, strong wrists, nice. 'I was bored so I was flicking through Tinder. You came up in my matches, I liked the look of you, and I decided I'd rather spend an evening getting to know you over a drink than doing anything else.'

'What were your other options?' I asked.

'Are you always this cynical?' he asked.

I nodded hard.

'Fine. I could have gone for a drink with some of my mates, I could have gone to the birthday party of someone I work with, or I could have stayed home and, I don't know, worked? Watched telly?'

'Had a wank?' I suggested.

'You really don't do this that often, do you?' he replied. 'But yes, obviously.'

'Then I am honoured,' I relented slightly. Despite the odds, I wasn't having the worst time ever. 'So, what is it that you do?'

'When I'm not being grilled by Tinder dates or having

a wank, I'm a graphic designer,' he said as the live music, wherever it was, ended to a surge of applause and the chatter in the bar grew slightly louder. 'Freelance. But I'm working for the local paper at the moment, some online rebranding stuff.'

'Do you like it?'

'I do,' he replied, rubbing his stubble beard. 'I like working with different people, I love the design element of it. It's never the same day twice. You?'

'You'd think every day would be different for a vet but at the moment it feels like Groundhog Day.' I rattled the ice around in my glass to shake out any last dregs. Either I'd hoovered it up like a first-class lush or it had been mostly ice in the first place. Only there didn't seem to be a lot of ice. 'I work in a village, the village I grew up in actually, so it's more or less the same people, same animals.'

'Do you like it though?' Henry asked, thankfully finishing his drink before I wrote myself off as a drunk.

'It's more of an "I love you but I don't always like you" situation,' I explained with what I hoped was a wry smile. 'It is what it is.'

'Why?' he asked with a small shrug of his broad shoulders. 'You can't leave? Surely you could be a vet anywhere.'

For a moment, I'd forgotten he didn't know me.

'It's sort of complicated,' I said, hoping he didn't think I was complaining about my diamond slippers being too tight. 'Family business, that sort of thing.'

'Nothing's set in stone, you know,' he said, scratching his beard. 'Life isn't a straight line, we don't have to be tomorrow who we were today.'

'That's a bit heavy for the first drink,' I replied, tapping my nails on my almost-empty glass. 'But yeah, I don't know. If we're doing deep and meaningful, right now I feel as though I'm on a rope bridge and there's a massive drop on either side with crocodiles waiting for me to slip and fall.'

'Now that *is* a bit heavy for the first drink,' Henry laughed. 'At least get rid of the crocodiles.'

I sat back in my chair and smiled down at my hands. 'You asked.'

'It seems to me I've met you at an interesting time,' he said. 'How many more drinks is it going to take for you to tell me what's really going on?'

'More drinks than they have here,' I replied, pointing at his empty glass. 'But I think I will have another, same again?'

'Yes,' he stood and scooped my glass up in his hand. Big hands. 'I'll get them.'

He had already started towards the bar before I could object. Not that I was planning to object that hard, but still, it would have been nice to have had the chance. I quickly emptied the contents of my handbag on the table, phone on one side, powder compact on the other. Quick as a three-legged cat, I popped the compact, checked my lipstick and powdered my nose. Second, I swiped my phone into life to find a text from Abi and two Facebook notifications. I opened Abi's message first.

Leaving work at 8.00. Let me know if you need an out. Hope he's not mental!

Poor cow, I thought, working this late on a Friday night. Maybe I should have asked her to come and work with me instead of Cass, get her away from the test tubes and mouse spleens.

I glanced up to check on Henry's whereabouts. The bar

was even busier than it had been when I arrived, people were crowding around the walls, hanging around and hoping for a table. I hadn't noticed it get so busy but then, I'd been preoccupied. I still wasn't certain as to whether or not I was having a good time but I was definitely having an interesting one. The Facebook notifications were from David. He had posted a photo of me. Thankfully, his artful editing and flattering filters remained and I smiled at the thought of actually looking like that. This girl, she could absolutely be out on a Friday night with a fit graphic designer who had a lovely pair of forearms. This girl was brilliant, charming, and if she spilled her drink, she'd be ready with a lightning fast pun to distract everyone. And the internet agreed. Six likes already! Six! At seven forty on a Friday night! David, of course, Abi, Cassie and Chris, David's friend Jeremy and – oh, Adam.

Adam Floyd likes your picture.

And there was the guilt and the nerves and the over-whelming sense of misery again.

'Here you go.' Henry placed a glass in front of me and I stuck my phone in my coat pocket, forcing a smile onto my face. 'It's still rum but it's a bit different. What do you think?'

'I think I like it,' I said as I took a big sip and let the rum wash away all those awful feelings. The first sip took the edge off but they were still there. How many rum cocktails did it take to cause short-term memory loss? 'Thank you.'

'Cheers,' he took his seat and held up his glass in a toast. 'To new friends.'

I clinked my glass carefully against his.

'To new friends,' I repeated, wincing at the tartness of the cocktail. 'And strong drinks.'

'Anyone would think I was trying to get you drunk,' he said, tasting his own drink and sticking out his tongue. 'Christ.'

I pinched my shoulders up to my ears and let them go in a loose shrug.

'You never know,' I replied, steeling myself for a longer sip as his face relaxed into a lopsided smile I hadn't seen yet. 'I might let you . . .'

Two drinks later, light-headed and ready for bed, I tottered down the staircase and out into the cold air of Pelham Street. Town was really only just getting going but four rum cocktails were more than enough to put me on my arse. Henry had argued a persuasive case for one more but I was just about sober enough to know what a bad idea that was.

'I'm going to the train station,' I announced, the wind whipping up around us and ruffling my skirt, thankfully anchored down by my coat. Those poor girls with their bare, painted-on midriffs, I thought. You couldn't pay me to be eighteen again. 'Which way are you going?'

'You are not getting a train back to Long Harrington at this time of night,' he said with a shake of his wavy head. 'We'll get you a taxi.'

'No, it's fine,' I assured him. 'I've got the train home a million times at night, you don't need to worry.'

Even though he had almost a foot on me, he was definitely the most drunk, I knew for certain when he declared his intention to end the night with a kebab. At least I knew he didn't fancy me, I thought confidently, no one had ever attempted to seduce someone when their thoughts were already full of lamb doners. And given that I'd spent most of the night wondering what exactly Adam was up to, in spite of his charming conversation and absurdly handsome face, I was relieved.

'I'm calling you an Uber.' Henry produced a giant smartphone from his inside chest pocket and waved it in my face. 'You'll do as you're told.'

'Oh, will I now?' I replied, tipsy and coquettish. Or tipsy and belligerent, depending on how he took it. I didn't like him telling me what to do but I didn't hate the thought of being chauffeured home at someone else's expense. Would Germaine Greer have an issue with this? Would I be able to look Emma Watson in the eye again? Not that I'd looked her in the eye yet, but still.

'I wouldn't feel right, letting you get the train,' he said, one hand lightly rubbing my arm as he carried on swiping at his phone. 'If I can't walk you home, I at least want to know you got there safely.'

'You really don't need to get me a taxi,' I told him without the slightest hint of conviction in my voice. I could throw myself under the king's horse another night – right now, it was cold, I was tipsy, and someone was offering to pay for a cab. Case closed. 'Also, did you know that you're more likely to get murdered by your Uber driver than your date? True fact.'

'A lot of women expect this, you know,' he said, tapping his screen triumphantly, his other hand still wending its way from my shoulder down to my elbow and back again. 'I've been on dates where girls have actually demanded I get them a taxi home.'

'I don't want to offend you . . .' I watched his hand go up and down, hypnotized. 'But I don't think those dates went very well.'

'You don't need to tell me that,' he replied. 'I wouldn't be here now if they had.'

The broad, sleepy-eyed smile he'd brought out at the beginning of the evening had been completely replaced with a beautiful lopsided grin that lit up his entire face. I noticed how he cocked his head slightly to one side every time, as though his smile was weighing him down.

'I had a really good time tonight,' he told me, tightening the grip of his hand so that he was squeezing my shoulder and I felt tingles run all the way down to my fingertips. 'Thank you for not being boring.'

'That's the nicest thing anyone has ever said to me,' I said, a dizzy smile on my face. 'Thank you, Henry.'

'You're welcome,' he said as we moved ever so slightly closer together. I looked up into his eyes. There was a chance I had been wrong about the kebab. 'And thank you for those shoes you're wearing. I love those shoes.'

'Really?' I looked down at my black patent Mary Janes. I'd chosen them because the heel wasn't too high and, worst-case scenario, the ankle straps would help hold my foot in place if I needed to make a run for it. 'When were you looking at my shoes?'

'I saw them when you came in,' he said, winding my hair around his hand and pulling it lightly. It was all I could do not to fall down in the street. 'Every other man in the bar was hoping you were his date, you know.'

'Oh,' I said, not moving. 'Right.'

He didn't say anything else. Instead, with my hair still in hand, he slipped his palm around the back of my neck and drew me to him. His lips were soft and we both tasted the same, warm and tangy. I rested my hands on his hips as we stumbled backwards against a recessed wooden door, the heat of his body mixing with the rum cocktails to sweep away any concerns I might have had about snogging a stranger in a doorway on a Friday night. Adam and his Angelina-lookalike be damned. Henry's stubble prickled my face but I didn't push him away; instead I pulled him closer, tipping my head back to encourage more kisses, eyes closed, mouth open, body all his.

Until a shiny black Honda Jazz beeped its horn behind us.

'You call an Uber?'

Henry broke the kiss and laughed awkwardly before turning to give the driver a thumbs up.

'Give us a minute, mate?' he called before turning back to me. The driver sighed audibly and turned up his car stereo.

'I should go,' I said, staring at those green eyes.

'What?' He automatically reached up to brush something nonexistent from his face. 'What's wrong?'

'Nothing,' I replied, reaching up on my tiptoes to kiss him again much to his delight. I had forgotten the thrill of kissing a man I didn't know and had no idea of what came next. Adam's kisses could be easily categorized: a morning peck, a goodnight kiss, an open-mouthed, proper tongue, we're-definitely-having-sex-in-the-next-ten-minutes snog. This was all brand new. It felt strange. Objectively, it was a good kiss, there was no getting around that, but something about it was off.

'I could come with you,' Henry suggested as I pulled away, pressing my lips together in a thin line. 'If you wanted.'

'I don't think that's a very good idea.' I shuffled sideways out from under him and waved at the Uber driver. He looked up from his phone and rolled his eyes before getting back to hammering out a text message so hard I had to assume his phone had done something to offend him.

Henry opened the back door of the car and I climbed inside as gracefully as possible. That was to say, I very nearly managed not to show him my knickers.

'Thank you. For tonight,' I said as he hung on the door and I knew he was still anticipating an invitation to join me. 'It was nice to meet you.'

'I'll call you,' he promised, finally closing the door, accepting defeat. I pressed myself up against the window, watching him watch me as the car pulled away. Then I realized what was wrong with Henry's kisses. They weren't Adam's. The strange, unsettled feeling inside me grew stronger and stranger before souring into something far more familiar. It was guilt. I felt guilty and lonely and so far away from the man I still loved.

'Where am I going?' the driver asked we drove off down the road, stereo pumping out hard dance music that burned the soft edges off my moment. I gave him my address and was flung against the back seat as we tore out of the city centre. Trying to ignore the sensory overload of the tiny car, I tapped my bottom lip and relived Henry's kiss for a moment.

As we burned through the streets with a booming hip-hop soundtrack, I fumbled for my phone to text my friends and let them know I'd survived the date, but instead of typing a group text, my finger hovered over the Facebook notification, letting me know Adam had liked my photo. I closed my eyes and gipped as the little car that could hopped over a speed bump, bouncing me out of my seat and hitting my head on the roof of the car.

'Sorry,' the driver said automatically.

'No worries,' I replied, fastening my seatbelt and attempting to go limp.

I wondered how Adam would feel if he knew I'd been on a date. Jealous, I told myself. So jealous and so angry. I wondered how he would feel if he'd seen me kissing Henry. The same way I'd felt when I'd seen him kissing that girl? Well, now we were even. He wasn't the only one who could go around snogging good-looking people in public; he wasn't the only one who could get on with his life. But righteous indignation did nothing to soothe the swirling pit of misery in my stomach. I felt as though all the fucks I'd ever not given had come home to roost. What if he did find out? Would he be angry? Would he even want to speak to me again?

'Sorry,' the driver shouted over the ear-splittingly loud music as we sailed over another speed bump and landed back down with a bounce in the middle of the road. The driver swerved out of the way of an oncoming bus and then tutted loudly. 'Fucking buses, though.'

'Buses,' I agreed, clutching my seatbelt in sheer terror. Probably wasn't a good idea to upset him by pointing out he was the worst driver on earth – he was clearly mentally unwell.

At least I wouldn't need to worry about feeling guilty about kissing Henry if I died on my way home, I thought to myself, closing my eyes and praying for safe passage along the A52.

21

'What I would do, is have someone kidnap M and then, when Bond goes to find out who's got him, he finds out it's his dad,' Chris said, hitting the steering wheel with the heel of his hand. 'That would be amazing.'

'Isn't his dad dead though?' I asked. 'Isn't him being an orphan a massive part of it?'

'He's *supposed* to be dead,' he agreed as he pulled into the left lane to undertake a Volkswagen Beetle travelling at the speed limit. 'That's why it's amazing. It's the last person you expect, father figure versus actual father. The only person Bond can never kill.'

I looked out the window and watched the countryside blur past in a swipe of green and grey and blue. 'What about his mum?'

'Still dead,' he confirmed. 'Box office gold.'

Chris put his foot down as we passed a large, green sign, declaring London seventy-five miles away and I leaned forward to turn up the radio. He had insisted on giving me a lift down to London on Saturday morning while we were both at Mum and Dad's on Friday night and I couldn't turn him down in front of my dad. I had agreed to check out the upstairs space at the bar with Jane and her brother, to see if her dream of a sixties speakeasy could become a reality, while Chris was on his way to some ridiculously overpriced jewellers to buy a christening gift for Gus and a something for Cassie. He had told me what, but I couldn't remember, I hadn't been listening.

'Listen, I don't want to stick my oar in,' Chris began. I couldn't even bring myself to laugh. 'But I told Cassie I'd have a word. About tomorrow.'

'What about tomorrow?' I asked. It was a classic Chris tactic, whenever he had to have an awkward conversation, he would open by blaming whatever topic he wanted to discuss on someone else. I was almost certain this was the only reason he'd got married in the first place. Cassie was now his lifelong scapegoat.

'The christening,' he said, lowering the volume I had just raised with the controls on his steering wheel. 'You and Liv.'

'What about me and Liv?' I asked, my shoulders stiff.

'You're two-thirds of the bloody godparents and you haven't spoken to each other in a week,' he reminded me. 'You're not going to give me any grief, are you?'

I strained against my seatbelt to give him a questioning look. 'When in my life have I ever given you any grief?' I asked. 'What do you think I'm going to do?'

'I don't know, do I?' he exclaimed as we sailed down the A1. 'But I need to know you're both going to behave yourselves. Cassie doesn't want a scene.'

'Then Cassie shouldn't have married you, should she?' I suggested, buttoning and unbuttoning the cuff of my shirt. 'There's not going to be any scene.'

'You could have bloody well waited to break up with her until after the christening,' he sniffed, flicking his eyes up to the Beetle in the rear view.

'I do apologize,' I replied. The car was right up our arse. Didn't appreciate being undertaken, obviously. 'Anyway, we haven't broken up. And again, for the millionth time, I don't want to talk about it.'

'Right, right,' he nodded, a smirk curling at the edges of his lips. 'Well, if you don't want to talk, I shan't say a word.'

One of Chris's biggest problems was that he could not keep a secret to save his life. He knew something I didn't and he was desperate to let me know but he savoured the moment, flexing the withheld information over me for a moment.

'What's going on with you and this dark-haired bird?'

Shutting my mouth, my jaw tensed as though it were wired shut and my eyes widened for just a second. Chris's smile broadened.

'What dark-haired bird?' I asked, an amber alert flashing in my guts.

'Come on,' he egged. 'Cassie saw you with some scorching hot brunette in the Bell. You're not going to deny it, are you?'

Cassie had seen us? If Cassie had seen us, then Liv knew and that could not be good.

'You mean Jane?' I replied casually.

'I believe that is to whom I am referring, yes.'

'She owns the bar, you know the one you're driving me to right now?' I explained, keeping to the facts and trying not to panic. 'I don't know what your missus thinks she saw but that's all it is. She came up to choose the wood for the bar and then we went for a drink. How scandalous is that?'

It wasn't an entirely accurate timeline of events but it was all the information Chris needed. Not that a little thing like the truth mattered if the village jungle drums had already got back to Liv. I hadn't seen Cassie in the Bell on Wednesday, wherever she'd been lurking she hadn't seen fit to come over and speak to me, so there was no telling what she thought she'd seen. And no telling what she'd passed on to her supposed best friend. I felt a bit sick at the thought – it had been three days since the drink with Jane in the Bell and it would only have taken Cassie three minutes to turn an innocent drink into something else. What had she told Liv? Was this why she'd told me not to call again? What if she wasn't at home, working things out, but at home thinking I was already shagging somebody else? My brain hummed with questions and potential disasters and Chris's driving wasn't the only thing making me nauseous.

'What exactly did Cassie say?' I asked, with a dry mouth. 'Has she spoken to Liv?'

'She said you were in the Bell with the closest thing the East Midlands had seen to a supermodel since Kelly Brook was signing trainers in Debenhams,' he said, steering with one hand. 'And of course she's spoken to Liv. Not that it matters, Liv was there as well.'

Oh no. Fuck fuck, fuck fuck, fuck fuck fuck. I was screwed.

'Liv saw me with Jane?'

'What does it matter?' Chris asked gleefully. 'She's only someone you're working with, there's nothing going on.'

'There isn't,' I insisted. My phone burned in the palm of my hand. 'But you don't know what it looked like, do you? To other people?'

'I know exactly what it looked like to other people,' he replied. 'It looked like you were out with a total fox, chugging drinks in your local when you're supposed to already have a girlfriend.'

'If it weren't for all this break bollocks, none of this would be a problem.' I punched the roof of the car and Chris jumped in his seat, the car starting forward even faster than before. 'Liv has never not trusted me. So what if I was having a drink with a woman? I work with women all the time, she's never been jealous.'

'Hey, don't take your cockups out on my car,' he warned, calming his pace. 'I know you think I'm a knobhead, little brother, but I'm not a complete idiot.'

I had nothing nice to say so I said nothing.

'This has been going on, how long? Nearly two weeks?'

Nodding, I stared down at my phone as though, if I concentrated long enough and hard enough, Liv might call so I could clear up all this nonsense, once and for all.

'It's time to work it out,' my brother advised. 'If you're going to end it, end it. If you're going to propose, propose. This limbo bollocks will do your head in.'

'My head is already done in,' I replied. 'And call me crazy, but I don't think proposing would go down very well right now.'

I stared at the phone in my lap. Should I call her? She'd said not to but that was before I knew what she thought she knew.

'Tell me about this Jane,' Chris said, turning off the radio altogether. 'Are you sure there's nothing going on?'

'There's nothing going on,' I repeated, still trying to telepathically link with Liv through the O2 network. 'Nothing at all.'

'Show me a photo then,' he demanded. 'Let's have a look.'

'Strangely enough, Chris, I don't carry around head-shots of my clients,' I said, furious with him, furious with Cass and furious with myself. 'You knob.'

'Get her on Facebook then, Nutsack,' he replied, swerving to dodge a kamikaze pigeon. 'Or have you not added her?'

'Of course I haven't added her. I'm not fourteen, I hardly ever use Facebook.'

Chris sat in the driver's seat, a smug grin spread right across his face. 'You haven't added her because you fancy her. If there was nothing going on, you'd add her.'

'That's ridiculous,' I said, refusing to look at him. 'You fucktard, I haven't added her on Facebook because I'm building her bar. She's a client, I don't need her going through every photo from your stag do.'

'Yeah, because you fancy her,' he said with complete conviction. 'If there was nothing going on, you'd have added her. You don't want Liv clicking on your Facebook and seeing you adding loads of fitties.'

'If I'd have added her, she might have got the wrong idea,' I replied, finger hovering over the Facebook icon on my home screen. 'And that's the last thing I want.'

'Well, what's she like then?' Chris asked. 'I mean, Cass was going on like she was Scarlett Johansson crossed with Jennifer Lopez crossed with, I don't know, Stoya or something.'

'I find it highly unlikely that your wife compared a woman I was with in the pub to your favourite porn star,' I said, frowning. 'But yeah, I suppose she's fit.'

'And?'

'And, I don't know,' I replied, trying to choose just one

of the thousands of words that were desperate to trip off my tongue. 'She's cool. She's done a lot of travelling, been to loads of the same places I have. She's really into mixology and this bar she's opening, she's really easy to talk to, she's really honest. Pretty funny as well. Can I stop now?'

'You could have stopped any time,' he said, concerned. 'Fucking hell, Ad, maybe you should propose to her instead of Liv.'

'She's basically Marsellus Wallace's wife.' I fished for a way to explain that he would understand. 'I've got to be nice to her because I'm working for her, but I'm not going to do anything.'

'"Say you had a lovely evening, drink your drink, go home and jerk off, that's all you're going to do",' he quoted. 'I get it but I'm not so sure. You're the one with the missus for a start. I think that makes you Uma Thurman and she's John Travolta.'

'And Liv is Ving Rhames?'

He furrowed his brow. 'It wouldn't be the first celebrity I'd think to compare her to, but if the shoe fits . . .'

'The shoe wouldn't fit. The shoe would be about seven sizes too big. It's a shit shoe.' I looked out of the window of the Jag so Chris couldn't see the colour in my cheeks. 'You asked me what she was like, I've told you. There's nothing going on.'

'And if you weren't interested, the correct answer would have been tall, dark hair, nice tits, not she's the world's most incredible woman oh, and she's *funny*,' he said emphatically. 'Adam, I'm serious. You need to do some thinking. If things are really this rocky with Liv, and you're mooning over this Jane bird, why shouldn't you give this a go? You know what I always say about taking a car for a test drive.'

'Because I love Liv,' I replied with only the slightest hesitation. 'Because two weeks ago, I was going to ask her to marry me.'

'"Was" is the operative word in that sentence,' he said. 'Past tense. You *were* going to ask her to marry you.'

The quickest way to shut him up was to agree with him, however much it pained me. And it never pained me more than when there was even the slightest chance he could be right.

'While I remember,' Chris forced an air of nonchalance into his voice, fooling no one. 'I meant to ask you something.'

I rested my hands on the top of my head, knuckles brushing against the roof of the Jag. It was a nice car but it was not made for tall men, something he had not considered when his wallet went out shopping to overcompensate for what was not in his pants.

'You do know Liv was supposed to have a date last night, don't you?'

He paused and looked over at me.

'No she was not,' I replied, staring straight ahead. 'Don't be ridiculous.'

'Oh, all right then,' Chris turned on the radio to listen for the final scores. 'She didn't agree to go out with a bloke on Tinder and then cancel. Even though she did.'

I sucked in my cheeks and bit down, refusing to ask any follow up questions. There was no way. Liv was not on Tinder, Liv wouldn't not go on a date. She was the one who said no seeing other people, she would never, ever do that. Unless she thought I'd gone on a date too . . .

'I'm only telling you what I've been told. Cass didn't want me to tell you but it's hardly fair, is it? Her running

317

around town with god knows who and you sat at home like a numpty. But it's probably nothing,' he said, turning up the radio. 'I mean, Cass did say she'd cancelled it.'

She'd better have cancelled. I couldn't stand even the thought of her flipping through photos of other men; it was enough to send me over the edge. Was that what the new Facebook photo was in aid of? Tinder? I'd *liked* that bloody photo. Sitting round Chris's house, watching Mum's dodgy home video of her yoga retreat and desperately wishing I was with Liv instead, I had liked, nay, *loved*, that photo.

'Probably nothing,' I agreed amiably while the world around me burned. 'Thanks, Chris.'

'You can drop me off here,' I instructed as we passed Jane's Mini, parked right in front of the bar. 'This is perfect.'

'Hang on, there's a space up there,' Chris said, slowing down and whipping the car across the street, pulling straight into a slightly too small parking spot. He looked at me, grinning from ear to ear. 'Come on, though, that's a nice bit of parking.'

I unbuckled my seatbelt and opened the door. I'd been desperate to get out of the car and away from my brother ever since he'd decided to share the news about Liv's non-date. If he followed me even a foot there was every chance I'd throw him in front of the first passing lorry. 'Well done. Call me when you're done and I'll come and meet you.'

'Hold on.' He turned off the engine and unclipped himself. 'I'm coming with.'

'You are not,' I replied, startled. I unfolded my long legs, cramped from two hours of hitting imaginary brakes

on the passenger's side, and immediately crossed the
road. 'I'm working. This is work. You're not coming
with me.'

'If you think I'm taking off without seeing this goddess
you're absolutely not interested in,' Chris started, checking
the street for traffic before bolting after me, 'you're more
mental than I thought.'

'Chris, I am a hundred per cent serious.' Surrounded
by the seductive inner-city scents of southern fried
chicken and unemptied bins, I turned to threaten my big
brother as politely as possible. 'Please don't be a dick. I
don't need you to ruin this for me.'

The two-inch difference in our height disappeared as
my shoulders rounded and his spine pulled him all the
way up straight. 'Ad, what do you think I'm going to
do?' he asked. 'I'm not going to Kanye your bar, am I?
"Excuse me, I'm going to let Adam finish but I'm the
best furniture designer in all the world right now."'

'I don't know what you're going to do,' I began to panic
when I saw Jane walking towards us, sunglasses on and
a giant cup of something in her hand. 'But precedent
does not suggest you'll be incredibly supportive.'

'You're not a lawyer any more, little brother,' he said,
proving my point and not caring one jot. 'So don't quote
precedent, I want to see this hot piece.'

'Then you've come to the right place.' Jane threw her
spare arm around my neck and kissed me on the cheek
before pushing her sunglasses up into her absurdly shiny
hair and taking a good look at my brother. 'He is talking
about the bar, isn't he?'

Chris, struck dumb, nodded.

'Adam,' Jane whispered theatrically, 'is there something wrong with him?'

'If I started to explain we'd be here all day,' I said, no calmer for her presence. 'Jane, this is my brother, Chris. He gave me a lift and apparently that means he's entitled to be a pain in my arse for the rest of eternity. Is it OK if I give him a quick tour of the bar?'

She sipped her coffee, pressing her lush lips against the white plastic lid of the cup, never taking her eyes off Chris.

'I'll behave,' he promised with creaking words. 'I'll be good as gold.'

'All right then,' she relented, pulling a bunch of keys out of her pocket. 'But only because you're Adam's brother and Adam's the best.'

She flashed me a quick smile before fitting her keys in the lock, wooden hoarding panels obscuring the windows, and opening the door with her hip.

'Welcome to Camp Bell,' she announced, holding her arms out wide to unveil the cold, dark and completely empty space. 'So, Adam's brother, do you love it?'

He turned around a couple of times, catching my eye and raising his eyebrows before turning back to Jane.

'It's amazing,' he said. 'Best bar I've ever been in.'

'Right answer.' She switched on the lights and three bare light bulbs hanging from the ceiling glowed yellow. 'And when your brother has worked his magic, it's going to be even more amazing.'

'Is Jim here?' I enquired as she put down her coffee and dropped to her hands and knees, burrowing under a pile of boxes with her arse in the air.

'No,' she called back, muffled by her hair. 'He's running late. He'll be here in a bit, though.'

Chris elbowed me aggressively in the ribs, his eyes firmly attached to Jane's rear end.

'Pack it in,' I whispered with a shove that sent him staggering several steps over to his left. 'Can you go now?'

'There, that's the heating on.' Jane sat back on her heels and smiled up at the two of us from her knees. 'What was that?'

'Chris has to leave,' I answered readily. 'He's going to buy his wife a present. It's his son's christening tomorrow.'

'You should come,' he said before she could react. 'It's going to be a real party. Not like your average christening at all.'

'Is that right?' she asked, looking at me for confirmation and not finding it. 'A christening that's a real party? On a Sunday?'

'Oh yeah,' he went on, entirely unaware of the gentle mocking in her voice. 'We've got a marquee, I've hired a band, full bar, catering, everything. It's not every day you christen your first-born, is it?'

'No, you're right,' she agreed. I reached out a hand to help her to her feet and there was the same fizzing in my stomach when our hands touched. 'I'm sorry, I can't make it. I've no doubt it'll be a fabulous occasion regardless. Is Uncle Adam excited?'

'Beside himself,' I assured her, clapping Chris on the shoulder as I made a move towards the back of the room. 'Shall we have a look upstairs? I don't want to keep you all day.'

'I've got nowhere better to be,' she replied, following. We both turned back at the same time to see my brother glued to the spot. 'Are you joining us, Chris?'

'No,' I said before he could open his mouth. 'He isn't. Call me when you're done.'

'I'll call you when I'm done,' he agreed, still staring at Jane. 'I'll see myself out.'

'Seriously though, is he all right?' she asked as we disappeared through the back door and up the short, steep staircase to the second level. 'He's not like, special or anything?'

'Oh, he's definitely special,' I assured her, feeling around the wall for a light switch of some kind. 'But not in that way. I'm sorry, he's married, so he's forgotten how to talk to women.'

'And how to look at them, listen to them and be within fifteen feet of them,' she added, reaching out and turning on the lights. 'He seems nice though.'

'Does he? He was only here for a minute, you couldn't get to know him properly,' I joked. 'Wow, this is all yours as well?'

'It is,' she said, skipping into the middle of the room with her arms stretched up over her head. 'What do you think?'

'I think it's great,' I told her. It really was. I pushed all thoughts of Liv out of my mind and concentrated on work. The space was about half the size of the main bar downstairs but it was perfectly sized for what she had in mind. A cool, 1960s speakeasy, all sunken seating, low lighting and cool, ugly patterns. Definitely a hot spot for the cool kids. 'We can definitely work with this.'

'I'm so happy you like it.' Her face was flushed and she held her hands behind her back. 'It's not like I'm not excited about the main bar, but that's Jim's baby, really, and I can't stop thinking about this. It would be so nice to have something that's just mine.'

'I understand,' I assured her. 'I get that.'

She grinned and did a little dance on the spot, eyes shining with such genuine joy that I couldn't fight the same smile on my own face. I looked at her, her plush red lips, the shiny hair, wide set, dark eyes and insane body – and none of it mattered. She stopped being the sum of her parts and became something so much more. She looked at me and I saw someone who was entirely happy. Happy with her life and happy I was there to be a part of it. If Chris was right and things were over with Liv, if Liv was already looking for someone else, I would have to be insane to walk away from this moment.

Fuelled by a confidence I didn't really feel and the very idea of Liv so much as swiping right, with one quick and certain step, I moved towards her, slid my hands around her face, thumbs nestling under her cheekbones, fingertips winding into her hair, and kissed her.

'What are you doing?'

Jane broke away, shoving me clear across the room and wiping her mouth with the back of her hand. She was unnervingly strong for such a slim woman.

'What?' I recovered myself, one hand on the wall, one hand in the air, my balls shrinking back up inside myself.

'What are you doing?' she demanded. 'You've got a bloody girlfriend.'

'I thought you wanted me to.' I was very confused. Confused, embarrassed, and still incredibly horny. It was shit being a man sometimes.

'Why would I want to kiss someone who has a girl-friend?' she asked, scrubbing at her mouth again until the skin around it was bright red. 'God, Adam. That's not on.'

'But I thought . . .' I ducked my head, ashamed. What an absolute, first-class wanker I was turning out to be.

'Yeah, I like you.' Jane began to calm, very, very slightly. 'But I don't get off with other people's boyfriends.'

She looked at the floor, examining her ankle boots, and then back up at me. 'You *have* still got a girlfriend?'

'Sort of. I don't actually know.' I wondered how much damage I would do if I were to throw myself out the window. Even if I didn't, I might still just die of pure embarrassment. Was that possible? It certainly felt possible. 'Jane, I'm sorry. I'm such a dick, please don't . . . I don't know. I'm really sorry. I'll go.'

With her eyes closed, she sighed loudly as I skulked back towards the staircase, face flaming. It was beyond me how I thought kissing Jane might make anything better. Other than my brother before he got married, what kind of arse kisses someone when he's still got a girlfriend? Even if said girlfriend might be seeing other people, it was still a dick move. Especially given that said girlfriend might be seeing other people because she thinks *I'm* seeing other people. The thought that the entire situation might be a hole, all of my own making, made me feel light-headed and sick and desperately in need of a quiet lie down. Tom was right, what the fuck was wrong with me?

'Adam, don't go,' Jane called, just as I reached the staircase, ready to run far, far away and never return. I looked back to see her, one hand on her hip, the other pressed against her forehead. 'You don't have to go. You just got carried away, right?'

'Yes,' I said quickly, ready to agree to anything. 'I did and I'm really, really sorry.'

'OK then.' She seemed to be talking more to herself than to me. 'But you need to know I won't get involved with someone who is already involved.'

'Right. I'm really—'

'If you say you're sorry again I'm afraid I'm going to

have to glass you,' Jane said with a tentative attempt at a smile.

'One hundred per cent professional from here on out,' I swore as the tension in the room began to ebb away into something more like awkward discomfort, still less than desirable but something I could live with for the time being as long as it meant I wasn't fired. What a twazzock.

'We can be friends,' Jane relented, winding down her shoulders. 'I want to be friends. But I'm not that girl, Adam. I wouldn't do that to your girlfriend. It's not right.'

I nodded and she placed a hand on my shoulder as she walked back towards the steep, narrow staircase

'No, I agree, you're right.' I breathed in as she passed to give her as much room as humanly possible. 'Just friends, totally cool.'

She paused for just a second and held my eyes with hers and pressed a hand against my chest.

'But I'm not saying that things couldn't be different if you were single,' she said before pulling away her hand. 'But you're not.'

'I'm not,' I agreed, breathless.

With a nod, she jogged lightly down the stairs and I heard Jim's voice call her name from the front door. Glued to the spot, I closed my eyes and waited for the feeling to come back into my legs. We were so far past a teaspoon moment. I'd need an entire canteen of cutlery before I could greet her brother with a straight face.

Why couldn't anything ever be simple?

22

I was lying on the settee, enjoying a particularly intense staring contest with the cat when I heard a knock at the door. Almost anyone who might be at my door in the first place had their own key and even those who didn't would let themselves in, so I stayed put for a second knock before displacing Daniel Craig and traipsing down to see who it might be.

'Mum?'

'Clearly,' my mother replied, shaking off her umbrella in the doorway and waiting for me to step aside and let her in. 'I do hope Cassie gets better weather tomorrow, it's been very up and down of late. The forecast is for sun but who knows what we'll get?'

'Yeah,' I said, following her quick step up the stairs and holding out my arms for her discarded mac. 'I didn't know you were coming over.'

'Clearly.' She cast a disapproving eye over the flat as she stepped inside. I'd started cleaning up, really I had, but after a busy Saturday morning at the surgery, sitting down with a cup of tea and the last chapter of *Wish It*.

Want It. Do It. had proven far too tempting. 'Your father said the flat was a disgrace.'

'It's not that bad,' I argued, draping her jacket over an epic ironing pile and Daniel Craig slunk underneath, out of sight.

'For you, no,' she agreed, busying herself in the kitchen. 'But then he didn't spend a lot of time in your room as a teenager.'

'Let me make the tea,' I offered as she rifled through half-empty boxes of teabags, looking for something that met her approval. 'You sit down.'

'Your dad is concerned about the surgery.'

Apparently she didn't want to sit down.

'And I'm concerned about you.'

'No need to be concerned,' I assured her. She turned her grey-blue eyes in my direction and I could see I wasn't going to get off that easily. 'Everything's fine.'

'Tell me the truth,' she said, fully aware I was incapable of lying to her once she had insisted on 'the truth'. It was as though she'd had a wicked fairy cast a spell on me at birth, I was powerless against that command. 'It's not like you to behave like this.'

'Like what?' I asked, fighting the compulsion to tell her everything and genuinely curious as to how she thought I was behaving.

Mum carried on making the tea, warming the pot with freshly boiled water, resetting the kettle and emptying the teapot into the sink before adding two teabags and pouring in the water.

'You're not yourself,' she replied, one hand on the teapot, the other on her denim-clad hip. I looked down at my own ripped knee skinnies and then back at her sensible high-waisted, straight leg jeans. Thinking about it, hers were probably more on trend than mine. 'I should have known when you turned up at your dad's birthday in that dress.'

'It was a very nice dress.' I crossed my arms over my feeble bosom. 'Possibly not entirely appropriate, I will give you that, but still, very nice.'

'Not the word I would have used.' She sat my one and only tray on the coffee table between us, two clean mugs with exactly half an inch of milk in the bottom of each and a steaming pot of tea in the middle. 'First you run out on the party, then your dad says you're giving him grief about the new vet.'

I made a grumbling sound that couldn't quite be considered words and reached out to pour my tea.

'Leave it,' Mum said briskly. 'It needs two more minutes. Olivia, what's the matter?'

Until I met Adam's family, I'd always felt like me and my parents were close but it turned out geographically that 'nearby' and 'close' weren't exactly the same thing. Compared to Abi's family, we were the Waltons. Not once had my mother slapped my father in the middle of parents' evening and neither of them had ever declared the other a whoring witch in the nearest big Tesco, but at the same time we didn't merrily spend time together the way the Floyds did. Adam actually *chose* to hang out with his parents; there was no such thing as a dutiful Sunday lunch around his house, it was all unlocked doors, 'just popped in to say hello' and Tuesday night fajitas. They had been on holiday together, as adults, *more than once*.

I loved my parents, but even though I worked with Dad, we didn't spend an awful lot of time together. If we were both in the surgery, it was because we were both busy and conversation outside of work stayed strictly superficial – who in the village had what illness, the price of eggs these days, whether or not someone had been cheating on *Bake Off*. And so Mum's surprise visit was alarming enough without her wanting to have an actual conversation about actual real life.

'Is it Adam?' she pressed.

'No, well, yes – but not just Adam.' I couldn't stand another second of this without the galvanizing power of tea. I grabbed the teapot, turned it twice, and poured it as my mother's thin lips disappeared into her face. 'I've got a lot going on. But I'm not giving Dad grief, I'm just not sure I agree with the way he wants to do things.'

'That I don't understand,' she replied, pushing her wispy blonde fringe out of her eyes. 'Your dad has been running that place since before you were born; why would you not want his help?'

'I do want his help,' I said, pulling on a loose thread left by a missing button on my shirt. 'But I don't want him telling me what I have to do with the rest of my life.'

I knew how I sounded, the look on her face just confirmed it.

'I'm not being difficult.' I read her mind to save her some time. 'But I don't agree that getting a new vet in and taking me away from the animals to sit in an office doing paperwork is the best way to run the business. If he wants me to run the business he needs to let me do it my way. Mum, I'm thirty.'

Mum held my gaze, her eyes calm and steady, while I fidgeted in my seat. This was the part where she waited for me to confess, apologize and promise never to do it again. Only I hadn't done anything wrong and there was no apology coming.

'You could start acting like it,' she suggested, ignoring my shocked gasp. 'What's going on with you and Adam?'

Ooh, distract me with an insult then throw in the real question. Sneaky diversion from Addison the Elder.

'I'm not entirely sure,' I told her, noting her tactics for future use. 'We're on a break.'

She looked at me before she spoke and I flushed uncomfortably under the weight of her blue eyes. It wasn't the usual 'look at the state of you' glance, she was really paying attention.

'There are a lot of things I might have done differently with my life, if I'd had the chance,' she began. 'If I were your age, believe me Olivia, I'd be out there doing it all. But the one thing I have never doubted was the fact your father was the right man for me. I want the same thing for you.'

'How do you know, though?' I wasn't convinced. As far as I was aware, and as far as I ever wanted to be aware, my dad was the only boyfriend she'd ever had. 'There are what, seven billion people in the world and I'm supposed to know some bloke I met in the local supermarket is the one, just because? I haven't even met all my Facebook friends in real life, let alone every eligible man on the planet.'

'The world was a much smaller place for me and your dad,' Mum replied, smiling for the first time since she'd walked through my door. 'But it wouldn't have mattered if I'd been an international jetsetter, he would still have been the one for me. There's a lot to be said for someone who understands who you are and where you're from – don't underestimate how much those things matter. It's a lot more important to find someone who appreciates the things that made you who you are today than someone with a nice bum and a Ferrari.'

'Why, do you know someone with a nice bum and a Ferrari?'

My mum, the relationship guru, blushed into her cup of tea and I reluctantly let myself wonder if she was right. I had never had to explain myself to Adam; I'd never had to be someone I wasn't. Out of the seven billion people on earth, how many would have taken the day off to hold my hand through my wisdom tooth surgery and told me I looked beautiful when I actually looked like a deranged gerbil? How many would have flown me all the way to Budapest to introduce me to a wombat on my thirtieth birthday? And how many would still stroke the edge of my ear until I fell asleep every night, even after three years? None of them, because none of them were Adam.

'Your generation has made the world a very big place, Olivia,' she explained. 'And I don't know if that's always a good thing. I was very relieved when you came back home after university – I was worried you'd run off travelling around the world or something, because you always had that mad streak in you and between you and Abigail I wouldn't have put any sort of escapades past the two of you.'

'I didn't move home,' I reminded her, pulling myself upright. 'I never moved back into the house, and I started work as soon as I graduated, you know that.'

'I meant came back to the village,' she replied, pulling the loose thread out of my shirt altogether. 'All I ever wanted for you was to see you settled and happy. That might not sound very exciting, but in this day and age, it's not a given.'

'I *am* happy,' I said, realizing as soon as I spoke that

it wasn't entirely true. 'Or I thought I was. Now I don't know what to think.'

'Hmm.' Mum tucked the loose thread into her jeans pocket.

Hmm? That was the best she could do?

'What would you have done differently?' I asked, struggling to imagine my mum as anything other than my mum, reliable, predictable Lesley Addison, baker of cakes, mender of socks and village authority on the best time of year to plant your daffodils. 'If you had the chance?'

She took a deep breath in through her nose and looked up at the crack in my ceiling. 'All kinds of things,' she said, her soft smile turning wistful. 'I would have liked to have travelled more but hopefully there's still time for that. I think I would have liked to have had a job – I feel quite odd to have reached my age without having done *something*.'

'I thought you were happy not working,' I said, thinking of Cass and Chris and Gus. 'I didn't realize.'

'I was happy taking care of you,' she said with a quick touch of my knee. 'But once you started school things got very boring, very quickly. I did consider a few things but it's hard to get started when you're in your thirties and you've no experience at anything other than raising a child. All the qualifications I got in college were out of date by the time you went up to secondary school and your dad was a bit funny about me doing anything in the village.'

Curiouser and curiouser.

'Funny how?'

'He didn't want me to work in the old supermarket when it opened.' She arched an eyebrow at the memory.

'I don't think it'll be news to you that your dad can be a bit of a snob.'

It didn't feel like the right time to point out that more than a few of his snobbish tendencies had rubbed off.

'And we had always planned to have more children but we couldn't, so that was that.'

She brushed nonexistent crumbs from her lap as though she hadn't just dropped a massive truth bomb in the middle of my living room.

'You couldn't have more kids?' I asked quietly. 'Why?'

'Because we couldn't,' she said quickly. 'We don't really know why. Your dad didn't want to do the tests and I didn't want to go through the rigmarole of doing it the doctor way anyway, so that was that. But yes, I do wish I'd found something worthwhile to do with my time. Although I don't feel too badly about it when I look at how well you've turned out.'

'Really?' I allowed myself to be distracted by the rare, seemingly genuine compliment even while I processed her confession. This was all a lot at once. 'You could still get a job now, Mum. You could do a lot of things.'

'All I want to do now is get your father out of that white coat and into his swimmers.' She took a deep drink of tea and rattled her neatly filed nails against the mug. 'He's worked very hard his whole life. It's time he did something for himself, for both of us actually. It'll be nice to turn the light out and know he's not got to rush out and take care of someone's silly rabbit in the middle of the night.'

'I've got so much to look forward to,' I said, my expression grim. Rabbit call outs were the worst. There was hardly ever anything you could do for a rabbit.

'If you and Adam have as happy a life as me and your

father, you'll have done bloody well for yourself,' she replied, flushing at her own uncharacteristic light swear. She would have died if she'd heard the way I talked to David and Abi. 'And whatever is the matter between the two of you, sort it out. From what I can tell, it's terribly easy to walk away from things these days with your Tinders and Grindrs and the like but nothing worth having was ever easy and that is a fact.'

'Mum!' I was truly shocked. 'Do you even know what Grindr is?'

'I'm fifty-five, I'm not dead,' she said, draining the dregs of her tea. 'You see all sorts on *Loose Women*, Olivia. All these couples breaking up at the first sign of trouble because they think there's something easier around the corner – but easier does not endure. Easier is not worth the time of day.'

'What if he doesn't want to sort it out?' I asked, keeping my voice light, my eyes on my bare toes.

'Then he's a bloody fool.' She stood up and kissed me on the top of my head before reaching for her coat. My ironing pile tumbled to the floor and Daniel Craig raced out from under the mess, a pair of knickers looped around his neck. Mum tightened her mouth again and shook her head. 'I'm saying nothing.'

'Thanks.' I gathered everything up in my arms and dumped it on the settee. I would totally do it before the christening.

'Talk to your dad about the surgery,' Mum said, glancing out the window at the weather before belting her mac. It was still raining. 'Talk to Adam about whatever is going on and get that button sewn back on your shirt, if you even know where it is.'

'Life's too short to worry about missing buttons,' I

said, throwing my arms in the air. I had no idea where it was. 'Isn't that what this whole chat was about?'

'This chat was about listening to your parents from time to time,' she corrected. 'Every so often, we might have something useful to tell you.'

'God forbid,' I replied as she saw herself out, shaking out her umbrella and closing the door behind her.

Resuming my position on the settee I looked at her lipstick-stained mug and wondered. What would I regret when I was sixty? The photo of me and Adam and my beloved birthday wombat stared down at me from the wall. What stories did I want to share with my daughter? Daniel Craig pranced indignantly out of my bedroom, still wearing my pink thong around his neck. I reached out to pull it away but got nothing but a swipe of his paw and a high-pitched yowl for my troubles.

'Keep them then,' I said, settling back down and closing my eyes. 'You weirdo.'

Because I didn't have enough to worry about without a three-legged cross-dressing cat called Daniel Craig giving me grief.

23

Easy does it, I thought to myself, concentrating on my footing with Abi and David close behind me. The steps up to the village church were steep and irregular and my heels were too high for the job at hand. I really hadn't taken the practicality of stilettos versus ancient stone steps when I'd chosen my outfit that morning and the last thing I needed was a visit to A & E. Actually a couple of hours in the Queen's Medical Centre might have been preferable to an afternoon with Adam and the family Floyd. I considered asking David to push me, but I was worried he might do it.

Chris's car rolled around the corner and David tapped out a drumroll on his knees.

'Here we go,' I said, watching as Chris leapt out of the car and began gesticulating wildly at a man holding a fancy-looking video camera while a tiny woman in a Pokémon T-shirt wielded a giant boom mic, twice her own height.

'Oh god, I forgot,' Abi groaned. 'Cass told me he'd hired an independent film-maker to document the first year of Gus's life. He's convinced it needs to be recorded for posterity.'

'Given that he's almost guaranteed to grow up to be a Bond villain, I'd have to agree with him,' I said, pushing my sunglasses on top of my head. I couldn't sit around waiting for Adam to arrive, I was going mad waiting. I needed something to do. 'I'm going to give Cass a hand, I'll see you inside.'

'Tell Chris I do not give him permission to use my likeness,' David said. 'We'll be up here, waiting.'

'Liv!' Cass exclaimed, resting the basket on the back seat as I tiptoed back down the stairs. Gus was still fast asleep in his basket, oblivious to all the commotion around him. 'You look beautiful, godmother.'

'That's funny because I feel like balls,' I said with a smile, kissing her on the cheek. 'You look amazing.'

'Do you like my earrings?' She tilted her head so that the chunks of ice glinted in the afternoon sun. 'Chris gave them to me this morning. Aren't they beautiful?'

'All right, Liv,' Chris waved to me over the top of the Jag.

'Hello Chris,' I said flatly. 'What a very interesting tie you're wearing.'

Unable to choose a single colour to celebrate the occasion, he had decided to wear all of them at once. That or Gus had thrown up on him on the way here. He looked down at his tie and back at me, not amused.

'It's designer, you wouldn't understand,' he sniped as I turned away. 'Actually, I was just wondering something about you. How come you cancelled your date on Friday?'

I turned back in slow motion. Chris was all teeth, a self-satisfied crocodile of a man, while Cassie offered nothing but a thin-lipped wince. Gus blew a spit bubble from his basket and I silently agreed he had the most appropriate reaction.

'You told him?' I asked in a half-whisper. 'What happened to sisters before misters?'

Cassie's mouth opened and closed and Gus laughed at her goldfish impression before punching himself in the head and bursting into tears.

'I didn't mean to.' She ducked into the car and picked up the baby. 'I asked him to ask his mum to babysit and he asked why and Gus was crying and I was trying to do ten things at once and it just came out. I'm sorry. What does it matter? You cancelled!'

If she thought using the baby as a human shield was going to deter me from violence, she was very wrong.

'Afternoon.'

I turned to see Adam pushing his way through the gaggle of well-wishers at the bottom of the steps to the church. Knowing I was going to see him and seeing him were altogether two separate things. As he stood in front of me, shielding his eyes from the sun, we looked at each other. It had been so long since we were in the same place and here he was, not six feet away, and all I wanted to do was touch him. The magnetic pull of habit wanted me to kiss him but my uncertainty about everything made me back away. He frowned at my mini retreat, still not moving, still not speaking.

'Ah, I see we have everyone here.'

Reverend Stevens appeared at the top of the steps in front of the church, beaming in his bright white smock with a rainbow-coloured scarf draped around his shoulders. He clasped his hands together and smiled down at us all, four arseholes and a baby.

'What a beautiful day we have for it.' He let his glance rest on each of us in turn and his smile slipped down into a frown. 'Oh dear. Is everything quite all right?'

'Good afternoon, reverend,' Cass sang, sailing up the steps with the baby. 'Everything is wonderful. Chris, come!'

Chris heeled, running after her with his videographer closely behind, only pausing to throw me and Adam the kind of shade Abi could only dream of.

'I need to talk to you,' Adam said, rubbing his eyebrows madly as a herd of christening guests rushed us.

He looked stunning, hair still shining with its Mexican highlights, his skin tanned and even. We had inadvertently matched, my deep blue dress complementing his navy suit, and as every second passed it became harder and harder not to reach out and touch him, just to make sure he really was there.

'No,' I shook my head stiffly. 'Not here.'

He studied me for a moment before turning to take the stairs two at a time. I forced myself to follow on uncertain legs.

'David,' Adam nodded as he passed my friends. 'Abigail.'

'You're going to be fine,' Abi promised, David flipping both middle fingers at Adam's back. They flanked me on either side and pulled me through the door. We didn't burn up on entry so that was a good start. 'Don't worry about a thing, no one would make a scene at a christening.'

'I'm not sure that's true,' I replied. 'Random question, is there enough water in that font to drown someone?'

They shuffled into a pew three rows from the front and I continued on alone, until I found my seat beside a stony-faced Adam. Not exactly how I'd imagined him meeting me at the end of the aisle but as long as we got through the next hour unscathed, I was prepared to consider silence a good result.

The church filled up quickly. Chris had predictably invited the entire village, despite barely even knowing the names of his neighbours, and as with any sort of social event, they had all turned out. My mum and dad sat with Chris, Cassie and the rest of her family across the aisle, leaving me stranded with Liv on the other. She looked beautiful. Her sky-blue dress was the same colour as her eyes and I wondered if she'd realized how well we matched. But it didn't matter how great she looked, I was still struggling to get past the Tinder thing. I needed to hear her side of it; break or no break, enough was enough. I had a right to know what was going on.

'That's a very nice suit, Adam,' her mum commented as she reached our row, the organist bumbling through something that sounded suspiciously like 'When Doves Cry'. 'Is it new?'

'No, he's had it ages,' Liv answered, absently leafing through the Bible in front of her before looking up, startled. 'Sorry.'

'I've had it ages,' I replied, while Liv concentrated hard on her programme. 'I like your hat, Lesley.'

'Thank you.' She reached up to make a faux adjustment to the cream puff attached to her hair and smiled. 'Hopefully I'll get some more wear out of it soon.'

'Mum,' Liv warned.

'Olivia?' she replied with a questioning eyebrow.

'We're starting,' she said, inching away from her dad up the pew. They hadn't spoken since he'd sat down. Something was clearly up and it was so frustrating not to know what. 'Shush.'

The rims of Liv's eyes were red and I was surprised that my first and only instinct was to reach over and hold her hand. But I didn't. I hated to see her cry and I hated knowing that I was most likely the cause. Unless she already had a new boyfriend who was responsible? Miserable and confused, I picked up my own programme of service and rolled it up into a tight cylinder.

The vicar stood in front of us, up on his platform, and I pulled at my tie, loosening it ever so slightly. Two weeks ago we were in Mexico. I'd been awake all Saturday night, running through everything I wanted to say to Liv the next day, counting down the hours until my grand proposal. And now, here we were, not speaking, barely even able to look at each other at our godson's christening.

The vicar, whatever his name was, rattled on about the grace of our Lord and Saviour, the rest of the congregation occasionally making agreeable noises, while Gus protested loudly in Cassie's arms. When they asked us to be godparents, we'd agreed we wouldn't christen our children for christening's sake but that we would support them if they chose to do it later in life. I wondered what Jane thought about christenings. I didn't even know if she was religious. She could worship an alien in a volcano for all I knew.

I looked over at Liv, her blonde hair shining, her hands shaking as she held her order of service and felt a cold chill that had nothing to do with the buggered roof the vicar had already rattled on about for ten minutes. If she was seeing someone else and we were over, that meant I was well within my rights to make a move on Jane, but sitting there with Liv I couldn't think of anything I wanted less.

'Parents and godparents?'

I looked up to see Gus's other godfather, Cassie's cousin, sliding out of his seat and Liv already standing, urging me up with wide eyes. Shuffling sideways, I followed her up to the front of the church, took my place next to Cass and my brother, tightening my tie until it choked me.

'Parents and godparents,' the vicar began, a weighty, sombre expression on his face. 'The church receives this child with joy.'

I looked down at Mingus in his fluffy white frock. He didn't look very joyous. He looked like he'd rather be flat on his back in a nappy full of his own filth.

'Will you pray for him, draw him by your example into the community of faith and walk with him in the way of Christ?'

'I will,' Cass, Chris and Cassie's cousin, whose name I just could not remember, replied in unison.

'Uh, yes?' Liv said. The closest Liv had ever come to the way of Christ was the soundtrack to *Jesus Christ, Superstar* and we both knew it.

'Um.'

Everyone turned to look at me.

'Yeah? Yes? I do.'

Liv and Cassie rolled their eyes at exactly the same time while Chris mouthed the word 'wanker'. At first I thought it was 'wake up' but the subtle hand gesture down by his hip confirmed otherwise.

I inhaled sharply and tried to concentrate. Perhaps

Jane had been a test, I thought, staring at the stained-glass window. I didn't know much about religion but I knew there were tests, tests of faith. Maybe Jane had been sent to test mine. And she was tempting, there was no doubt about it, but when it came down to it, she wasn't Liv. She was the girl I wanted to shag in the nightclub toilets when I was twenty-five but she wasn't the girl I wanted to wake up next to every morning for the rest of my life. So what if the business went tits up? Liv wouldn't care. If she'd stood by me the summer I'd decided to grow a moustache, she would weather any storm.

'As their parents and godparents, you have the prime responsibility for guiding and helping him in his early years.' The vicar gave me a stern look. 'This is a demanding task for which you will need the help and grace of God. Therefore, let us pray.'

Lowering my head, I tapped the tops of my fingers together. Yes, let us pray. Let us pray that Gus didn't turn out to be quite as big a wanker as his dad, had better taste in romantic partners than his mother, and far more backbone than his uncle. In fact, his best bet was to take as much after his Aunt Liv as possible.

'Mingus Christopher Floyd, today God has touched you with his love and given you a place among his people,' the vicar went on. 'God promises to be with you in joy and in sorrow, to be your guide in life and to bring you safely to heaven.'

I shouldn't take all that too seriously, I thought, as Gus kicked his mother in the face. My parents had me christened and I was sorely lacking a guide in life at present. I glanced sideways, stealing a quick peek at her. She really did look amazing, all glowing and shiny and fresh. She always looked amazing, whether it was first thing in a morning or last thing at night. She didn't even bite her nails. Although she had explained once that if I had my hands where she had her hands all day, I might not bite my nails either. I looked at her, in the light shining in through the window and landing on her like a bloody angel, and I was more certain than I had ever been, and from one heartbeat to the next, I knew I didn't want to spend another single second apart.

After what felt like a lifetime, the organist began to play and a chorus of muted sighs echoed around the church as the congregation stood up to leave.

Chris was busy glad-handing everyone who walked by, reminding them that they were expected at his house for the christening bash of the century. He'd spent more on this party than the cost of an average university education – a fact I had chosen not to point out to him, given my situation.

Now was my moment. I had to make her understand, we were meant to be together. All I wanted to do was grab Liv's hand and start running. Ideally, we'd run fast enough to turn back time like Superman, but since that seemed unlikely I'd settle for getting as far away from the christening as our legs would carry us.

'Liv,' I grabbed hold of her wrist as people began to leave, fussing over Cassie and Gus stationed by the doorway as they went. 'I need to talk to you.'

'Not here you don't,' she said, her eyes skirting around the room. I followed her gaze and saw David and Abigail leaving and fist-bumping the baby on the way out. 'Let me go.'

'But I need to talk,' I insisted. 'Will you listen to me please?'

'No, I won't,' she said, shaking her hand free, her eyes burning fiercely. She took two steps back down the little steps onto the aisle. It was easy to imagine her in a white dress, walking towards me, but instead she was practically running away. 'Everything that's gone to shit over the last two weeks has gone to shit on your schedule. You can't have everything you want when you want it, Adam. I'm done with that.'

Even though I wanted to chase her, I couldn't. Instead, I watched as she ran down the aisle and out into the sunshine, leaving me all alone as what very much felt like my last chance slipped away.

'I have never seen anything like this,' David gasped as we followed the streams of people into Cassie and Chris's back garden. Or at least, what used to be their back garden. 'Are we in the right place or did we wander into Disneyland by mistake?'

'They used an event planner,' I said, trying to take it all in but getting somewhat stuck on the carousel and Ferris wheel. I was still shaking from our font-side confrontation, but as far as I could tell, Adam had given the after-party a miss. I didn't know whether to be relieved or disappointed. 'I had no idea it was going to be this big.'

'Cass told me they were putting on "a bit of a do",' Abi replied, accepting a glass of champagne from a passing clown. 'I'd hate to see what she considers a proper party.'

The entire garden and at least half the field beyond had been turned into a Mingus Floyd-themed carnival. Clowns, lion tamers and a top hat-wearing ringmaster all patrolled the grounds, while girls in silver leotards handed out drinks and candyfloss.

'I'm going to invent an app,' David announced, necking his first glass of bubbles and holding out his hand for another. 'I need a horribly exploitative way to make a million quid so I can set up my own private Alton Towers in the back garden. Ideas? Thoughts? Suggestions?'

'What are people too lazy to do themselves?' Abi asked. 'That's the key.'

'I'm too lazy to do anything,' he replied as a man ran by inside a giant plastic bubble. 'This isn't going to work, is it?'

'Just keep drinking,' I ordered, searching the crowds for Adam. 'It'll come to you eventually.'

Between the dodgems and the hook-a-duck stall, instead of my almost certainly *ex*-boyfriend I spotted Cassie, all alone and staring blankly into the crowd.

'I'll be back in a minute,' I said, touching Abi on the arm while David juggled his champagne glass and a handful of mini hot dogs.

'I don't know, Cass,' I said, approaching with a careful smile. 'You could have made a bit of effort, it *is* your son's christening.'

'There's a slight chance Chris got carried away,' she replied, opening her arms for a hug. 'One minute we're putting on a spread upstairs at the Millstone, the next he's hired his own helter-skelter. Well, he says he's hired it, but I'm almost certain he's actually bought it.'

She took a breath, wrung her hands together, and turned to me with an apology on her face.

'I'm sorry I told Chris you were going on a date. I shouldn't have.'

'Please don't apologize,' I said, shirking the memory of shouting at her outside her own child's christening. 'I shouldn't have said anything. Besides, I actually did go on the date even though I told you I'd cancelled. I've got to stop blaming everything on he said, she said and actually start dealing with the truth.'

Cassie looked at me with hopeful eyes. 'Which is?'

'I have no idea,' I replied, turning my attention to Chris and his black top hat. 'Look at him.'

She nodded over to her husband, the ringmaster, resplendent in red tails, with a great big whip in his hands.

'Like a pig in shit,' she said with a sigh.

I watched as he cracked the whip at Mr Davies while Mrs Davies clung to his arm, tittering with delight. 'I'm amazed he hasn't got an actual lion. Couldn't they find one?'

'Don't think he didn't try,' she warned. 'The party planner said no live animals. Apparently they've had trouble in the past. He wanted an elephant as well.'

'Do you ever wonder what you've got yourself into?' I asked. Chris was encouraging Mrs Davies to spank him with the whip, much to the dismay of Mr Davies. 'I don't remember him being quite this intense when you started going out.'

'I know he can be a loud-mouthed shit sometimes,' she said, tilting her head and considering her husband with softer eyes. 'But I do love him. And he loves me and he's obsessed with Gus. He thinks he needs to prove himself to everyone all the time and I don't know why, but he won't be happy until he's got everyone's approval. Mostly, I just let him get on with it. He's not like this when it's just the two of us, he's – you won't believe it, but he's so quiet.'

'No, I get it,' I said, still looking around for Floyd the

Younger, wanting to see him and hoping I didn't at the same time. 'Adam does the same thing, just in a different way. He gives it a lot of "I don't care what people think" but really, he's terrified of letting people down. I always assumed it was because he'd packed in law school but maybe it runs in the family.'

'I blame their parents,' Cassie replied, watching her husband turn a very unflattering cartwheel in front of the neighbour's children. The children immediately began to cry. 'Their dad is so easy-going and their mum is all "Be whatever you want to be!" No one ever told the pair of them no or that they couldn't do something. Their parents are literally undisappointable and the boys can't deal with it.'

'They messed up their kids by being too good at parenting?' I laughed. 'You really can't win, can you?'

She pulled up the strap of her pink sundress and scratched her shoulder. 'That's the conclusion I've come to. I apologize to Gus every night when I put him to bed.'

Nodding, I took in the rest of the scene. Everything was shiny and bright, like it had been coloured in with felt-tip pens. The red and white bumper cars, the golden horses on the carousel. There were so many flashing lights, so much music and everything smelled like popcorn, it was like being in a five-year-old's fever dream, only with adult beverages.

'Where is Ming?' I asked, realizing I hadn't seen my godson since we arrived back at the house. For all the banners and balloons and inflatable signs declaring it his day, there was no actual sign of the baby. 'Dodgems?'

'In bed.' Cass rubbed her thumbs into her temples. 'Where I wish I was. My mum and dad are upstairs with him – this isn't entirely their cup of tea.'

'Ooh,' I pouted, my stomach grumbling loudly. I hadn't been able to eat all morning for nerves. 'I'd kill for a cup of tea right now.'

'We could always nip in and put the kettle on?' she suggested, looking more excited at the prospect of a custard cream than a turn on the Ferris wheel. 'It's not like anyone would miss us for ten minutes, would they?'

I turned to look for Abi and David and saw them clapping in time as a beautiful woman in a sequined bodysuit lit a three-foot rod on fire and swallowed it whole.

'Let's do it,' I agreed. 'We'll be back before anyone's even noticed we're gone.'

'Cassie! You must meet Chris and Andrew!' the ringmaster bellowed across the garden, his arms thrown around the shoulders of two very confused-looking men in heavy suits.

'Oh god, I think they're his investors,' she winced, pulling up the errant strap once more. 'Come with me, please? I hate talking to work people.'

'Fine,' I said, following her across the lawn. 'But you will officially owe me more than a cup of tea.'

'All right, Liv?' Chris took off his top hat and gave a shallow bow as we approached. 'Good to see you've untwisted your knickers.'

'Very funny,' I said through a polite smile. 'Nice hat. You had that already, didn't you?'

'Ah,' he placed it back on his head and began to loop up his whip. 'Knickers still twisted?'

'Please shut up.' I kept the smile on my face while Cass made awkward small talk with his investors, one eye on our exchange at all times. 'I'd like to get through this afternoon without a scene.'

'Who's causing a scene?' he bellowed, clapping a heavy hand on my back and almost knocking me to the ground. 'Just because you and Nutsack aren't together any more doesn't mean you aren't family.'

Recovering my footing, I stared as a marching band appeared from the side of the house and began circling the garden, serenading us with a rousing rendition of 'Oops, I Did it Again'. I blinked up at Chris, his cheery face so at odds with everything I was feeling.

'Did you tell him?' I asked. 'Did you tell Adam I was supposed to go on a date?'

'Why?' He cracked his whip loudly at the man who ran the chip shop. 'Was I not supposed to?'

The thing that annoyed me the most was the fact I was still shocked. Of course he had told him. I bet he couldn't wait to tell him. He'd probably driven over to deliver the news in person, just to see the look on his face. I didn't care what Cass said or how many times Adam defended him, Chris Floyd was a complete and utter tosser.

'Why would you tell him?' I asked, mad at Chris, mad at Cass and, more than anything else, mad at myself. 'Why can't you just stay out of things?'

'If you didn't want me to tell my brother that his supposed girlfriend was going out with another man,' he replied simply, 'then you shouldn't be putting it about on Tinder, should you?'

'And you should just mind your own bloody business,' I said, losing my temper with him once and for all. 'You haven't got a clue what's going on, so stop interfering.'

'Liv . . .' Cassie placed a tentative hand on my shoulder. 'Shall we go and get that cup of tea?'

'I'm not much in the mood for tea now,' I replied, the

skirt of my pale blue dress spinning up around me as I twisted towards her. 'You know he told Adam?'

'You didn't?' She turned on her husband and his whip went limp. 'Christopher Floyd, you promised!'

'He would have found out anyway,' Chris said, shrugging off any kind of responsibility like the man-child he was. 'Don't shoot the messenger.'

The worst part of it all was that he was right. And not only had I been considering a date, I'd actually gone on one, that was an indisputable fact. But the temptation to not only shoot but bludgeon the messenger to death with my shoe was so overwhelming I could hardly breathe.

'Liv, are you OK?' Cass whispered, wrapping her arms around me and pulling me away. 'You've gone such a funny colour.'

'None of this would have happened if you hadn't told me he was going to propose in Mexico in the first place!' I pushed her away as the people standing closest began to abandon their own conversations and tune in to our drama instead. 'Why can't you all just leave well enough alone?'

'You told her he was going to propose?' Chris yelled, dropping his whip in the grass. 'Cass! I told you that in confidence.'

'Says you!' she shouted back as the crowd around us grew. I covered my face with my hands, trying to find myself while they shouted across me. 'No one should tell me anything, I just had a baby! I hardly know what day it is, let alone who's supposed to know what and who isn't supposed to know anything. Now apologize to Liv.'

'Honestly, Liv, you're probably better off without him.' Chris turned his attention back to me and tried to dig himself out of his hole before his wife went nuclear. 'He'll never grow up, he thinks he's Peter bloody Pan. Let's be honest, he hasn't even really got a proper job, has he?'

'He's doing exactly what he wants with his life,' I countered, my voice low and hot. 'How many people really do that? How many people are that brave? What did you want, Chris? Was he supposed to carry on with something that was making him miserable just to make you happy?'

'No, but he could have mentioned it before Mum and Dad spent half their savings putting him through law school,' he replied, flicking an invisible speck of dust from his sleeve. 'Maybe he can make them another coffee table to make up for it.'

It was at times like these I was so glad to be an only child.

'Your parents want him to be happy,' I pointed out. 'So what's *your* problem? Or are you just jealous?'

'Please.' He gave a braying laugh, genuinely stunned by the idea. 'Why would I be jealous of Adam?'

'I don't know,' I replied, going through the various options. The crowd at the bottom of the road had grown to include a number of village gawkers, along with the christening guests and three teenagers on push bikes, the closest thing we had to a local gang. 'You've got a lot going for you but, well, he's taller than you, he's better looking than you, he's certainly nicer than you. Or is it a penis thing?'

'Ha,' he replied, burning up. 'Very funny.'

'Well,' I heard David somewhere behind me, 'it's *clearly* a penis thing.'

'You know size doesn't matter – Cass has always been

a really understanding person,' I assured him before glancing back at his wife. 'Sorry, Cass.'

She spun her hair around her finger and kept her mouth clamped shut.

'I'm not jealous of my little brother,' Chris said stiffly, bending down to pick up his whip. 'And right now, I think he's well out of it with you.'

'Oh, OK.' I started to cool down, keenly aware of my parents crossing the field towards us. 'Whatever.'

But as I was wrapping up, Chris was just getting started. 'Yes, I was annoyed when Mum and Dad gave him Granddad's house.' He emphasized each word by cracking his whip into the air. If I weren't so mad at him, I'd have been quite impressed. 'And I wasn't impressed when he bailed out on law school and then sodded off travelling instead of getting a proper job to pay Mum and Dad back. If that were me, I wouldn't have been able to face myself.'

'Thank goodness he's not you,' I replied, taking a cool step back. 'Adam works bloody hard and you know it. Sticking with law school would have been the easy way out. He took a massive risk, he moved halfway up the country, lived on next to nothing for six years, and now he's finally getting somewhere, you want to be a knob about it? Your brother is the best man I've ever known. He's caring, he's passionate about what he does, and he always puts other people before himself. Even you.'

'I don't know why you're so desperate to stand up for him,' he went on, two red spots flaming in the centre of his cheeks. 'He packs you in then changes his mind, then you pack him in and he's got someone else lined up before his bed's even cold. He doesn't need you fighting his battles, Olivia, in fact, he doesn't need you at all.'

Without moving an inch, I bit my lip, desperately trying to come up with something clever to say but Chris got there first.

'Shouldn't you be off cleaning up a dog's diarrhoea or something?'

'Hey!' David barged through the crowd and jumped in front of me, taking the verbal bullet. 'If anyone cleans up dog diarrhoea in this village, it's me.'

'Chris?'

Everyone turned around to see Adam scratching his head, his best friend Tom hovering closely behind.

'Have I missed something?'

'You're well out of it with this one,' Chris replied, shaking out his shoulders and straightening his red sleeves, while Cassie and David formed a human shield between us. 'Ad, she's completely mental.'

'Shut up, Chris.' Adam dismissed his brother with a simple command and I watched, impressed as Chris shrank back into himself. Why couldn't I have done that instead?

'It doesn't matter.' He turned his focus to me. 'I don't care if you went out with someone else.'

'Of course you don't,' I replied, an unwelcome squeak in the end of my sentence. 'Why would you care if I went on one date when you've already got a new girl-friend?'

'What?' He looked towards Chris as he spoke to me. 'You mean Jane?'

So it was true. Even after all I'd seen and all I'd heard, I had hoped and hoped that I'd somehow got it wrong but the look on his face confirmed everything.

'She's not my girlfriend,' he replied, his tanned face a washed-out white.

I kicked at the grass and sent a chunk of turf flying right into Chris's crotch.

'I saw you together! And you took her to the Bell, everyone saw you.'

Now I was shouting. Now I was shouting and everyone could hear. The whole party pricked up its ears and began to move towards us en masse.

'And he kissed her,' David added. 'Sorry.'

'Yes,' I pointed at David triumphantly. 'You did. You kissed her!'

'How did you know I kissed Jane?' Adam looked up at his brother, confused. 'I didn't tell you that, did I?'

'How come I'm the one getting all the grief?' Chris bellowed. 'I haven't done anything!'

'And Bill saw her leaving his house on Thursday morning,' Abi contributed from the edges of the party. 'Sorry, Liv. I wasn't going to say anything.'

'But you thought now was the time to share?' Adam asked, raking his hair back from his face. 'She stayed over because she lost her car keys, nothing happened. If you'd let me explain—'

'A likely story,' I replied before realizing that actually, it was. 'Adam and Jane. Jane and Adam. Adam and his new girlfriend, Jane.'

There was a chance I'd gone completely mad.

'I've had enough, I'm leaving.'

I threw my arms up in the air, forgetting for a moment that I was holding onto my handbag. The entire contents rained down on top of me, tampons, car keys and half a dozen lip balms littering the floor around my feet while my wallet clapped me right on the nose.

'I'm OK,' I whispered, clutching my face while David leapt to the floor scooping up my possessions. 'Don't panic.'

'I need to talk to you. I tried to talk to you the other night,' Adam replied, red-faced and defensive as I pawed at my face, hopeful that it didn't look as bad as it felt. 'But you told me not to call again.'

'What are you talking about?' I squealed, my entire face throbbing as I spoke. 'When did you call?'

'Um,' Abi raised her hand at the side of me. 'Actually—'

'Please, just give me five minutes.'

'I'm leaving,' I insisted, shaking my head no. This was all too much for one fun-fair themed afternoon. 'And it's all your fault anyway. If you'd proposed in Mexico like you were supposed to, none of this would be happening!'

The entire village gasped.

'You told her I was going to propose?' Adam turned on Chris again, giving me a moment to swipe angrily at my eyes, swatting away hot, unwelcome tears.

'Hardly the issue now, is it?' Chris said, twirling his whip in the grass, shamefaced.

'Oh, you can all sod off,' I shouted, snatching my handbag back from David and marching away. 'Fuck you and you and you. Sorry, Cass.'

'What was that, dear?'

My mum and dad stood at the edge of the crowd, clutching at each other as though I'd just come out as a Nazi.

'I'm sorry,' I said, refusing to let the tears that prickled at the back of my eyes fall in front of everyone. 'I'm really sorry. I've got to go.'

'Liv, wait!' Adam followed me through the swarm. Every pair of eyes at the party was on us and I was certain I saw at least one iPhone in the air. Of course some arsehole was filming.

'If you've got something to say, why don't you tell Cass?' I snapped. 'I'm sure it'll get back to me eventually.'

Nope, there was no stopping it, I was definitely going to cry.

'Liv, stop!' he shouted. In spite of myself, my heels dug into the ground and I froze. Adam ran around in front of me, a tall, frazzled mess of blue and blond.

'What do you want to know?' I asked, determined not to choke on my words. 'Which parts are you not caught up on? Yes, I went on a date on Friday night and yes, I kissed him but that was it. At least I had the good grace to wait a week before I got off with someone else, and only *after* you started dating a bloody supermodel.'

'I don't care,' he repeated, even if the look on his face suggested he might care a little bit. 'I don't need to hear about it, but I don't care. Nothing happened with Jane and me, nothing. Well, no, I kissed her as well – but you kissed him, but it was the same. I mean, it didn't mean anything.'

I smeared my tears across my cheeks, bringing Adam into focus, everyone else behind him a blur.

'Cass was right, I was going to propose in Mexico and I bottled it,' he went on, edging slightly closer, holding out his hands. 'I messed everything up that last night, everything went wrong and then I was such an arsehole, Liv. I don't blame you for wanting a break from me.'

'It wasn't just you.' Tucking my bag under my arm, I wrapped my arms around myself, out of his reach. 'It was everything. My job, my family, this village, *everything*. I never stopped being in love with you, I didn't want to not be with you any more, I just needed to be certain I was making good decisions and after you said you wanted a break, I got so confused about everything. I didn't ever want you to think I wanted us to break up.'

Glancing over my shoulder, I saw the whole village advancing slowly. How could we possibly still be the biggest attraction in the middle of an actual circus?

'Please can we forget about all of it?' Adam said, his cheeks blooming red. 'Can we pretend none of it happened? None of it matters.'

'But it does matter.' I rubbed my temple, trying to find the right words to make him understand. 'It matters to me.'

'Olivia!'

My parents marched down the path, closely followed by Abi and David, an alarmingly stern look on his face.

'When you're quite done making a scene, might I have a word inside?' My dad brushed straight past Adam and cocked his head towards Cass's kitchen. 'Now?'

'No.'

After I'd said it once, it was surprisingly easy to say it again.

'No.'

A sudden sense of calm washed over me and the tightness in my chest eased slightly. I'd been right all along. I needed a break.

'I wanted time to think and work things out and none of you were prepared to give me that,' I told them all. 'It's obvious I'm not going to get anywhere while I'm here so I'm going away. Tonight.'

'*What?*'

Dad and Adam exchanged a glance, each looking as though the other might know what was going on.

'I'm going to Japan,' I announced. 'I've always wanted to go. If not now, when?'

'You're not going to Japan,' Dad stated, as though it was the most ridiculous thing he had ever heard. 'You just came back off holiday, don't be ridiculous.'

'I'm going,' I said simply. 'I booked the flight after I talked to Mum the other day. I didn't tell anyone because I didn't want anyone to talk me out of it.'

'My baby's all grown up,' Abi whispered to David, beaming.

'Are you serious?' Adam asked. I nodded. 'Why?'

'Because I can,' I replied. It really was the only answer I had.

'Olivia, you can't just walk out on work because you've had a fight with your boyfriend.' Dad cast Adam a scathing look before turning his attention back to me. 'Come inside and calm down. You owe Cassie an apology.'

'You're talking to me like I'm a child again.' I shook my head. 'Sorry, Dad. No.'

'Because you're acting like one,' he replied. I knew he was right to a point but no one wanted to listen to grown-up Liv. Everyone wanted to tell her their opinion and what they thought she should do. At least they were paying attention now. 'Maybe I was wrong, perhaps you're not ready to run the business after all.'

'You might be right,' I agreed. 'I don't want to run your business, Dad. I want to run my own. That's something that will have to wait until I'm back.'

'Liv, don't go.' Adam took over as my dad searched for the right response and failed to find it. 'Stay. Marry me.'

And just like that, my dad wasn't the only one who was lost for words.

'You're joking,' I said hesitantly as Adam clambered down onto one knee. 'Oh dear god, you're not joking.'

'I'm not, I'm serious,' he said, patting down his pockets. 'But I mean it. I want to marry you, Liv. I'm miserable without you. I love you, I don't want to go another day without knowing we're in this together for the rest of our lives.'

Two weeks earlier, it was all I wanted to hear. If he'd asked me two weeks earlier, I'd have said yes, come home with a shiny ring and a head full of weddings and probably agreed to everything my dad demanded. But that was two weeks earlier.

'I can't believe you're doing this now,' I said as he began to wobble on one knee. He couldn't be comfortable, emotionally or physically. 'Please get up.'

'Only if you say yes,' he said, fishing around inside his wallet for something I did not want to see. 'Liv, come on, it's *us*, you know it's right. I'm your yeti. Say yes.'

'I can't.' Even though I felt strangely calm, I could still hear the shaking in my voice. 'I really can't. I meant it, I'm going to Japan. The flight is booked.'

Shuffling uncomfortably on the ground, Adam lowered his arms.

'You're saying no?' he asked, flushed with emotions. At first he looked sad and then confused. 'You're actually saying no?'

I nodded, just barely.

Finally he settled on angry.

'If you say no now, that's it.' He stood up with one dirty knee, a dead look in his eyes I would never forgive myself for. 'We're done. We're properly over.'

'Which just goes to show you're not listening to me,' I said. My voice was raw with tears and the realization that everything in our lives was about to change. 'Adam, I love you, but everything that's happened these last two weeks . . . maybe we're not so perfect for each other as I thought, so I'm sorry, but I'm saying no.'

Before Adam or my dad could say anything more, I turned away and ran up the driveway towards the road. When I finally looked up, I realized David and Abi were right behind me.

'Let's get you in the car,' David said as Abi took hold of my hand.

Biting my lip hard, I nodded, clinging to my friend and concentrating on putting one foot in front of the other until Chris, Cass and my ex-boyfriend were far, far behind us.

24

October was not messing about.

The day after the christening the weather turned completely and I couldn't remember the last time I'd seen a full day of sun. The last lingering leaves fell from the trees and near-constant drizzle had turned their autumnal gold into brown sludge. By the middle of the month, everything looked as grey and miserable as I felt and not even the pumpkins and skeletons gathering on the lawns up and down my street could raise a smile. Liv hated Halloween. She claimed it was a money-grabbing non-holiday but really, I knew it was because she hated scary things: horror movies, skeletons, spiders. She couldn't even drive past the cemetery without shivering. That was my Liv, brave enough to get on a plane and fly to Japan but too much of a wuss to watch a scary film with her boyfriend.

'What do you think your mum is up to now?' I asked Not Daniel Craig, the small, stuffed toy tortoiseshell that sat on the end of my settee. 'Reckon she's having a good time?'

Not Daniel Craig did not answer. I'd tried to fight for custody of the real thing but David wasn't having any of it. Liv had left him in charge of my fluffy son and he had made it quite clear he was prepared to go full *War of the Roses* over it if need be. I'd considered an elaborate *Ocean's Eleven*-style heist but then I remembered I wasn't George Clooney and I didn't know any Chinese gymnasts and gave up before I'd even started. I did watch *Ocean's Eleven*, but that didn't really help.

I pulled my dressing gown tighter around myself as the wind howled outside the window. It was too cold to be in the workshop today and anyway, I was so far ahead on work on the bar – guilt and embarrassment driving me onwards – that I could afford a day off. And it was too cold to do anything today other than watch TV, drink hot toddies and talk to Not Daniel Craig. Only I didn't have any of the ingredients for a hot toddy other than whiskey and there was nothing I wanted to watch on TV, so really, I was drinking neat whiskey at eleven a.m. and talking to a cuddly toy. It was not my finest hour.

Shuffling the contents of my boxers, I forced myself into the kitchen, filling Liv's mug to the brim with Jack Daniel's and padding back into the living room, pausing when I saw a shadow at the front door.

'Adam?' a voice called through the letterbox. 'Is that you?'

'Not today thank you,' I called back. 'Now's not a good time.'

'Then you probably shouldn't have given me a key for emergencies,' the voice replied and as I heard it turn in the lock, I realized it was Tom. He pushed open the door and stepped inside, giving me the once-over and shaking his head. 'Christ almighty, mate.'

'You look nice,' I said, raising my mug. 'Tom Ford suit?'

'Topman,' he replied, following me into the living room. 'I've been calling you all morning. I was up in Edinburgh for a couple of days, wanted to see if you fancied getting lunch on my way home?'

'Really?' I looked around my mess and couldn't see my phone. I'd given up carrying it with me morning, noon and night when Liv's phone stopped connecting a week after she left for Japan. 'It must be on silent.'

'In your pants in the middle of the day?' Tom hovered over an armchair for a moment before sitting down. 'Are you ill?'

'Nope,' I replied. 'Couldn't be arsed to get dressed.'

'My favourite thing about you is your unrelenting honesty,' he said. 'What's going on?'

'Not much.' I looked into my mug and then took a deep drink. 'You?'

'Are you drinking?' Tom asked, taking off his suit jacket.

I nodded. 'Yes but not out of the bottle so I'm making progress.'

'The first time I met Mads, she was sitting under a tree drinking out of a bottle, talking utter bollocks. Maybe that's why I liked her so much, reminded me of you.' He stretched out his legs and leaned back in his chair. 'I don't know if you ever actually told me how you met Liv?'

'We were in the supermarket,' I said, swirling the dark liquid around in my mug. 'I was with my mum and dad and my mum was looking for something random to put in one of her rancid juices, I think, and my dad pointed Liv out and said "Nice pair of legs" or something equally embarrassing.'

'He said that to her?' Tom asked, laughing loudly. 'I'm surprised she didn't slap him.'

'No, he said it to me.' I started to smile. 'It might have even been "That's a fine filly." That's one of his favourites. I do remember it was mortifying. I ignored him, obviously, then my dad picks up a box of pasta and basically lobs it across the aisle, right at Liv.'

'Class act, your dad.' He stood up and crossed the room to take a glass out of the drinks cabinet and poured himself a double from my granddad's decanter. I'd forgotten I had glasses. I'd forgotten there was whiskey in the decanter. Why had I wasted so much time walking into the kitchen? 'That's a vintage move, right there.'

'She thought he'd dropped it so she picked it up, brought it over and then that was it, we were talking.' I pressed my sweaty palm against my eyes. 'I wouldn't have said anything, I would have given her a nod, and then gone about my day.'

'Imagine that,' Tom said. 'You might never have met her.'

'Doesn't feel like that bad an idea right now,' I replied. 'I hate everything.'

Tom considered the statement for a moment. 'So you haven't spoken to her?'

'I left about twenty-five voicemails and sent half a dozen emails.' I picked up a tiny screwed-up piece of paper, one of my abandoned letters of apology, and attempted to toss it into the cup in the middle of my coffee table. I missed by a mile. 'She isn't answering.'

My friend scooped the ball of paper up from the floor and took a shot. 'I can see you've been keeping yourself busy though, that's good.'

'It is essential,' I replied. 'I'm almost done with the bar, waiting on the electrician to do some work before I can finish. Nothing else on at the moment.'

'It went well?' he asked.

I gave him a so-so gesture. It had actually gone amazingly well, but it was very hard to look at it with pride when I knew how many sleepless nights had gone into the project, and not because I was so desperately concerned with doing a good job.

'And you're clearly hustling like a pro.'

'I'm waiting for inspiration,' I replied. 'How's Maddie?'

'Amazing,' he said, leaning across the floor to pick up another ball of paper for another shot. Swing and a miss for Mr Wheeler. 'Everything's amazing.'

'Bully for you,' I muttered. 'When's the wedding?'

'Hopefully next summer.' He reached into his pocket and pulled out a ring box that housed a stunning diamond ring. 'Do you think she'll say yes?'

'Fuck me, mate, *I* would say yes,' I shot up in my seat and instinctively reached out for the ring, pausing for his approval. He nodded and I took it between my thumb and forefinger, holding it up to the window, trying not to blind myself. 'This is amazing. I thought global warming was melting all the icebergs? If you squint, you can actually see the polar bear tracks.'

'Ha ha.' He took the ring and placed it back in the box. 'It's not that big. Is it? Do you think it's ostentatious?'

'Don't start second guessing yourself,' I warned. 'Ask her sooner rather than later, before you talk yourself out of it.'

'Won't happen,' he assured me. 'I'm going to ask her on Friday, it's her birthday. We're going for dinner and I've booked a hotel, whole nine yards. I wasn't going to say anything, what with everything you've got going on, but quite frankly man, you need a kick up the arse.'

I looked over at the vase on the mantelpiece where

my grandmother's ring was still hiding. I hadn't even been able to look at it since Liv left.

'How did you know?' he asked, considering his ring before snapping the box shut and putting it safely away. 'How did you know she was the one?'

'How does anyone know?' I countered, scooping up as many balls of paper as I could reach without getting off the settee. 'What made you decide to do it?'

'It was my dad's birthday last week.' Tom picked up one small ball and took aim. 'He would have been sixty-five this year, you know. I always call my mum on my dad's birthday, even though I sort of dread it. I hate knowing how upset she's going to be. But for whatever reason, this time she wasn't. She was so happy.'

'High?' I suggested. 'You're never too old for it.'

'Maybe,' he admitted. 'But what she told me was she'd spent all day looking at photo albums, remembering all the happy times they had together rather than upsetting herself with what they'd missed.'

'Oh.' I watched him throw the paper, just barely missing its target. Sometimes I forgot Tom had lost his dad. I felt stupid and selfish and tossed him one of my balls to take an extra shot. 'Well, that's nice.'

'I've always felt guilty about the idea of putting Mum through a wedding,' he said. 'I didn't want her to have to do it all without my dad, I didn't want everyone telling me how proud he would have been. But talking to her put it all into perspective. I could keep putting it off and leave things how they were or I could go and buy a bloody ring and tell Maddie she's the person I want to be with.'

I pulled back my arm and tossed another ball of paper, overthrowing this time and missing the coffee table entirely.

'I bought a ring the next day. I just knew.'

'Fair play mate.' Tom took his turn and missed again. 'But seriously, what difference does getting married make? As far as I can see, these days all that happens when you get married is you turn into Chris and Cass and everyone hates each other.'

Tom rolled up his sleeves and drew his eyebrows together in concentration. 'If that's how you feel, why were you going to propose to Liv in the first place?'

I shook my head slowly, stood up and walked over to the fireplace. Holding my breath and half expecting not to find it, I pulled my grandmother's sapphire engagement ring out of the vase.

'It was a couple of months ago,' I said, dropping it into his open palm. 'We were supposed to be going out for Cassie's birthday dinner and I said I'd pick her up after she finished work. You know Liv, she's always early for everything, so I pulled into the car park at the surgery, expecting her to be waiting already and she wasn't there. I waited a minute and then I called her and she didn't answer. That's when I started to panic because that girl is never more than two feet away from her phone.'

'Maddie's the same,' Tom nodded as he placed the ring carefully back in my hand. I slipped it back into the box and laid it on the mantelpiece, open, where I could see it. 'At one point, I even thought about texting my proposal, she's on it so bloody often.'

'Romantic,' I said. He shrugged modestly. 'So, I let myself into the flat and there she is, totally zonked out on the settee, all dressed up, make-up on, present wrapped, card written. The cat's got a fresh bowl of Whiskas in front of him and she hasn't even got as far as making herself a cup of tea. I mean, the teabag was in the mug and the kettle had boiled but she'd been so busy doing everything else she hadn't even made a cup of tea before she fell asleep.'

'That's ridiculously adorable,' he said, carefully choosing his next ball of paper and hurling it at the cup and just missing as I sucked in my breath.

'Well done,' I said with an approving clap as Tom grasped at the air in anguish. 'I put the kettle on and made her a cup of tea and I was getting the milk out of the fridge and I thought, you do so much for other people, I am always going to make sure you've got a cup of tea.'

'Adam,' he glowed at me across the room. 'You soppy old bastard.'

'I'd been thinking about it for months, you know,' I said, lying back on the settee and folding my dressing gown over my bare chest. 'But that was when I knew.'

Tom picked out a large, scrunched-up wad of paper and tossed it to me.

'You do know what I'm going to say, don't you?'

'It's too late,' I told him, closing one eye and sizing up my throw. The moment it left my hand, I knew it was going to miss. 'I fucked up and she's gone. Please don't ask me to be your best man.'

'Will you be my best man?' he asked.

'Of course, you tool. Maddie's brilliant, I'm chuffed to monkeys for you both.'

'To be honest, Adam,' Tom said, hovering above me, 'I'm a bit disappointed in you.'

He put his drink down on the floor and walked over to the window to look out at my garden. The lawn sorely needed mowing. I looked down at my whiskey and felt sick at the sight of it. How did people manage to drink so much in movies? Everyone was forever knocking back entire bottles of booze, I could only drink two shots and I was wankered.

'You've never been afraid to go after what you want,' he said. 'But now, when it's really important, you're going to run away?'

'I think you'll find she did the running,' I told him, examining my fingernails. It was days since I'd done anything that could be considered manual labour. They were clean and sparkling and, quite frankly, needed a trim. 'Have I been in Japan for a month? No, I've been here.'

I looked at the ring on the fireplace and imagined the moment. Me on one knee, Liv smiling down at me, probably calling me a dickhead and then saying, hopefully, yes. How could I have messed all of this up so badly? And what could I do to make it better? Other than decapitate my brother and post his head on a pike outside her window?

A mad banging on the door interrupted my beheading fantasy.

'Hello?' I heard Cassie in the hallway. 'Adam, are you home?'

I didn't get it. Was she psychically attuned to any threat of violence against her husband?

'In here,' Tom called. I flashed him a look and sat up quickly, making sure all relevant body parts were covered.

I hadn't seen much of Chris or Cassie since the christening. I hadn't seen much of anyone other than the woman who worked the late-night checkout at the supermarket and my mum. It was a sorry state of affairs.

'Oh, hello.' Cassie walked into the living room, neat and tidy and not wearing a dressing gown. 'What are you two up to?'

'I was just visiting,' Tom said, standing up. He was

such a bloody gentleman it made me want to punch him. 'Can I get you a cup of tea?' He looked over at me on the settee. 'Assuming there is tea?'

'There's tea but there's no milk,' I replied. 'Sorry.'

'No worries, I'm fine,' she said, fishing around for something in her oversized fancy handbag. 'I can't stay too long, my mum's got Gus. Only, I had to come over and show you something.'

I stared at her expectantly while Tom moved awkwardly from foot to foot before sitting back in his chair.

'I'm sorry I told Liv you were going to propose,' Cassie said, her forehead creased with apologies I'd heard before. 'We were talking about your holiday and it just came out – I honestly wasn't trying to ruin anything. I know she hates surprises and I wanted it to be perfect for you both.'

'None of this is your fault,' I assured her. Even though it bloody was. 'Obviously we had bigger problems than I realized.'

'They might not be as bad as you think,' she said, looking at my TV. 'Is that a Blu-ray player?'

I nodded. 'Can you imagine my brother allowing me to have anything less?'

'Last night we got all the raw footage back from the film-maker we hired for the christening,' she explained. 'Chris fired them after they submitted the first edit. He thinks he can do better – he's got really into vlogging.'

'Makes sense,' I said as she slid the disk into the player. 'Finally he's been given his very own global platform. I'm surprised he didn't start sooner.'

'Yeah, I was a bit worried when I checked the internet browser history,' she replied. 'I mean, what's a thirty-eight-year-old man doing watching Zoella?'

'Could have been a lot worse,' Tom offered.

'Oh, I know,' she said with a sigh. 'He says he's going to be the first big daddy vlogger.'

'You know what he's like once he puts his mind to something,' I said. 'What are we watching?'

'This would be my husband and your girlfriend having a chat at the christening,' she replied. 'I didn't realize you weren't here for it all until I saw them playing back the footage.'

I grabbed Faux Daniel Craig from the end of the settee and sat him in my lap.

'They are really going at it,' Tom whistled as Liv laid into my brother.

'If it's at all possible, try to ignore everything your brother says,' she replied, not looking especially proud of the man she had married. 'He doesn't mean any of it, you know that, don't you? He was just very riled up.'

'He means some of it,' I corrected as I watched, my heart stinging and swelling at the same time. 'But it's a big brother/little brother thing. He's not saying anything to Liv that he hasn't said to my face.'

'Really?' Tom looked surprised while my brother and my ex went at it on the big screen. 'It's a bit harsh, mate.'

'It's very harsh,' Cassie agreed. 'He's always bragging about you to his friends, you know. Telling everyone you're a master craftsman.'

'He told me I should put "master-bator" on my business card because wanking was the only thing I'd ever mastered,' I said, not sure why but I was smiling. 'It's a brother thing, seriously.'

'For someone who doesn't love you, Liv was pretty quick to defend you,' Tom pointed out gently.

'She said I was amazing,' I breathed. 'She said she was proud of me.'

Cass was nodding. 'It was the right thing, wasn't it? Bringing it over?'

'Yeah but I'm not sure how it helps,' I said, watching as I appeared on the screen. My hair looked good, I really needed a trim. Eyebrows were insane, though. Not as mad as now but still, why hadn't I trimmed them before a christening? 'She's gone.'

'No,' Cass replied with a nervous smile. 'She *was* gone. She's coming back.'

The clouds parted and choirs of angels sang in my dirty living room, shining down on me and my scabby dressing gown.

'She texted Abi this morning,' she said, not dwelling on the fact that Liv hadn't sent her a message. 'I don't know when, exactly, but she's coming back.'

'Honest Cass, nothing happened with Jane,' I said, jumping to my feet. There was no need to go into exact details for the moment. 'I don't know what Chris told you or what you told Liv, but it was nothing, ever. I swear on Chris's life.'

'Chris's life?' She looked dubious.

'Gus's life?' I offered.

'Good enough for me.' Cassie clicked the mouse and froze the video right as Liv was questioning the size of Chris's manhood. 'I still feel horrible about it all. I feel responsible.'

'You're not,' I assured her, eyes still glued to the screen. Liv looked even more amazing than I remembered, eyes blazing, fire in her cheeks, her hair flying out behind her as she gave Chris what for. 'I've got to fix this.'

I stood up and walked over to the fireplace, grabbing

my grandmother's ring, determined. Slightly manic, desperately panicked but totally determined.

'But I might need help.'

'I thought you'd never ask,' Tom said, raising his glass in his hand and taking a wild-eyed swig. 'Maddie has staged some amazing proposals. What do you need? White stallion? An hour behind closed doors in Tiffany? Private dinner at the top of the Eiffel Tower?'

'Five hundred boxes of penne and a pot of Yorkshire Gold,' I replied as he lowered the whiskey in disappointment. 'ASAP.'

'I think the first thing you need is a shower,' Cassie suggested. 'Are you sure you're OK? I don't think Liv will have missed Italian food that much, Adam.'

'Trust me,' I assured her, casting off my dressing gown as she averted her eyes from my greying boxer shorts. 'I'll get in the shower. Tom, you get the pasta and Cassie, you don't actually need to do anything but thanks for coming over and that.'

I looked at my assembled crew. Who needed Brad and George and Julia?

'Seriously,' I promised as Tom and Cassie exchanged an uncertain shrug. 'This is going to be epic.'

25

I'd slept almost all the way home on the train from London but the taxi from the train station had been a different matter. I kept reminding myself that nothing would really have changed, that I'd only been away for a little over a month. When the driver dropped me off, I'd debated where to go first but really, there was only one place I wanted to go.

It felt strange to walk back into the surgery as though nothing had happened, backpack over my shoulder, suitcase in one hand, bag full of wacky-flavoured KitKats in the other. I had thought it might seem smaller or older or at least less familiar, but, in reality, it was exactly the same. Same posters on the pinboards, same magazines on the coffee table. The doorbell chimed as the front door closed behind me, alerting whoever might be inside that they had a visitor, and I took a deep breath in, ready for whatever was coming.

'Just a minute, I'm coming.'

Oh god. I wasn't ready. I looked back at the door and considered making a run for it but it was too late.

'Livvy!'

My dad stood in the hallway between the examination rooms and the waiting room, rubber gloves up to his elbows, arms held aloft.

'Hello, Dad,' I said with a weak, all-teeth smile. 'Everything all right?'

'I was just about to set a Doberman's broken leg,' he said with a sniff.

'Are you crying?' I asked, as he tried to wipe his face with the inside of his elbow. 'Dad?'

'No,' he said, rushing across the waiting room and pinching me in an all-elbow hug. 'Of course not. Oh, it is good to see your face.'

I wrapped my arms around his waist and hugged him back. It had to be our first hug since secondary school but it was worth the wait.

'I'm so sorry,' I told his scrub-covered chest. We were so British I had to get the apologies out the way first thing or they would have to wait for someone's deathbed. 'I should never have run off the way I did.'

'No, you shouldn't,' he agreed, before taking stock for a moment. 'But I understand you had a lot going on and I should have discussed things with you rather than simply have expected you to do as you were told. You're not a child.'

I broke away from the hug to see a tight, cat's arse look on his face.

'Did Mum tell you to say that?'

'Yes,' he admitted. 'But I think she's right. Have you been to see her yet? She's been so worried.'

'I sent emails,' I said, curling my shoulders in on themselves. 'I texted.'

'She'll want to see you,' he said firmly. 'I'm going to

be in surgery for an hour at least, so why don't you go
over now?'

'Do you need help setting the leg?' I asked, dropping
my backpack on a waiting-room chair. 'I could run
upstairs and get changed.'

Dad shook his head. 'I've got help. Dr Khan's son,
remember? He's assisting me. I know, I know,' he said,
seeing the look on my face, 'but I had to get someone
in, Livvy, it's been very busy for the past few weeks and
we didn't know when you were coming back.'

'Oh . . .' I sucked in my bottom lip and nodded. It
wasn't as though I'd expected to walk back through the
door and have everyone magically give me everything
I wanted. Whether I thought I was in the right or not,
I'd walked out on the surgery; I really should have been
grateful my dad was still speaking to me, let alone happy
to see me.

Of course, I wasn't.

'He's working here now?'

'He is,' Dad replied. 'And a fine job he's doing as well.'

Hmm. A fine job.

'But I have explained his position is currently tempo-
rary,' he added. 'And that things may change when you
take over.'

I chewed on a smile, trying not to look too happy.

'I'm still far from impressed with the way you behaved,'
Dad warned. 'But we don't need to talk about this right
now. You need to go and see your mother.'

'Where's David?' I asked, hedging. I did want to see
Mum, if only to deliver her KitKats before I ate them
all, but I wasn't quite ready for the lecture I knew was
coming and was fairly certain I deserved. 'Is he not here
today?'

'Oh. My. God.'

'He's here,' Dad replied.

I turned to see my friend silhouetted in the front door, clutching a twenty-pound sack of cat litter. Without a second thought, he threw it to the ground and ran straight through the cloud of litter dust, sweeping me off my feet in a huge hug.

'You're back!' he yelled in my ear. 'Why didn't you call me?'

'You know me,' I coughed with a lung full of litter. 'I don't like a fuss.'

'I've got to get back to Dr Khan's and Mr Punk's broken leg,' Dad said, smiling as he backed away, the smile never leaving his face. 'I shall speak to you later.'

'You look amazing,' David said, dragging me into the breakroom and immediately turning on the kettle. 'Is your hair pink? It's shorter. What did you eat? Did you do naked karaoke? Tell me everything.'

'It was pink, it's washed out now,' I replied, combing my fingers through the ends. 'But yes, it's shorter. I ate loads of stuff and I don't know what films you've been watching but I don't think there is such a thing as naked karaoke. Will that do?'

'No,' he said bluntly, flicking a teabag in my face. 'Specifics. I need details. And why didn't you tell us you were coming home?'

Before I could reply, the phone started singing in reception. Automatically, I reached over the front desk and answered.

'Dr Addison and Associates,' I answered without thinking. 'How can we help today?'

'It's Mr Beavis.' The voice on the other end of the line

was not a happy one. 'Gerald Beavis. It's my Valerie, she's not well, not well at all.'

'Of course, Mr Beavis,' I replied in my most professional voice while David gagged and shook his head back and forth. 'Do you want to bring her in?'

'Is Dr Addison not working today?' he asked with hesitation.

I closed my eyes, took a deep breath and exhaled.

'My dad's in surgery right now, Mr Beavis,' I said. 'Can I help?'

'She keeps being sick,' he said, his voice wavering. 'I don't know what's wrong, she won't stop.'

'Can you bring her in?' I asked as kindly as possible. 'We might need to do some tests.'

'I don't want to move her,' he replied, pausing to clear his throat. 'She's really not well.'

'I'll come out,' I said, standing up and shaking off my jet lag.

'Thank you, Dr Addison,' Mr Beavis said with only a slight hesitation. 'We'll be waiting.'

David looked at me with a sour face as I hung up the receiver.

'I hate that cat,' he said. 'It's really old anyway. Fuck it, Liv, let's go and get wasted.'

'I can't,' I replied, grabbing my white coat from the rack. All that was missing was my cape. 'I've got to go and see a man about a cat.'

'And then you need to come and see me about a drink,' he said forcing one more hug on me before grabbing his phone from the side. 'I'll round up the troops.'

'I'll let you know when I'm done,' I promised, swapping my suitcase for my bag of instruments and heading out the door. 'Hopefully I won't be long.'

I'd been back in the village for less than thirty minutes and it already felt like I'd never left. I looked up at the window of my flat and saw a fluffy tail flicker past a curtain. With something like a smile on my face, I set off down the road.

Mr and Mrs Beavis only lived five minutes away and the walk was just what I needed to clear my head. It was already turning cold but I barely felt it, I was so wired. Japan had been incredible. For years I'd watched it in movies and built up a version of the country in my head, something between *Memoirs of a Geisha*, *Lost in Translation* and *Godzilla*, full of karaoke and Harajuku girls and Hello Kitty and fish. To be fair, giant lizards aside, I hadn't been far off. Every day, for five weeks, was sensory overload, from one extreme to the other. I landed at Narita international airport after two connections, with nothing more than my suitcase, backpack and a two-night reservation at a Tokyo hotel. I went from the mind-boggling madness of cities that didn't know how to stop, to a kind of serenity I'd never known, lodging with monks in Mount Kōya. And while Tokyo didn't give me much time to think, lodging in the temples gave me nothing but. No internet, no mobile service, and not even a TV. I had never felt so far away from myself and I was forced to find another me. If I'd gone looking for a break I'd found one, but it only presented me with a new problem. I'd assumed that once I got my time-out everything would magically fall into place, that my world would suddenly make sense, but instead it turned out to be just like my mum had said. Nothing good or real was that easy.

The Beavises' semi was just a couple of streets over

from Adam's house. Valerie was in her bed, perched on top of a newspaper-lined kitchen table and not looking the slightest bit pleased with her lot in life.

'She started being sick this afternoon,' Mr Beavis said as his wife busied herself by putting on the kettle for what I had to imagine was the hundredth time that day. 'I can't imagine there's anything left in her now, the poor thing.'

'And it only started today?' I asked, pulling out my beloved stethoscope and listening for poor Valerie's weak heartbeat. 'She's been fine the rest of the week?'

'Absolutely fine,' he nodded. 'She's been eating fine, doing her business, playing outside.'

I gently pressed on Valerie's abdomen, squinting out the kitchen window.

'There's no blood in the vomit?' I asked.

'We saved some,' Mrs Beavis said, holding a rancid yoghurt pot under my nose. 'It's in here.'

Wrenching my head back, I took it from her, quickly shifting to breathe through my mouth.

'Is that an oak tree?' I put the Not-a-Yoghurt down on the kitchen sink and pointed at a large tree at the bottom of the garden.

'Yes,' Mr Beavis replied, gently stroking his cat's head as she mewed her displeasure. 'Do you think she ate the leaves? Are they poisonous?'

'OK, I can't be sure until she's had a scan but I think Valerie has eaten something she shouldn't have. It looks like, and it definitely smells like, she's got a blockage and most often it's something like an acorn. I think it'd be best to take her to the animal hospital in Nottingham and get an endoscopy done.'

'Can't you do it?' he asked, clutching his wife's hand.

'I'd be much happier if you could do it. Valerie doesn't like strangers messing with her.'

'Yes,' I said, surprised.

I watched as they ran around preparing the cat carrier, packing up her favourite toys and favourite food and looked at Valerie with a small smile on my face.

'We'll sort you out,' I promised in a whisper. 'Don't you worry.'

'Didn't you say this was going to be epic?'

'He did,' Tom confirmed to Cass, standing back to survey our work. 'He definitely used the word epic.'

The three of us stood in front of my workshop, staring at my masterpiece. The idea was simple but spectacular. I'd win Liv back by recreating the aisle of the super-market where we had first met, fill it with equal parts candles and pasta then beg her to forgive me. We'd skip over the bit where she'd been shagging around with some bloke from Tinder, turned down my proposal and run off to Japan, and then I'd propose. Again. It was the most romantic idea in the world.

Except the execution wasn't quite as romantic as the concept.

Tom had done an excellent job with the pasta but unfortunately, even after I sent him out twice, we still only had about forty boxes of penne and thirty boxes of orecchiette and though seventy boxes of pasta sounded like a lot, when I pulled my workshop shelves into the middle of the room to create a makeshift supermarket aisle, we only managed to fill two of the five shelves on either side. And thanks to a leaky can of wood stain and the month of shit weather, the whole workshop smelled like damp death. In my head, it was going to be an exact replica of the moment we met, with better lighting and fewer lecherous comments from my dad, transporting us back in time to a moment before I'd been such an incredible dickhead. But instead of a loving recreation of our most special moment, it looked like I was building a corner shop set for a post-apocalypse zombie movie. And a shit one at that.

'The candles look nice though,' Cassie said, desperately looking for a bright side the way Liv said she always did. 'You've done a lovely job with the candles.'

Even that was a lie. I'd always thought there were more candles in those bags of tealights you got from Ikea. The overall effect was definitely more 'unexpected power cut' than anything else.

'This is ridiculous!' I kicked one of a thousand plastic bags across the room. 'What a stupid idea.'

'It's a lovely idea,' Cass argued. 'And Liv will love it.'

'I don't know . . .' Tom slipped his hands into his pockets and clucked. 'If you're going to propose to a woman, you need to do it right. And I'm not sure this is right.'

'Bloody men,' Cass said loudly. 'There is a woman in the room, you know. Who happens to be one of the best friends of the woman you're planning to propose to. Anyone thought to ask me my opinion?'

Tom and I shared a glance. We really hadn't.

'Liv will love the effort,' she agreed, gesturing to my sub-Netto pasta aisle. 'But all she really needs to hear are the words. Did Chris tell you how he proposed to me?'

'On holiday in Italy,' I answered, Tom nodding in agreement. 'In Venice, wasn't it?'

'We were in Venice,' she confirmed. 'And he'd hired a gondola and booked a fancy dinner and all that nonsense, but do you know when he actually proposed?'

'Not on a gondola or at the fancy dinner?'

'When I was in the toilet,' she replied flatly. 'I was in the lav, you know, finishing up, and he started babbling about something outside the door, saying how he had been thinking about this for weeks and nothing felt right but he had to say it, and when I opened the door, face covered in zit cream, he was standing there with the ring in his hand. He looked like he'd been bent over and shagged backwards.'

'Funny how he never mentioned *any* of this,' I said, looking at my disastrous handiwork.

'And you still said yes?' Tom was amazed.

'I said yes because I wanted to marry him,' she replied. 'I didn't care how he asked me, I didn't care about the ring, I said yes because I love him and I want to be with him.'

She thought about what she had said for a moment, glancing down at her ring.

'I cared about the ring a little bit,' she conceded. 'But the main thing was that he asked. The how, the where, the when wasn't important at all.'

'I don't believe her,' Tom whispered in my ear. 'My girlfriend is an event planner.'

'And how many of the events your girlfriend plans are women proposing to their boyfriends?' Cass asked. 'Or even women proposing to other women? Trust me, this thing has got totally out of hand. Just go round to her house, say you're sorry, and ask the woman to marry you.'

'I'm not going to argue with her,' Tom said, stepping

back. 'Not just because I'm scared of her but because, well, anything's better than *this*.'

He picked up a box of orecchiette and turned it around in his hands.

'You're going to be eating pasta and sauce for the rest of your life. I should have got you some Ragú.'

'All Liv cares about is you, her friends, her mum and dad, and Daniel Craig,' Cassie said before turning to Tom with an explanatory pat on the back. 'Her cat. But she does care about human Daniel Craig as well.'

'Who doesn't?' Tom replied.

'You're right,' I said to Cassie, scattering tiny candles all over the workshop and nodding at Tom. 'She's right.'

'Also, this place is a complete fire hazard,' he said as he turned on the overhead light. 'You really need to get your workshop cleaned up, mate.'

'We don't even know when she's coming home,' I said, the absurdity of the situation hitting me like seventy boxes of pasta. 'I'm stockpiling pasta in a damp workshop to impress a woman who has turned me down once and is currently halfway around the world. I got carried away.'

Sinking down onto my workbench, I watched as the wind knocked itself out of Cass and Tom's sails.

'I ought to get back to Gus,' Cass said, starting towards the door. 'Seriously, Adam, don't give up. She'll love this.'

I couldn't help but wonder whether or not she truly believed herself or if she still just felt guilty.

'I've got to get off as well, mate,' Tom said, clapping me on the back. 'You know Liv better than me. If Cass says she'll love it, I'm sure she'll love it.'

Hmm.

'The ring is beautiful though,' he added. 'You can always lead with that.'

I watched as they walked down my driveway, leaving me alone in the saddest supermarket the world had ever seen.

26

'For someone who isn't sure if she wants to be a vet any more, you're awfully bloody good at it,' David said, sliding Valerie back into her cage to rest after we had removed her blockage. As predicted, someone had been eating acorns and it wasn't Squirrel Nutkin. 'And it doesn't seem as though you hate it.'

'I never said I didn't want to be a vet any more.' I reached in to stroke her sleepy head and quiet a twitchy paw. 'I felt trapped.'

'And now you don't?' he asked, turning the lights down low and following me out into the breakroom. 'Five weeks in Japan and poof, everything's sorted?'

Collapsing onto the settee, I loosened each shoulder and rolled my head around on my neck. We'd been in surgery for almost an hour, followed by a good twenty minutes on the phone to Mr and Mrs Beavis. I was grateful, not just because we'd saved Valerie's life, but also because I couldn't begin to imagine what kind of a state they'd have been in if things hadn't gone so well. Explaining to a grumpy man in his mid-fifties that he could not sleep on the floor of the surgery was not how I'd envisioned spending my first night back at home. Still, I hadn't planned to spend it sleeping in the same hospital myself but it looked like I was going to have to, at least until Valerie came round from her anaesthetic.

'I wouldn't say everything,' I said, curling up into a little ball on the settee. 'There's plenty that still needs sorting out.'

'*Domo arigato*,' he replied. 'What are you going to do?'

'I don't know,' I took a deep breath. 'Go and see Mum? Go and see Abi? Make Cass come and see me? Make up the fold-out bed and wait for an anaesthetized cat to wake up?'

'You can call me crazy, but there seems to be a certain option missing from the list,' David replied. 'Go and see Adam isn't an option this evening?'

I closed my eyes and groaned.

'Planning to leave that until I've had a shower and got changed,' I said. 'And you know, worked out exactly what I want to say to him.'

'Didn't you have five weeks to do that?'

'And it was not long enough,' I opened my eyes to see him brandishing a Penguin above my head. I almost snatched his hand off. 'The only thing I really worked out was that none of us have any kind of clue what we're doing.'

David contemplated my wisdom while biting his own Penguin in half. 'Learn that from a Buddhist monk?'

'I watched *Eat, Pray, Love* on the plane over,' I replied. 'Turns out Japan's not really a very good place to find yourself. Getting lost and hanging out in hot springs and being touched up by businessmen on the subway, yes. Finding yourself? Not so much.'

'Then what took you so long?' he asked, kicking me in the shin. 'We've been dying over here without you.'

'It was much easier to pretend all the horrible stuff I left behind never happened from a few time zones away,' I confessed. 'When you're trying to order something to eat that doesn't have eel in it you don't have a lot of time to worry about suggesting to the entire village your boyfriend's brother has a tiny penis.'

'Point taken,' David said. 'And speaking of said boyfriend?'

I closed my eyes and held my hand out for another Penguin.

'He's missed you,' he admitted with great reluctance. 'He wanted to take Daniel Craig. Cass says he's barely left the house the whole time you've been away and I've seen him walking around with a face like a slapped arse.'

'I want to pretend that makes me happy but it really doesn't,' I replied. 'I still don't know what to do.'

We sat quietly for a moment.

'Everyone's had time to think about stuff while you were away,' my friend said slowly. 'Adam included. Go and see him.'

'Now?'

'Liv, while you've been off on your adventures, I've been sitting here for five weeks with no idea when, or even if, you were planning to come back, putting up with your dad, and having to deal with a very nice but – let's be brutally honest – not especially entertaining new vet. He doesn't watch telly. At all. We had nothing to talk about. And you haven't even come to a bloody decision about what you want. So help me god, I'm going to take the endoscope and shove it somewhere very uncomfortable if you don't go and see Adam Floyd right now.'

David's threats always carried more weight than they should, ever since he threw Abi's phone out of a moving car on the way to Glastonbury.

'I'll go and see Adam then.'

Standing on unsteady feet I scraped my hair back into a bun and pulled out one of a million lip balms from a drawer underneath the kettle.

'Go,' David commanded as I started to mess around with my hair in the mirror. 'You're bringing me and the cat down and she's been unconscious for two hours, so just think about yourself for a minute.'

'Point taken,' I said, leaving my phone behind and walking out into the night.

After Cassie and Tom left, I'd rearranged my pasta shack five times over but never managed to make it look any better. Eventually, I just walked away. I didn't even bother to turn off the light. Without really knowing where I was going, I started walking and before I knew it, I found myself at Liv's door.

There was a light on in the surgery, even though it was late. It had to be David, I thought, pounding on the door. Her dad always clocked off at six, no matter what. I bounced from foot to foot as a shadowy figure emerged from the back office.

'Keep your knickers on, I'm coming.'

David opened the door with a surprised look on his face. 'What are you doing here?' he asked. 'Where's Liv?'

'In Japan?' I suggested, bouncing from foot to foot.

Even though I'd been walking around for an hour before I ended up here, I felt so restless. 'I came to see Daniel Craig.'

'Adam,' David reached out, placed his hands on my shoulders and held me in one spot until I stopped moving, 'Liv's back.'

It was like a kick in the nads with an added slap to the chops on the way down.

'She's back?'

David nodded before taking an uncomfortable shuffle backwards. 'I thought . . .'

'Thought what?'

I couldn't believe she was back. I had to see her.

'I thought she was going to see you,' David replied, pulling a shawl-collared cardigan closer around him. 'She said she was.'

'When did she leave?' I asked. Now was not the time to ask him where he got his cardi, however nice it was. 'Could I have missed her? Did she go home first?'

'I don't know,' he said slowly. 'Maybe you should go back home, in case she decides to pop round.'

'Do you think she will?'

He didn't reply.

'I like your cardigan,' I said, waving in his general direction and looking away before I could even think about crying. It hadn't even occurred to me that Liv might be back; all I'd wanted was to see Daniel Craig and possibly borrow a DVD or two.

David straightened his collar. 'Topman. It's new, probably still got them in.'

'Do you think it'd be all right if I ran upstairs and checked on DC?' I asked. 'Maybe I should wait for her here.'

'I don't think you should wait for her in the flat,' he said, pity all over his face. 'Unless you want to give her a heart attack. I'm sure she wouldn't mind if you wanted to run in and see the cat though.'

'Yeah, good point,' I agreed, already on my way round to the back door. 'Thanks, David.'

The path from the front of the surgery to the back door of Liv's flat had to be less than a hundred feet but tonight it felt like a thousand miles. For the first time I felt uncomfortable turning my key in the lock, a stranger on her stairs. It had to have been nearly two months since I'd been in the flat but Daniel Craig was right there, waiting for me as always, sitting with his two front paws neatly together, his single back leg tucked in between.

'Evening son.' I reached down and picked him up, holding him on his back like a furry cat baby. 'You been all right?'

He purred agreeably and I walked around the small living room with him in my arms. Liv hadn't taken down our photographs or thrown out any of my gifts. That had to be a good sign, didn't it? Although, she hadn't been there in a month. Chucking out a *Captain America* cushion probably wasn't her top priority before she legged it halfway around the world.

'I came to see your mum,' I told the cat. 'I bet you know where she is, don't you?'

He wriggled around in my arms, meowing to be put down. Even though the boy only had three legs, he was more than capable of cutting me up when he was in the mood and so I let him go, following him over to the settee.

'So, did you meet that other bloke?' I asked, absently

opening a ring binder lying on top of the coffee table. 'I hope you scratched his eyes out.'

I must have leafed through at least five pages before I realized what the binder was. Cakes, rings, big white dresses. It was all wedding stuff. Liv had started collecting wedding stuff. Not only did she know I was going to propose, she actually wanted me to. Daniel Craig meowed loudly, relieved that I was finally catching on.

'I'm such a bloody idiot,' I said, falling backwards onto the settee, ring binder in my lap. 'All of this could have been avoided if I hadn't been such a massive pussy.'

The cat yowled in agreement.

'Sorry,' I said. 'That's probably an offensive term to you and your people.'

I stared at him as he head-butted me in the stomach. Whatever else she might be doing while she wasn't at my house, I knew it wouldn't be long before she came home to Daniel Craig.

'Do us a favour, DC . . .' I reached into my pocket and pulled out my grandmother's engagement ring. 'Can you give this to Liv for me?'

Holding him still between my knees, I unfastened his collar and slipped the narrow gold band of the ring onto the stretchy black fabric before clipping it back together. David was right. I couldn't be here, it wasn't fair. Besides, Liv hated surprises.

'Looks good on you,' I said, kneading him between the shoulders and closing up the binder. 'Hopefully I'll see you soon.'

I turned out the lights, half wanting to leave one on for when Liv got home but knowing that she would only panic that someone had been in the flat. Miserable, ringless, and with a head full of pasta recipes, I headed back down the stairs, taking them two at a time before letting myself out for the last time.

'Oh my god!'

'Liv, you scared me.' Six feet four inches of Adam Floyd leapt out of my doorway as I turned the corner and for the first time in my life I understood the phrase to jump out of your skin. I pressed my hand to my pounding heart and Adam dropped his keys to the floor. We both bent down at the same time and our heads clashed.

'First you try to give me a heart attack and then you head-butt me,' I muttered, rolling arse backwards into the gravel. 'Thanks.'

'Sorry,' he said, squatting on the front step and rubbing his forehead. 'You made me jump.'

'I made you jump?' I stood up, gravel stuck in my palms, any jet lag fatigue a million miles away. I was more than wide awake. 'You're the one creeping around in my flat. What are you doing here?'

He looked at me in the strangest way. Or perhaps it wasn't that strange. Perhaps I'd just forgotten. I looked back. Had there been flecks of grey at his temples before I left? His stubble was longer than before, almost a beard.

'You've got pink hair?' he said.

It should have been a statement but instead sounded like a question.

I couldn't stop staring at him. We hadn't seen each other for five weeks but it might as well have been a lifetime.

'Are you all right?' he asked. 'Where were you?'

'Yes,' I replied, still picking gravel out of my palms. 'I went to Japan.'

'I know,' he said, brushing his hand through his hair. It was definitely longer. 'I meant, just now. David said you'd gone somewhere.'

'You were upstairs?' I deflected, pointing at the door. 'In the flat?'

'Yeah.' Adam ducked his head away from me, seemingly just as embarrassed as I was. 'I was saying hello to the cat. I didn't know you were back.'

'That cat?' I pointed as Daniel Craig came running down the stairs and pelted past the pair of us, a little tortoiseshell blur.

'Shit!' Adam shouted, scrambling to his feet and throwing himself after DC. 'Where did he go? Can you see him?'

'Calm down,' I said, brushing off my knees. 'He'll come back.'

'No!' Rubbing his hands against his face, Adam shook his head over and over. 'No, no, no. We've got to find him.'

'He'll come in eventually,' I said, watching as he ran off into the car park. 'Probably as soon as I manage to fall asleep.'

'He – I – on his collar,' Adam looked back at me, clawing at his throat. 'We've got to find him.'

'He'll come if we shake his food,' I assured him. 'You'll never find a cat in the dark if he doesn't want to be found.'

'You're the expert.' He put his hands on top of his head and stood next to my car, staring out into the woods. 'God.'

I trotted upstairs, pulling my jumper down over my bum as I went, too conscious of Adam trailing right behind me.

'Here.' I handed him the glass jar of treats I kept on the shelf by the door. 'Shake this and he'll be back in two seconds.'

He took the jar and ran back downstairs, shaking it like it was a pair of maracas and he was playing backup for Ricky Martin as I watched from the doorway.

After I left the surgery, instead of walking over to Adam's, I got straight in my car and drove up and down the A1, blasting my music and trying to clear my head. One thing I'd missed in Japan was my car. Nothing made more sense to me than tearing down country roads with my music blaring. It didn't matter how many gongs I struck at how many Buddhist temples, nothing ever gave me that kind of clarity. Eventually, when I got back to the village, I drove straight over to Adam's house.

But he wasn't there.

Standing at the top of the staircase, I looked down at the man who was patrolling the car park, shaking a jar of cat treats as though his life depended on it.

'I went to your house,' I called out. 'Why is your garage full of pasta?'

He turned and stared up at me, squinting against the bright light of the staircase.

'You went to my house?'

I nodded.

'Why?'

'Why did you come to mine?' I countered.

'I told you, to see the cat.' He spoke stiffly and didn't bother to turn to face me. 'Did you have a good time? In Japan?'

'I did,' I confirmed. 'I can see why you love travelling so much. It's different to going somewhere on holiday, isn't it?'

'Totally different,' he agreed. 'I'm glad you enjoyed it.'

The strained formality between us kept me pinned to the spot.

'I missed things, though,' I said slowly. 'Being away makes you appreciate what you've left behind, I think.'

He shook the treats once more before giving up.

'I really missed the surgery,' I explained, taking one small step down the staircase. 'I was surprised how much, to be honest. And, you know, it's tough being away from your friends and family for a long time.'

'And Daniel Craig,' he suggested, wandering back towards the staircase and sitting on the bottom step.

Two more steps.

'And Daniel Craig,' I agreed.

I hopped lightly down the last few steps.

'And you.'

He was shaking as I sat down beside him.

'Sometimes,' I said in a voice so light I was worried my words would float away, 'you need a break to see what was already broken.'

'I messed things up.' Adam's hands hovered over his kneecaps, the jar of treats tucked in under his legs. 'I was so scared of getting it wrong, I convinced myself it was better not to do it at all.'

'I thought everything was fine before Mexico,' I whispered, picking up the jar and turning it around in my hands. 'But it went so wrong, so quickly. It shouldn't have been that easy to ruin what we had. That's not your fault.'

'But if I'd got it right the first time round, we would never have gone through all this,' he argued, emphasizing the last word by waving at the air in front of us with both hands. 'There was no need for any of it.'

'There was every need,' I corrected him gently. 'If you'd proposed in Mexico and I'd said yes, everything that happened when we got back would still have happened but it would have been even more complicated. Dad would still have caught me off guard with the surgery, you would still have met her.'

'Nothing ever happened between me and her,' he said, insistent. 'I don't know what Cass and Chris told you but nothing happened at all.'

'Feels like it doesn't matter now,' I replied, looking out into the night and spotting a pair of bright green eyes flashing underneath my car. 'Anyone else was a symptom of the problem, not the cause.'

'Liv . . .' Adam looked down at me with the saddest eyes. 'I have been so unhappy.'

'I haven't,' I admitted and Adam wiped a hand over his tired-looking face. 'I was before I went away, and then the last few weeks were amazing.'

He leaned forward, elbows on his knees, head in his hands, took some cat treats from the jar and put them by his feet.

'But I still missed you so much.'

It was hard to get the words out and I steeled myself for my own reaction to the truth as what I was saying filtered through to Adam. For the first couple of weeks I had written off the sleepless nights and constant aching as homesickness and then just the feeling of being a stranger in a strange land. It was only when I booked my ticket home and I realized I would have to see him eventually that it all came into focus. I wasn't sad – I was scared. Scared that it was truly over between us.

'Everything I did, everywhere I went, I wished you were there with me,' I admitted. 'Every day.'

'Oh.'

That was it? Oh? I wet my lips and started again.

'I didn't know if you'd want to see me,' I said, letting go of the glass jar and taking hold of his hand. He kept his eyes straight ahead but he didn't pull away. 'I didn't reply to your emails.'

'Rude,' he sniffed and swiped at his eyes with his forearm. 'I thought you might not have internet or something.'

'That was only for a week when I was staying with some monks but, trust me, that's another story,' I replied, staring at our interwoven fingers. 'I just didn't know what to say.'

'But you do now?' he asked, turning to face me with tears on his cheeks.

We were both crying but I was smiling. It had been so long since I had looked at his face and seen my Adam looking back. All the fear melted away and all that was left was relief.

'Before I left, I had a chat with my mum and I didn't get it at the time,' I said. 'She said people run away from things when they're hard because they want something easier and she was right. It's so much easier to stay angry than it is to forgive someone. Only, it's not nearly as important.'

'So you forgive me?' Adam's voice cracked as he spoke.

'And I really hope you can forgive me,' I nodded.

The night was still and cool, not quite cold but not nearly warm enough for us to be outside. Even though I knew we were both freezing, neither of us moved.

'I was wondering,' I started, my voice thick and stilted and raw, 'if that offer of yours was still good?'

'Offer?' Adam's mouth hung open for a moment before it turned up into a smile. 'Really?'

'Why not?' I replied with a happy shrug. 'We can't make a bigger cockup of things than we already have, can we?'

The green eyes shot out from underneath my car and ran across to the pile of treats by Adam's feet. Daniel Craig looked up at the pair of us, glancing back and forth, and pulling his treats towards him with one paw.

'Good timing, son,' Adam said, picking him up and placing him in my arms, Daniel twisting and yowling and desperate to get back to the treats. He was such a junkie. 'There's something you might like on his collar.'

Dodging an attack paw, I ran my finger around the cat's neck, stopping when I found something that certainly wasn't there when I went away. It was a gorgeous sapphire and diamond ring.

'It's a bit Liberace for him,' I said, turning it around in my fingers. 'I don't think DC is into that much bling.'

'Is it a bit Liberace for you?' Adam asked, shuffling off the step and onto one knee. 'This didn't go very well last time, but third time's a charm.'

I opened my mouth to say something funny, but instead, all that came out was an echoing sob. I held Daniel tightly against his will as Adam unhooked the ring from his collar. The second I let go, he tore off upstairs, meowing in dismay at being made an unwitting participant in Adam's proposal.

'It's my grandmother's ring,' Adam said, sliding it onto the third finger of my left hand. 'And even though you never got to meet her, I know she would have loved you.

Although I don't know if you'd have been so keen – she was a bit weird, my nan. Used to think she could control the buses and you know, slightly racist. Other than that, though, really lovely.'

'You're really selling this,' I replied staring down at the ring. 'Luckily, it's beautiful.'

'Every day without you has been horrible,' he carried on, his smile growing by the second. 'You make me better, and hopefully I don't make you worse. Liv, I want to marry you.'

I laughed, the sound bubbling up out of me like a language I didn't know I knew.

The ring was beautiful, whether it came with some sort of telepathic control over the bus timetable or not. A vintage, oval-shaped dark blue sapphire, flanked by three diamonds on either side, almost like a little bow tie.

'Adam Floyd,' I replied, holding his hand tightly. 'I want to marry you too. Also, no one else has asked me.'

'Do you want to make a few calls before you commit to anything?' he asked, tears on his dirty cheeks. 'I can wait a minute.'

'I'll probably just put something on Facebook,' I said, rubbing my nose against his. 'So, if I get any messages in the next couple of days, I reserve the right to change my mind.'

'And that's why you're the best.' He pressed his lips to mine and I felt a welcome, familiar warmth all over my body. 'You're so practical.'

'I try,' I said, kissing him back with head full of jet lag and a heart full of joy.

'So,' Adam said, pulling away and holding my face in his hands. 'You'll marry me then? I'm going to need a definite yes.'

Holding out my hand I looked at his grandmother's ring and then back at him, grubby and messy, wearing a dirty T-shirt and jeans, sitting on the floor outside my flat. It was exactly how I wanted him.

'Why not?' I replied. 'I really hated Tinder.'

'That'll do,' he said, pulling me towards him for another kiss. 'And I'm holding you to it.'

'You'd bloody better,' I threatened, our faces close together, arms around each other's necks, my lips tingling. 'Although I have another important question: have you got any food in? I'm starving.'

'I've got pasta,' he offered, cupping my face in his palms. 'And nothing but pasta for at least the next six months.'

'You're weird,' I said, laughing.

'You're weird,' he echoed, planting a kiss on the end of my nose.

Sometimes, I realized, life didn't work out quite how you'd imagined it would.

And sometimes life was all the better for it.

Acknowledgements

As always, there are a million people to thank and very little brain power left to remember them so here goes.

Rowan Lawton, thank you for being my sounding board, my motivator, my cheerleader, my agent and my friend. The very fact this book exists is because of you and the Griffith Observatory. Nice one.

To Lynne Drew and Martha Ashby at HarperCollins, this is a thank you and an apology, although I was only two weeks late on this one in the end! New record? Thank you for making this book the best book it could be.

To everyone at Furniss Lawton and James Grant: Liane, Isha, Eugenie, Georgie, Blaise and Will (and everyone else), thank you for making this so much easier and so much more fun than it otherwise would be, I appreciate everything you do hugely.

HarperCollins, my global publishing fam, you're all amaze. Sarah, Katie, Liz, Louise, you're all owed drinks or hugs or drugs or something. Jean-Marie, Liza, Laura and (sniff) Victoria at Harper 360 and Leo, Sara, Kelsey and everyone else at HC Canada, you're all on the 'must buy booze' list also. And not forgetting HarperCollins Australia, I'm sure I'm overdue a visit, OK Kimberley? Get the kettle on. Thank you all, for everything you do.

I genuinely couldn't get through a day without my online family. The authors, the journos, bloggers, vloggers, anyone who is working hard to make something good and everyone who puts up with my madness on Twitter, Facebook, Instagram, Snapchat, YouTube and my Hello! Blog. You're all champions and I can't wait to see you IRL.

And as for the poor people who have to tolerate me day in, day out, I'm sorry and I'm thankful and I'd have gone mental(er?) without you by now. Mentaler isn't a word, scratch that. I'm not going to name names because I'd be here all day. You know who you are, you're the best ones and I love you. Well, I suppose Jeff gets a mention because he might lock me out. Thank you, Jeff.

And thank you for reading this! You have been acknowledged, I acknowledge thee. Next time, I'm just going to print a list of names and an 'I.O.U' drinks voucher to save everyone time.

Look out for Lindsey's

girl

series

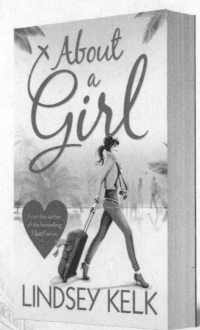

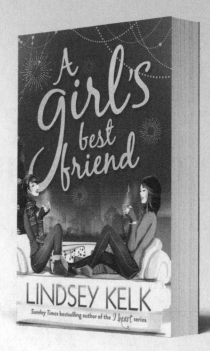

A girl's best friend

LINDSEY KELK

Sunday Times bestselling author of the I heart series

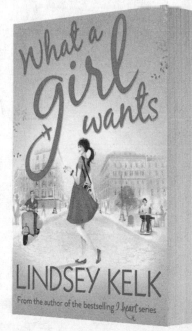

What a girl wants

LINDSEY KELK

From the author of the bestselling I heart series

DISCOVER LINDSEY'S

I heart SERIES

There are lots of ways to keep up-to-date with Lindsey's news and views:

lindseykelk.com

facebook.com/LindseyKelk

@LindseyKelk

@LindseyKelk

LindseyKelk